AGAINST
THE ROPES

SARAH CASTILLE

sourcebooks
casablanca

Published by Sourcebooks Casablanca, and imprint of Sourcebooks, Inc.

P.O. Box 4410, Naperville, Illinois 60567-4410
(630) 961-3900
Fax: (630) 961-2168
www.sourcebooks.com

Library of Congress Cataloging-in-Publication data is on file with the publisher.

Printed and bound in the United States of America.
VP 10 9 8 7 6 5 4 3 2 1

To Mum and Dad, for everything you have given me.

And to John…always.

Chapter 1
OH, BETRAYING LIPS

"YOU COME IN. YOU fight. It's simple."

Me fight? He can't be serious. Do I look like I pound on people for fun?

"Sorry. I think there's been a misunderstanding." Forcing a tight laugh, I shuffle back to the red line marking the fighters' entrance to Redemption, a full-service gym and training center that is home to one of Oakland's few remaining unsanctioned, underground fight clubs. Maybe I should have read the rules posted at the door.

"No, you don't." The hefty blond grabs my shoulders and pulls me toward him. My nose sinks into the yellow happy face tank top stretched tight over his keg-size belly. The pungent odor of unwashed gorilla invades my nostrils, bringing back memories of school trips to the San Diego Zoo. Lovely.

Gasping for air, I glance up and flash my best fake smile. "I'm just here to sell tickets. One of your fighters, Jake, asked my friend Amanda to work the door and she asked me to help her. Why don't we just pretend you didn't see me cross the red line and I'll get back to work?"

If I were a different type of girl, wearing a different—and lower cut—shirt, I might try another kind of technique to get out of this predicament, but right now, a smile is all I've got.

It backfires.

"Mmm. Pretty." He releases my shoulders and paws at my hair, mussing it from my crown to the middle of my back. What a waste of two hours with the flat iron.

"I'm not too sure about pretty." My voice goes from a low quiver to a thin whine as he strokes my jaw with a thick finger. "But I am small, fragile, delicate, easily frightened, and given to high-pitched screams in situations involving violence." In an attempt to make my lies a reality, I suck in my stomach and tuck in my tush.

He frowns, and for the first time I notice the missing teeth, jagged scar across his throat, and the skull and crossbones tattoos covering his arms like sleeves. Not quite the cuddly teddy bear I had thought he was. More like a Viking berserker.

My heart kicks up a notch, and I hold up my hands in a defensive gesture. "Listen. I was chasing after some deadbeat who didn't buy a ticket. He came in just before me. Tall, broad shoulders, black leather jacket, bandana—I only saw him from the back. He was in line talking to people, and then suddenly he breezed past the ticket counter and went through this entrance. Did you see him?"

A smile ghosts his lips. "You'll have to talk to Torment. He deals with all line crossers and ticket dodgers. Usually takes them into the ring for a lesson in following the rules. He likes to hear people scream." His chuckle is as menacing as his breath. Maybe he ate a small child for lunch.

"Let's go. I'll introduce you." His hand clamps around my arm and he tugs me forward.

A shiver of fear races down my spine. "You're kidding, right? I mean, look at me. Do I look like I could take on someone named Torment?" My smile wavers, so I add a few eyelash flutters and a desperate breast jiggle to the mix. Unfortunately, my ass decides to join the party, and my thighs aren't far behind.

Wrong message. His heated gaze rakes over my body, and a lascivious grin splits his wide face from ear to ear. "Torment likes the curvy ones."

Now there's a slap in the face. But maybe I can use the curves to my advantage. If I can't talk my way out of this mess, I'll just wiggle.

"Come on. He'll decide what to do with you."

Heart pounding, I scramble behind the self-styled Cerberus deep into the belly of Hell. I wish I had written a will.

Upon first glance, Hell disappoints.

The giant sheet-metal warehouse, probably around 20,000 square feet, boasts corrugated metal walls, concrete floors, and the stale sweat stench of one hundred high-school gym lockers. The ceiling is easily twenty-five feet above me. At the far end, a few freight containers are stacked in the corner, and a circular, metal staircase leads up to a second level.

Our end of the warehouse has a dedicated training area and a fully equipped gym. Half-naked, sweaty, pumped up alpha-males grapple on scarred red mats and spar in the two practice rings. Fight posters and pennants are plastered on the walls. In one corner a man dressed as a drill sergeant is barking orders at a motley group of huffing, puffing fighter wannabes.

My stomach clenches as the drumroll of speed bags, the slap of jump ropes, the whir of the treadmill, and the thud of gloves on flesh create a gut-churning symphony of violent sound.

"Hey, Rampage, you get us a new ring girl?" A small, wiry, bald fighter with red-rimmed pupil-less psycho eyes points to the "FCUK Me" lettering on my T-shirt and makes an obscene gesture with his hips. "Answer is yes, honey. Find me after the show."

I berate myself for my poor choice of attire. But really, it is my sister Susie's fault. She sends me the strangest gifts from London.

Rampage leads me toward an enormous raised boxing ring in the center of the warehouse. Spiky-haired punkers, clean-cut jocks, hip-hop headers, businessmen in suits, and leather-vested bikers fill the metal bleachers and folding chairs surrounding the main attraction. I've never seen a more eclectic group. There must be at least two hundred people here with seating for probably two hundred more. But there's no sign of Amanda. Some best friend.

We stop in front of a small, roped-off area about ten feet square. Rampage opens a steel-framed gate and shoves me inside. "You can wait in the pen. It's for your own safety. We can't have people wandering too close to the ring."

"I am not an animal," I mumble as the gate slams shut. He doesn't even crack a smile. Maybe he doesn't go to the movies.

I walk to the back of the pen for a good view of the ring and instantly recognize the man with the black bandana, despite the fact he has changed into a pleasantly tight pair of white board shorts with black winged skulls emblazoned on the sides. "That's him," I shriek. "That's the guy who didn't buy a ticket."

Amusement flashes in Rampage's beady black eyes. He stalks over to the pen and throws open the gate. "You get that guy to buy a ticket, and we'll call everything off. I won't make you face the ring."

My brow crinkles. "Isn't he a fighter? Does he even need a ticket?"

"I made you an offer. You gonna stand around talking or are you gonna take it?"

I lean up against the gate. "This has got to be a joke. And guess what? I'm not playing anymore. Just let me find Amanda and I'll get out of here."

Rampage glowers at me and his voice drops to a menacing growl. "You get up those stairs or I'll take you up myself and I can guarantee it ain't gonna be pretty."

I sigh an exasperated sigh.

"I'm going. I'm going." What the hell. Even if this is some kind of joke, the guy in the ring has mouth-watering shoulders and a great ass. I can also make out some tattoos on his back. It can't hurt to get a closer look. Maybe make a new friend.

Stiffening my spine, I climb the stairs and slide between the ropes and onto the spongy canvas mat. Hesitating, I take one last look over my shoulder. Rampage smirks and waves me forward.

My target is leaning over the ropes on the other side of the ring talking to an excessively curvy blonde wearing a one-piece, pink Lycra bodysuit. Her mountain of platinum hair is cinched on top of her head in a tight ponytail. Her huge, brown doe eyes are enhanced by her orange, spray-on tan and a slash of hot pink lipstick. She is pink and she is luscious. She is Pinkaluscious.

She rests a dainty, pink-tipped hand on Torment's foot and gazes up at him until he slides his foot back and away. Ah. Unrequited love. My heart goes out to Pinkaluscious, but really, she could do better than some two-bit, cheapskate fighter.

"Hey, Torment. I brought you a treat." Rampage's voice booms over the excited murmur of the crowd.

In one smooth, quick movement, Torment spins around to face

me. My eyes are slow to react. No doubt he caught me staring at his ass, and now I am staring at something even more enticing. Something big. My cheeks burn, and I study the worn vinyl under my feet. Someone needs to make a few repairs.

Footsteps thud across the mat. The platform vibrates under my bare feet sending tremors through my body.

Swallowing hard, I look up. My eyes widen as well over six feet of lean, hard muscle stalks toward me.

Run. I should run. But all I can do is stare.

His fight shorts are slung deliciously low on his narrow hips, hugging his powerful thighs. Hard, thick muscles ripple across the broad expanse of his chest, tapering down to a taut, corrugated abdomen. But most striking are the tattoos covering over half of his upper body—a hypnotizing cocktail of curving, flowing, tribal designs that just beg to be touched.

He stops only a foot away and I crane my neck up to look at his face.

God is he gorgeous.

His high cheekbones are sharply cut, his jaw square, and his eyes dark brown and flecked with gold. His aquiline nose is slightly off-center, as if it had been broken and not properly reset, but instead of detracting from his breathtaking good looks, it gives him a dangerous appeal. His hair is hidden beneath a black bandana, but a few tawny, brown tufts have escaped from the edges and curl down past the base of his neck.

His full lips quirk into a faint smile as he studies me. A lithe and powerful animal assessing its prey.

My finely tuned instinct of self-preservation forces me back against the ropes and away from his intoxicating scent of soap and leather and the faintest kiss of the ocean.

"Excuse me…Torment. I…thought you forgot to buy a ticket, but…um…I don't think you really need one. Do you?"

"A ticket?" His low-pitched, husky, sensual voice could seduce a saint. Or a young college grad trying to supplement her meager salary by selling tickets at a fight club.

My heart thunders in my chest and I lick my lips. His eyes lock on my mouth, and my tongue freezes mid-stroke before beating a hasty retreat behind my Pink Innocence glossed lips.

He steps forward and I press myself harder against the springy ropes, wincing as they bite into my skin through my thin T-shirt.

"Are you Amanda?"

With herculean effort, I manage to pry my tongue off the roof of my mouth. "I'm the best friend."

He lifts an eyebrow. "Does the best friend have a name?"

"Mac."

"Doesn't suit you. Do you have a different name?"

"What do you mean a different name? That's my name. Well, it's my nickname. But that's what people call me. I'm not going to choose another name just because *you* don't like it." My hands find my hips, and I give him my second-best scowl—my best scowl being reserved for less handsome irritating men.

His gaze drifts down to the bright white "FCUK Me" lettering now stretched tight across my overly generous breasts. With my every breath, the letters expand and retract like a flashing neon sign. I hate my sister.

He leans so close I can see every contour of bone and sinew in his chest and the more intricate patterns in his tribal tattoos. The flexible ropes accommodate my last retreat, and I brace myself, trembling, against them.

"What's your real name?" he rumbles.

"Makayla." *Oh, betraying lips.*

He smiles and his eyes crinkle at the corners. "Makayla is a beautiful name. I'll call you Makayla."

Heat roars through me like a tidal wave. He likes my name. "So… about that ticket—"

He snorts a laugh. "I don't need to buy a ticket."

Why is he standing so close? Has he not heard of personal space? My body trembles from the exertion of pressing back against the ropes, and my brain clicks into babble mode. "I guess the joke's on me. Rampage said I would have to fight you if I didn't get you to buy a ticket. Not that I believed for a second I would have to fight. Well, maybe I did until we got here and I saw the ring and the blood spots on the concrete and

I remembered my stepdad is a policeman. I mean I'm a girl and you're a guy—"

He looks at me aghast and cuts me off. "Shhh. It's okay, Makayla. I'm not—" He takes a step toward me. In my effort to dodge away, I lose my footing and the ropes propel me right into Torment's chest. He steps backward and falls to the floor pulling me on top of him.

No way. I am not that heavy. Sure, I enjoy my desserts, but not enough to send a two-hundred-pound man tumbling to the ground.

For a long moment, neither of us moves. One of my legs is tucked between his muscular thighs. My breasts are pressed against the warm, bare skin of his hard chest. My head is nestled on his shoulder and my hands rest lightly on his thick biceps. We breathe together. Our hearts pound together. I melt into him, not wanting what should be a humiliating moment to end.

Torment snakes an arm around my waist and I hold my breath, daring to hope he will pull me closer, but instead he rolls us so we are each on our side and rests one hand in the curve of my waist, propping his head up with the other.

"Are you hurt?"

I shake my head, not trusting myself to speak.

"Is this what you plan to do to every person who doesn't buy a ticket?" he murmurs. "If so, I might have to offer you a permanent position."

"You…own the club?" My eyes find yet another tiny tear in the mat. Really, he should keep his equipment in better repair.

"Yes, I do."

"But Rampage—"

"Set you up." He finishes my sentence for me. "I'll deal with him when we're done here. I don't allow mixed fighting at the club, and I don't force people to fight who have not already agreed to do so. I also have a zero-tolerance policy for hazing beautiful new staff members."

He thinks I'm beautiful. Or maybe it's just a figure of speech.

His warm hand strokes the dip of my waist and the curve of my hip, back and forth, up and down—a seemingly absent and casual caress. And yet, he appears to be a man very much in control of his body. A solid, heavy, muscular body.

"I didn't really knock you down, did I?" My mouth blurts out my thoughts before they make it through the filtering process. As usual.

He gives me a slow, sexy, devilish smile but his sensual lips remain firmly closed.

Well, I'm not going to complain. He can pull me on top of him any day.

"Hey, Torment. Thirty minutes. Time to wrap." Rampage's voice cuts through my perfect moment like scissors.

In one swift, easy movement, Torment rolls to his front and pushes himself to standing. He easily pulls me to my feet. "I've got to go and get ready for my fight."

A sliver of disappointment slices through me. "Sure. I've got to get back to the door, anyway. My boss might be upset if he knew I was rolling around on the mats with one of his fighters."

Torment chuckles. "Your boss wants you to stay and watch the fight."

"No can do, Boss." I can't help wrinkling my nose even though it isn't my best look. "I've got a serious aversion to violence. Unless you've got a mop and a bucket handy, you do not want me anywhere near that ring."

"If you don't like violence, why are you working here?"

I shrug and my cheeks heat. "I needed the money. Amanda promised I wouldn't have to go inside. I was planning to go home when you guys locked down for the big event."

He studies me intently for a moment and then lowers his head until his lips are so close I can feel the heat of his breath on my cheek.

"Stay."

Yes! God, I want to stay. So hot. So sexy. I could watch him all night. But no. I can't. One punch. One drop of blood. One vomit bag, please.

"No. I can't. Really can't. Not a made-up can't. It's a physical thing. Basically, I can only stomach violence if I know no one is actually getting hurt. Boxing, wrestling, even karate or judo, all fall into my no-watch zone. Just not me."

He stokes a finger along my jaw. Blazing heat shoots straight to my core, and my breath catches in my throat.

"Have you ever seen an entire fight?" He tucks a wayward strand of hair behind my ear and strokes his hand over my head.

Oh, lovely hand petting me. So gentle. If I had a tail, I would thump it.

"No. Not even on TV."

"All the more reason for you to stay. You can't sell tickets to an event you know nothing about. I would be remiss in my duty as your employer if I didn't ensure you were familiar with the services we are offering, especially if I needed you to come back and help out again."

Again? I thought this was a one-shot deal to cover for the regular ticket girls who couldn't make it tonight. "I was doing okay."

His hand drops to my shoulder and tightens. "Dressed like that, I can imagine you were."

Jeez. Again with the shirt. Doesn't anyone understand it's a joke and not an invitation? "Amanda will be waiting for me. She's taking me home."

"She and Jake went into my office as soon as ticket sales ended. I don't think you'll be seeing her anytime soon."

I knew it. She couldn't keep her hands off him. No wonder she needed a wingman tonight. She didn't want help on the door. She wanted full coverage.

He tucks a warm finger under my chin, tilting my head back so he can mesmerize me with the chestnut depths of his beautiful eyes.

"One fight. My fight. I promise it won't last long."

Mesmerized, I say, "How long is not long?"

Triumph flares in his eyes, but in an instant it is gone, replaced by concern. "How long can you last?"

"I don't know. A couple of minutes, maybe, if no one gets hurt."

A rough sound erupts from his throat. "You don't want me to hurt my opponent?"

"And I don't want him to hurt you," I say softly.

Burn cheeks burn.

His eyes widen and the look he gives me is speculative, thoughtful, considered. "One minute and I'll win by submission. No one gets hurt."

"Cocky."

His smile sears me to the core. "You have no idea."

Chapter 2
MY HEART ISN'T SO EASY TO PLEASE

TWENTY MINUTES LATER, I am seated in the front row between a thoroughly chastised Rampage and a "submission artist" named Homicide Hank. Wiry thin and lanky, with overly long arms and a shock of wildly unkempt red hair, Homicide claims to have been sent by Torment to translate the fight into Makayla-understandable terms. More likely, Torment needed someone to keep me from screaming and running away as I am now *persona non grata* in Rampage's books for getting him in trouble.

Courtesy of Torment, I have a protein shake, a protein bar, an energy drink, a bucket, and a wet cloth. He sure knows how to treat a girl.

While we wait for the fight to start, five ring girls warm up the crowd cheerleader style. Rampage puts his fingers in his mouth and whistles, "Go, Sandy," at Pinkaluscious.

Homicide shakes his head. "Torment doesn't like all the pre-show hype, but it distracts people from the lockdown. We secure the doors in case of a raid by the California State Athletic Commission."

"Why doesn't Torment just get a license and have his events sanctioned?" I ask.

"He won't do it," Rampage says. "He wants to be able to fight when and how and who he wants to fight. He wants to be able to take on a two-hundred-sixty-pound judoka or a Five Animal kung fu master without some big ass government official telling him he's in the wrong weight class, or he doesn't have enough fights under his belt. He wants to keep it real. He's not in it for the money or the glory. And he doesn't want to follow a whole lot of rules. Most of us think the same. That's how we all found our way here."

"No rules?" What would stop someone from bringing in a weapon or causing a fatal injury?

"Four rules," Rampage says. "No eye gouging, no groin shots, no biting, and no fish hooking—that's when a guy sticks his fingers in his opponent's mouth or nose and tries to tear the tissue."

My stomach clenches and I reach for the bucket. "Please don't tell me any more."

Rampage frowns. "If you can't even hear about it, how are you going to watch the fight?"

Bucket on head. Face cloth over eyes. Torment has given me lots of options.

"Torment said it would only last a minute, and he would win by submission. I'm not sure what that means but it didn't sound so bad."

Homicide chuckles. "It means he's gonna put Flash in a bone-breaking arm lock or leg lock or a choke that can put him out cold. If Flash doesn't submit—" He makes a disgusting cracking sound with his throat.

I dry heave into the bucket.

"I'm not sitting next to her." Rampage gets to his feet. "She's gonna spew all over me."

But it's too late for him to leave. The crowd suddenly comes to life, cheering and clapping as Torment and his opponent, Flash, climb into the ring.

My breath catches in my throat. Flash is none other than Mr. Psycho Eyes and supposedly my post-fight date for a little FCUK.

Jake joins Torment in his corner. Jake's blond hair is mussed and his T-shirt is inside out. Nice. Amanda must have pulled out all the stops in Torment's office. At least his fly is closed.

"Jake is Torment's cornerman," Homicide explains. "He'll coach him and tend to his cuts."

"Why does Flash have three guys in his corner?"

"He's a show-off. Likes to pretend he's a sanctioned amateur."

Jake checks Torment's gloves and helps him with his mouthpiece. Beside each other, they are a tableau of masculine perfection, all broad shoulders, tight muscles, tattoos, and slim hips. They are almost the same height, but Jake is slightly leaner and his muscles less defined. Still, with that chiseled jaw, deep voice, and those dazzling baby blues, I can totally understand how Amanda fell under his spell.

And where is Amanda?

"Thanks for covering for me." A poke in my back and a clipped, sarcastic tone reveal the location of my missing friend.

I look over my shoulder and glare as she settles herself on the chair behind me.

"You left me and now look what's happened," I say. "I'm sitting in a fight club about to throw up into a bucket of protein bars."

"You left *me* to chase after a guy." Amanda crosses her arms under her ample and perfectly-formed breasts, drawing the attention of every male in the vicinity.

"I thought he was a ticket dodger. You know I would never just run off."

Rampage and Homicide insist on introductions. Of course they would. Amanda in a burlap sack could make any man drool. Amanda in a simple, fitted, green sheath dress and gold kitten-heel pumps, her soft golden curls cascading down her back, her perfect features glowing from an hour of doing the nasty with Jake, will bring them to their knees. If I am a desert on the dating front, Amanda is a monsoon.

The bell rings. The cornermen step out of the ring. My pulse races. How is Torment going to win a fight without anyone getting hurt?

Torment wastes no time. He throws a right hook and catches Flash a glancing blow to the jaw. He follows it with a one-two punch and then a kick. Flash backs away and dances around.

"He's just playing with Flash," Homicide says. "Torment is one of the top underground fighters on the circuit. He is only a few fights away from the underground championship belt. Flash only has about ten fights on his card."

"Why would he challenge Torment?"

Homicide shrugs. "He thinks he's something special because he was an enforcer in a street gang in San Diego. In this club you can challenge whoever you want, regardless of weight or experience. We never turn down a challenge. But in the ring, skill usually wins out over strength, speed, and aggression. Flash doesn't have a chance."

Even I can tell Torment is highly skilled. There is stark beauty in the precision with which his body moves. He keeps to a tight circle near the center of the ring, moving back and forth only to strike or defend. If he wasn't wearing gloves, I might think he was dancing.

Suddenly Torment lunges forward and grabs Flash's left leg. Flash keeps his balance. Torment grabs the other leg and slams Flash to the floor, falling on top of him.

"Nice double leg takedown," Homicide calls.

But Flash is quick. He rolls to his side and gets up on one knee. Torment tries to push him back. He flattens Flash but just for a moment. Like a jack-in-the-box, Flash pops back up. Torment grabs him around the waist and falls back and to the side, pulling Flash on top of him.

"Oh no." My hand flies to my mouth.

"Don't worry. He's nasty off his back." Rampage says, as if that means something to me.

A few seconds later it does. Flash lifts his right arm to throw a punch. Still on his back, Torment grabs Flash's right wrist and pulls Flash toward him. Then he wraps his right leg over Flash's neck, hooking his foot into his left leg, which he has just wrapped around Flash's midsection. He pulls Flash's head down against his chest with two hands. Flash flails, trying desperately to escape, but he's obviously in pain.

"He's locked him in a quick triangle." Homicide says. "Match over."

My heart thuds in my chest. "He's putting pressure on the carotid artery. Flash will lose consciousness. Stop him."

Homicide gives me a sideways glance. "That's the point. It's a submission hold. Flash knows what will happen if he doesn't tap out or break the hold."

"How did you know about the artery?" Rampage asks. "I thought you weren't into fighting."

"She's an intermediate-level EMT and a pre-med grad." Amanda ruffles my hair. "And she's damn good. She's just figuring out what to do with her life, but I already know she's meant to be healing people. She's got a gift."

"Stop it." Tears well up in my eyes, and I bat Amanda's hand away.

She's the big sister Susie never was and the mother I always wanted all wrapped up in one golden, best friend package.

I turn my attention back to the ring. Flash's legs are no longer flailing.

"If he loses consciousness, I will consider it as 'someone getting hurt.'" I grumble quietly but Homicide hears me.

"He'll tap out," Homicide says. "If he doesn't, the referee will stop the match."

As if on cue, Flash taps the mat twice. Torment releases his grip and Flash rolls off him and lies spread eagle on the mat. The crowd is a frenzy of cheers and clapping. The retro bass of "Eye of the Tiger" pounds through the warehouse. The ring girls run a circle outside the ring, bosoms bouncing, miniskirts flapping, high heels clacking as they cheer, "Torment. Torment. Torment."

My God. If this is what happens after every fight, his ego must be blimp size.

The referee holds up Torment's hand and announces a win by submission in forty-six seconds. Flash staggers to his feet and wavers. He takes a step forward, then back, then sideways. He blinks several times and reaches for the ropes.

"Something's wrong with him." I tug on Homicide's sleeve. "Where's the doctor?"

"We don't have a ring doctor." His face tightens. "After the CSAC decided to sanction amateur MMA events, the ring doctors became afraid to work the underground circuit. The penalty for working an unsanctioned event is a license suspension. No doctor wants to take that risk."

"You must have someone here to look after injuries."

"It's every man for himself," Rampage answers. "Torment always takes the seriously injured guys to the hospital, but other than that, it's the luck of the draw if we've got a medical professional at a match."

I glance over at the ring. Torment is watching Flash and frowning. He calls out and Flash spins around then crumples and falls limp through the ropes. He lands on the concrete floor with a thud.

I jump up, knocking over my barf bucket. Protein bars spill across the floor. "Do you have a first aid kit?"

"Down by the ring. I'll get it for you." Rampage bulldozes a path through the crowd, and I race over to Flash.

Torment and the referee are already with him. His cornermen hover uselessly in the background.

"Makayla, you shouldn't be here," Torment snaps when I kneel beside Flash. I ignore him. He broke his promise. Someone got hurt after all.

Flash is conscious but moaning. He rubs his head and lets loose a string of swear words that would put a fifth grader to shame.

"Flash, I'm an EMT. Can I examine you?"

Flash's eyes focus on me and his lascivious smile makes my skin crawl. "Yeah, FCUK. I knew you'd come lookin' for Daddy Flash. You're wanting what I promised you. Don't worry, baby. A little injury isn't gonna stop me from putting my—"

A low growl startles us both. I look up. Torment's jaw is clenched and his eyes have narrowed to slits.

"Calm." I place my hand over his. "Although rude and obnoxious, he is my patient. I won't be very happy if you hurt him…yet."

Other than a bump on the head and the telltale signs of drug abuse around his nostrils, Flash seems fine. His cut man—the cornerman responsible for tending injuries—helps him to a folding chair near the training area. While the next fight gets underway, I check his vitals and ice his head. Torment hovers beside me. Although I don't look at him, I feel his presence like a protective cloak over my body.

I warn Flash about the possibility of a concussion. I tell him I think he blacked out because of the combination of restricted blood flow to his brain and drug abuse. His lips tighten and I know I've hit the mark.

After ten minutes, Flash starts to come down from his high. He apologizes for his behavior. He moans about his defeat and his humiliating fall from the ring. A tear trickles down his cheek. I try to console him as best I can. I pat his back and tell him he was brave to challenge one of the best fighters in the league and he isn't the first person to fall through the ropes.

I glance up at Torment. He is watching me, his brown eyes darkened by intense emotion. For the briefest second, he lets me in, and the need and longing I see behind his mask take my breath away. Suddenly his eyes shutter and the moment is gone. Maybe I imagined it.

Flash's friends arrive to take him home. Torment helps me tidy up. He tells me Flash will be banned from the club for life. Drugs are prohibited even on the underground circuit. He bends down to pick up the last ice pack and winces.

"What's wrong with your shoulder?"

He gives a manly I-could-be-bleeding-to-death-but-I'll-never-complain shrug. "It's fine."

"That's the shoulder you landed on when he threw you. It could be injured. Let me take a look."

"I'll deal with it later."

"Torment." I grip his elbow and turn him to face me. "I have my Intermediate EMT certificate, and I volunteered for the last four years with the ambulance service. If it's not serious, I can treat it."

He studies me for a long moment and then his gaze drifts to my hand on his arm. When he looks up again, I catch a mischievous sparkle in his eyes. "Not here. The next fight is about to begin. We have a first aid room out by the front office. You can examine me there to your heart's content."

"My heart isn't so easy to please."

He laughs, a chuckle as deep and warm as a vat of melted chocolate. "I'll consider it a challenge."

I make a quick detour to let Amanda know where I'll be. She is in a lip-lock with Jake and gives me a nod. When I catch up with Torment, he is in the training area shaking hands and chatting with his fighters. He has a personal comment or a piece of advice for everyone who comes to congratulate him. Through the frenzy of fighters clamoring for his attention, I catch his gaze. He gives me a wink that sends a sizzle of delicious heat darting through me, and I cannot help but smile.

"Everyone gets nervous before a fight," he explains when he returns to my side a few minutes later. "Even the most seasoned fighters. Sometimes all it takes is a little encouragement to ease that tension."

So considerate. He can ease my tension any time.

With his hand on my lower back, he escorts me through the rest of the club. I could definitely get used to this kind of courtesy. Maybe after I've found a real job, paid down my student loan, and figured out what to do with my life, I'll move to the Southern States.

We cross the red line and enter the only part of the building benefitting from proper interior construction. Shower rooms, bathrooms, and changing rooms for both men and women are on the right, as well as a kitchen and a small lounge area. The walls are covered with floor-to-ceiling chalkboards setting out the daily class schedules and work out regimes. I catch the words "Boot Camp," "Kick and Lick," and "Punch Fest." Definitely not the gym for me.

Torment leads me to the left and past a few offices with closed doors. Our shadows blend together, his magnificent body beside my small, curvy one. Even his shadow is sexy, dominating my other self as we weave our way through the loitering crowds to a door marked with a red cross.

Torment pushes open the door and turns on the lights. The small, whitewashed room is bare except for an examination table, chair, and a small cabinet with a sink and cupboards.

"Door open or closed?"

My breath catches in my throat, and I head over to the sink to wash my hands. "Open is fine unless you're concerned about showing any sign of weakness to the rest of the pride. Someone might deem you unworthy to lead and take you down."

Torment chuckles and his eyes sparkle, amused. He closes the door with a bang. My heart skips a beat.

"Up on the bed." I choke on the last word and my cheeks flame. Really. Flaming cheeks. How unprofessional. What if he had a groin injury? My body heats and sweat trickles down between my breasts. Well, there's my answer.

Torment eases himself onto the examination table. I open the cupboards and root around, pretending to search for supplies as I try to slow my racing heart. Deep, slow breaths. Unclench the jaw. Swallow the drool. Focus on the sharp scent of antiseptic.

"Okay, then." I spin around and give him my best fake smile. Torment lifts his eyes from where my bottom used to be. He licks his lips. I almost melt under the heat of his gaze.

Swallowing hard, I walk over to the bed. "I'm…just going to examine you. I'll be gentle."

He gives me a curt nod, and I place my hands on his shoulder. His skin is hot, his muscles tight. His raw, primal scent of sweat and musk sends my already heightened state of arousal into overdrive.

Taking a deep breath, I clear my mind and focus on the task at hand. My training finally kicks in and I rule out a dislocation, not just because there are no physical signs, but because he does not appear to be in pain. I lean closer, pressing gently as I check for localized tenderness. My hair slides over my shoulder and brushes across his chest. He sucks in a breath and his muscles tense.

"Sorry." I glance at his face to assess how much pain I caused. His eyes are closed and his jaw is tight.

"Did I…hurt you?"

"No. It's…your hair…it's—"

My hair? Did I hurt him with my hair? Or maybe he's shocked by the color.

"Auburn?" I say, as he opens his eyes. "Most people think it's a bad dye job because there's so much red mixed in with the brown, but it's real."

Torment twists a strand of my hair around his fingers. "So soft," he murmurs.

My lips curve into a smile. He likes my hair. He likes my name. He thinks I'm beautiful. My ego hasn't had such a boost since…well, ever.

I trace my finger over three smallish scars on his shoulder. "You've had surgery on this shoulder."

He shrugs. "It takes my weight when I fall. It's seen a lot of misuse."

"Poor little shoulder." I brush my lips over the scars.

Torment's body stiffens and he chokes. "Makayla."

Oh God. What did I just do? After four years with the ambulance crew, I thought I had the empathy problem under control.

"Sorry." I give myself a mental smack and rein my body in.

"Don't ever be sorry for who you are," he rumbles softly. From the way the phrase glides of his tongue, I sense it is something he also tells himself.

The rest of the examination proceeds uneventfully. I poke. I twist. I prod. I am the epitome of a clinical, detached, very horny professional.

By the time I finish running my hands over his sculpted body, I am wound tight with need. My breasts ache. My panties are damp. But I am in control.

"I don't think it's anything serious," I say. "Probably a mild ligament sprain or a light tear. Pain killers and ice packs for twenty minutes every two hours should help. You might want to get someone to strap it down if it gets worse."

I pull an ice pack from the freezer and hold it against his shoulder. Unable to resist, I close my eyes and inhale deeply, breathing him in. I had forgotten how heady the raw, natural scent of a man can be.

"Makayla? Everything okay?"

"You smell so good," I blurt out, then clap my hand across my mouth. Did I just say that?

Grimacing, I force myself to look up. His warm, brown eyes lock on mine and he gives me a heart-stopping grin.

"So do you. Like flowers in the sunshine." The soft, velvety texture of his voice takes my breath away.

"You can take ibuprofen for the pain." My words tumble over each other as I try to maintain the rapidly diminishing facade of professionalism. "Although I find a tub of Ben & Jerry's works just as well."

"Ice cream?"

"Not *just* ice cream. Amazing ice cream. So rich you can only buy it in pints. They keep changing the flavors, but my current favorite is Chunky Monkey."

"Sounds…unhealthy."

"That's the point. It's an indulgence. It's not supposed to be healthy."

Torment traces a finger over my lips. "I can think of several indulgences that are very healthy."

I inhale a sharp breath. Oh. My. God. Is he coming on to me? What should I say? What should I do? I freeze and stare straight ahead.

"What did you think of the fight?" He drops his hand and I lick my lips, tasting his salty deliciousness on my tongue.

"It wasn't what I expected. I thought there would be more punching and kicking people in the face. Lots of blood. Bones breaking. I didn't know about the whole grapple and submission aspect."

"You asked me not to hurt him."

I twist my lips to the side. "So…it is how I imagined?"

"Probably worse."

I slide the ice pack to a better position. "Well, then my first instinct to stay outside was a good one. I'll remember that the next time I'm tempted to sell tickets at a fight club to make a little extra cash."

He frowns. "Do you need work?"

"I have a job at the admissions desk at the County Hospital, but the occasional odd job helps make ends meet."

He tucks an errant strand of hair behind my ear, and the gentle, casual gesture makes my toes curl.

"I've been looking for someone with emergency medical experience to handle first aid at the club." His hand lingers on my shoulder and my stomach does a backflip.

"This was just a one-off for me," I say. "I couldn't work here permanently because of the whole violence aspect."

He cups my chin in his warm palm and strokes my cheek with his thumb. My heart flutters and desire sends shivers through my body.

"Is it just the violence, or do you have a boyfriend who doesn't like the idea of you working here?" He drops his hand, and his tattoos undulate across his chest. The longer I stare at them, the more the center line begins to resemble a dragon, twisting its way down his sternum and over his abdomen, only to disappear under the waistband of his shorts. Oh, to be that dragon!

"No boyfriend." I manage a hoarse whisper. "I mean not right at this very moment. I had one. Well, three, actually. In my life. Serious boyfriends. But not all at once and never for longer than a month or two. It just didn't work out with any of them. It never does."

"I find that hard to believe." The caress in his voice turns my bones to mush.

Scrambling to orient myself, I focus again on his tattoos. So many. So intricate. But why only on the right side of his body? Maybe it was too painful. I remember the night Amanda and I foolishly decided to get matching tattoos to celebrate our high school graduation and how I screamed and ran the minute the needle touched my skin.

Unthinking, I stroke my finger down the dragon, stopping just before it disappears below his waistband.

Torment hisses in a breath.

I gasp. "I'm sorry. I shouldn't have…I wasn't thinking…I know it hurts to get a tattoo and I was imagining your pain, and they are so beautiful and scary at the same time."

This is mortifying. I am on the verge of running away when the door opens and Amanda steps inside. "All ready to go?"

Oh, thank God.

"Yup." I hand the ice pack to Torment. "I'm sorry I can't stay longer, but Amanda is my ride home."

Amanda disappears and I repeat my instructions of when and how long to ice his shoulder. I get no response. His face is impassive and I can't tell if he is angry, disappointed, or indifferent.

After I tidy up the room, I turn to him and for lack of anything better to do or say, I hold out a stiff hand. "It was nice to meet you."

He slides his hand against my palm and strokes his thumb over the sensitive skin near my wrist.

A delicious shiver slides down my spine. I can feel his eyes on me, willing me to look up, but I don't want him to see how much he affects me. Especially since I'll never see him again.

"Bye." I pull away and race through the door.

Jake and Amanda are chatting outside the ticket office.

"Can we go now?" I shift from one foot to the other.

Amanda looks at me and her eyes widen. "What's wrong, Mac?"

"Nothing. I just…I thought we were leaving."

She gives me a long, assessing look. Her eyes flick over my shoulder and back to my face. She raises a perfectly arched eyebrow and gives me a conspiratorial nod.

Uh-oh. Maybe I should stay at the club. My ride home promises to be an inquisition—Amanda style.

"Sorry, Jake." She pecks him on the cheek, leaving behind the faint, pink imprint of her lush lips. "Have to go. Friends come first. But I'll see you at my place after your fight. Don't shower. I like you all sweaty and pumped up."

Jake rakes his hand through his thick, blond hair and grins. "I aim to please."

Amanda pushes open the door, and I glance back over my shoulder. Torment is standing in the doorway to the first aid room, still as a statue, his body chiseled from the finest marble, his tattoos begging to be explored.

No way in hell can I bring myself to go back and ask for my paycheck. I can't face him ever again.

He studies me, thoughtful, focused, intent, and then he smiles, transforming breathtaking good looks into utter irresistibility in a heartbeat. My breath catches in my throat. I take one last, lingering look. And then I walk out the door.

Chapter 3

I'M AFRAID SHE'S TAKEN

"YOU'RE FIVE MINUTES LATE, Mac. That's coming off your pay."

Big Doris taps her clipboard while I take my seat at Admissions Desk One in Oakland's leading county hospital. Although only five-foot-two and weighing no more than ninety-nine pounds, Big Doris is possessed of an unnaturally loud voice, and her words boom throughout the crowded waiting room, drawing titters from the patients waiting to see the triage nurse.

"I'm not late. The clock is five minutes fast. According to my watch, I'm exactly on time."

"According to the hospital clock, you are late." Big Doris writes up a shame-inducing green slip for my personnel file and then peers down at me over horn-rimmed glasses that I suspect are only for show.

"No wonder you failed out of pre-med in college. You don't even have the discipline to get to work on time."

"I didn't fail out," I explain through clenched teeth. "I graduated with a science degree and an Intermediate-Level EMT qualification. I didn't have the money to pay for medical school."

"Ha!" she snorts. "As if there aren't dozens of organizations willing to provide scholarships to train new doctors. You must have been at the bottom of the class."

Why is she always antagonizing me? She was so pleasant the first month, and positively evil for the last twenty-three months since I joined the department.

"I was at the top of my class. I just wasn't sure if it was what I wanted to do. I didn't want to take money away from people who were truly committed."

She tears the green slip off her pad and flutters it in the air just out of my reach. "So much more fulfilling to be working the Admissions Desk and making a fraction of the salary, isn't it?"

Snatching the slip from her fingers, I give her a cool smile. "I'm grateful to have any job in this economy."

Two seconds after she stomps away in her four-inch, fire engine red pumps, my counterpart at Admissions Desk Two and second best friend, Charlie, pokes his head around the partition.

"Don't let her get to you. She's jealous because you are so much prettier than her. Just don't eat any of her apples. She might be suffering from wicked queen syndrome."

"Maybe if I eat a poisoned apple, my prince will come." I turn on my computer. "Nothing else has worked so far."

My computer hums to life and I stow my purse in the bottom drawer of my desk. Charlie rolls his desk chair into my cubicle, while seated, with a coordinated jerking of his hips and heels. His Mickey Mouse scrubs are bunched up around his thighs and a length of hairy calf protrudes above Disney-themed socks. His bright orange Crocs squeak when he pulls himself to a stop.

"Here I am." He throws his arms out to the sides and almost knocks over the partition. "One prince, ready to kiss you and carry you away to my tiny bachelor pad in the sky."

My grin and snort of laughter do nothing but encourage him. He closes his eyes and purses his lips, waiting for the kiss that is never going to happen.

"Sorry," I lie, not wanting to hurt his feelings. "My heart is taken by the prince who shall not be named."

"It's Doctor Drake, isn't it?" he whispers. "I can lower my standards. I'll dye what little hair I have left the color of spun gold, add some blue contacts, lose one hundred and fifty pounds, work out, get a fake tan, take a chisel to my jaw, accept a job as a highly paid surgeon, and hang out in the waiting room for twenty-three months pretending to be assessing the staff."

"Doctor Drake is the head of administration now," I interject. "That's why he's always lurking around. And rich guys make me nervous. I'm more of a pizza and beer kind of girl, not caviar and wine. I wouldn't be able to walk the walk or talk the talk. I just want to find someone I could be comfortable with. Someone like me."

"Poor but proud," Charlie sighs. "I suspect you're going to have to change your attitude. Drake's lurking around because he likes you. One day he's going to work up the nerve to ask you out and I'll have to challenge him to a duel in the parking lot."

I flip my sign to "Open," and give Charlie's chair a shove. "I thought we agreed we were better off as friends. Now, get to work. Only eight and a half hours left until the weekend."

Charlie hangs his head in mock disappointment and rolls back to his desk.

An hour later, my cell phone rings. I wave the phone over the partition to let Charlie know to watch out for Big Doris. He thumps the partition in agreement. I settle in my chair and accept the call on the last ring.

"Makayla Delaney?"

"Yes."

"This is Sergio Martinez from Collections R Us. I received your file from the Education Commission. They inform me you have defaulted on your loan payments. It is my job to collect the money."

My heart thuds in my chest and I swallow hard before answering. "I think there's been a misunderstanding. I tried to make the payments after I graduated. I used all my savings, moved to a cheaper apartment, and sold my car, but I was unemployed. I applied for deferment and they agreed to defer the loan for five years."

"Apparently, they changed their minds."

"But that's not fair. They never told me."

Sergio yawns. "Not my problem. They sent me the file with the word 'Default' stamped on the front in big red letters. I take that to mean you didn't make your payments."

Sweat trickles down my back and I grip the phone. "I can send you the paperwork or you can contact them yourself. The five years aren't up and my circumstances haven't changed. I can barely pay rent and—"

"Frankly, Ms. Delaney, I don't care about your circumstances and it's not my job to conduct an investigation or to contact the Education Commission. My job is to collect the money, and the government permits me to use every means at my disposal to get it. Let's see what you owe. I have a loan calculator right here." He taps on what sounds like a keyboard and then rattles off a number that makes my heart seize in my chest.

"That's almost twice the original loan."

Sergio laughs. "Interest and penalties have been accumulating." More tapping. And then he gives me a monthly payment amount that sends my pulse skyrocketing.

"I can't pay that much." My voice rises to a pathetic whine. "That's almost my entire monthly salary. I won't have money to pay rent or eat."

"I'm afraid that is the minimum payment to rehabilitate your loan. Nine payments in ten months and you repair your credit and get me off your back. My boss wants more but you sound like a nice girl and I want to give you a break. You have until Monday to decide or I'll seize part of your paycheck forever and you'll never have another chance to rehabilitate your loan."

"Monday?" I squeak. "I can't do it. I need time to contact the Education Commission and find out what happened to my deferment."

Sergio sighs. "Are you sure you want to do that? You will be required to make a formal complaint and who knows how long it will take them to respond. In the meantime, your default will show up on credit checks, and the interest and penalties continue to rise. I can offer you the opportunity to rehabilitate your loan right here, right now. Don't you want a fresh start?"

"But where will I get the money?"

"I'm sure you have family, friends, relatives, or neighbors who could help you. Maybe you have things to sell. Have a garage sale. Clean out your wardrobe. Be creative. That's what I tell all my debtors."

My heart sinks to my stomach. "I have nothing. I have no jewelry or fancy clothes or paintings. I don't own a bicycle or a car. I don't even own the TV in the house I'm sharing with four other people. I can't ask my friends for money. Most of them don't have enough to make ends meet. And as for my family—"

"Again, Ms. Delaney, don't waste your breath. I've heard it all—injuries, accidents, sick children, dying parents, unexpected pregnancies, fatal illnesses, hungry boa constrictors, divorces, exploding houses, and rabid dogs running off with bags of cash."

"Have you heard the one about the elephant and the trombone?" I scramble to save the situation the only way I know how.

Sergio is silent for so long I can't tell if he is amused or really annoyed. "Actually, Ms. Delaney, I can't say that I have. Please enlighten me."

I tell Sergio a long joke about an elephant, a debt collector, and a trombone. When I get to the punch line, he snickers, then he snorts, then he laughs out loud.

"Very amusing." He chuckles again. "I haven't laughed like that for years. Usually people scream, swear, and threaten me. I heard the words 'Fuck off' two hundred and three times yesterday. No one has ever told me a joke."

I cross my fingers. "I aim to please."

"And please you have done. In return I'm going to do something for you. I'll give you an extra week to come up with your first installment. After that, as long as you make your payments, you'll have no trouble from me. If you miss even one payment, the entire loan comes due with immediate effect. I will then be entitled to seek orders from the court to garnish your wages, seize your income tax refunds, drain your bank accounts, and I can do the same to your parents. As guarantors of your loan, their assets are up for grabs, including their house."

My lungs seize up and I gasp. "Oh God. No. That house means everything to them. It has been in my stepfather's family for generations. He gave it to my mother so she would never have to worry about having a roof over her head again. They plan to live there until they die."

"Or until I foreclose to pay their daughter's debts."

I clench my fists under the table. Never. I'll never let him take their house. "I'll make the payments," I say, through gritted teeth. "And I appreciate your offer."

"I'm glad you do," he says. "As with most student debt collection agencies, we are incentivized to collect the debts. Usually we receive a percentage of the amount collected plus performance bonuses, and it can add up fast. My supervisor made half a million dollars last year and the CEO made one million dollars. I used my bonus to buy myself a Jag. This year, I'm aiming to buy a Porsche."

"How nice for you." I do a quick mental calculation. Even if I pare down the grocery shopping to the bare essentials, cut out meat, forgo Friday nights at the bar with Amanda, and collect my money from Torment, I won't have enough to make the payment. I need a second job. Fast.

"I can hear the wheels clicking in your brain." Sergio's thin, reedy voice jolts me back to reality. "I see from your college transcript, you're a very clever girl. You should have applied for some scholarships and gone to medical school. Your loans would have been deferred until you were done and then you would have been making so much money they wouldn't have been an issue."

"Thanks for the advice."

Sergio chuckles. "I like you Ms. Delaney. I can't say that about many of my debtors. I look forward to speaking to you again soon."

A few hours and several dozen patients later, I doodle a picture of a boxing ring on my notepad. Maybe I should have stayed at the club last Friday instead of running away. Maybe after everyone had gone, Torment would have taken me into the ring and kissed me. His hard body would have pressed me back into the ropes. We would have made the offer on my "FCUK Me" T-shirt a reality, and afterward we would have gotten matching tattoos.

"Mac, wake up." The urgency in Charlie's voice snaps me out of my daydream.

"What's going on here?" Big Doris swoops into my cubicle and stares down at me through clear, plastic lenses that do not refract her eyes in any noticeable way. She whips out her book of green slips and clicks her pen. "I've had a complaint about a patient backlog."

"We're having problems with the computers." Charlie pokes his head around the partition and lies with the aplomb of a used car dealer sensing a sale. "They keep freezing up. We need someone from IT down here right away."

Big Doris narrows her eyes but even she doesn't dare challenge Charlie. He has been here too long. He knows too many people. And he has a very sharp tongue.

"Fine. I'll deal with it." Big Doris deflates and storms away.

"You just ruined her morning," I call out. "She wanted to give me another green slip."

"Don't worry about Big Doris. I've got her figured out. She just needs a man. And since you won't have me, I'll have to settle for tenth best."

Hah. Charlie and Big Doris. Never going to happen.

While I wait for the computer to dredge up a new patient form, I resolve to find Charlie a girlfriend. Someone normal. Someone who likes nice, soft, slightly balding guys who are eager to please. Someone whose heart doesn't pound at the sight of hard-bodied men covered in tattoos.

A collective sigh from the waiting room pulls me out of the start of yet another daydream about Torment. I look up, just as Dr. Donald Drake, preeminent heart surgeon turned administrator, glides toward me. He stops in front of my desk and smiles.

Ah. My insides quiver. Although he has no visible tattoos or piercings and exudes an aura of calm competence as opposed to one of seething danger, I am not immune to his chiseled charms.

"How are things going today, Mac?"

My smile stretches my cheeks. "Very well, thank you, Doctor Drake."

Dr. Drake places his hands on my desk and leans forward. I inhale his fresh, clean scent of laundry soap and after dinner mints. I sneeze.

"Doris mentioned you were having difficulties with your computer. Perhaps I could take a look at it for you."

"You?" My eyes widen. He has departments filled with minions to do his grunt work, not to mention an entire IT department.

Charlie makes lewd, loud kissing noises behind the partition, and I cover my mouth, pretending to cough.

Dr. Drake glances over at the partition and frowns. "Problem, Mr. Brown?"

"No, sir," Charlie calls over. "Just sucking on a lemon. I'm trying to increase my consumption of citrus fruits."

My stomach clenches with repressed laughter.

Dr. Drake looks down at me and smiles again. Such a happy doctor. The light glints off his unnaturally white teeth. "I know a thing or two about computers, Mac. I didn't spend all my time with my head in my medical books."

"Heh, heh, heh." I join him laughing at his own joke. What a pathetic laugh. Thank God I can't see Charlie's face.

A few moments later, Dr. Drake's lean, toned body is settled in my desk chair. He pounds away at my keyboard, and I glance over the partition at Charlie. Big mistake. He mouths "heh, heh, heh," and then wheezes in a breath, and doubles over in a fit of laughter. I resolve to find Charlie a psychopathic girlfriend with a sharp knife.

"I think this may require an IT specialist after all." Dr. Drake's perfectly smooth brow wrinkles. "Why don't I take you for lunch? I'll ask IT to send someone up while you're away from your desk."

My mouth drops open. Dr. Drake is asking me out for lunch? With his medical pedigree and women lining up to get in his pants, he doesn't lack for potential lunch partners. Why me? And why couldn't he be a beguiling fighter with the manners of a Southern gentleman?

A fighter I will never see again. The rational thought sobers me up and I muster a lukewarm smile. Only last week I would have been overjoyed at the chance to lunch with the hospital's number one most eligible bachelor. Or maybe not. We are fiscally incompatible. He is caviar and I am instant noodles.

"I'm afraid she's taken."

Brain freeze. From somewhere deep in my core, recognition of the deep, sensual rumble of that voice sizzles through me, awakening every nerve ending in my body. Awareness comes back slowly. A shadowy image hovers in front of my desk. Gradually, my vision comes into focus.

Torment.

Torment is here.

My heart takes off down the speedway.

His loose, wavy brown hair is neatly tucked back into his black bandana. He is wearing his black leather biker jacket over a Harley-Davidson T-shirt stretched tight across his broad, muscular chest. His black jeans are a feast of tight seams in all the right places. He exudes pure, raw sensuality. And he is looking at me.

"Ready to go?" He drops his pack onto the chair in front of my desk and holds out his hand.

Inhaling a sharp breath, I blurt out an eloquent, "What?"

His lips curve into a smile. "Lunch, Makayla. You do eat, don't you?"

"You want to have lunch with me? How did you know where I work?"

His gaze sears through me, hot and electric. "You told me last week. I have a good memory for details. And yes, I am here to take you to lunch."

"Mac, do you know this…*person*?" Dr. Drake rises slowly from my chair and positions himself between me and Torment. From the unnatural wrinkles in his perfectly smooth forehead, I assume he is not pleased to have our discussion interrupted.

"This is…um…Torment." My cheeks burn and I glare at Torment, willing him to reveal his real name and save me from the perils of bad manners. His eyes glimmer with barely repressed amusement, but his sensual lips stay firmly closed.

Dr. Drake gives me a quizzical look. "Torment? Is that a last name? Or perhaps an affliction?"

"I believe it's a ring name." I try to block out the muffled sound of Charlie's snort of laughter. "He's an MMA fighter."

"Ah." Dr. Drake rests his hand on my shoulder and gives it a gentle squeeze. I stiffen at the unexpected touch. Torment's eyes narrow and focus like laser beams on Dr. Drake's hand.

"A sweet girl like you shouldn't be associating with these rough, fight types," Dr. Drake says in the gentle tone usually reserved for wayward children and small animals. "They are violent men who think nothing of flaunting the law or exposing innocent girls to the more uncivilized elements of our society."

How can he talk like that with Torment standing right in front of him? Aside from being impolite, it's dangerous. I try to pry his hand off my shoulder. "I think you might be overreacting."

Dr. Drake slides his thumb under my hair in a gesture that is disconcertingly soothing. "So compassionate. I sensed that quality in you during your interview. But don't let your empathy obscure who these men really are and what they can do. Come to the ER one Friday or Saturday night and see for yourself the effects of uncontrolled violence." His thumb rubs up and down, gently massaging my neck. My back arches involuntarily and I inhale a sharp breath.

Torment growls—a deep, barely audible, entirely thrilling sound. He leans across the desk, grabs Dr. Drake's hand, and rips it off my shoulder.

"She's coming with me. Now." He whips off his jacket, tossing it on the chair beside his pack, and folds his arms over his chest, his biceps tensed like he is about to punch someone.

Dr. Drake snorts his derision and his eyes flick to me instead of staying focused on the deadly threat in front of him. "Exactly as I said. Uncivilized."

Torment sucks in a breath and takes a step closer to my desk.

I reach over and rest a soothing hand on Torment's corded forearm. Electricity darts through me the second I make contact. My heart almost goes into cardiac arrest. Not good. Given his reaction to Dr. Drake's unexpected neck stroking, how would Torment react if Dr. Drake had to perform CPR and rub my chest? I jerk my hand away.

"I forgot we were going for lunch today." I give Dr. Drake my best fake smile as the lie slides off my tongue with a healthy dose of drool. "I'll have to take a rain check on your kind invitation."

Dr. Drake's eyes soften. "I'm free on Monday. I'll arrange for IT to look at your computer while you're away from your desk." He gives Torment a dismissive glance before weaving his way through the crowded waiting room, seemingly unaware of the sighs and flushed cheeks he leaves in his wake.

"What the hell was that?" I yank open my desk drawer and grab my purse. "You almost got me fired."

Torment scowls. "He won't fire you. He wants you too much. He probably wouldn't even accept your resignation if you tried to leave."

"Are you crazy?" I round my desk and pull up in front of him. "He's never paid any attention to me until today."

"You just haven't seen him. I know his type." He pauses and his voice takes on a deeper, cutting edge. "Are you going to have lunch with him on Monday?"

"None of your business." I am righteous in my indignation. "And what's this about lunch today? Usually, if you want to have lunch with someone, you call and ask if it's convenient. I only have half an hour. It's barely enough time to go to the cafeteria."

"You left so quickly I didn't get a chance to ask for your number. I have your paycheck, a picnic, and a proposition for you." He squares his shoulders and raises my hand to his lips. "If it is convenient, would you care to join me for lunch, Makayla Delaney?"

This is just like the movies. Entranced, I just stare and smile, like the vacant fool I am.

Torment chuckles. "Makayla?

I shake my head. "Um. Yes. Lunch. Good. Picnic area. Outside. For staff."

Oh God. Someone, please put me out of my misery, or at least cover my mouth with surgical tape.

"Lead the way." Torment picks up his pack and jacket, and I lead him through the hospital to a grassy outdoor quadrangle dotted with picnic tables, flower beds, and leafy trees.

"What's the proposition?" I glance over at the feast of testosterone walking beside me. Really, who needs lunch?

"I desperately need a medical professional to cover our underground events. Two more guys had to go to the hospital last week, and I'm concerned someone is going to rat us out to the CSAC. We've heard rumors on the underground circuit that if an event is restricted to club members and a doctor is present, they'll look the other way provided the fighters are not given any compensation. We're okay on the compensation side. I've always given the money we collect at the door to charity. But we can't find a ring doctor, and I haven't been able to find anyone with first aid experience willing to commit to being at every match. We usually have events once or twice a week on the weekend."

"Oh." My heart thuds into my stomach. He just wants me to work. Not that I don't need the work with Sergio now in the picture, but it would have been nice to be wanted for something else.

His face falls. "You can't do it? I'll pay you anything you ask."

"No. I mean, yes, I'll do it."

"You will?" His face brightens. I slide into a picnic table bench under a shady tree and Torment takes a seat across from me.

"Could you come tonight for an orientation? It's the only time I have free."

"Sure."

He beams. "I wasn't sure if you would agree because of your violence issues." He pulls two wax paper packages from his pack and slides one across the table.

"I need the money, and if I stay in the first aid office and only come out when I'm needed, it shouldn't be a problem." I take the sandwich he offers and peek inside at the one-inch thick piece of cheese slathered in what appears to be half a tub of margarine. Horrors.

"I made it myself," he says. Pride shines in his warm, brown eyes.

Not wanting to hurt his feelings, I smile. "I love cheese."

Torment opens a steel container and places it between us. Chopped veggies. Very healthy, but not very delicious. I select a baby tomato and bite down. Tomato juice shoots across the table and hits Torment square in the chest.

Damn. The Clumsyosaurus strikes again.

"I'm so sorry. Obviously, I don't get out much. Nor do I eat many vegetables." I reach over the table and dab at Torment's tomato-juice stained chest with a tissue from my purse. He sucks in a sharp breath.

My eyes follow his gaze into the gaping maw of my unbuttoned shirt. My cheeks heat. "Enjoying the view?"

"There wasn't anywhere else for me to look." Amusement flashes in his eyes and he gives me a cocky, toe-curling smile. "And even if there was, I thought it would be impolite to turn down the invitation."

"You could have closed your eyes." I sit back down and feign annoyance, but he is too cute, and too happy, and I can't help but smile back. Plus, I'm quite proud of my girls.

"That would have been worse." His voice drops to a low, sensual rumble. "My imagination might have run wild."

My heart thuds in my chest. Me? The object of Torment's wild fantasies? Really?

Torment takes my hand and lifts it to his mouth. He kisses my fingers one by one, and then brushes his lips down my palm. Electricity shoots from my hand straight to my core. I think he's coming on to me. Or else, he's really, really pleased to have a new first aid attendant.

"Since you're willing to handle the first aid, I have another proposition for you," he murmurs.

Frozen, rapt, unable even to breathe, I watch his sensuous lips work their way up the inside of my arm to the sensitive crease of my elbow. His kisses are as light as butterfly wings. I shiver—a bone-deep awakening of dormant desire.

"What is it?" There is almost nothing I could refuse him at this very moment. Sex on the picnic bench? Check. Strip off and do the Macarena on the grass? Check. Crawl under the table and do naughty things? Not much experience in that department either, but…check. Ride off into the sunset? Double check.

"Dinner."

"Okay."

"If you give me your address, I'll pick you up at home before the club opens."

"Okay."

"We'll grab some pizza, and then I can go over the rules of the club."

"Okay."

"We'll do the orientation and I can show you around."

"Okay."

"I'll bring you home at the end of the night.

"Okay."

"Makayla?"

Filled with the joy of renewed hope, I lift my eyes to his.

"You have something on your cheek."

Chapter 4
COME AND GET IT

IT IS AFTER SIX p.m. by the time I get home from work. Unable to face the cheery chatter of my housemates, I make my way to my bedroom, strip down to my panties, and throw on a tank top and a pair of faded, torn gym pants. All comfy for a round of "he likes me, he likes me not" with a wilted daisy from the garden, and if "not" then a sulk about hot, witty, charming guys who make me picnic lunches only to get into my first aid kit and not my pants.

Once I have arranged the purple cushions on my bed, I settle my laptop on my knees, and amuse myself by typing "Torment," "California," and "Redemption" into various search engines. Nothing of interest comes up. I read Redemption's web page and find no mention of the unsanctioned events. "Torment" yields all sorts of references to games, books, music, and torture, but no pictures of men with tattoos and warm, brown eyes.

A flash of black catches my eye, and I look up. My hands fly to my mouth when I glimpse the shadow of a man by the door. I drop my computer, a shriek ripping from my throat.

"Shhh. I'm not going to hurt you." Eyes wide, Torment holds up his hands, palms forward. He takes a step back just as my four housemates barrel into my room.

My heart pounds a frantic rhythm against my ribs. "What's he doing here?"

"He said you were expecting him." Rob's voice wavers with uncertainty as he glances over at the leather-clad giant dwarfing my tiny room.

"Yes, but not for a few hours." I draw in a ragged breath. "And you're not supposed to let strangers just walk into the house. You're supposed to ask them to wait at the door. What if I was changing? What if I didn't really know him?"

Rob grimaces. "I'm sorry, Mac. I didn't think." He runs a hand through his thick, black curls. "You want me to throw him out?"

With his slender frame and gentle manner, Rob is hardly in a position to throw me out, much less six feet two inches of hard, lean muscle. Laughter bubbles in my chest, and I shake my head. "You'll need both your arms to take over my garbage duty next week, which you will be doing by way of apology."

Rob gives me a wink and follows my disappointed housemates down the hallway. Fights are always good entertainment.

"When you said you would pick me up before Redemption opened, I didn't realize you meant two hours before it opened," I moan as soon as Rob's curly head disappears around the corner. "I just got home from work."

"You didn't give me your number," a bemused Torment retorts. "We have a lot of ground to cover to get you up to speed on the club's rules and operations. I wouldn't want to see you in the ring again." He scrubs his hand through his thick, chestnut hair. Without the bandana, it is longer than I imagined, falling well past his collar, and cut with apparent carelessness to follow the line of his jaw. Could he look any more breathtaking?

"Fine. We'll exchange numbers to avoid any future surprises. Just let me find my phone." I hunt around for my cell while Torment makes a slow, careful, inspection of my room. Not that there's much to see. Twin bed. Desk. Shelf. Wardrobe. Dresser. Purple walls, purple bedspread, purple area rug, purple curtains. A few dollar store prints. At least I keep it tidy.

I cross the room and catch sight of myself in the mirror. Dear Lord. I'm not wearing a bra. And worse, my interest in the tribute to testosterone planted in the middle of my floor is clearly evident in the hard buds of my nipples visible through my tank top.

A squeak escapes my lips and I slam my arms across my chest and turn to face the wall.

"Is this where you sleep?" The inflection in his voice betrays a lack of appreciation for my sanctuary. Or maybe he doesn't like purple.

"Yeah. It's not much, but it's cheap." I shuffle toward my dresser, keeping my back to him.

"This isn't a room," he admonishes, "it's a hallway."

"Actually, it's a back entrance." I point to a door in the side wall. "That's the back door. Our communal bathroom is right beside you."

"Communal bathroom?" he splutters. "People have to walk through your bedroom to use the bathroom?"

My dresser is finally within reach and I yank a hoodie out of the drawer and pull it over my head. "I only pay half the rent the others pay. I volunteered to take the room because I couldn't afford to pay the full amount, and I'm the only one without a regular bed friend."

"How many people live here? I saw at least ten when I walked through the house." He stops in front of my bookshelf and studies my books: an eclectic collection of college texts, medical reference books, running logs, travel guides for all the places I dream of visiting, thrillers, and romance novels. Lots of romance novels.

"Officially five, but usually there are about nine or ten people around if you count boyfriends, girlfriends, cousins, friends, and the odd vagrant." Relaxed now that I am decently covered and no longer besieged by naughty thoughts, I turn around and lean against the dresser.

"But it's not safe," Torment's voice rises sharply. "And you need privacy. How can you live like this?"

Why does no one ever understand? I like having people wander in for a pee and a chat. I'm a sociable girl. "It took a while to get used to. The biggest downside is that I can't let my parents visit. My stepfather is a policeman. If he saw this place, he would drag me home."

Torment crosses the room in two strides and twists the handle on the back door. The lock gives way and the door creaks open. "Who's your landlord? Anyone could come in this door. The lock isn't secure."

I want to tell him his delightful protective streak is showing, but I don't want to embarrass him. "Some guy who's never around. Slumlord. We haven't had a working stove for the last six months, and the dishwasher broke on Tuesday, but we'll be lucky if he even stops by in the next year."

Torment scrubs his hand over his face. "You said you don't make much at the hospital, but isn't it enough for a decent place to live?"

My cheeks heat. "I have a few college debts to pay. I also haven't decided yet what I want to do with my life, so it's okay for now. It's got…character."

I finally spot my cell under the bed and get down on my hands and knees to retrieve it.

"I'm sorry." He sounds genuinely contrite. "It's just…a woman should feel safe—" He cuts himself off and makes a choking sound. "What the hell are you doing?"

"Getting my phone. It must have fallen under the bed when you suddenly materialized in my room." Looking up over my shoulder, I follow his gaze to my bottom, waving around in the air, my panties partially exposed by the tears in my gym pants. Can this day get any worse?

There is just no elegant way to extract myself from this situation, so I don't even try. I grab my phone and back into the center of the room, delivery truck style but without the beeps.

"I'm guessing you don't have to share a bathroom at your house," I say with the casual tone of someone who isn't waving her half-naked bottom in the air in front of a hunky, semi-stranger and soon-to-be-boss. I push myself to my feet and edge my way back to the dresser, this time keeping my back to the wall.

He snorts a laugh. "No. Nor do I have a back door in my bedroom or a collection of random people walking around my house."

"Sounds lonely." I grab a T-shirt and a pair of jeans from the top drawer and shuffle over to the bathroom.

"I'm too busy working to be lonely."

I toss him my phone. "You can do the number exchange while I get ready. No long distance calls. I don't have many minutes left on it."

He stares at my cheap plastic cell with a puzzled look on his face. "Is this real?"

"Of course it's real," I snort. "It's a basic prepaid cell phone. It comes with a set number of minutes and I buy phone cards to top it up when I need to. Why? What do you use?"

The sleek, silver and glass device he pulls from his pocket is like nothing I've ever seen before. Slightly bigger than an iPhone but half as thick, it has an incredible, crystal clear screen that sparkles under the naked bulb overhead.

"What is it?" I breathe a gasp of longing.

He shrugs. "Prototype. Can't really talk about it."

"It has multiple windows. You could display all your social media at once. You wouldn't miss anything."

"I don't do social media." He calls himself with my phone and his device quivers in his hand.

"No Facebook? No Twitter? No Pinterest?" My eyebrows shoot up to my hairline.

"What's Pinterest?" He finishes the number exchange and hands me my cell.

"Seriously? You haven't heard about it? It's like a bulletin board. You post pictures on it. You could put up all sorts of pictures of yourself in various fighting poses." Curling up my forearms, I drop my spare clothes and mock up a few fighting stances.

Torment stares at me, his face devoid of expression.

I freeze. What am I doing? This is exactly why guys never take me seriously.

His laugh takes me by surprise. A deep, rumbling roar of a chuckle. I can't help but smile.

He bends down to pick up my clothes. "You are quite the package, Makayla. I'm surprised your doctor friend didn't snap you up sooner."

My mouth drops open. Maybe tonight won't be a write-off after all.

"How do you run your business without social media? How do you advertise? How do you let people know when there's an event?"

"We're already at capacity in the gym and training center. As for the events, Jake's the promoter. He handles that side of things. And we don't advertise. The invitations are sent by text a few hours before the match starts so it's almost impossible for CSAC to regulate us or shut us down."

He hands me my jeans, but when I reach for my shirt he frowns. "Is this the shirt you wore last week?" He holds the shirt up, and I grimace when the bright, white "FCUK Me" lettering shines under the overhead light.

"You aren't wearing this."

"Why?"

"I don't want the men at the club thinking what they think when they see you in this shirt."

"What do they think?" My hand finds my hip and my eyebrow finds the ceiling.

"Makayla." He purrs out my name in a warning tone. "Not at the club. The men there—do you have anything less provocative?"

My face heats up. "My shirt is provocative?"

"The words are provocative. The shirt is flattering."

A grin spreads across my face. Provocative and flattering. Quite the package. I have died and gone to heaven.

Torment balls the shirt in his fist. "Find something else."

I laugh and hold out my hand. "You do realize I have to wear the shirt now. Hand it over."

Torment gives me a slow, sexy smile as he tucks my shirt into his leather jacket. "No."

"Give me my shirt…please." I'm not sure what kind of game he is playing, if it is a game, but damned if I am leaving here without that shirt on.

"Come and get it," he rasps.

Something shifts in the air between us. As I walk over to him, no more able to resist his challenge than I can stop from breathing, his face wavers, changes, reveals the predator behind the sculpted cheekbones and the warm, sparkling eyes. I glimpse power, barely restrained and a force of will that takes my breath away. He draws me to him with the intensity of his gaze and the dangerous rumble of his deep, dark voice.

God, he's hot.

By the time I am close enough to feel the heat from his body, my heart is racing at double speed. His eyes lock on mine, and I grasp the edge of my shirt. He smells of leather and a citrus scent that is at once sharp and sensual.

I draw my shirt away from his chest, inch by slow, thick inch. His dark eyes smolder, and his gaze drops to my mouth. I lick my lips and the tangy taste of Bubblegum Blast lip gloss bursts over my tongue. Need unfurls in my belly.

And then the shirt is in my hand, drooping with disappointment toward the floor. My breath leaves me in a rush of unfulfilled desire.

"It actually needs a wash." I toss it into the laundry bin. "I'll wear something else."

His approving smile melts me inside. I want to see that smile again. But more than that, I want to hear him laugh.

Pulling an identical shirt from the drawer, I saunter into the bathroom and slam the door, mentally thanking my big sister for her habit of never buying one of anything when she can buy two.

After I've dressed, brushed my hair, and applied my makeup, I take a deep breath and fling open the door to the bathroom. Torment is staring out the window, lost in thought.

"Ahem."

He spins around and his eyes widen. A grin spreads across his face and his deep, soft chuckle warms me to my toes.

—⁓—

Two hours, two pieces of pizza, and one exhilarating motorcycle ride around San Francisco later, we arrive outside the club. Torment glides his motorcycle to a stop and turns off the ignition.

For a moment we just sit. I squeeze my eyes shut and try to memorize the heady, erotic sensation of having my arms around his waist, my breasts against his back, and his ass tucked tight against the juncture of my thighs.

Finally, he pulls off his helmet and twists in his seat to help me. "Was that too fast?" He slides the helmet off my head and clips it under the seat.

"Are you kidding?" I squeal, bouncing on the seat like a little kid. "I think I might forget about buying a car and get one of these. What did you call it?"

His lips curve into a smile. "It's a custom MV-Agusta F4CC, but you might want to feign a little concern for the fact we were going almost one hundred and fifty miles an hour down the freeway. I might start to think you want to live dangerously."

My smile broadens. Maybe I do. Maybe that is what has been missing from my life—a little excitement and a whole lot of danger.

"What should I do with this?" I pat the stiff, leather jacket Torment gave me when he picked me up. Just my size.

"Keep it. You'll need it for the ride home." He helps me off the motorcycle and props it up on its kickstand. Although I don't know much about motorcycles, I can appreciate the sleek lines, shiny chrome, and death-defying speed of his Agusta. My hand rests on the seat, still warm from our ride. When I look up, Torment is watching me and the intensity of his gaze makes my heart pound.

"Come." He holds out his hand. "I have a surprise for you inside."

As if he hasn't given me enough surprises today. The only thing missing is the tiniest personal detail about him. I've never met anyone who didn't like to talk about themselves— even a little bit.

We walk through the brightly lit parking lot, and Torment gives me a warning lecture about the dangers of Ghost Town and being alone outside the club at night—as if I haven't lived in Oaktown all my life and been immersed in the daily reports of muggings and shootings in the Foster Hoover Historic District.

Once we are inside the club, he sends me to inventory the first aid room while he unlocks the doors and turns on the lights.

The room is cool and quiet and smells faintly of antiseptic. I rifle through the drawers and cupboards. Someone has taken the time to think about the types of injuries that might occur in a fight club. Since my last visit, the room has been restocked, and everything is organized and labeled.

"You'll need this." Torment appears in the doorway with a cooler in his hand.

"Another picnic?"

He places the cooler on the counter and waggles his crooked finger, motioning for me to open it. A smile tugs at the corners of his lips and his eyes sparkle with an almost palpable excitement. I can't resist happy Torment. I open the lid.

"Ice cream? You bought me five pints of ice cream?" I pull out a container of Ben & Jerry's Chunky Monkey and lick my lips.

"Is that the right one?"

An idiotic grin splits my face. "Yes. This is the right one. The only one. But why did you buy it? And why so many?"

"Welcome present for new staff." His brow wrinkles and then he spins around and walks out the door.

First pizza, then a motorcycle ride, and now my favorite ice cream. The night is just getting better and better.

My mouth waters and I pull the lid off the carton. The ice cream is at its optimal state—partially melted. Unable to resist, I dip in a finger and pop it in my mouth, closing my eyes at the first, creamy, rich, chocolaty banana burst of flavor. Ahhh. Heaven.

"I brought you a—"

My eyes fly open. Torment is standing in front of me with a bowl and a spoon and eyes as wide as the ice cream lid.

"Spoon." He chokes out the last word, and his eyes lock on the finger in my mouth. I pull it out with a loud, elegant pop.

"Looks like you don't need it," he chuckles.

"I…it's so good…I couldn't wait." My face heats. "Usually I use a spoon. Always, actually. I always use a spoon." I hold my breath and pray for a natural disaster—earthquake, flood, hurricane, even a plague of locusts. Anything to save me from death by mortification.

"I think I would prefer to watch you eat it the other way." His low, husky growl sends a shiver down my spine.

"Spoon…please," I whisper. Why can't I be like normal people and lose my appetite in times of stress or profound embarrassment?

He hands me the spoon and leans against the bed, thick arms folded. Although I don't look up, I can feel his eyes on me. Maybe he's hungry.

"Would you like some?"

"I don't eat ice cream. It's full of chemicals and unnecessary fats." The soft, velvety texture of his voice is almost a match for the smooth, creamy ice cream on my tongue. What a combination: Torment, ice cream, unnecessary fats, and me.

"It's very unhealthy," he continues. "Any nutritional value is canceled out by the high sugar content."

"Have you actually ever tried it?" I scoop out some ice cream and lick it off the cold metal spoon with slow, careful, little flicks of my tongue. When I lift my eyes, Torment's lips have parted and his eyes burn with sensual fire.

"No."

"Here, try it."

Torment looks from the spoon to me and back to the spoon. "I'll try it if you'll watch us sparring tonight. I think it would help you get a feel for the potential injuries you might face in the ring if you saw the different strikes, grapples, and submissions the fighters use. It's just training. No serious injuries. Rarely any blood or broken bones."

Anything to gain a convert to the cult of Chunky Monkey.

"Okay." I waggle the spoon in front of his lips. "I'll come, but you have to hold up your end of the bargain."

"Your way." He pushes the spoon to the side.

Everything below my waist tightens. "My finger?"

His sinful smile makes my pulse throb in unexpected parts of my anatomy.

"This one." Lifting my hand, he strokes along the finger I just pulled out my mouth.

How damn erotic is that? I dip my finger into the soft ice cream and hold it out. Torment leans forward and takes it in his mouth, sucking gently. His lips are soft and warm. His mouth is wet and oh so hot.

A soft sigh escapes my parted lips and the endorphin rush almost knocks me off my feet. Desire sings its way through my veins straight to my core. My eyes lock on his lips as they glide gently over my skin and then pull away, leaving me bereft.

Torment gives me a heart-stopping, sensual, self-satisfied smile.

"You like?" I lean in toward him as if I might miss his answer.

"I like."

Is he still talking about the ice cream, or is he talking about me? Please be talking about me. Please be talking about me.

"More?"

"Later." He cups my cheek and his thumb presses my chin up, forcing me to meet his eyes. "I'll be looking for you in the training ring."

My legs melt, and I am swept up in the warmth of his gaze. "I'll be the one staring at the floor."

"And I'll be the one thinking about dessert." His mouth curves up in a wicked smile, and he presses my forefinger, still sticky with ice cream, to his lips. "Your way."

Chapter 5
IT HAS NOTHING TO DO WITH SEX

WEDGED BETWEEN RAMPAGE AND a thick, heavyset Mexican named Jimmy "Blade Saw" Ramirez, I turn my attention to the ground-level practice ring in the training area. A few fighters join us on the bench to watch and learn as Torment spars with Homicide Hank.

Torment warms up in the corner, and Homicide Hank beats on the punching bag, stopping every few strikes to scream at the ceiling for no apparent reason.

"They don't seem to be a good match," I say to Jimmy. Unable to refer to him as "Blade Saw"—either in my head or out loud—without convulsing into fits of laughter, I don't use his name at all. Rampage has still not apologized for his ill-conceived practical joke, and relations between us remain cool.

My first impression is that physically, Torment has the edge. His height will give him a better reach and his long legs will let him cover more ground. He is also broader, heavier, and more muscular. By contrast, Homicide is small, wiry, and highly strung. He jumps up and down in the corner, punctuating every bounce with a scream.

"Homicide is tougher than he looks," Jimmy says. "He's quick and an expert on submission. He won't win, but he'll get a chance to practice a few new moves."

Torment's abs flex as he twists and stretches. He has changed into a pair of red fight shorts with stylized dragons down each leg, and the deep cuts of his hip bones are clearly visible above his waistband. The fabric clings to every curve of his tight, muscular ass. At least I know where to look if I can't watch them spar.

Torment turns to talk to Jake, and the light reflects off the tattoos covering his back. Larger and more intricate than the designs on his front, the tattoos cover every inch of his right side down to his waist, including his arm. I remember the feel of soft skin over hard muscle when I traced my finger along the dragon's tail. My cheeks heat. I should have kept going.

Jake calls the start of the fight. For the first few seconds, Torment and Homicide dance around, feeling each other out, throwing occasional kicks and punches. Finally, Homicide breaks the pattern and lunges at Torment. Reacting quickly, Torment hits him in the jaw. Homicide's head snaps to the side. My stomach clenches and I bend over and take a few deep breaths. So much for no one getting hurt.

"Did you see that, Makayla?" Jimmy asks. "Torment pulled his punch. He could have really done some damage, but he held back."

"Yeah. Lucky Homicide."

Torment calls a time-out. He explains to the crowd what Homicide did wrong. His explanations are clear enough even I understand. He is a good teacher. Authoritative. Patient. Encouraging. Attentive. And damn sexy.

They return to the center of the ring. Torment doesn't waste any time. He rushes forward and knees Homicide in the stomach. Homicide staggers back into the ropes. He springs forward and into Torment's chest. I wince, expecting Torment to fall over backward, but his massive body absorbs the blow and he doesn't move.

Rampage wasn't the only one who set me up last week. Cheeky Torment pulled me down on purpose when we were in the ring. At least now I know I won't have to go on a liquid diet.

Homicide feints to one side and then dodges around Torment. He grabs Torment around the waist from the back and crouches down low. I tug on Jimmy's sleeve.

"He's going for a double leg takedown," I say, my voice filled with pride as I reference the only move I know.

"Won't happen."

Torment grabs Homicide's arm, pivots, and spins. He drops to his seat on the mat and sweeps Homicide's legs out from under him in a move worthy of any professional dancer. Homicide goes down hard and lands on his back. Torment throws himself across Homicide's throat. Homicide taps the mat, and Torment releases him.

"Nice rolling kimura," Jimmy mutters.

Torment explains the kimura hold to the assembled group and then he and Homicide show a few variations. I tune out and look around the gym. Despite the crowd gathered around the training ring, almost all the equipment is in use—treadmills, cross trainers, steppers, free weights, punch bags, a second training ring, and black human-shaped grapple dummies. Kinda like blow-up sex toys without the naughty parts.

"Most of serious fighters train every day," Jimmy says, following my gaze. "In addition to learning all the submissions, strikes, kicks, grapple techniques, and defenses, they also need to build strength, speed, and endurance if they want to have a chance in the ring. Most of them also take classes in Brazilian Jiu Jitsu, Muay Thai, boxing, and wrestling, which are the dominant fighting arts in MMA right now."

"I didn't realize it was so involved," I say. "The fighters must be super fit."

Like Torment.

I turn my attention back to the ring. Torment is still talking. Homicide Hank is kneeling on the floor with his back to Torment's knees.

"So from this position," Torment says, "I can move to mount, transition to back, and then get a submission by rear naked choke."

Sounds dirty to me. From what I've heard so far, fighting seems to have a lot in common with sex. I like sex. Maybe I'll grow to like fighting too.

Torment flips Homicide onto his back and lies flat on top of him. He talks about being dominant for a ground and pound.

I imagine him lying flat on top of me, grounding and pounding. Fight terms skitter through my brain. Naked. Back. Rear. Mount. Submission. Dominant. Pound. My body heats. I cross my legs and feel the slip of arousal between my thighs.

I am so caught up in my daydream, it takes a second for my brain to register Torment is watching me. The mischievous sparkle in his eyes suggests he knows what I'm thinking. But he can't. How could he possibly know how filthy I really am?

Homicide takes advantage of Torment's momentary lack of focus and breaks the hold. He flips Torment onto his back, jumps to his feet, and before Torment can get away, he leaps. Torment lifts a knee and thrusts upward, catching Homicide in the diaphragm. Homicide falls to his side clutching his chest.

Then he moans and rolls on the floor.

Torment drops to his knees beside Homicide and waves me over. I race to the ring and climb through the ropes.

"I thought I'd just knocked the wind out of him, but he's turning blue," Torment says. Worry creases his face and he rakes his hand through his hair.

I straighten Homicide's body just enough to allow me to run my hands over his chest and abdomen. His eyes are wide, panicked, but his pupils are stable. My hands find a hard knot of muscle just below his ribs.

"I don't think he's ruptured any tissue," I say. "I think he's compressed his diaphragm and the lower lobes of his lungs, and it has forced out all his residual air. He might also have pulled the muscle in his diaphragm. I'll need a wide ACE bandage and some ice before we can move him."

"Jake. You heard her. Ice. Bandages." Torment barks the order and Jake tosses a bag of ice into the ring from a cooler on the floor before racing out the door. Torment catches the ice with one hand and holds it over Homicide's stomach.

"You need to breathe deeply," I tell Homicide. "Fight real hard for that first, real deep breath. It will release the spasm and you'll be able to breathe normally again."

Homicide grips my hand and locks his frightened eyes on mine. His muscles tense. I give him an encouraging nod as he struggles and strains. Finally, he sucks in a deep breath and collapses back on the mat.

Torment lets out a long, slow sigh. He catches my gaze and gives me the most devastating smile.

Jake arrives with the bandages. We tape up Homicide's chest, and Torment and Rampage walk him to the first aid room and help him onto the bed.

"Fuck." Homicide pounds his fist on the bed and wheezes in a breath. "I should have seen that knee coming a mile away. I'm such an idiot. Damn stupid newbie mistake."

I pat Homicide's shoulder. "Don't be so hard on yourself. We all make mistakes. If we didn't, no fight would ever have a winner. We just need to learn from them and move on. And I was pretty damn impressed with your moves."

Homicide's lips quiver. He looks over at Torment and something passes between them that brings out Homicide's smile in all its toothy glory.

My cheeks heat and I look away. "Is there someone you want me to call? I don't think you should drive."

Homicide coughs. "Nah. I'll just catch a ride with one of the guys. My wife, Sally, wouldn't be caught dead here. I've invited her so many times, and she never shows."

His face crumples, and I give his hand a squeeze. "Were you expecting her to come alone?"

"I thought she'd get bored during the warm-up so I just told her to come when the show started." He coughs again, and I warn him to breathe slow and easy.

"Maybe she's afraid to come here by herself. It's a pretty dangerous area of town. I sure wouldn't come alone. And if she was afraid, she'd probably think you knew that and you were only asking her to be polite but not expecting her to come."

Homicide, Rampage, and Torment stare at me as if I've suddenly grown a second head.

"Women don't think the same as you." I use small, simple words so they can understand. "I'll bet if you asked her to come with you and showed her around, she would love to watch you fight."

Homicide scratches his head. Rampage grunts. Torment studies me like I'm a delightful curiosity in a zoo.

"Maybe you *should* ask her to pick you up," I continue. "People like to know they are needed."

By the time Homicide's wife arrives to take him home, the gym is almost empty. Rampage and Jake wash down the mats and equipment and then head to the kitchen to have a drink with an impatient Pinkaluscious and her friend, Shayla, otherwise known as Shilla the Killa.

I lock up the first aid room and find Torment and Jimmy on the mats practicing grappling holds. Torment is lying on top of a stuffed leather grapple dummy. Unlike the dummies that resemble a man standing straight, this one has legs curved into a bow shape and arms bent up and over its head. Torment's hips are between the dummy's legs, his pelvis pressed against the juncture of the dummy's thighs.

I have never seen anything as titillating in my life.

"It's a submission dummy," Torment says, looking up. "We just got it in. The arms and legs are flexible. It's very useful for practicing arm bars, chokes, side mounts, and submissions."

"I'm sure it is," I murmur. Sweat trickles down my back. I berate myself for my dirty mind. He is practicing a fight position using fight equipment. This is NOT sexual. Not in the least.

Torment talks Jimmy through the position and then slides down the dummy's body until his head is where his hips used to be.

My breath catches in my throat. My head spins. I grasp one of the ring poles and hold on for dear life.

"Hmmm. It's not working," he says to Jimmy.

Really? It's working pretty good for me. So good, in fact, I need to get home right away.

Jimmy joins him on the mat and they practice a few holds. For some reason watching Torment lie on top of Jimmy isn't quite as arousing.

Torment wraps his arms around Jimmy's head and pulls him down. Jimmy struggles and finally slaps the mat. Torment rolls off him.

"I can't get it," Jimmy says. "It seemed easy when you had the dummy, but I can't break that triangle. I need to see it with a real person." He looks up and catches my gaze. "Hey, Makayla. Can you give us a hand?"

I stiffen and shake my head. "I don't know anything about grappling. I wouldn't be any use."

Torment gives me a wicked grin. "We just need a warm body."

Oh God, so do I.

He holds out his hand. "Come on. I won't bite."

Maybe not. But if he lies on top of me in my current state of arousal, I just might. I make an effort to feign modesty when, really, all I want to do is throw myself into the fray. "No, I don't think—"

"Please."

I study his impassive face. He has to know how suggestive the positions are. How he isn't constantly aroused I don't know. If I had to spend my evenings sliding over a grapple dummy, I wouldn't need my Rabbit. Maybe I've been single too long.

"You'll learn something," he says. His voice takes on the authoritative teaching tone he used with Homicide. "If you understand the positions, you can better understand the injuries."

Hmmm. Do I want to roll around on the mat with two half-naked, super-fit men? Yes, please!

"Okay, if it will help you out." I slip off my shoes and kneel on the mat while Torment and Jimmy discuss what to do with me. My pulse pounds so hard I can barely hear them over the rush of blood through my veins. This is sports. It has nothing to do with sex. Sports. Sports. Sports.

Torment puts his hand on my shoulder. "Lie on your back, hands over your head, legs apart."

Sex.

I lay on the mat just as he explained, and he kneels between my legs. The position leaves me vulnerable, exposed. Shivers of need course down my spine.

Jimmy sits to the side and Torment talks us through the move. He is so damn sexy when he's teaching. Confident, assured, knowledgeable, and patient. He explains he is going to mount me. *Yes!* And take a dominant position. *Oh, yes!* Then, once I have him in a triangle, he'll show Jimmy how to defend.

My brain fuzzes with lust.

His gaze catches mine. My cheeks flame. For the longest time, he studies me and then his eyes widen, as if he had just seen into my hidden depths—the pounding of my heart, the sheen of sweat on my skin, the wetness between my thighs. His eyes shutter and his jaw tightens.

"Are you okay there?"

Words fail me. "Mmmhmm."

"Right then. I'm going to mount you now."

Oh God.

He mounts me.

I bite right through my lip. The sharp tang of blood flows over my tongue.

Torment lies on top of me, his knees pressed tight against my hips, his elbows snug against my ears. I lock his head between my arms the way he explained, tilting it and pressing his face down to my breasts. His warm, heavy body covers me, holds me, encloses me. His breath is hot on my neck. His hair is soft between my fingers. It is the most erotic experience I have ever had, and from the state of affairs pressed up against my sex, I would venture to say it might rank with Torment's top experiences too.

He lifts his head and his eyes blaze with sensual fire. "This may not have been the best idea." His voice is low and husky, thick with need.

"Maybe not," I whisper.

"Now what?" Jimmy interjects. "How do you get out of it?"

"I don't think I want to get out of it," Torment murmurs. His mouth hovers only an inch above mine, his breath dusting sweet promises over my lips.

Kiss me. Kiss me. Kiss me.

"What the hell are you doing?" A woman's shriek breaks the spell.

I twist my head back and catch a flash of pink and a mane of golden hair.

Pinkaluscious. And she doesn't look pleased.

"We're practicing grappling techniques," Jimmy says as if Torment and I were not smoldering beside him. "You're welcome to join us. I could use a partner."

"Not you. Him. It looks like he's having sex with her."

Torment closes his eyes briefly and sighs. Then he pushes himself back to his knees. I shiver at the loss of his warmth.

"What do you want, Sandy?" Torment stands up and joins her at the edge of the mat.

I roll out of my compromising position and kneel on the mat beside Jimmy. Sandy's glare turns my blood to ice.

"I need to talk to you."

"You can see we're busy."

"With her?" She shoots me another glare so I shoot one back.

"With Blade Saw. Makayla is just helping us out."

She winds her arms around his neck and presses herself up against him. "I need you," she whinny whines.

He lifts her arms away and his voice takes on a soft, gentle tone. "Not now, Sandy."

Not now? Not now implies what she's doing is okay later. Not now means not in front of Makayla. Not now means not ever for me.

Pinkaluscious's long, brown lashes fan over her rosy cheeks. She blinks her big, brown Bambi eyes at him and whispers, "Please. It's important."

Torment tightens his lips and gives her a curt nod. "Five minutes…if that works for Blade Saw and Makayla. I don't want to keep them waiting."

We both nod our assent. Jimmy because he's an easygoing guy. Me because my mouth has gone dry.

"Thank you." She stands on tiptoe and brushes her lips over his, before clasping his hand and leading him to the door. Jimmy jumps up and follows behind them.

Nausea cramps my stomach, and I choke back a snort.

The sound draws her attention. Her eyes flick to mine and she looks me up and down, lingering over my physical imperfections as only a woman can do. She laughs, tosses her mane, and then trots away taking my hopes and dreams with her.

"Who is that?" I call out to Jimmy.

He mumbles something unintelligible and then says, "Girlfriend."

My heart crashes into my stomach. I should have known. I'm no Amanda or Pinkaluscious. He really did want me here just to work. And the rest was what? A game?

I stomp back to the first aid room, pack up my stuff, and head for the front entrance. I'm not waiting around for more humiliation. But before I step outside, I freeze. How am I going to get home? Cabs are too expensive. Walking is too dangerous. It is Friday night and my friends will all be plastered and unable to drive. No way will I ask Torment. No. Damn. Way.

But I can ask Jake.

Always accommodating, Jake agrees to drive me home after he takes a shower.

Cowardice drives me to wait for him outside in the parking lot, where Torment won't find me. Zipping my sweater to my chin, I lean against the cold, metal wall and fold my arms in my best "I'm not a hooker" pose.

"Hey, honey, you ride bareback?"

My best is clearly not good enough. Detaching myself from the hooker wall, I head over to Torment's motorcycle for a good-bye caress. So beautiful. So shiny and sleek. My fingers brush over the seat where Torment sat, the handlebars he touched, and a shiny silver plate bearing the inscription "1 of 100."

"What the hell are you doing?"

My head jerks up and my hand freezes in midair. Torment stalks across the parking lot toward me, his face a mask of fury. He has changed into his sexy, low-slung jeans and a pair of casual black shoes, but his chest is still bare, and heaving as if he's just been running.

Hands shaking, I back away from the motorcycle. "I...I was just saying good-bye to your Agusta. I'm sorry. I wouldn't have damaged it."

"Not the bike," he shouts. "You. Why are you out here alone?"

So loud. So angry. My throat freezes, and sweat trickles between my breasts.

"Well?"

"I could do without the shouting." I twist the bottom edge of my sweater in my hands and stare at the ground.

Torment draws in a ragged breath and lifts my chin with his finger, tilting my head back. I can't meet his gaze, and I turn my head away.

"I told you, it's not safe for you to be out here alone." His voice softens. "You should have waited for me inside."

"Jake is taking me home." I swallow hard and shove my hands in my pockets.

Torment frowns. "You don't need to go home with Jake. I said I would take you home after the fight. You helped me out. It's the least I can do."

Duty. Nothing more. Despair and disappointment war over who should crush me first.

"Jake has to go past my house to get to Amanda's place, and you don't owe me anything. Rampage gave me the check for tonight. And… um…I won't be back, so we're good."

I force myself to look at him. Confusion fills every line and plane of his face. "Why?" he asks softly.

"Because I'm not the kind of girl who likes to play games."

Mercifully, the door bangs open and Jake bounds into the parking lot. "Sorry I took so long. Ready to go?" He gives me the wide, easy smile Amanda couldn't resist. This is the kind of guy I should be going out with—nice, friendly, easygoing. Instead, I've been wasting my time lusting over a mercurial fighter with a sexy girlfriend.

Torment's eyes narrow. Jake takes a step back.

"Is it okay if I give Makayla a ride home?"

"We're not finished here." Torment's voice is perfectly controlled, but anger simmers just beneath the surface.

"We are finished."

"No, we're not."

I sigh. "We are. I hope you don't have too much trouble finding someone else."

I pivot and follow Jake into the parking lot.

This time, I don't look back.

Chapter 6

ANGRY GIRLS DON'T BOUNCE

I AM JOLTED OUT of a fitful sleep by a loud banging on the front door and the grating sounds of heavy equipment. My clock flashes eight o'clock. Who the hell gets up at eight o'clock on a Saturday morning?

By the time I find my bathrobe and stumble down the hallway, my housemates are already in the foyer.

"What's going on?"

Rob hands me an official-looking piece of paper. "We have a new landlord, a company called Legacy Holdings. They're renovating the property starting today. They've arranged for us to move to the Sunset View Apartments on Lake Merritt while the renovations are being done."

Jennifer staggers back against the wall and slaps a hand to her chest. "No way. Those apartments are insanely expensive. I went out with a guy who rented there. He lived on the twenty-fourth floor. The views over the Bay are amazing. They have a doorman, a fitness center, and a sauna."

Doormen and saunas sound expensive. "Do we have to pay more rent?"

Rob reads the rest of the document. "Nothing changes. We pay the same rent. And they are splurging for three apartments on the same floor. Carlos and I are in one. Jennifer and Ashley are in the other, and you get your own place."

"Seriously? My own apartment?"

Rob hands me the papers and I skim over the boring legal bits and dive straight into the important stuff. Yup. My very own apartment, fully furnished, and my rent doesn't change. Not only are they putting us up during the renovations, they are sending a moving truck for our personal stuff today at noon.

Too bad this didn't happen a day earlier and Torment could have seen me living in style. But I will not think about Torment. I will not remember the feel of his soft warm lips as they sucked ice cream off my finger. I will not remember his chiseled pecs or his smoldering eyes… or the deep rumble of his voice…or the feel of his hard body pressed up against mine…or the way my core tightens when he touches me. He is gone. Forgotten. I have already moved on.

Dr. Drake is easy on the eye. He has a nice smile. Nice body. Very nice teeth. Not much in the way of a dangerous persona, but he seems to like me.

I will have lunch with him on Monday.

I hope he likes picnics.

Nine hours later, my first housewarming party is in full swing. My luxuriously furnished, one-bedroom apartment on the twenty-third floor of the Sunset View Apartments buzzes with activity. While Jennifer and Carlos mix cocktails with their friends in the high-end kitchen, I grab another glass of champagne from the bar and head over to the balcony to catch up with Amanda.

My path takes me through the random assortment of boyfriends, girlfriends, friends with benefits, and soon-to-be one-night stands clustered in the center of my open space living area. A pang of loneliness grips me. Why am I always single at parties—the best friend, housemate, filler, or stand-in? Why am I never the one making out in the bedroom or chatting to the guests as my boyfriend slings a casual arm over my shoulder and whispers sweet nothings into my ear? What's wrong with me?

"So, what happened with Torment?" As always, Amanda gets straight to the point. I lean over the railing, soaking up the view of San Francisco Bay, and steel myself for her interrogation.

She pokes me in the side when I am not immediately forthcoming with information.

"I thought I'd finally get the 'don't call me in the morning' text after you texted me about your afternoon picnic and your motorcycle ride."

A warm breeze ruffles my hair, bringing with it the fresh scent of the ocean and an unwanted memory of my cheek pressed up against Torment's jacket when we raced around the bay on his Agusta.

"You must have missed the text where I said he just wanted me to work." My third—or is it my fourth?—glass of champagne is a little too sweet and a little too fruity, but I gulp it down just the same. Some nights call for a little extra indulgence, and this is one of them.

Amanda's laugh tinkles in the still of the night. "I didn't believe it. I saw the way he watched you when we left the club last week. When you told me he tracked you down at the hospital with a picnic in tow, I knew he was into you."

"Well, your instincts were wrong this time," I snap. "He has a girl-friend. That over-processed blonde who was prancing around in pink Latex. I call her Pinkaluscious."

Amanda snorts champagne through her nose. "Catty. Not like you—which tells me you like him."

I shake my head. "He isn't really my type. Too violent. Too rough. Too dangerous. He probably hangs out with unsavory biker dudes. I'm better off sticking with my usual."

"Bland."

"What do you mean by that?" I take another sip of champagne. Gah. I'll have to switch to something harder—something to numb my brain and erase all my memories of yesterday.

"The only guys you ever go out with are boring, dull, and safe. The kind of guys parents love. Ryan? Yawn. Phil? Dull as ditch water. Mike? He was so innocuous I can't even remember his face." Even your friend Charlie, who you had the sense not to date, is the same. Nice and dull."

"They're the only ones who ask me out." I stare out into the night. Lake Merritt glimmers below us—an inky black stain surrounded by twinkling lights. So pretty. If I owned a place like this, I would spend all my time just looking at the view.

"Not true." Amanda raps my knuckles with her finger. "You forget we've been friends since we were four. I've seen the guys you lust after, but the minute they express any interest, you run away. Remember Timmy Jones?"

"He put a dead frog in my lunch box."

"Jack from high school?"

"He set my locker on fire."

"How about Dan from first-year biology?"

"He tried to turn me into an anarchist and start a revolution." I turn to face her. "And Timmy doesn't count. We were in first grade."

Amanda sighs. "My point is, the edgy, dangerous guys you liked all wanted to ask you out, but you ran away before they got a chance."

My fingers curl around the cold, iron railing. "Well, this time I got blindsided by a pink Barbie doll. Just leave it. I don't need to be psychoanalyzed. And it doesn't matter. I'm having lunch with Doctor Drake on Monday, and he's definitely not bland—well, at least not physically."

"I thought you said he touched you inappropriately."

"It wasn't so much inappropriate as it was…protective." I graciously give Dr. Drake the benefit of the doubt.

"Protective or possessive?"

"Doctor Drake doesn't want to possess me." I fold my arms and give her my best scowl.

"Not since he lost the pissing contest."

"What pissing contest?" Amanda always forgets her experience with men vastly exceeds my own. Vastly with a capital *V*.

Amanda rolls her eyes. "The one you told me about. Torment and Doctor Drake, sniffing each other out, trying to establish who was top dog."

"It wasn't like that. It was just about lunch. And it wasn't really a contest—"

"I don't imagine it would have been," she interjects. "Torment is as alpha as they come. Drake probably ran off with his tail between his legs."

"Doctor Drake was just being friendly. Charlie says he likes me.

He'll be good for me. Everyone thinks he's gorgeous. He's you but a man."

"Mmm." Amanda twists her lips. "Then he'll be amazing in bed."

"Who's amazing in bed?" Jake comes up behind Amanda, wraps his arms around her waist, and nuzzles her neck.

Sigh.

"You are, baby." She grins and wiggles her ass against him.

Jake whispers in her ear and Amanda blushes. For all her feigned indifference, she really likes him. More than any other guy I've seen her with. Much more.

"Makayla was asking me about Torment," Amanda says. "Help her out and I'll make it worth your while."

"Amanda!"

She gives me a wink and turns in Jake's arms, planting little kisses along his jaw.

"What do you want to know?" He squeezes her ass and she squeals.

"Name, rank, and serial number," Amanda murmurs against his lips. "Current girlfriend. Day job. Gossip. That will do for a start."

Jake moans. "No can do. He's an intensely private person. If he found out I had spilled his secrets, he would kick me out. Privacy is such a big thing to him, he set up Redemption as an invitation-only club. Even the spectators are screened. They have to have a connection with someone in the club and they have to sign a nondisclosure statement before they are put on the list to receive texts about the events. And it works. Most people don't even realize he has a real job. They think he works at the club full time. "

Amanda's eyes narrow. "He has a secret identity?"

Jake shakes his head and swallows. "I didn't say that. Pretend I didn't say that."

"And you know who he is?"

He looks at the floor and shuffles his feet.

Poor guy. She will stop at nothing to get that information from him. He does not even understand the hunger of the beast he has unleashed. He'll be lucky to escape with his tongue intact.

My phone vibrates in my back pocket and I almost trip over my feet to get away from them. I step back into the apartment and check my texts. Torment's name shows up on my Caller ID. Unable to resist, I open the message.

> I need you at the club tonight

Ha. I'm sure you do. And that's all you want from me. I quickly type a response:

> *No. Sorry. Busy*
> What are you doing?
> *I'm having a party **dances** **drinks***
> Without me?

Don't even think about guilt-tripping me. My thumb wavers as I type. I've definitely had enough to drink.

> *U have club things 2 do. Like hurting people*
> Is the doctor at ur party?

My eyes widen. Is he jealous? Why? He has Pinkaluscious. Why does he care if Dr. Drake is at my party? Should I lie and say yes?

"Sorry, Mac. Jake wouldn't tell me anything." Amanda joins me in the living room and gives my shoulder a squeeze.

Just what I need. An expert. I hand her the phone.

Amanda reads the messages and gives me a curious, sideways glance. "Mention the girlfriend."

"Why?"

She laughs. "Just a hunch. Work the girlfriend into the conversation. I'll bet he shows up at your door in less than half an hour."

Amanda has never let me down, especially when it comes to men. Trusting her instincts, I send my text.

> *No doctor here. Just me and friends and lots of drinks*
> I want to see lots-of-drinks Makayla. Come to the club

2 much violence
I have ice cream

My hands shake, and a giggle erupts from my chest. Maybe if I wasn't so drunk I would find him less amusing.

Give it 2 Pinkaluscious
Who?
Your girlfriend **frowns**

After waiting five minutes for him to respond, I hand the phone to Amanda and let her read the new texts. She tells me not to text him again. For the next ten minutes, I conduct tests on my phone to ensure it is still working by forcing everyone at the party to text me. Another ten minutes pass by and I finally give up. He isn't going to respond. And why would he? If it was a game, he knows he's been found out.

"Someone hit me over the head the next time I express any interest in a man." I throw myself into the black, leather chair beside Rob and steal his bowl of calorie- and fat-laden chips.

Rob laughs and reaches behind him to turn up the music on the insanely expensive sound system that comes with the apartment. "With pleasure, darling."

Half an hour and an entire bowl of chips later, the low-pitched, high decibel rumble of a motorcycle from the street below cuts through Gotye's sad and highly appropriate "Somebody That I Used To Know." A pathetic hope unfurls in my belly, and I immediately quash it down. He has a girlfriend. Why would he come looking for me?

A light breeze blows across the balcony and through the open windows, ruffling my hair. Gotye's voice warbles behind me, and I imagine the motorcycle's engine quiets to a soft, steady, low rumble. Or is it my imagination? My heartbeat quickens. Self-destructive curiosity claws its way through my belly.

Cursing myself for my stupidity, I leave Rob and step onto the balcony. Amanda and Jake are entwined in the corner. Taking a deep breath, I clutch the railing and look at the street below.

Oh. My. God. I know that motorcycle. And I know that tall, powerfully lean, mouthwateringly tight body dismounting the seat.

For a moment, I can only stare. Stunned.

"Amanda," I gasp. "It's him. Torment is outside." A huge grin spreads across my face and I suck in a breath. He's here. He's here.

Amanda detaches herself from Jake and frowns. "How did he know your new address?"

"Rob put a sign on the door at my old place." I narrow my eyes. "You knew he would go there and find it empty."

Amanda shrugs. "I thought he deserved it after what he did to you. I didn't know about Rob's sign."

My lips tighten into a thin line. "I'm going to call the doorman, and tell him to send Torment up."

"Don't let him in," Amanda snaps. "You told him no. He came anyway. Men like that need boundaries. If you don't set them at the beginning, he will never know where the boundaries are and he'll walk all over you. It takes a very strong person to build them in the middle of a relationship. If he's interested, he'll ditch the girlfriend and come looking for you. I guarantee it."

"Maybe he just needs someone to handle first aid tonight," I say.

"Stop biting your nails." Amanda slaps my hand away from my mouth. "And stop bouncing. I thought you were angry with him. Angry girls don't bounce."

But excited girls do. And what is more exciting than being hunted down by a devastatingly handsome tattooed fighter with a heartwarming laugh?

Amanda studies me and sighs. "Even if it is about work, my previous advice stands. Don't let the two-timing bastard in."

Jake strokes his hand down her hair. "I don't think that's good advice. I know Torment. If he had a girlfriend—and I think I would have heard about it—he wouldn't be here. He's not that kind of guy." He looks at me and raises his eyebrows. "You saw him at the club, Makayla. What do you think?"

"I think I'm confused." I lean over the railing. The night is still and quiet again. Torment has removed his helmet and is looking up at my balcony, but from this distance I cannot see his face. Can he see me? For the longest time he looks up and I look down. Finally, he scrubs his hand through his hair, and then his body stills. He sees me.

HE SEES ME!

Using my fancy new intercom, and despite Amanda's protests, I ring down to the doorman and tell him to send Torment to my apartment. Five minutes later, Torment crosses my threshold, his leather creaking with every step.

The room freezes. Every conversation stops. The last few notes of Taylor Swift's "I Knew You Were Trouble" linger in the air. Amanda detaches herself from Jake's arms, stomps across the room, and stands in front of me.

"Torment." She crosses her arms. I don't have to see her face to know she has shot him her best don't-mess-with-my-friend glare.

"Amanda."

Tension hangs in the air between them, and the skin on the back of my neck prickles.

"What are you doing here?" she snaps.

"I want to speak to Makayla."

"She's busy. She doesn't have time for men who are going to mess with her head." Amanda is in full protective mode and although she is only one third Torment's size, the force of her will makes me shudder.

"It's okay. I want to talk to him." I pat her shoulder but she doesn't move.

"She wants to talk to me." Torment's firm voice silences the whispers at the back of the room.

"She doesn't."

"She does."

"She doesn't."

Torment explodes into motion. "Dammit, Amanda. Get out of my way." He reaches around her, grasps my hand, and pulls me into his chest.

My pulse races. My body flames. Moisture pools between my thighs.

So hard. So rough. So warm. So dominating. I want more. More of this erotic manhandling of my body. More forceful, alpha-male.

No. I give myself a mental shake. Dominating bad. Manhandling bad. Forceful bad. Did I learn nothing when I was a child?

I press my hands against his chest and push myself away.

Torment frowns. "I need to see you. Now. Alone." His body vibrates with tension and I slide my hand into his to calm him down.

"Okay. We can talk in my bedroom. It's just down the hall." I give his hand a squeeze. He gives my hand a tug. Next thing I know, I am flying down the hallway behind him. He pulls me into the bedroom, slams the door behind us, and spins me around to face him.

"That was dramatic and just bordering on unacceptable behavior," I say, breathless.

He rakes his hand through his hair. "I couldn't wait. I had to talk to you."

With a shaky inhalation, I press my back against the door. Every nerve in my body is on fire. "Here I am," I breathe a whisper. "Talk away."

"I don't have a girlfriend."

My eyes widen. "You came here to tell me that?"

"I came here to see you."

I melt against the door in a pool of warm fuzzies. "You saw me last night."

"I saw you leave last night. I didn't understand why until I got your text." He takes a deep breath and leans his forearm against the door beside my head. So close. So hot. His broad chest blocks out everything in the room, and I have to tilt my head back to see his face.

"You should have given me a chance to explain." His eyes soften and he twirls a strand of my hair around his fingers. "I would never lead you on. I'm a one-woman man and right now you're the woman I want to get to know. I've never met anyone with so much compassion. You're beautiful, strong, and brave. You see into the heart of people. You listen. You did more for Homicide and Flash than patching them up. You made their lives better in the short time you were with them."

Stunned by the onslaught of compliments—more than I've ever had in my life—I have to force my words out. "But I saw you with… Pink…Sandy…and Homicide said she was your girlfriend."

His face darkens. "Maybe you misheard. Sandy and I had a casual and brief relationship. It didn't work out. She has had a hard time accepting that it's over."

"No one else?"

His slow, easy smile steals my breath away. "No one."

He tucks my hair behind my ear and strokes a finger along my jaw. "Will you come to the club now?"

Argh. What a confusing man. Did he do all this just to get me to work after all?

He cups my jaw with his hand and tilts my head back, stroking my cheek with his thumb. "You have the most expressive eyes," he murmurs. "Beautiful, emerald-green eyes. I can see what you're thinking. And you're wrong. I would have come here tonight even if I didn't need you at the club."

I squeeze my eyes shut and press my lips together. How nice to be so transparent. What if he can see how badly I want him to kiss me? Hmmm. My eyes fly open.

Torment studies me and smiles. "Come to the club and afterward we'll go for coffee and talk."

Club? Coffee? Talk? Not really what I had in mind. How about testing out the king-size bed covered in six hundred thread count sheets?

"I wasn't lying to you when I said violence makes me uncomfortable." The gentle movement of his thumb sends heat swirling through me, and my voice thickens. "Watching you fight made me feel ill."

"I just need to know you're there." His rich baritone deepens "I don't understand it, but you make me feel calm, grounded. I haven't felt like that since…I was a teenager. I won't let you run away again. If there is something bothering you, talk to me. I promise I'll listen."

The power of his voice sweeps through me. His voice warms me. His touch electrifies me. And knowing he won't let me run makes it that much easier to stay. "I'll come with you," I whisper.

I am pathetic. I am weak. I am so overcome with lust, I don't care. But it is more than lust. Something inside him calls to me—something that needs to be healed. And for all his rough edges and brooding intensity, I sense he's a good person. I saw it in the way he treats his fighters, the way he runs his club, and the way he looks after me. Dangerous? Yes. Passionate? Definitely. Committed? Still not too sure.

He smiles slowly, his cheek creasing. "I would have thrown you over my shoulder and carried you to the club if you'd said no."

An erotic shiver runs down my spine. The visual image of Torment carrying me away caveman-style awakens something deeply sensual within me. Something forbidden.

"That would have been totally unacceptable behavior, and I would have been most displeased. Plus, you would never have made it past Amanda."

Torment raises an eyebrow and grins. "I could have managed Amanda, or I could have asked Jake to help me. He handles her well. She needs someone like him—firm but gentle."

Handles her? Since when has anyone handled Amanda?

He threads his fingers through my hair and gives it a gentle tug, tilting my head back and exposing my neck to the heat of his breath. "You, on the other hand, need something else." He presses a kiss to the base of my throat.

My body trembles and vibrates as if I might fly apart at any second. "What do I need?" My voice, when it comes, is so quiet I can barely hear it.

"Me." He trails hot, wet kisses up my throat and along my jaw.

Red, hot flames of need lick through my body and escape my parted lips with the softest of whimpers.

Torment groans. "Christ, Makayla. Don't tempt me. I have to fight tonight." He wraps his arms around me, squeezing me tight as if I might lure him to the dark side with my touch. He rests his forehead against mine and closes his eyes.

I could stay here forever. Safe. Warm. Wanted.

"Hey, Torment!" Jake bangs on the door. "Blade Saw called. They're waiting for you at the club. Misery's already arrived. He's saying you're afraid to show."

"Misery?" My perfect moment disappears with a sigh of disappointment.

Torment takes a long, deep breath and steps back. "He's a licensed amateur who is trying to get enough experience to get picked up by a professional league. But there are only so many amateur tournaments. On the underground circuit, he can fight as much as he wants, against whoever he wants. He can test his skills and practice new moves on bigger stronger opponents. A lot of amateurs won't take the risk. If he's caught, he'll face a suspension. But he's willing to do what it takes. And he's good. Damn good. When he challenged me, I couldn't resist. If I beat him, I move up in the underground rankings. We have our own championship belt. One day it's going to be mine."

"Sounds like it's going to be a very different fight than the one you had with Homicide. Maybe we could just stay here." My eyes flick over the bed and back to Torment. How is that for suggestive?

Torment's brows draw together. "I have to fight, but I want you with me, Makayla. And when I want something, I don't let go."

My body responds to his words, melting, as heat pools in my core. God, I want him too.

Chapter 7

DID YOU JUST KISS ME?

Where are you?

Safe in Redemption's first aid room, I stare at Torment's text message.
Crowds snake past my open door and into the club. Torment versus
Misery is a big match and with only a few minutes to go before the club
is locked down for the show, people are pushing and shoving to make
sure they get inside.

My hand shakes as I type in my answer.

Hiding
I am fighting in ten minutes

Torment is such a slow texter. Maybe I should buy him a book of text
language and make him do some thumb exercises.

My fingers fly over the keys, and I type my answer. Why couldn't
he have a different hobby? Something with a low level of risk—like golf.
The image of Torment playing golf makes me giggle. He would probably destroy any ball that dared not make it into the hole.

I know
I want you to watch
I can't
I need you to watch
I'm in the club. Isn't that enough?
No. I need to see you when I'm fighting
I need 2 c u not fighting

I'll send Rampage to get you
I'll run away
He'll catch you
Only if I'm crawling
That's not nice
Neither is fighting

How does he have time for all this texting? Isn't he supposed to be warming up? From the snippets of conversation I've heard about Misery's previous fights, Torment will need every advantage he's got. My cell vibrates yet again. He is nothing if not persistent.

Did you watch me last time?
Yes
What did you think?
U r good
What if Misery is better?

My hand flies to my mouth at this tiny glimpse into Torment's psyche. He is human after all and in need of reassurance. I text him back.

U'll be fine
Only if you are here
How can I make a difference?
You will
U hardly know me
I know I need you here
*Wish I knew more about u **sighs***
Ask me something
*What's your real name? **bites fingernails***
If I tell you, will you watch?

Ah. Ha. The urge to jump up and down and pump my fist in the air is tempting but very unladylike. However, I can choke back another match to get Torment's real name, especially now I know he's worried about the fight.

Yes

He responds a few seconds later.

Max

Max. Max. Max. The name doesn't stick. He is still Torment to me.

I push my way through the crowded hallway, race through the gym and training area, and head toward the ring. Rampage sees me coming and clears a path with a few swings of his mighty arms. Maybe one day I'll forgive him.

Torment is already in the ring, his back to me. Jake is talking to him, but he is looking down. I type my message.

Nice 2 meet u Max **smiles** **waves**
Now will you come and watch?
Right behind u

He turns around and gives me the most brilliant smile, all crinkled eyes and boyish charm. Good thing I have no socks to knock off. He points at my phone.

I read the message, and my heart stutters.

XX
Did you just kiss me? **blushes**

I look up. He is looking down at me. His sensual lips part and he mouths his answer.

"Yes."

━━∿━━

Misery is one of California's top-ranked amateur heavyweight fighters. At six feet two inches tall and weighing two hundred and sixty pounds, he towers over the fans and cornermen clustered around him. Torment is tall, but Misery is taller. Torment is broad, but Misery is broader. The only advantage Torment appears to have over Misery is his breathtaking good looks. From the size of Misery's fists, I suspect Torment won't have that advantage for long.

My official first aid attendant status gives me a front-row seat. I breathe in the aroma of lemon disinfectant with just a hint of stale sweat. Nice. At least Torment keeps the ring clean.

"Torment said this was a good match." I tug on Jimmy's sleeve, but he is too busy sticking his tongue in Pinkaluscious's ear to talk. I look over at Rampage beside me. He is watching Jimmy and Pinkaluscious, and the pain on his face tells me everything I need to know. Love triangle.

"Hey," I say softly. I nudge him with my elbow and he tears his gaze away and glares.

"Don't torture yourself. Sometimes these things don't work out."

His cheeks redden, and he tightens his lips and looks away.

"Think about something else. Tell me about the fight. How long is it going to last?"

He looks sideways at me and sighs. "Three rounds of three minutes each. Professionals go three rounds of five."

"Does Torment have a chance? He's a lot smaller and lighter than Misery."

Rampage shakes his head. "Misery is incredibly tough and hard to finish. In sanctioned fights, Torment would be classed as a light heavyweight, two classes down from Misery. That weight will make a difference, especially if Misery gets him to the ground. Torment is also at a disadvantage because he's dominant in boxing. That's his background. Misery is more well-rounded."

Homicide Hank steps into the ring and warms up the crowd with flavorful details of past unsanctioned fights. He announces the money collected at the door will be donated to the County Hospital. I glance up at Torment. Jake is helping him with his gloves. Torment winks. I smile. How sweet is that?

I check beneath my feet for my first aid kit. I am prepared for everything—cuts, bruises, fractures, and head trauma.

At a nod from Homicide, Pinkaluscious tears herself away from Jimmy and climbs into the ring. The crowd roars in approval as she goes through her routine. She revs them up with her fake smiles and jiggle wiggles, before waving her pink flag to start the match. Rampage stares at her with naked longing. How could any man not want her?

The energy in the crowd is almost palpable. Every seat is taken and it is standing room only for the last few stragglers. The gym and training equipment sit idle. No one wants to miss a second of this fight.

The bell rings and the match starts with wild punching exchanges. Torment takes a hard shot to the head and his eye swells almost instantly. I have to force myself to stay in my seat instead of running down to the ring.

Torment recovers quickly and settles into a rhythm, peppering Misery with a frenzy of kicks and punches that seem to frustrate and exhaust the bigger fighter. By the end of the round, Misery is on the defensive, swinging tired arms to bat away Torment's fists.

Misery gets his second wind in the second round. A solid right punch opens a deep gash under Torment's swollen right eye. Blood streams down Torment's face and the referee calls a break.

Nausea roils in my belly. Too real. Too visceral. On television, I can't smell the tang of blood or the pungent scents of sweat, smoke, and stale beer; bile doesn't burn my tongue, and I can't hear the sickening, live smack of bones hitting flesh. And I've never known anyone who voluntarily stood in harm's way. Except me. But that was a long time ago.

A sob wells up in my chest and I put my head between my legs and take deep breaths. A warm hand strokes down my back.

"He'll be okay," Rampage says, his voice uncharacteristically warm and soothing. He rubs my back until I sit up and then puts a comforting arm around me. "He's seen worse. I'll tell you when not to look."

Overwhelmed with gratitude, I instantly forgive Rampage all his sins.

Jake cleans up Torment's face and patches the cut. The referee signals a restart. Torment is still the fresher fighter. He dances around and throws a few kicks and punches. Misery deflects them, but his blocks are slow and his feet drag on the mat. Misery's bulk must be working against him.

In what seems like a last-ditch effort to win, he shoots in on

Torment and knocks him to the ground. They grapple for a few seconds and then Torment, in an incredible display of flexibility, tucks one shin under Misery's neck and swings his other leg over Misery's back. He pulls Misery's head down, applying pressure to his trachea with his shin and effectively choking him.

The crowd goes wild. People jump, scream, and cheer.

Rampage leaps to his feet and pumps his fist in the air. "No way. No fucking way. Torment locked him in a gogoplata." He high-fives Jimmy and Pinkaluscious and then pulls me up to my feet.

"Gogoplata?" Sounds like a dance from the fifties.

"It's one of rarest submissions in Jiu Jitsu. I've only ever seen it done once, and I've been doing MMA for fifteen years."

The crowd draws a collective breath, waiting for Misery's submission. Instead, we get three short blasts of whistle and a wild-eyed Homicide running toward the ring screaming, "Evacuate. Evacuate."

The warehouse erupts into chaos.

Lights go on. Doors are thrown open. People storm outside in a frenzy of shouts and stomping feet.

Homicide joins us, gasping for breath. "I just got a text from Flash that he reported us to the CSAC. He was pissed off about being kicked out. We gotta get everyone out and lock down before they get here."

I grab the first aid kit and look up at the ring. Torment has released Misery and is standing at the ropes. He points me to the door and mouths "Go."

Behind him, Misery has climbed to his feet. He stalks across the mat, his intent clear on his face.

"No!" I scream and point at Misery. "Torment, behind you!"

Torment spins around. Too late. Misery lets loose what must be his knockout punch. Torment's head snaps to the side. He staggers back into the corner, whacks his skull on the post, and slides to the ground.

"Why did he do that?" I scream my outrage. "The fight was over." I push chairs aside, trying to clear a path to the ring.

Jimmy grabs my hand and pulls me back. "Technically, the fight wasn't over. Misery didn't tap out or go limp."

"But the club is being evacuated. Torment clearly thought the fight was done. He was just trying to make sure I was safe. Surely that's against the rules, aside from being just plain unsportsmanlike."

Jimmy shook his head. "No one will criticize Misery for wanting to finish the match. Torment knows better than to turn his back on an opponent before the fight is done."

Torment moans and rolls to his back. His hand twitches, and then he is still. Warm tears slip from my eyes and drip onto my cheeks.

"We have to go," Jimmy says, his voice urgent. "They'll question anyone they find. We don't want to give them the ammunition they need to shut us down."

"But...Torment."

"Don't worry. His people will come for him."

Shaking off Jimmy's hand, I turn back to the ring. Misery is standing in his corner, massive arms folded. Torment is still lying dazed on the mat. Vulnerable. Hurt.

"We can't leave him like that," I say, aghast.

"I can't risk getting caught. I haven't told anyone but I'm applying for the amateurs. Being caught at an unsanctioned event might destroy any chance I have of getting in. Sandy and I will wait outside for you as long as we can." Jimmy pivots and disappears into the dwindling crowd.

My heart pounds against my ribs and I climb into the ring beside Torment.

"Torment? Max?" I turn his face toward me. "Are you okay? Talk to me."

His eyes open and he gives me a weak smile.

"Stay with me," I urge him. "Keep your eyes open. Focus on me." My hands are already running over his body, checking for breaks and injuries. He has a bump on his head and a cut on his temple. Possibly a concussion.

"You didn't kiss me back." His voice is so soft I barely hear him.

My eyes widen. "This isn't the time. You're hurt."

"Kiss me better, Makayla," he whispers.

Cupping his face in my hands, I lean over and brush my lips against his cheek. Electricity shoots through me like a bolt of white, hot lightning.

"A real kiss," he grumbles as I pull away.

"That's all you get," I snap. "I'm not going to ignore your medical needs so I can indulge myself."

He gives me a half smile. "I thought you were all about indulgence."

The platform shakes. Misery pounds his way across the ring toward us.

"Enough. He's talking, so the fight's not done. Get out, bitch."

My blood runs cold and I position myself between Torment and Misery. "He's hurt. The regulators are coming. The fight is over."

Misery's face darkens. "I don't take backtalk from bitches, especially not when their mouths should be doing something else. Looks like you need a lesson in respect." He stalks toward me, a bald, sweaty Goliath with murder in his eyes.

My knees shake, my pulse races, and my mouth goes dry. Fragments of memories burst from my subconscious. Long buried. Another night. A man stalking toward me in the darkness. I hold up tiny hands, terrified I won't be able to protect myself or the person on the floor. I scream.

Misery stops short. His eyes focus on something behind me and widen to the size of tea cups. Torment steps in front of me and throws a punch and then another. His fists fly, hitting Misery in the head and face, over and over and over again. Misery staggers backward into the ropes. He bounces forward and into Torment's waiting knee before crumpling to the floor with a groan.

My heart thumps in my chest while my mind spins backward, desperately trying to fill in the missing pieces to a nightmare I haven't had since I was a child. What happened when he reached me? How did we escape? The fight ring blurs, and I grab the ropes to steady myself.

"I've got you."

Strong arms lift me and slide me under the ropes. My dizziness subsides. My vision clears. Torment jumps down to the floor and carries me easily in his arms. I frown at his concerned expression. "What happened?"

"I thought you were going to faint. You were a little…unfocused." His arms are warm around me and his footsteps echo in the near-empty warehouse.

Oh God. He's carrying me. "Put me down. I can walk."

"No. You've caused enough problems for one night. Taking on Misery wasn't the wisest of moves, especially for a girl who professes to abhor violence." He ducks under the bleachers and heads toward an exit door hidden in the corner.

"Sorry. I was just trying to help."

"You did help. You gave me enough time to clear my head and get to my feet." He pauses and his voice takes on a more serious tone. "But next time don't put yourself in danger. You're the healer. I'm the fighter."

"I'm not a healer."

Torment frowns. "You have a gift—a passion—for healing people. Don't downplay it. You don't just heal bodies, you heal people inside. Somehow you can see what people need—"

My cheeks heat and I manage to wiggle my way out of his arms. "Okay. You got me. I like to help people. I like to make them feel better. But it doesn't make me a healer." If it did, I would heal myself.

"You're wrong." He pushes open the door and I follow him out into the cool, still night air.

"Mr. Huntington, sir, the limo is over here. You'd best hurry."

A cut-glass English accent is not something one hears often in Oakland. My head whips around just as a tall, broad-shouldered man emerges from the shadows. He is shorter than Torment by about three inches, and heavier. He has a shaved head, rounded body, and a cheerful countenance. From the slight sag to his skin and the wrinkles creasing his brow, he might be in his early forties—older than Torment, and much older than me. His suit—a stiff white shirt, striped blue tie, long gray suit jacket, and matching gray dress trousers—is more appropriate for an office or a wedding and not a Ghost Town alley reeking of stale beer and rotting garbage.

"Makayla, this is Colton. Colton, Makayla."

Colton nods. "How do you do, Miss Makayla. It's a pleasure to finally meet you."

Finally? How does he know about me? Why does he know about me? Instinctively, I thrust out my hand. "Hi."

Amusement glitters in Colton's clear, sparkling blue eyes, and he gives my hand a gentle shake. Then, he snaps his fingers and a sleek, black Bentley limo purrs out of the alley and stops beside us.

My eyes widen. "What is this? What's going on?"

"Why did you bring that?" Torment grumbles.

"I thought it might be more comfortable if you were unconscious again, sir. We had difficulty keeping you upright last time in the Lexus."

A door slams and a man in a black suit and flat-brimmed hat races around the limo and pulls open the passenger door.

Torment sighs. "Makayla, this is Lewis. He insists on wearing a uniform despite my preference for casual attire. Lewis, this is Makayla."

Lewis narrows his eyes and gives me a tight-lipped smile. I immediately don't like Lewis in his fancy uniform. I also don't like limos appearing out of nowhere in dark alleys and men in suits who call Torment "sir." I especially don't like not understanding what the hell is going on.

Torment places his hand on my lower back and urges me forward. "After you."

My breath catches in my throat, and I stare at the vast expanse of polished chrome, the uniformed chauffeur, and…Colton. Words fail me and I shake my head.

His jaw tightens. "It's okay. You're safe with me."

My voice, when it returns, is soft and hoarse. "But what about your motorcycle?"

"Mr. Huntington's motorcycle is already on a truck and on its way home," Colton answers.

Everyone stares at me. Waiting. Expectant. But my brain is still playing catch-up and my feet refuse to move. "Why are you riding around in a limo with a chauffeur and a—"

"Butler, Miss Makayla." Colton is quick to fill in the gap in my knowledge.

"Butler. You have a butler. Who are you?"

Torment tugs off his bandana and rubs his hand over the back of his neck. "We can talk in the limo. We don't have time to discuss it here. The regulators are coming, and we need to clear the area before they get here. Jake is inside getting rid of the last stragglers and shutting things down. He'll help Misery's cornermen get him out. We're free to go."

Something inside me tightens. He isn't who I thought he was. I don't know him at all. But I do know not to get into a car—or a limo—with a stranger.

He reaches for my hand, but I back away.

His face falls. "Makayla—"

"Who. Are. You?" Raising my voice, I enunciate each word no longer caring if the regulators find us.

"You haven't told her?" Colton asks.

Torment shakes his head.

Colton's eyes flick to me and his blue eyes soften before his gaze returns to Torment. "Might I suggest you give her your phone and let her look you up on the Internet, sir? I retrieved your personal belongings when the whistle blew. I suspect in your current state, you will be unable to do justice to yourself and given our time constraints it is best if she receives her information from a reliable source. She might then be able to assure herself of her safety in your company."

Torment's shoulders slump and he nods. Colton reaches into the limo and retrieves Torment's phone.

"You can just speak to it." He hands the futuristic gadget to me. "Tell it to search for Max Huntington."

"I'll do it the old-fashioned way." Hands trembling, I type "Max Huntington" into the search engine and get dozens of hits.

My mouth drops open when I read about Max Huntington, one of America's youngest leading venture capitalists and partner of IMM Ventures. I scroll through article after article about him in the business newspapers and financial magazines. His name also appears in society and gossip columns as one of California's most eligible bachelors. Here he is at a charity event with a woman I recognize from the movies. And here he is looking breathtaking in a tux with a beautiful model clinging to his arm on a luxury yacht. My eyes drink in pictures of him at lavish parties, gala openings, media events, and even the Academy Awards. But none of him fighting in Ghost Town.

I exhale slowly and my heart thuds into the ground. For a moment I can only stare at him, stunned. "Why didn't you tell me?"

Torment shrugs. "You liked me as Torment. Except for Sandy, the women I've been with couldn't see past the money and would have been horrified to know I was on the underground fight club circuit."

Sirens wail in the background. Lewis sniffs.

Colton tenses. "It sounds like they've brought the police with them this time, sir. It would be a PR nightmare if you were caught here."

My hands clench into fists. "You lied to me. You made me think you were a regular guy."

A pained look crosses Torment's face. "I never lied to you. I just didn't tell you everything."

"Sir. We have to go." The urgency in Colton's tone makes the hair on the back of my neck prickle.

"Come with me. Please, Makayla."

My head spins. Too much. Too many things to process. Torment coming to my house. The fight. Our almost kiss. The rebirth of an unwanted memory. And this. My beast turned into a prince. Or is it the other way around?

Tears well up in my eyes. "I know Torment. I know pizza and picnics and motorcycles. I don't know you, Max, with your fancy limo and your staff and your movie star girlfriends. I don't know what kind of man you are. All I know is that you're incredibly rich and I'm... well, me. I buy my shoes at Handi-Mart. I eat cereal for breakfast and, recently, for dinner too. I have had to sacrifice my principles to make money to pay my...rent. And I don't know what will happen to me if I jump into your rabbit hole."

His steady gaze falters, almost as if I've hurt him, and guilt crawls through me.

"I'm the same man," he rasps. He pauses, and the disappointment in his voice is almost palpable. "But I understand. Colton can call for a taxi and he'll wait with you until it arrives."

Colton nods and speaks into a headset I didn't even notice he was wearing. He gives me a sad, guilt-inducing smile. "Taxi will be here in two minutes."

Torment brushes a kiss across my cheek then turns and steps into the limo, leaving me with a sense of loss deep in my stomach and a hole in my chest.

"Wait."

He pauses, one foot in the limo and one foot on the street.

I close the distance between us and take his face between my hands. I search his eyes, looking for Max. Instead, I see Torment.

Torment in pain. Torment in need.

Blood trickles down his cheek. His eye is badly swollen. His jaw is cut and bruised. I stand on tiptoe and run my hand through his hair. He winces when I touch the lump where he hit his head on the metal post and again when my hand runs over the slight swelling where Misery hit him.

He is rich, successful, and until the fight, breathtakingly gorgeous. He has everything. Why does he need the fight club? Why does he need me?

"You'll need a stitch here," I whisper, brushing my thumb over his cheek. "And maybe here too." I run my hand over his chin, rough with stubble.

His eyes darken and he takes my hand, pressing his lips to the underside of my wrist. "Maybe you could just kiss it better." The deep rumble of his voice sets my nerve endings on fire.

I take a deep breath and step into the limo. "Maybe I could."

Chapter 8

WHERE'S MY MUFFIN TOP?

"GOOD MORNING, MS. DELANEY."

"Sergio, it is exactly one minute past eight o'clock on a Monday morning. Surely you have better things to do than call me at work, especially since you promised to give me an extra week." A weekend of Internet research about student loan collection and a brief chat with Amanda have made me cocky. I lean back in my chair and wave the next patient over to Charlie's desk.

Sergio laughs. "Calling you *is* my job and since you are the most pleasant of all my debtors, who better to call first on a Monday morning. I just wanted to remind you about your payment."

"And I wanted to remind you that you cannot enforce a minimum payment without first assessing my financial position. I've also filed an online complaint with the Education Commission. I understand collections have to be frozen until the complaint is resolved."

Sergio's voice turns cold. "I haven't received any notice of your complaint, and until I do, you must make the payments as they fall due. Otherwise, sneaky debtors like yourself could claim to have filed a complaint to avoid making their payments. I know all the tricks, Ms. Delaney. All the tricks."

My confidence wavers. "Well, you still have to do a financial analysis. I'll send you my financial statement and you will see there is no way I can make the minimum payment."

"I know that trick too." Sergio sighs. "You spend weeks pretending to look for the documents. Then you pretend to have sent them. After a few weeks, you suggest they are lost in the post, and we have to go through the whole process again."

"I wouldn't do that. I spent all weekend getting them together and I can send the statement to you today."

Sergio laughs. "How refreshing. Please do send it to me. I would be delighted to read it. You have my details in the letter I sent. But I will tell you now the minimum payment will not change. That is our final number." He emphasizes the last two words in a voice so loud I have to hold the phone away from my ear.

I do some quick mental calculations. I have the paychecks from Redemption. If I work another weekend at the club, and stick to my noodle diet, I just might be able to make the first payment. And maybe lose some weight. Helllooo, skinny jeans. Surely by then the Education Commission will have acknowledged my complaint and realized their mistake.

"Okay. I'll do my best."

"Do you hate me now? Are you going to hang up? Swear at me? Everyone does." The slightly needy tone in his voice makes the skin on my neck prickle.

"No. I don't hate you. You're doing your job and I'm trying to understand that."

Sergio sighs. "You seem like a nice person, Ms. Delaney. Honest, trustworthy, and from your file photo, very pretty. I enjoy talking to you. I can't say that about my other debtors. Please don't disappoint me. I would hate to have to get heavy-handed with you."

I suck in a sharp breath. "Is that a threat?"

"Of course not. By law, I'm not allowed to make threats, and I would *never* do something I'm not allowed to do." Sergio's tone lightens. "Now, how about a joke?"

"A joke?"

"You brightened my day last week with your amusing story. I was able to return the favor in my own way. My personal circumstances are such that I don't have many opportunities to smile. Perhaps you might wish to build up some more goodwill. You never know when you might need it."

My jaw tightens. The last thing I want to do right now is tell a joke, but the tone of his voice suggests it is not really a request. I lean back and stare at the ceiling. "A debt collector walked into a bar…"

How's my girl today?

I'm not ur girl

Max frowns

Silly. Learn to text. Frown like this **frowns**

frowns

That's a lot of frowning

Your fault

Sorry. Bad day

Will cheer you up. What r u doing for lunch?

Eating with a friend

Lascivious doctor friend?

No

Crazy black hair friend?

No

Amanda?

No

Male friend?

Yes

frowns

Stop frowning. U saw him. Works beside me

Lunch with male friend approved

Gee, tx

Please seek prior approval for all lunches with male friends

Ha ha **rolls eyes**

No ha ha **frowns**

Gotta run. Male friend is here **winks**

"So, how was your weekend?" Charlie beats a rhythm on his Justin Bieber lunch kit while I grab my brown paper lunch bag and purse from my desk drawer.

"Same old. Same old." My lips quiver with a repressed smile. "How was your course this morning?"

"Same old. Same old." Charlie shrugs. "I think that's the fifth time I've had to take Customer Relations 101. This time, I've learned to smile. Imagine that! People like people who smile. No wonder I haven't been able to get a date."

"I had a sort-of date." I give Charlie a wink and then vacate the cubicle for Jenny, our new temp trainee. Charlie and I walk down the corridor toward the cafeteria.

"No!" Charlie clutches his chest in mock horror and staggers backward. "You had a date? Was he breathing?"

I punch him in the shoulder. "You're just jealous."

"I have to admit I do have an itch to punch the as-yet-unidentified bastard in the face for moving in on my territory. I should have marked you—maybe pissed on your feet."

"I meant you're jealous I had a date."

"I had a date too."

Charlie drops hints about his mystery date, but I'm only half listening. I see Torment in every shadow. I hear his husky voice in every corridor. I smell the fresh, citrus scent of his cologne. I imagine his arms wrapped around me. I wish he hadn't just dropped me off on Saturday night but Colton had insisted on having him checked out by his private doctor.

"Mac. There you are! I've been looking all over for you."

"Good afternoon, Doctor Drake." Charlie spares me the embarrassment of being totally unaware of my surroundings by being overly genial and shaking Dr. Drake's hand.

Dr. Drake frowns and turns to me. "I've been looking for you."

My heart sinks in my chest. Did Big Doris file a complaint after handing me two green slips in the space of an hour? How was I to know two chair casters have to be under the desk at all times?

"Ready for our lunch date?" He winks and flashes his pearly whites.

Oh God. I totally forgot. "Um. Actually, I…I brought my lunch. Maybe we could do it another day."

Dr. Drake plucks my lunch bag from my hand with this thumb and index finger. Without even looking over his shoulder, he tosses it backward and into the garbage can.

"Score!" Charlie shouts. "Good shot, Doctor Drake. You missed your calling in the NBA."

Dr. Drake's cheeks flush ever so slightly and he gives Charlie a bemused smile. "Actually, wrestling was my thing in college, but I've always enjoyed handling balls."

Don't look at Charlie. Don't look at Charlie. DON'T LOOK AT CHARLIE.

"I'm sure you do." Charlie's voice shakes with repressed laughter. "As does Mac. We were just discussing how much she enjoys—"

"Charlie! Don't you have somewhere to be?"

"Three's a crowd. I get it. And look, I see the lovely Doris watching us from the entrance to the cafeteria." Charlie gives me a wink and walks briskly toward the glaring woman in the lime green suit, his every step punctuated with a little squeak from his Crocs.

"He's quite a character," Dr. Drake muses.

"He's got a good sense of humor."

Dr. Drake studies me for a long moment. "You two seem quite close."

"We're good friends." I twist my school ring around my finger—round and round and round.

"And that's all?" He puts a hand on my lower back and steers me away from the cafeteria.

"Just friends."

Dr. Drake smiles and his hand slides around me to squeeze my hip. "Good to hear."

"Um…the cafeteria is the other way." I slide out of his grasp and spin around.

Dr. Drake motions to an exit door at the end of the hallway. "I'm taking you to the Surgeon's Club. It's a new private club just down the block run by a few friends of mine. You and I have some business to discuss and I thought we could do so without the distraction of all your male friends vying for your attention in the cafeteria. I've already talked to Jenny and she has agreed to cover for you."

Um…what male friends? Who's vying for my attention? Charlie?

I swallow hard and follow him outside. The door slams closed, and

I catch a glimpse of my faded Tweety Bird scrubs in the glass. "I'm not really dressed for a private club."

"Nonsense. It's run by medical professionals and a favorite with the hospital lunch crowd. There are always a few people in scrubs."

We walk down the block to a tall, brick building with a heavy oak door. Dr. Drake slides his card through the card reader and heaves the door open. I freeze, poised on the threshold of the ultimate masculine man cave, scented with the fragrant odor of bloody meat. The dark wood details, worn Persian carpets, and leather furniture imbue the room with an air of exclusivity. The white walls covered with taxidermy remind me of the zoo. A deer looks balefully down at me as I follow Dr. Drake to a table by the window.

"I'm the only person wearing scrubs." I take my seat and glance around the room. I recognize almost everyone from the hospital. "I'm also the only woman, and the only person who is not a doctor."

He takes my hand and gives it a squeeze. "Relax. You're with me. No one is going to say anything."

Maybe not, but they'll be wondering why Dr. Drake is slumming it with the staff.

Dr. Drake smiles at the waiter, waiting patiently by the table. "We'll have the Chateaubriand, medium rare, baby potatoes, and spring vegetables. No wine. We're on duty. Just water." The waiter scratches everything down on his pad and, before I can say anything, he is gone.

"I like my meat cooked." My voice rises in pitch. "Well cooked. Charred to a crisp. If it's pink and squishy with blood oozing out of it—"

Doctor Drake cuts me off. "It would taste even better. The chef here is extraordinary. I promise you're going to love it."

I imagine Dr. Drake tearing into a raw steak, bloody juices dripping down his chin. Bile rises in my throat. If anyone should be eating raw steak, it's Max, not the capital *C* conservative doctor. Does Max like his steak rare? I would guess he does. Predators usually like fresh meat.

"We should get down to business before the food arrives." Dr. Drake steeples his fingers and his normal, genial expression turns serious. "I've been reviewing personnel files in anticipation of the upcoming annual reviews. I must admit I had forgotten you were in pre-med, but I never knew you were near the top of your class. Why didn't you apply to medical school?"

I shrug. "I didn't know if it was what I really wanted to do, and I didn't have the money."

Dr. Drake shakes his head. "You have a healing gift, Mac. You have a responsibility to share it. I want to help."

"How?"

"I know people on the scholarship committees. I can direct you to the scholarships you have the best chance of winning. I can help you fill out the forms. I can put in a good word for you with my friends on various admissions committees. I'll even tutor you when you get in."

My mouth drops open. "That's very kind of you, but why do you want to help me?"

He beams. "I think you would be a great doctor, and we need more doctors. You have compassion, intelligence, and empathy. Your EMT coworkers and your coworkers in the hospital have had nothing but praise for you."

My cheeks flame and I stare at the table. "I don't know. I just…I need time to decide what I really want in life."

"It's been almost three years since you graduated," Dr. Drake says. "You're spinning your wheels. You can't stay on the admissions desk forever. You need to move forward. I'm giving you a chance to grab the brass ring. Don't let it go."

Thankfully, the waiter arrives with our food. As specified, the meat is barely cooked. Bloody juices seep into the two minuscule potatoes and three steamed green beans artfully arranged on my plate. Already tense from our conversation, my stomach gurgles, threatening rebellion. The elk above Dr. Drake's head glares at me, and I give my excuses and beat a hasty retreat to the luxurious, wood-paneled washroom.

After I splash water on my face and reapply my makeup, I take a few deep breaths and prepare to return to the menagerie. My phone buzzes in my purse and I check the Caller ID. Max. Is he checking up on me already?

How is lunch?

Bad

What's wrong?

Change of plans. Different lunch companion

Male companion?

Yes

Black hair?

No

Brown hair?

No

Blond hair?

Yes

Doctor?

Yes

Lascivious doctor?

Actually, he's being quite nice

Not approved

Too late

Not approved

We're already in the middle of lunch

Not approved

I see someone figured out how to use his Repeat button

I'm coming to the hospital

I'm not at the hospital

Where are you?

Not telling. Chill

Chill?

I'm a big girl. I can handle myself

You're a sexy girl. I want to handle you

Naughty Max

You need me, I'm there

Sweet Max

Maybe I should come and find you
No Max
Yes Max
BAD MAX

———————

Anticipation ratchets through me after I end the conversation. Is he just teasing or is he seriously going to try and find me? I tuck my phone into the pocket of my scrubs and make my way back to the table. Dr. Drake has finished his meal. My steak has stopped bleeding, but now it is floating in a congealed puddle of pink fat. Yummy.

"I'm not feeling very well." I put my fork and knife at four o'clock on the plate. "I think I might have a touch of stomach flu. I've lost my appetite."

The elk smiles and nods approvingly. I pick up my water glass and take a sip.

"Maybe you should come to my office," Dr. Drake suggests. "I can give you a thorough examination. We wouldn't want anything spreading through the staff."

I choke and splutter water over the plate. "Actually, I'm suddenly feeling a lot better. Maybe I was just dehydrated." I pick up my fork and knife and slice into the unroasted beast with the zeal of my housemate, Rob, on a bar crawl. It quivers. I put a tiny piece of steak in my mouth, press my lips together and chew. Soft. Squishy. Like flesh.

No. Chicken. It tastes like chicken. It tastes like chicken.

I gag.

"Mac!" Dr. Drake leaps from his seat.

I force the meat down and put my utensils on my plate. "I'm fine. You were right. It was delicious, and very filling."

"Well then, we'll have to come back another day. If you liked that, you'll love the raw lamb. They serve warmed lamb blood on the side. Delicious and full of iron."

My stomach heaves. "You're kidding."

"Yes, I am." Dr. Drake chortles. "They don't warm the blood."

I slap my hand over my mouth in case I lose what little I ate all over Dr. Drake's shoes. "Can I go back to work now?"

Dr. Drake gives me a wink. "Off you go. Next time we'll just have salad and you can tell me if you've thought about my offer."

He dismisses me with a casual wave of his hand and I flee the man cave under the disapproving glare of the assorted forest animals. How can I turn him down? He is almost guaranteeing me a scholarship and my student loan payments would be put on hold until I finish medical school. Problem solved.

So why does it feel so wrong?

Five hours, no Max and no answers later, I sling my pack over my back and head into the parking lot. Thank God the day of horribleness is over. Now I can go home, have a bath, and cry. Not necessarily in that order.

"Makayla."

Squinting into the sun, I catch the outline of a tall, broad-shouldered man in a suit standing in front of a sleek, black limo. Familiar. He closes the distance between us, and holds out a hand. Broad palm, elegant fingers. I know those fingers.

Max.

Max in clothes.

My heart pounds in my chest. Max in his leathers is hot. Max in his fight shorts is scorching. Max in an elegant black suit, blue shirt, and striped silk tie sets my blood on fire. The tailored cut of his jacket molds to his broad shoulders and emphasizes his narrow waist and lean hips. He looks mature, sophisticated, and powerful. I can imagine him hammering out deals in boardrooms, escorting movie stars to parties, and running his successful company.

What the hell does he want with me?

My mouth goes dry and my feet refuse to move. Max stops only a foot away. He smells of citrus cologne and ever so faintly of coffee.

"What's wrong?" He frowns and wipes away a tear I didn't even know was on my cheek.

"Wow." I try for a light, joking tone, but in my depressed state, my voice comes out flat. "You clean up well. I've never seen you in…well, clothes. I almost didn't recognize you."

His face tightens. "You aren't going to distract me. Why were you crying?"

The sympathy in his voice makes me want to lean into him and bare my soul. But I don't want him to think I'm asking for anything, especially after what he told me outside the club. I don't need his help. I'll figure it out on my own.

"Nothing. Just a bad day at work. It happens."

His eyes darken, and he wipes another tear from my cheek. "Did someone bother you?" His chest puffs up and his biceps twitch. "Tell me who it is and—"

"It's okay, Max." I pat his arm. "I'm just going home to wallow in self-pity. I'll be fine tomorrow."

Max shakes his head. "You have to eat first. Self-pity is better on a full stomach. Let me take you for dinner."

Hmmm. Instant noodles alone in my apartment or a hot, cooked meal with GQ model Max in a restaurant? Not really a choice. More like a foregone conclusion.

I take his hand. "Lead the way."

We climb into the air-conditioned interior and my mood immediately improves. "Same limo as before?" I run my hand over the butter soft, beige leather seat and check out the situation: television, small bar fridge, seating for eight, laptop, privacy glass, Internet port. All looks the same.

Max chuckles. "Sorry to disappoint. I only need one." He presses the button on the intercom. "Lewis, we're going to Bianco Nero, but first we'll visit Eva."

"Bianco Nero? The ritzy Michelin-starred restaurant?" My voice rises and trembles. "I can't go there in jeans and a T-shirt. Do you know the kind of people who go there? Certainly not the likes of me. I was thinking of something more casual."

Max cups my face in his hands and turns me to face him. "Yes, the likes of you. Exactly the likes of you. With me. And I would never put you in a situation where you would feel uncomfortable. I have the dress-code issue all sorted out."

"What does that mean?"

Max's lips quirk into a smile and he takes my hand and twines his fingers through mine. "You'll see. Now relax."

Relax? In a limo beside a man who now looks so far out of my league I shouldn't be able to see him?

We sit in silence while Lewis expertly navigates the traffic. I sigh and twist my ring around my finger as I anticipate yet another humiliating inappropriate clothing experience. Max lets my hand go and puts his arm around my shoulders, pulling me into his chest.

"Relax, baby. Trust me."

Baby. He called me baby. Warmth ripples through my body and I drift on happiness clouds until the limo pulls to a stop.

Lewis dashes out of the vehicle and holds open the door as we step onto the sidewalk outside an exclusive boutique in Rockridge. My contentment vanishes like a thief in the night.

Max clasps my hand and leads me to the door. My tension flares to life. "I can't buy anything here. I can tell just by looking at the six items of clothing in the window. I probably can't even afford to buy a tissue in this place."

Max presses a buzzer and the door is opened by an exquisite, darkly exotic woman with long, black hair.

"Eva."

"Max." She doesn't even wait for us to step inside before she throws her arms around him. Her expensively clothed, toned body presses up against him. Long, dark lashes flutter down over her perfectly smooth, honey-colored cheeks.

"It's been so long," she breathes through plump, rouged lips.

Jeez. Not again. He's really pushing his "I'm a one-woman man" promise to its limits.

"Ahem."

Max pulls away. "Makayla this is Eva. She's an old friend."

We exchange greetings and Eva excuses herself to get things ready. I sigh and walk over to the rack as I contemplate how Eva can run a business with only six items of stock.

"What's wrong?"

"She's very…friendly. And she appears to be more your type. She could probably afford to buy the clothes she sells. I can't."

"You are my type," he says, emphasizing each word. He cups my jaw and strokes my cheek with his thumb. "And I want to buy you something you would feel comfortable wearing to Bianco Nero. You don't have to worry about the cost." His voice drops to a soothing murmur and I lean in to the touch of his hand.

"I don't need you to buy my clothes, Max. If you take me home, I'm sure I have something I can wear."

He pulls me close and kisses me lightly on the forehead. "You are a beautiful woman and I want to buy you something beautiful to wear. Let me have that small pleasure."

Am I so heartless I would deny a man the small pleasures in his life? Of course not. I'm altruistic to the core. "Okay. You win."

Max settles himself in a gilded throne-like chair and pulls out his fancy phone. Eva hands me a tiny piece of green, sparkly material. "It will be perfect," she breathes. "It matches your eyes and will highlight your beautiful curves."

I give her a tight smile. "I'm not really a scarf person."

Eva laughs, a light, musical sound, so unlike my snorts and guffaws when I really get going. "It's not a scarf. It's a dress."

I unfold the flimsy material. No way is this going over my rolls. Even if I do find a way to get it on, no doubt I will immediately shred it with the jagged edge of my freshly chewed fingernails. My eyes flick to Eva and back to the dress. "Do you have anything more…substantial?"

Eva trills another laugh and leads me to a tiny, curtained alcove. Clearly, normal people do not shop at this store. I cannot move without brushing open the soft, beige cotton curtains, much less strip off and slide on the handkerchief without revealing things best kept hidden.

"He's not watching," she whispers. "Take off your clothes and I'll help you put it on."

Still doubtful, I close my eyes and prepare for a snicker when I pull off my shirt.

Nothing. I crack open an eye. Eva is staring at my jeans. Or maybe she's contemplating my muffin top and how many scarves will be needed to hide it.

"Jeans too," she says without a hint of humor.

Maybe she's seen worse. Taking a breath, I strip down to my bra and panties. At least they match and it isn't my granny pants time of the month. "Do you have any foundation or support garments? Maybe a Spanx bodystocking?" I whisper. "I don't think this dress is going to adequately hide my...whole self."

Eva slides the dress over my head. "You don't need any. You have a beautiful body. You should show off your curves, not hide them."

Like she would know. Whenever she turns sideways, she almost disappears. "I don't want to hide them, just smooth them out. I'm going for the loaf look instead of the muffin top."

Ignoring me, Eva makes a few adjustments and hands me a death-defying pair of matching stilettos. I don't know much about shoes, but the simple, elegant, emerald encrusted stilts do something miraculous to my legs. Suddenly, I have some. She pulls out my ponytail holder, fluffs my hair, and gives me the fastest makeover I've ever had. Then she pulls back the curtain and I step out into the arena.

I bite my lip and hold my breath. Max is focused on his space-age communicator, no doubt sending secret messages to galactic emperors with thin and sophisticated daughters. Eva clears her throat and he looks up. His eyes rake over my body and his mouth curls into a smile. "You look beautiful."

My cheeks flame, but it is a pleasant burn.

"Turn around." His low, husky voice sends a tremor through my body.

I spin and catch sight of myself in the mirror beside the changing room. What the hell? Where's my muffin top? The woman in the mirror is tall and elegant. The sheer, sparkly dress gives her curves to rival even Pinkaluscious. Dark, thick eyelashes frame rich, emerald green eyes, and the rosy tinge on her cheeks brings out the color of her ripe, pink lips. And her legs take no prisoners.

"Look at me," I breathe. I twist and turn in front of the mirror. Even my bottom looks succulent. No wonder rich people always look so good.

"I'm looking, baby, and I like what I see." He turns to Eva, who has the self-satisfied smile of a woman who is just about to make a whole lot of money. "Do you have something she can wear if she gets cold?"

Eva hands him a matching piece of material and Max stands behind me and wraps it around my shoulders. "Maybe this wasn't such a good idea," he murmurs. "I'll be too distracted beating off your admirers to talk."

I smile and look up at us in the mirror—his tall broad body enveloping me like a blanket. "I guess I'll have to go myself then. I wouldn't want to waste all Eva's effort."

The low rumble of Max's voice carries through the confined space. "You're not going anywhere without me."

Chapter 9

YOU'RE DIFFERENT

AN HOUR LATER, WE arrive at Bianco Nero. Still reeling over the price of the dress and shoes, I ease myself carefully out of the car and allow Max to assist me across the sidewalk. One brush against the wrong surface or one misstep, and five thousand dollars will be down the drain. I should have told him I have a tendency to be less than coordinated.

The manager races out to fawn over Max and ushers us inside. My eyes dart from side to side seeking a flash of color in the cavernous room, but everything is decorated in white—even the staff. I am a brilliant green paint smudge in the middle of an otherwise perfect canvas.

"Are you sure this is a restaurant?" With only twenty tables in a space that could easily accommodate one hundred, and no one speaking above a hushed whisper, the place has the feel of a modern art gallery, and we are the art.

Max laughs. "It was designed that way. The idea is to keep the focus on the food."

Food sounds good. After the disaster of a lunch, my stomach is protesting the lack of sustenance at an increasingly loud volume.

Our waiter for the evening is small, thin, and blond with a narrow face and the tiniest mouth I have ever seen. He introduces himself as Brad, and his dark, cold eyes flick over me dismissively as if he knows I don't belong. Brad plods through the fixed price menu in a nasal monotone. After two minutes, Max interrupts him and excuses himself to take a call. The second Max is out of earshot, Brad stops his monologue and stares at me with sudden intensity.

I swallow hard. "Is there a problem, Brad?"

"You're different."

"Different as in I've got two heads, or different as in I've changed since we last met, which I'm sure was never?"

"Definitely different." He purses his tiny lips and tilts his head to the side.

I can't tell if Brad's comment is an insult or a compliment. Maybe I should let Max know that Brad thinks I'm different and ask him what he thinks. I suspect Max wouldn't give Brad the benefit of the doubt. Wouldn't that be fun? For me. Not for Brad.

Max takes his seat and Brad finishes his menu monologue with a smile. He has such a tiny smile. I'm not sure if he even has teeth.

I excuse myself and go to the restroom. I can't get Brad's comment out of mind. I'm pretty sure he means I clearly don't belong. My eyes water and I dab them with a tissue. Maybe I could pretend I'm ill and ask Max to take me home. No. Damn it. I won't give Brad the satisfaction. I redo my makeup, but I can't hide my red eyes.

"Something wrong?" Max asks when I return to the table.

"No. I'm good."

Max frowns, but before he can question me further, Brad returns with a tiny shot glass filled with pink froth.

Dear God, please don't let this be the appetizer or I will pass out from hunger. "What is this?"

Max takes a sip. "Salmon mousseline. It's an amuse-bouche. A taster. Something to tease your taste buds and get your palate ready for the meal."

I down my amuse-bouche like a shot of tequila. Bitter, fishy, and frothy. My mouth is not amused.

The sommelier arrives. I am at a restaurant with a sommelier. My mom, the wine buff, would think she had died and gone to heaven. Good thing Max seems to know a thing or two about wine. I suspect there is no "House White" at Bianco Nero.

Our first wine, a Meursault, is soft, smooth, and buttery and totally unlike any white wine I've ever had. An orgasm for my tongue. Every sip makes me shiver. I sip. I sip. I sip some more. I have heard about multiple orgasms but never experienced them. If the wine is any indicator, I've been missing out.

Max excuses himself again to make a call. He leaves his phone on the table. As I contemplate what he might be doing, I guzzle down the rest of my wine. I'm ruined for house whites forever.

A few minutes later, Max returns and takes his seat. Brad reappears. Disappointingly, he doesn't have any wine in his hand. His face is white, and his dark eyes are wide. He blends in perfectly with the decor.

"I apologize if I offended you Ms. Delaney. That wasn't my intention." He looks at Max. Max gives him a curt nod.

My stomach clenches. "Thanks Brad. I wasn't offended. Just suffering from a bad case of self-doubt and an overprotective dining companion."

Brad gives me a weak smile and races back to the kitchen.

My lips press into a thin line. I raise an eyebrow and glare at Max. "If I wanted you involved, I would have asked. I had it under control."

Max glides his thumb along my bottom lip and my mouth opens to his touch. "He upset you. He's lucky to be standing. No one will hurt you when I'm around…in any way."

Tiny, warm quivers race through my body. Mmm. I like a protective alpha-male, but his actions were a bit over the top. No way am I going down that road. I know where it leads.

"You can't strong-arm everyone who ruffles my feathers," I say. "Sometimes it's a misunderstanding. Sometimes a person is having a bad day. Only rarely are people purposely nasty. I get hurt. I try to understand. I move on."

Max's eyes darken with emotion. "You're wrong, baby. The world is filled with cruel, nasty people. They think nothing of taking a life, destroying a family, or breaking a heart. If you don't protect yourself, you'll get hurt—maybe so bad you'll never recover."

His impassioned speech makes my heart ache. I can almost feel the pain behind his words. I reach out and cover his hand with my own. "Max–"

He cuts me off, as if he knows he has revealed too much, and yet his words have revealed nothing at all.

"I want to know about you. Where were you born?"

I startle at the abrupt change in conversation, and my brain scrambles to shift gears. "What?"

"Where were you born?" Max repeats.

With my wineglass refilled again by a now-silent Brad, I can give Max my full attention. Big mistake. The questions come thick and fast starting at birth, which I don't remember, and moving to the childhood, which I do. I skip the bad stuff and tell him Dad died when Susie and I were young and how hard it was for my mom to raise us alone. I tell him about Amanda and how she was my surrogate sister and how she practically lived at our house to get away from her cold, distant parents. I tell him about my stepdad, Steve, and how he changed our lives and made Mom smile again.

"I'm sorry about your dad." He takes my hand and presses his lips to my knuckles.

Brad returns with our first course, oysters with cabbage and some kind of foamy jelly. *No* to the most disgusting vegetable ever created. *No* to the foamy jelly. *Yes* to the oysters simply because they are supposed to be an aphrodisiac. The cold, slimy blob slithers down my throat. My gag reflex kicks in. Twice in one day. Good to know it works. I manage to control it with a sip of orgasmic wine. However, I am not overcome with the need to have sex right now. I cross oysters off my list of aphrodisiacs.

Max's questions continue. Brad removes the remnants of the oysters and replaces our plates with sea scallops (yum) and fancy deviled eggs (double yum). *How did I meet Amanda?* I stole her boyfriend in kindergarten and she stole him back. *Did I like school?* Yes. *Did I do extracurricular activities?* Soccer, volleyball, golf, tennis, archery (Amanda made me do it), volunteer stuff, and lots of social activities. *What were my favorite subjects?* Biology and gym. *Least favorite?* Physics and history.

Brad tops off my glass. Is that a smile or is he about to whistle? His tiny mouth is kind of cute. Not so much his bony ass.

Although the little bites of food are delicious, my stomach is growling for something more substantial. My heart sinks when Brad arrives with two more miniscule dishes. Disappointingly, the frilled cod is not dressed in a tutu. I hit my fish threshold and dive into the asparagus instead.

Max doesn't let up. His questions narrow in on college, my EMT work, my courses, and my boyfriends. What guy wants to know about the competition? Finally, I've had enough. "Max, please stop." My wineglass wobbles when I put it down. The problem with having Brad constantly refilling my glass reveals itself as my head spins. Or maybe it's lack of sustenance.

"I feel like I'm going through an Amanda-style inquisition. I want to have a conversation. I want to know about you."

Max frowns. "I'm not done."

"You are done."

"I'm not done, baby. I have more questions." Can a man look petulant? I'm leaning toward a big yes on that question.

"You are done because you aren't getting more answers until you answer some questions about yourself."

He raises an eyebrow. "One question. What do you want to know?"

"Why do you fight?"

"I enjoy it."

I groan and let my head fall back on the seat. "Work with me here. Why do you enjoy it? What is the appeal in hurting people?"

Max swirls the wine in his glass with an expert flick of his wrist. So cool. I want to learn how to do that.

"I don't do it to hurt people." He takes a sip and puts down the glass. "I enjoy the physical challenge and I enjoy the total mental focus it requires. My father was a professional boxer and he had me in the ring as soon as I could walk. He taught me the beauty of boxing. He called it the sweet science. He said it is more about focus and technique than outright violence. When I took up MMA as a teenager, I saw the same beauty in combining so many martial arts into one sport.

"Oh come on." I give an elegant snort. "You can't deny fighting is violent."

Brad places a bread basket between us. At least, I think it is bread. I grab a long white finger and shove it into my mouth. Not bread. Unidentifiable substance with a Styrofoam texture and no taste. I smile and wash it down with an elegant glug of wine.

Max leans forward and clasps my hand. His thumb rubs gently over my knuckles, soothing the savage Makayla beast. "We are all fighters.

It is basic human nature. We strive to get ahead in life or we fight for survival."

What have I ever strived for in my life? What have I ever wanted enough to pursue? A long time ago, I had a chance to fight for survival, and I threw it away. I gave up. I'm a quitter. "I'm not a fighter," I whisper.

As if he can sense my resignation, Max brings my hand to his lips and brushes a kiss over my palm. "Violence is part of you, baby, whether you admit it or not. You might have repressed it, but the instinct is still there. So why not embrace it and enjoy the rush?"

I give a noncommittal grunt and wallow in self-loathing. "If you're fighting just because you like to fight, why are you going for the underground championship belt? Why not enjoy each fight for what it is and move on to the next?"

He scrubs his hands over his face and shrugs. "I want to be the best. I want to know if anyone tried to hurt the people I care about, I could defend them."

"The best are not in the underground circuit, Max. The best are in the professional leagues. Everyone says you're good. Why don't you go pro and fight them?"

He picks up his wine and swirls it around the glass. "What if I'm not good enough?"

The mouth-watering aroma of lamb draws my gaze away from Max's earnest face. Brad places our dishes on the table. I search through the foliage on my plate and locate the tiny morsel of lamb shivering behind a baby carrot. Three huge slices of beetroot are artfully arranged in one corner. Maybe the carbs are served separately. I put down my knife and fork and wait.

"Something wrong?"

"I was waiting for the…carbohydrate part of the meal."

Max flags down Brad. Not difficult to do since Brad's job appears to involve hovering near our table. "Ms. Delaney would like a carbohydrate side dish."

"No. No." I shake my head and motion Brad away. "I just thought it would come with the meal because…well, usually there is rice or potatoes or pasta, but I don't need anything. Really. This is good. Protein and vegetables. Very healthy."

"We don't do carbohydrates." Brad's lips pinch together so tight it is a wonder he can breathe.

Max fixes Brad with a cold stare. "We'll have a side order of mashed potatoes with extra butter."

Brad shudders and scurries away. Does he even know what a potato is? From the size of the women in the restaurant, I believe him when he says carbs aren't part of the menu.

"You didn't have to do that, but thank you. I didn't have any lunch."

"I know." He slices his lamb into paper thin strips. I dismiss my plan to stick the thumb-size morsel in my mouth all at once.

"How do you know? You weren't there."

Max winks. "Secret."

Buzzed from too many glasses of orgasmic wine, I fix him with a mock glare and spear a slice of cooked beetroot. "Tell me."

"A man has to have some secrets," Max chuckles. "It makes him seem more mysterious."

"You are very mysterious," I agree, and then switch to a fake German accent. "But vee haf ways ov making you talk." I cackle and jerk my hand in the air. The beet flies off my fork and lands on the floor. I reach down to pick it up, just as Brad arrives with the mashed potatoes. He slips. The potatoes go up. He goes down. The elegant diners look over and snicker. Brad's face is as red as the squished beet on the floor.

Death cannot come too soon for me.

"I'm sorry. I'm so sorry. Are you okay?" I kneel beside Brad and brush mashed potatoes off his pants.

"Carbs," he moans. "I'm going to gain at least ten pounds."

A hushed murmur ripples through the restaurant. The forbidden word is on everyone's lips. For a moment I fear I will be forced to wear a giant scarlet letter *C* on my dress for the rest of the meal.

"Can you stand?"

Brad shakes his head. "My ankle. I think it's broken."

"I'm an EMT. Can I take a look?"

Brad nods and I examine his ankle. "It's not broken. Just slightly sprained," I tell him. "You need to rest, elevate, and ice it."

The manager arrives at the scene of the crime. He and Max have a hushed conversation, and then he helps Brad to his feet. He obsequiously assures us no one is at fault and he will call a cab and send Brad home with his full pay for the evening.

Max holds out his hand to help me up. I rise from the floor, and my throat thickens. My beautiful dress is stained red with beet juice and covered in mashed potatoes. My shoes have fared no better.

"I'm so sorry." I stare down at the disaster that is my dress. "I've ruined everything. I'll pay you back—"

"I don't care about the dress." Max cuts me off and wraps his arms around me, pulling me into his chest, stained clothes and all. "If you like it, I'll buy you another one. And you don't have to worry about Brad. I've taken care of everything."

He pays the bill and walks me to the limo, his hand firm on my lower back. I stare straight ahead so I don't have to see anyone laughing.

When we reach the limo, Lewis looks me up and down and frowns. "Are you okay, Ms. Delaney?"

Hmm. Maybe I was too harsh in my initial assessment of Lewis. "Yeah, I just look pretty bad."

Max strokes my hair. "You couldn't look bad if you tried."

"I just tried pretty hard."

Lewis starts up the limo and we pull away from the curb. The city lights blur as we purr down the street away from the site of my latest humiliation.

"I'm not good with first dates," I say to Max. "I always screw them up."

Max winds his fingers through mine and squeezes my hand. "This isn't a first date."

My heart sinks. Did I totally misinterpret this evening? The dress? The compliments? Did I botch it up so badly he wants to pretend it was something else? "Um. Yeah. Sure. I didn't really think—"

"Makayla, look at me."

His voice compels me to obey. I look up and an amused Max enters my line of vision. His lips twitch into the semblance of a smile. "This is our third date."

My brain kicks into gear and my face heats with a rush of blood. "Third date?"

"First we had a picnic. Then we had pizza. This time we almost had mashed potatoes."

"We seem to do a lot of eating together." Three dates? He thinks we've had three dates. Except for today, the time we spent together was more like two friends hanging out than fingernail-biting, heart-stressing dates.

"We'll have to do something else for date number four—or even tonight."

"Not tonight."

Max's face falls and he gives me a sideways glance. "Not tonight?"

"I just…today wasn't so good, and now I'm covered in potatoes and beets. I'm not really feeling my best. I just want to go home, take a shower, and go to bed."

"We'll go to your place, you can shower, and then—"

"No, Max." I pat his warm, broad hand. "Another time."

"But—"

Does he never give up? "Please. Just let me go home and wallow in my misery. If you change your mind about date four, that's okay. I get it. I'm sure that was just as humiliating for you as it was for me. You need to be with someone classy and sophisticated. Someone who doesn't throw beets around fancy restaurants."

"Actually, it was pretty damn funny."

"Seeing Brad fall?"

"Your German accent."

Snorting a laugh, I twist my hands in the shawl I've used to cover my stained dress. "You have to stop me when I do things like that. Amanda says my sense of humor gets a little quirky when I have too much to drink."

Max slides one hand under my hair and strokes my cheek. "I think your sense of humor is very refreshing. You are very refreshing. You have no guile. You put it all out there. What you see is what you get with Makayla, with a big dose of compassion thrown in."

All too soon, Lewis stops outside my apartment building and I step out of the limo and onto the sidewalk. "I'm sorry I ruined the evening. Like I said, I'll understand if you don't—"

"Is that what you want?" Max follows me out and walks me to the front entrance.

"I…don't know," I admit in a whisper. "The whole money thing makes me uncomfortable. I don't fit in."

Max smoothes my hair from my temple and tilts my head back with a finger under my chin. His warm, brown eyes study me until my cheeks burn, and I am forced to look away.

"If I'd taken you for pizza on the Agusta, and we were standing here in our leathers, would your answer be different?"

"Yes." I give him an honest answer. "You would have been more relaxed. I would have been more relaxed. I also wouldn't be covered in food."

"You don't like me this way?" His voice is hoarse, barely audible.

"Of course I do. It's just—" I stroke my hand down the cool, silk of his tie. "You're different in your suit. More focused and business-like. You fired questions at me like I was a potential investment, and you gave me almost nothing back. When you're at the club, you seem more comfortable with yourself. Business Max makes me nervous. I guess it showed."

He removes his hand from my chin and loosens his tie.

"What are you doing?" My throat goes dry. I should have kept my big mouth shut.

"I'm showing you I'm the same man, with or without the suit." He releases the buttons on his shirt, tugs it from his waistband, and shrugs free. Both his suit jacket and shirt fall to the ground. His devastatingly beautiful body gleams under the warm glow of the entrance light. He takes a step back into the shadows and holds out his hand.

Anticipation flutters through me. His brown eyes darken when I join him under the protective cover of the shadows.

"Touch me." His voice is raw, hoarse, and impossible to resist.

Without hesitation, I smooth my hands over the hard planes and sinews of his chest, just as I have imagined doing since the day I met him. He glides his thumb over my bottom lip, pressing down gently. Desire licks through my veins.

"Same Max?"

I snake my hands around his neck and press myself up against his warmth. "Same Max." I lie for the sole purpose of getting a kiss. His kiss.

He slides one arm around my waist and pins me tight against his body. His other hand cups my head, tilting it back, holding it firm. He brushes his lips over my ear and rasps, "Be sure, baby. Because after I kiss you, there is no going back."

My blood goes from a gentle simmer to a full on boil in a heartbeat. My knees buckle and Max tightens his grip and holds me steady.

"Tell me." His breath is hot and moist in my ear.

My hands clench and release restlessly behind his neck. "Kiss me," I whisper.

He gives a soft, satisfied grunt and feathers kisses down my jaw. "Open for me," he murmurs. My body trembles. Really trembles. Like an earthquake is happening and I can't stop the shaking.

My lips part and he brings his mouth down over mine. He kisses me gently, nibbling my lips. When my body melts against him, he deepens the kiss. His tongue dips inside stroking, exploring, leaving me nowhere to hide. I gasp, and he plunders my mouth, groans spilling from his throat as he drinks me down like the 1985 Château d'Yquem we had with our lamb bite.

So this is what it is like to be kissed. Really kissed. No soft pecks or wet, milky smacks on the lips. No tentative pokes of the tongue or the banging of teeth. This is a real kiss—a man's kiss—demanding, passionate, and hungry. No holds barred. All consuming.

Max's phone alarm beeps softly and he eases his mouth away. "I'm on the red-eye to Hong Kong in a few hours. But when I get back, we'll pick up where we left off."

Gah. My body aches with unfulfilled need. I hope I put fresh batteries in my Rabbit.

He releases me and I focus on staying upright while he pulls on his clothes.

"When?"

He presses a kiss to my forehead. "I fly back on Thursday morning. I'll pick you up after work. We'll have dinner."

"More food?" I cannot keep the disappointment out of my voice.

"Not if there is something else you'd rather do." The sensual purr of his voice sends my need from diminishing arousal to fierce craving in a heartbeat. A soft whimper escapes my lips.

His eyes blaze with sensual fire. "I'll take that as a yes."

By the time I've collected myself sufficiently to contemplate walking, Max's limo is a shadow in the darkness.

For the longest time I stare at the road, chewing my fingernails one by one down to a quick. I should have been honest when he asked "Same Max?"

I should have said no, but I like them both.

Chapter 10
FORWARD AND BACK

"You're going out with Max Huntington! SHUT UP!" Amanda shrieks. I cover my ears and slide into the padded booth beside her. Club music pounds through Doctor, Doctor. The new, medical-themed club, only a few blocks from the hospital, is the last place I want to blow off some steam but it was close, and Amanda has been trying to get me here since it opened.

"Thanks for meeting me," I shout over the music. "I waited for Max in the parking lot for almost an hour and he didn't show up. No text. No call. I guess I've officially been stood up."

"Well, he's missing out because you look HOT."

I smooth my hand over the sparkly silver, halter-neck dress Susie sent me from her favorite London store, French Connection UK. Tight, but not too tight, with a swishy skirt, it mercifully has the FCUK hidden in the label.

"You should have texted him," she continues. "Maybe he was delayed."

"Then he should have let me know. I only had enough minutes for one text, and I was tired of waiting. These stilettos are killing me, and it's been a stressful week. Big Doris has really been on my case. I've collected six green slips for nothing. I need a little girl-time relaxation."

Amanda grins and tries to flag down a waitress by fluttering her perfectly manicured and unbitten nails. "The drinks are on me tonight since you're poverty stricken and being chased by evil debt collectors."

"You don't—"

"And I just settled a big case so I feel like celebrating."

Her flutters attract the attention of a waitress wearing the smallest, tightest, nurse's uniform I have ever seen. She records our orders on a medical chart, and we relax into our booth as the DJ turns up the volume and spins some old-school funk.

Amanda listens patiently while I yell the details of my humiliating eating experiences into her ear. She stops me only to ask questions about what Max and Dr. Drake were wearing, how much the dress and shoes cost, and how far Max's tongue went down my throat.

Ten minutes later, my guts spilled, I suck back my citrusy "Liquid Lust" through a tube attached to an IV bag on a stand and await Amanda's analysis. She delicately sips her "Nitro Margarita" and considers my predicament, while at the same time scoping out the bar for potential sleeping partners. After I've pointed out the few actual doctors in the bar, she zeroes in on her target and lines him up with a flirtatious wink.

"What about Jake?" I suck back another shot and choke as the burst of sugary sweetness shoots down my throat. Someone forgot to turn the tap to low. Drips are supposed to drip.

Amanda sighs and almost immediately I sense she is hiding something. "I spent all night trying to get him to spill Torment's true identity. A waste of time since you found out anyway. Finally I called it quits and told him we needed a break."

"Amanda! You're punishing him for playing by the rules."

She gives me an evil grin. "He's being trained. When he's with me, the only rules he needs to follow are Amanda's rules. Don't worry. I'll only leave him hanging for another day. I don't want to have a dry weekend, and since I don't plan on being able to walk when he's done apologizing, I want to get the apology over with sooner rather than later so I can recover by Monday."

My cheeks flame and Amanda laughs. "You're too easy to embarrass. A little sexperience is all you need to cure that blushing problem. Speaking of which—" She pokes me hard in the shoulder. "Why didn't you invite Max in on Monday night?"

"I didn't get a chance. He kissed me and then ran off to catch a flight. Plus, I was covered in potatoes. It kind of spoiled the mood."

A waitress in green operating room scrubs stops at our table, and Amanda buys a few shots of "Tetra-Ouzo" in ready-to-administer, guaranteed-hygienic syringes. We take turns giving each other our "medicine." Within twenty minutes, I'm feeling the buzz.

"Why do you think he didn't show?"

Amanda fluffs her hair and pulls out her makeup bag—sure signs she is getting ready to go on the prowl. I follow suit, preparing to be the dutiful, tagalong friend who laughs at her jokes, checks out the guy, and entertains any of his annoying friends.

"If his tongue almost hit your tonsils, then he definitely wants to see you again. Tongue depth is a very accurate indicator of male interest." She slaps her cheeks repeatedly until they are pink and swollen and then pulls out a tiny fly swatter to swat her lips. She offers the torture device to me, but I wave her away.

"I swatted at home, thanks."

Amanda runs the lipstick over her plump lips and rubs them together. "I'd say whatever held him up wasn't his fault."

"I'm not sure," I sigh. "I got a funny feeling after he left. Like I was a deal he had just closed. Even though he took off his shirt and tie, he was still half dressed in his suit and he was different—very focused and demanding. Hard."

Amanda twists her lips to the side. "That doesn't sound good."

My eyes widen. "YOU don't think it sounds good. Now I know I'm in trouble."

She pats my hand and offers me another shot. "Let me think about it. Right now, I'm a bit distracted by the blond Adonis staring at us."

I follow the direction of her gaze and freeze. My breath catches in my throat. "It's Doctor Drake. Hide me. Don't let him see me." I try to slide under the table, but Amanda grabs my hand.

"Too late. He's on his way over. Pull up those big girl panties and paste on your best smile. If Max did dump you, here comes your second chance."

"He doesn't do it for me," I moan. "I know he's a gorgeous heart surgeon with an amazing body, and he's gone out of his way to offer to help me, but he doesn't make me tingle all over the way Max does. He's…safe and comfortable. Like…home."

"Are you insane?" Amanda hisses. "He is totally YUMMY and I've suddenly got a fever only a doctor can cure." She fans herself with a paper napkin.

"What happened to my girl-time relaxation?"

Amanda's eyebrows shoot up. "Seriously? You want girl-time relaxation when you could have him?"

Dr. Drake approaches the table, Amanda fluffs her breasts. I try to keep down the excessive quantity of alcohol I have just consumed on an empty stomach. Amanda's actions do not go unnoticed. Dr. Drake's eyes travel from her lips down to her chest and back again. He is wearing a lab coat over a white T-shirt, and a pair of tight blue jeans. He looks good. Too good. Like a soap opera doctor. But he has nothing on Max.

"He's all yours, but I think he might be more than even you can handle." I shove the IV tube in my mouth and take a big sip.

Amanda gives me a sideways glance and snorts. "No one has even come close. Except maybe Jake. But, since we're on a break, I'm free for a little examination."

"Mac, I thought that was you." Dr. Drake drags his eyes off Amanda's breasts and stares at the tube in my mouth. He reaches over to turn off the tap on my drip. "IVs have to be carefully monitored; otherwise, the patient might overdose."

"Some patients want to overdose." I turn the drip back on. Amanda splutters beside me. So what if I'm not being classy? He touched my drip.

"She's not thinking clearly," Amanda chimes in, patting my back. "She's inebriated because she had a hard week."

Grrrrr. Sometimes Amanda can be a total pain.

Dr. Drake's eyes flicker over to Amanda's face. His lips part. A smile creases his perfect face. "We haven't been formally introduced."

I introduce them between IV sucks. Amanda inhales. Her breasts rise. Her chin dips. She looks up at Dr. Drake through long, golden lashes and holds out her hand, waggling her fingers like little worms on a fishing hook. She is really laying it on thick. No one would ever suspect she is a crackerjack attorney at one of San Francisco's biggest law firms, and she likes to play it that way.

Dr. Drake presses his lips to her wrist. "How nice to meet one of

Mac's *girl*friends." He emphasizes the word "girl," making it seem as if I am inundated by men at work.

"Yes, we're very close." Amanda squeezes up beside me and puts her hand on my arm. I glance over at her and frown. Did I just miss something?

"Well, now I have two lovely ladies to dance with." Dr. Drake turns his gaze back to me and holds out both his hands.

"What's happening?" I whisper as I dutifully follow Amanda to the dance floor. "I told you he's all yours."

"Either he likes you a lot. Or he's into threesomes. Or both." She hits the dance floor and immediately begins to gyrate. Dr. Drake joins her, grooving to the hip-hop beat with some smooth moves of his own.

"Threesomes?" My alcohol-soaked brain cannot keep up and my voice rises in pitch. "You, me, and...Doctor Drake? Together? In bed? You picked that up after talking to him for five seconds?"

"I also picked up that he's into kinky sex. Watch." Amanda twists her scarf around her wrists, binding them together, then raises them over her head and shakes her breasts. Dr. Drake licks his lips. My stomach clenches. I. Am. Going. To. Hurl.

"So, are you interested?" she asks.

"In him or the threesome?" I force my feet to move in time to the beat. Dr. Drake gives me an encouraging nod. Good thing I'm not wearing a scarf.

"Either."

"Are you crazy?" I hiss in her ear. "He's my boss. You're my best friend. And my most exciting sexual experience to date was the kiss from Max. I don't think my heart could take it."

Dr. Drake grabs me and spins me around, pulling me against his lean body with a surprisingly muscular arm. He thrusts his pelvis forward and back, taking me with him. Forward and back. Forward and back. Our pelvises rock in time to the music. A giant picture of us flashes on the screen above the stage with a cartoon caption that reads, "Dirty Doctor Dancing." Bravo for new technology and instantaneous humiliation. My stomach clenches, and I try to pull away, but Dr. Drake smiles at the camera and presses his hand against my belly and my ass into his crotch.

And I thought Bianco Nero was a bad experience.

After twenty minutes Amanda and I escape to the restroom to

freshen up while Dr. Drake loiters outside, chatting with his doctor friends about his scintillating performance.

"I think he likes you." Amanda reapplies her lipstick for the hundredth time in two hours.

"Who?"

"Max. I'll bet you two shots of Unidentified Specimen he texts you tonight."

I ease myself up on the vanity counter made up to look like a hospital bed. "What if he's not interested in date four? What if he went home and thought to himself, 'Thank God that's over. I think I'll call up one of my poised, beautiful, movie star girlfriends who wouldn't know a carb if it hit her in the face'?"

"Then you get two free shots of Unidentified Specimen, and I'll return a slightly used Doctor Drake."

"How am I going to face Doctor Drake at work?" I bury my face in my hands. "They keep playing that video of us dirty dancing over and over again. It gets worse every time. Why didn't you stop me?"

Amanda shrugs. "You were having fun. Sometimes you have to stop worrying about things and just enjoy the moment."

"He was certainly enjoying it," I mutter. "I'm going to have a bruise on my lower back from his enjoyment."

Thankfully, Dr. Drake has disappeared when we emerge from the restroom. We make our way back to the table and collapse into the booth. I search for a waitress to top off my IV, and my eyes are drawn to a disturbance at the door. The manager pushes his way through the crowd, and a minute later Max emerges, flanked by two men dressed in black.

My mouth goes dry. "Oh. My. God. Max is here."

Amanda follows the direction of my gaze and her eyes widen. "Did you tell him where you were?"

"I didn't even know he was back, and my phone is dead."

His eyes focus on me like laser beams. My heart pounds a frantic rhythm against my ribs. Instinct screams for me to run, run, run. I wish my face would unfreeze so I could look anything other than horrified.

Max stalks toward our table, eating up the tiles with determined strides of his long legs.

I lean toward Amanda. "I think he's angry."

Amanda snorts a laugh. "I'd say that's an understatement. He's furious. It means he cares."

"I'd like it better if he showered me with flowers."

Max reaches our table and the two men in black loiter at a discrete distance. He folds his arms and glares down at me. His blue, button-down shirt and black dress pants are slightly wrinkled and his hair is mussed—as if he had just stepped off a plane. Uh-oh.

"Where were you?"

Sweat trickles down my back. "I waited for almost an hour. You didn't show. You didn't call or text. I walked here and called Amanda."

His jaw tightens. "You walked here? Alone? In the dark? After I told you to wait for me?"

"Um. Yes. Yes. Yes and yes."

"If I say I'm going to be somewhere, I'll be there. You don't leave. You wait."

My hands clench into fists and I crinkle my brow into a frown. "No way. I don't stand around in silver stilettos in a vacant parking lot waiting God knows how many hours for you to decide it's convenient to pick me up."

"You do."

"I don't."

Bang. Bang. Bang. My heart thuds a warning in my chest. With every word he steps closer to the line I will not cross. Protective I can handle. Possessive and controlling? Not a chance. My hand trembles so violently my watch vibrates against the table. "Why are you so angry? I'm the one who should be angry. You stood me up. I felt like an idiot standing around waiting for you."

Max bristles. "The plane was caught in turbulence. I couldn't call out. I texted you and Colton as soon as I was able."

"I didn't get your text. My phone ran out of minutes."

Max's eyes narrow. "Your phone ran out of minutes? What would you do in an emergency? What if you needed help? You need a reliable phone. A phone that doesn't run out of minutes. You need a phone that will keep you safe."

"We aren't all rich," I snap. Now I'm shaking and not in a good way. I imagine his foot hovering over the red line at Redemption. Just one inch and it will all be over.

Max pulls his phone out of his pocket and shouts "Colton" at it.

"Yes, sir." Colton's voice is as clear as if he was standing right in front of us.

"Makayla needs a cell phone. Something that will never run out of minutes. Long-term plan."

Long-term plan? Butterflies flutter in my belly. Maybe he isn't as annoyed as he appears.

"Yes, sir."

Max tucks his phone back in his pocket. "Done. He'll bring it to you tomorrow at work."

Amanda and I share an open-mouthed stare.

"I have a phone, Max."

"Now you have a better one. If you decide not to be somewhere I expect you to be, you will be able to contact me, and if I am delayed, I will be able to contact you, and if you are in danger, you will be able to call for help."

"See, I told you," I say under my breath to Amanda. "He is different in his suit."

Amanda looks from me to Max and then back to me. "The difference isn't the suit," she murmurs. "You kissed him. It changed things."

Yeah, it changed things. It made him insufferably bossy.

As if she could hear my thoughts, Amanda reaches under the table and squeezes my hand.

"What's this all about?" she says to Max. "You know it wasn't safe for her to wait alone in a parking lot."

Max runs a hand through his hair and looks at me as if I had asked the question. "I didn't know where you were. I didn't know if something had happened to you. We searched the hospital and the parking lot. I called the doorman, and he checked your apartment—" His voice cracks then softens. "I was worried, Makayla. I didn't...know...what to do."

And with that, my heart stops banging. Max's imaginary foot retreats from the line. All is right with me and Max.

Dr. Drake chooses this moment to make an untimely appearance with a test-tube rack filled with Medo-Jello shots. He plucks out the Larynx Lime. "Here you go, Mac. Just what the doctor ordered. Open that pretty little mouth for me and say ahhhh."

A sound erupts from Max's throat—a cross between a rumble and a growl. My eyes widen, and I suck in a breath and stare at Amanda. She gets the message and slides out of the booth.

"Who feels like dancing? Doctor Drake? Care to give me some medical attention?" She doesn't wait for his answer, but instead grabs his hand and tugs him toward the dance floor.

"Your turn for the dirty doctor," he laughs. He takes a step away and then turns back and stares at Max. "Don't I know you from somewhere?"

"No."

"Well, you'll know me well enough by the end of the evening." Dr. Drake's face brightens and he points to the giant screen. "Look, Mac, we're on again."

Oh God.

Max spins around to face the screen. The Dirty Doctor Dancing caption flashes and a supersize version of Dr. Drake and I hump and pump our way across the screen to LFMAO's "Sexy and I Know It."

When Max's gaze snaps to a rapt Dr. Drake, I shoot out of the booth and grab his arm.

"Please don't hurt him."

His lip curls and he shakes off my hand. "You think I'm going to hurt him?"

"You're looking at him like a lion that has just spotted his supper, so, yes; I think you're going to hurt him."

Max's jaw tightens. "You want him?"

"No, of course not. I thought I made that clear."

"Then why does he always have his hands on you?"

I shrug. "He's friendly?"

"Friendly is sitting across the table from someone and having a drink. Friendly is not grinding his dick into my girl's ass while he feels her up on the dance floor."

My girl. He thinks I'm his girl. I can barely breathe. I look up at

Max. His forehead is creased. His face is lined with exhaustion. His jaw is tight and his eyes are distant and hard. If I had any sense, I would walk away. The violence simmering under his skin scares me, but not as much as his need calls to me.

What is this all about? Amanda asked him.

I wrap my arms around him. He stiffens, but I hold him tight. I press my body against his. I let him feel me—the steady beat of my heart, the rise and fall of my chest. *I am here*, my body tells him. *I am safe. I am with you.*

It takes a long time for him to answer. But he does. He hugs me into his chest and rests his chin on my head. Time drifts away as we slow dance to fast songs, our bodies molded together until the DJ clears the dance floor with "Bleed It Out" by Linkin Park. Good for a fight club. Not so good for a night club.

I look up at Max. He is calm now, his eyes soft, his face relaxed.

"Don't you usually go to Redemption on Thursdays?"

Max presses a soft kiss to my forehead. "I wanted to see you."

"How did you find me?" I press my nose against his shirt. The stale, musty smell of airplane cannot overpower the fresh, clean scent of his cologne or the raw essence of Max.

"Secret."

"It's not nice to keep secrets." I pull away and mock a frown.

"You kept a secret from me." His breath is hot and moist in my ear.

My body stiffens. I am keeping so many secrets from him, I don't know which one he's uncovered. Best to play it dumb. "What secret?"

"What were you thinking when we were grappling at Redemption?" His eyes blaze with sensual fire and my mouth goes dry.

A thrill of excitement shoots through me. "Naughty things," I whisper.

"Tell me naughty things."

The DJ takes down the tempo with Alicia Keys' "Fallin'." A tremor shivers through me. "Like what? I don't really do naughty talking."

Max lifts my hand to his mouth and brushes his lips over my knuckles. "Like 'hand.'"

"'Hand' isn't naughty." I quiver as his lips feather up my arm and tickle my elbow.

"Oh, you don't know how naughty it can be," he rumbles, as he peppers tiny kisses over my shoulder. "Say 'shoulder.'"

"Shoulder. Max, what are you doing?"

He slides his hot, wet lips to the sensitive hollow at the base of my throat, sending tingles down to my core.

"Say 'neck,'" his deep voice demands.

"Neck." My heartbeat quickens; my lips part. We sway to the music, our bodies melded together as he plays his curious game.

He leans down and nibbles my lips, teasing them open. His kiss is soft and gentle. Sweet. But his lips are firm. "Say 'lips,'" he whispers.

"Lips."

Anticipation ratchets through me when he slides his hand down my body to cup my behind. He gives my cheek a squeeze. "Now, say 'ass.'"

I shiver in response to his firm touch. On his lips, the simple word takes on a sultry, erotic flavor that sends molten heat through my veins. I can do this. I have asked complete strangers in clothing stores if my ass looks big. I often told Susie to get her ass downstairs for dinner. In the bar, I told Amanda to wiggle her ass. Once, I even called Charlie an ass. My life is full of ass. "Ass," I whisper.

"Good girl." His lips brush over my ear, his breath hot and moist on my skin. Suddenly, I feel very, very naughty and very, very aroused.

He runs his hand over my hips, in and out on my waist, and along my rib cage. My body trembles, anticipating where he might go next. He brushes his fingers ever so gently over the exposed curve of my breast under my dress. "Say 'breast,' baby."

A soft whimper escapes my lips and my back arches, pressing my breasts against his chest. People dance around us oblivious to the blazing inferno at the edge of the dance floor, unaware that the slow, sensual brush of Max's fingers over my sensitive skin has peaked my nipples and fried my brain. His stroking fingers have turned the ordinary into the sublimely sexual.

"I'm waiting." His voice is soft but laced with demand.

I take a deep breath and close my eyes. I imagine I am diving into a pool filled with warm, decadent, dark chocolate. "Breast." The word drops from my lips like a falling petal.

"There we go." He spins us into a corner and under the shadow of an eight-foot bottle filled with giant pills, he tightens one hand around my waist and slides the other between us. His hand caresses the underside of my breast and then, inch by inch, he drops it down. Warm fingers brush down my sternum and press against my tummy. A firestorm of arousal courses through my veins like nothing I have ever experienced before. My breath comes in short, rapid pants. My panties are beyond soaked. My entire being is focused on Max's rapidly descending fingers. When he brushes the tips of his fingers over my mound my head falls back and I moan.

Triumph flares in the sensual depths of Max's eyes. "Now say 'pussy.'"

The soft, whispered word is erotic on his lips, sending a rush of molten heat through my veins. Max presses my body against his, trapping his hand between us. He is obviously erect and this, more than anything, sends my arousal spiraling out of control.

"Maaaax," I moan.

He cups the curve of my sex and I am gone, lost to the moment, lost to passion.

"Say it, baby." His demanding words bring me back.

My lips part. My body burns with lust. But some part of me says it is too much. This is not me and I have been pushed as far as I want to be pushed. The DJ spins Adele's "Set Fire to the Rain." Max tightens his arm around me and sings the lyrics in a soft, deep voice only I can hear. His deep baritone rumbles in his chest. Slow, delicious warmth spreads through me and something strange and new penetrates deep into my bones. Tilting my head back, I look up through my lashes. His dark eyes glitter, unyielding, and yet filled with sensual promise. "Say it."

I squeeze my eyes shut and whisper into his chest, "Not yet."

Chapter 11
THAT'S GOTTA HURT

"ARE YOU SURE YOU'VE got the right address?"

Amanda directs our cab to a large, clapboard house in prestigious Menlo Park. The tree-lined street is littered with cars. Lights flicker through the windows of the attached four-car garage. It looks like there should be a party going on, but there is no music, and no one hanging out on the lawn. Maybe it's a party Menlo-park style.

Amanda points to a group of pale, pasty-skinned men sporting bad haircuts, ripped jeans, screen-print T-shirts, and flip-flops. "It's called the Geek Club. I think we're in the right place."

I slump back in my seat. "I can't believe you dragged me out here."

"It won't take long, I promise. I'll surprise Jake, let him know he's forgiven, and then we'll all go home and you won't hear from me until Monday."

"Couldn't you have just called?"

Amanda pays the driver and we step out onto the street. "It's a *surprise*. He doesn't know I saw the details in his calendar the last time I was at his place. Plus I want to see him fight at this club. He told me it's one of the more dangerous underground fight clubs in California. No rules. No mercy. Nonfatal weapons are allowed."

"Anything wielded as a weapon can be fatal." We skirt around a child's wagon and three jolly garden gnomes. "Especially if people get carried away."

Amanda gives my shoulders a squeeze. "Such a grouch. I really appreciate you coming with me. I know you're upset Max hasn't called since we left the bar last night."

"I'm not upset. I'm glad I found out about his bossy and controlling side when I did. Makes the breakup that much easier."

Amanda shoots me a sideways glance. "You didn't tell me you broke up."

"He danced with me, tried to get me all hot and bothered right on the dance floor, then took me home, dropped me off, and all I got from him was a text this morning that said he was keeping Redemption closed all weekend in case the CSAC showed up. By the time they got to the club on Saturday, everyone was gone and Jake had the place shut down. I guess he was worried they might try again or maybe he was making it up to get rid of me."

"Hot and bothered, huh? And you didn't invite him home?" Amanda clearly is not interested in the fate of Redemption.

"I'm not good with dirty talking. When I didn't play his game, I guess he decided to leave me hanging to punish me. I swear if Doctor Drake had walked by, I would have been grinding with him on that dance floor like there was no tomorrow."

Amanda's eyes widen. "If you had done that, we would be visiting Doctor Drake in the hospital instead of Jake at the Geek Club. I thought Max was literally going to combust when he saw you and Doctor Drake on the screen. He is seriously into you."

I shake my head. "For once, you're wrong. He's done with me. I got the message from the old drop-her-off-at-the-door routine. I just don't know what I should do with this." I pull out my new phone.

Amanda sucks in a breath and reaches out her hand. "Oooooh pretty. When did you get it? You can give it to me. I have no qualms about taking secondhand gifts."

I pull it away, reluctant to share the most expensive and exciting piece of technology I have ever owned. "Colton brought it to the hospital this morning. It's been very distracting. I just speak to it and it does what I say. Watch." I stare at the phone and say, "CALL AMANDA CELL." The phone dials. Amanda's phone rings. She gives the phone a thorough inspection, then adds it to her Christmas list.

I knock over a garden gnome with a turtle on his head and stop to pick it up. "Maybe I should sell it to pay off the debt collector."

"You could ask a friend to bail you out instead."

Shaking my head, I tuck my phone away. "You know I would never do that. If I'm stuck, I can use the money Susie sent me to buy a plane ticket to visit her in London."

Amanda's face tightens. "You haven't seen Susie in five years. That money was her way of making amends."

More like her way of assuaging her guilt over abandoning the family and especially me.

We knock at the side door to the garage. A thin, reedy man wearing a plaid wool vest steps outside and closes the door behind him.

"We're here to visit the Geek Club." Amanda tosses her blond curls. I flip my bone-straight hair.

"Don't know what you're talking about." He sniffs loudly. "Just a private party going on inside."

Amanda's jaw tightens. "We both know it's not a party. I'm with one of the fighters, Jake Donovan."

"Does he know you're here?"

"Yes." Amanda lies with aplomb. No wonder she is such a good attorney.

"I'll go ask him."

"Wait." I put a hand on his arm. "Do you have anyone doing first aid at the club? I'm qualified and I'll work for free if you let us in."

He raises an eyebrow. "Let me ask the boss."

Ten minutes later we step across the threshold. The doorman, now identified as Stormin' Norman, informs us the boss is delighted to have both women and an EMT in the club. He hands me a first aid kit still wrapped in plastic and ushers us inside.

We enter the dimly lit garage, and my nose wrinkles at the pungent scent of sweaty bodies, spilled grease, and gas fumes. The crowd is thick around a makeshift boxing ring on the concrete floor. I count at least fifty men and maybe a dozen more groaning in the corner. War zone.

My heart pounds and I take a few deep breaths and fight the urge to run. I can do this. I've been in Redemption. I lived through two fights. It will only be an hour and then I can go home.

Amanda gives my hand a squeeze. "I know this isn't easy for you," she whispers. "You are the best wingman ever."

While Amanda looks for Jake, I head over to the side of the garage where the injured are nursing their wounds. From here, I have a clear view of the ring, which consists of a few ropes strung between metal pillars. The EMT in me approves of the fighters' protective gear—wire catcher masks and body armor, but is horrified at the sight of weapons. I blink several times. Not ordinary weapons—keyboards.

Yes, the weapon of choice in this fight club appears to be a keyboard. I should have guessed. We are in Silicon Valley, after all.

One of the fighters smashes his keyboard over the head of his much smaller but stockier opponent. A letter detaches itself from the cracked plastic and lands at my feet. *S* for sick. *S* for stomach.

I might need a bucket after all.

My arrival in the war zone is met with suspicion, but when I unwrap the first aid kit and commandeer a big bucket of ice, my patients warm to me. Or it might be my low-cut shirt.

While I ice a swollen knee, two new fighters enter the ring. The taller of the two is wearing a metal head mask resembling an upside-down trashcan with eye and mouth cutouts. I stare. It is a trashcan. He bangs two trashcan lids together like cymbals. I nickname him Oscar.

The other fighter adjusts his goalie mask and spins a vacuum cleaner hose over his head like a lasso. Somebody's carpets won't be cleaned tonight.

"Mac, what are you doing here?"

I spin around, my tension easing when Jake squats down beside me.

"First aid." I hold up the partially bandaged hand of my current patient, a short, pudgy blond who can't be over twenty-five. He looks familiar but I can't quite place him.

Jake frowns. "Does Torment know you're here? I can't believe he let you step foot in this club. It's too dangerous. If you couldn't handle the events at Redemption, you won't be able to handle this."

I use my patient as an excuse to ignore Jake, and busy myself taping his fingers together. "Why is Torment fighting here?"

Jake shrugs. "He challenged Iron Fist, the fourth-ranked fighter on the underground circuit, but with Redemption closed, they decided to do a tag team match here instead. It doesn't count toward the rankings, but he'll get a feel for Iron Fist's style."

The crowd cheers and I glance over at the ring. The goalie whips his vacuum cleaner hose around his head multiple times before smacking his opponent on the legs. Oscar goes down in a cloud of dust, and his trash can helmet bangs on the concrete floor with such force it dents.

Nausea grips my gut and I focus on keeping down my supper. "I thought Torment didn't use weapons."

Jake doesn't take his eyes off the fight. "He does here. It's expected, and he likes the challenge."

Torment uses weapons? Bile rises in my throat and my head spins. I fall back and into the wall.

"Mac? Are you okay?" Jake pulls me up and leads me over to a chair beside the door. Once I'm seated, he thrusts my head between my legs. "Breathe."

After I take a few deep breaths, the dizziness begins to fade. I try to sit up, but Jake forces my head down. "Don't move until I say," he orders. "Torment is in the ring."

"I want to see."

"From what I've seen of your inability to cope with violence, you would be flat on the ground in ten seconds."

"Please, Jake." I try to push up, but he holds me immobile.

"I don't like you very much at this moment," I grate through clenched teeth.

Jake chuckles. "Is that the best you can do? I was expecting a few swear words. Amanda sure knows a lot of them."

"She's here. She came to see you."

Jake snatches his hand away. "Fucking hell. Does she think I'm going to play her game? She's the last person I want to see."

I suck in a breath. I need to find Amanda. This is not going to play out the way she thinks. She's going to get hurt.

The clang of metal hitting concrete rings through the garage and my heart begins to pound. What if Max gets hurt? Who will look after him? Amanda or Max? Amanda or Max?

"What weapon did the other guy choose?" I jump up and down but I can't see over the sea of heads. "It sounds like a metal pipe. Oh, God. Someone's going to hit Max with a metal pipe."

Something whistles in the air and thuds against bare flesh with a sickening smack. The crowd murmurs in appreciation. My vision blurs and my lungs seize up. Jake grabs me and spins me into his chest. "Don't look. He'll be fine."

Another clang. A crack. A soft thud. A moan.

Jake sucks in a breath. "Oh, jeez. That's gotta hurt."

Using every ounce of strength I possess, I push myself away from Jake and grab my first aid kit. I launch myself through the crowd until I have a clear view of the ring. Max's opponent is indeed armed with a long, thick metal pipe. He is also wearing a mask, helmet, and body armor all emblazoned with the name Iron Fist. He does not, however, have an iron fist. Max has a baseball bat. He is wearing body armor and a helmet without a mask. It seems inadequate protection against a huge, metal pipe. Blood trickles down his temple and his forearms are bright red and swollen twice their normal size. I press my fist to my lips to stifle my distressed squeak.

Two men stand in opposing corners of the ring, both wearing body armor. Tag team. At least Max is not alone.

Iron Fist swings his pipe and hits Max in the ribs with a bone-crunching thwack. Max grabs his side and holds up his other hand in a defensive gesture. The other fighter hesitates and in that split second Max grabs the pipe, twists it out his hand, and tosses it to his teammate. They switch positions and relief trickles through me. Safe. For now.

Iron Fist's teammate hands him a printer. From the size and shape, it appears to be a multifunction unit that prints, scans, and faxes. I sure could use one of those. Maybe he wants to get rid of it because the cartridges are so expensive.

Max's partner swings his pipe, and Iron Fist uses his printer as a shield. He swings the printer in a wide arc and knocks the pipe to the ground. Max's partner trips backward over the pipe. Iron Fist smashes the printer over his head. Max's partner drops to his knees. My stomach clenches so violently I double over.

"I told you not to watch," Jake barks from behind me, shocking me with his deep, commanding tone. Holy smokes. Amanda misjudged him. He may appear easygoing, but underneath he has a core of steel.

"I don't always do what I'm told." I force myself up and look over my shoulder. Gone is his usual genial expression. Instead, his jaw is tight and his lips are pressed into a thin, straight line. "Then you aren't the right girl for Torment, and he's not the right guy for you."

"What's that supposed to mean?"

He gives me an enigmatic smile. "It means there's a lot you don't know."

"Enlighten me."

"Not my place."

I turn to the ring. Max's partner is still on his knees. His opponent has stepped back and is tossing the broken printer from hand to hand like a football, as if trying to decide whether to pass. Good thing he has big hands.

"I don't understand this place." I scrub my hand over my face. "I can sort of understand Redemption. There are a few rules. There seems to be some code of honor. But this place is just violence for the sake of violence."

Jake shrugs. "It means a lot to the people here. It fills a need. For some, it gives them the sense of control they otherwise feel they lack in their lives. For others, it provides an outlet for aggression that might otherwise be used in destructive ways."

"And for Torment?"

"Fighting is part of who he is. Unlike most of the guys here, he'll never be able to walk away."

The fighter slumps to the ground. He taps the floor twice and then goes limp. Only Max goes to his aid. I grab my first aid kit and climb into the ring. The look of shock on Max's face when he sees me is almost worth the nausea.

"Take off his helmet," I snap.

Max carefully removes his partner's helmet. The fighters around us grumble about delaying the next fight. Someone suggests we drag the injured man into the corner and attend to him there.

"Ignore them," Max says. "Do what you have to do."

"What's his name?"

"Frank."

Adrenaline surges through me and my pulse races. The rush I got treating Homicide in Redemption was nothing compared to this. Everything comes into sharp focus: Frank's gray pallor, his soft moans, and his shallow breathing. I register the loose threads on his body armor, the tiny cut on his finger, the wedding ring on his left hand, and the faded word "Daddy" written in pen on the underside of his wrist. Oh no. He's somebody's father and husband.

"Frank, can you hear me? My name is Makayla. I'm an EMT. Can I take a look at you?"

Frank moans. I check his pupils and run my hands over his head—huge lump and growing fast.

"Call an ambulance."

Max's eyes widen. "Usually the guys are a bit shaken after a hit like that, but after a few minutes, they're fine. He was wearing a helmet."

"He's not fine. Either his helmet was damaged or the force of the blow was more than it could withstand. If we don't get him to a hospital, he'll sustain brain damage at best. At worst, he'll die. Call 911. NOW."

For the next ten minutes, I try to stabilize Frank, but his condition deteriorates quickly. His pulse slows and his breathing becomes shallow.

"He shouldn't be going down this fast." My voice wavers and rises to a high pitch. "Something else is wrong and I don't know what it is. Where is the ambulance?"

"It's coming, baby. You're doing great."

"I don't have any equipment, Max, and even if I did I don't have the training for this. He's going to die and I can't save him." My hands shake so hard I can barely record Frank's vitals.

Max strokes my back and talks in a low, encouraging voice. "You're giving him a chance he never would have had. He's lucky you are here."

The ambulance arrives a few minutes later. I brief the paramedic, Ray, while his EMTs strap Frank to the stretcher and rush him out to the ambulance.

"You did a really great job of stabilizing him," Ray says. "You should think about taking that next step and qualifying as a paramedic. We need good people. People who can think on their feet and can handle a job where you never know what's coming next."

I am barely listening. I can't get the visual image of the "Daddy" penned on Frank's wrist out of my mind. "He's not going to make it, is he?"

Ray's eyes soften. "That's not our call. We do the best we can and then we move on. You did everything I would have done and then some. Rest easy." He slams the door and the ambulance disappears down the street.

Max strokes his hand down my hair. His gentle touch undoes me. Tears trickle down my cheeks and the tail end of my adrenaline rush sends a shudder through my body. Max pulls me into his arms and I sob into his chest.

"It's okay," he whispers. "I won't let you go."

When I open my eyes, it is still dark. My clock reads three a.m. A soft breeze blows through my window, and my curtains flap gently against the glass. I am warm and relaxed, and I am not alone.

A strong arm is wrapped around me, nestled between my breasts. A hard body is curled up against my back, holding me safe. I catch the scent of leather and soap and the faintest hint of citrusy cologne.

Max.

He breaths the slow, regular rhythm of sleep and yet his arm is locked tight around me. Not that I want to leave. Even though we are still in our clothes, I am almost giddy with the pleasure of being enveloped by his body.

"Go back to sleep, baby," he murmurs. "I've got you."

So he does. He's had me since I cried in his arms. He took care of everything. Amanda is safe at her home and I am safe at mine.

"I thought you were asleep."

He kisses my neck. "Not with your sweet body tucked up against me."

"You don't have to stay," I whisper. "I'm okay now. It's late—"

"You're hurting. I'm staying. Now go to sleep." He tightens his grip and pulls me closer to his chest. My body quivers at the sensation of his arm locked around me and the press of his belt buckle against my spine.

As if I could sleep with Max in my bed. "I thought you were angry with me."

"I could never be angry with you." He brushes my hair over my shoulder and peppers my neck with tiny kisses. "However, I am frustrated by your continual disregard for your own safety. Unreliable prepaid phone. Walking alone at night. Going to one of the most dangerous fight clubs in the city—"

I turn slightly and look back over my shoulder. "Is it that dangerous? For spectators I mean. I didn't see any fighting happening outside the ring."

Max sighs. "More goes on at the Geek Club than just fighting. I want you to promise you will never go there again." There is an unmistakable edge to his voice, bordering on fear.

Well, that's a no-brainer. I don't want to watch the mindless destruction of good printers again. "Okay. I promise never to go again."

Max grunts and rolls onto his back, pulling me with him. He arranges me against his body with my head on his shoulder, and my body plastered against his side. One arm snakes around my waist and the other rests on my hip. "Time to sleep."

"Don't want to sleep." I rest my hand on his chest and slide it over his T-shirt. My fingers encounter something soft—a bandage. I bolt upright. "I forgot. You were hurt. Let me take a look."

"I'm okay. I just need to rest and I need you to rest beside me." He tugs my arm, but I shake him away.

"I have medical supplies in the kitchen. I'll—"

He yanks my supporting arm and I fall down onto his chest. "I'm okay, baby. Relax."

"Max, please."

"Baby. Last time. Relax. Feeling you beside me is worth a hundred bandages."

I exhale my annoyance and snuggle into his chest. My body softens against him and he gives my head a chaste kiss. Not really what I want, but he's made it clear this is all I'm going to get.

A cuddle.

I've never dated a man who liked to cuddle, but I like it.

A lot.

———

Sorry I had to leave so early. Had to let maintenance crew into Redemption. Will be here all day.

Thank u 4 staying with me

Pleasure

I liked Max in my bed

I liked Makayla in my arms

I called the hospital. Frank is unconscious, but they think he's going 2 b ok

Because of you

I didn't do anything

Because of you

blushes

Dinner tonight?

Yes

My place?

Yes

Seven?

Yes

Lewis pick you up?

Yes

Agreeable today

Yes

Max likes yes

I know **winks**

Chapter 12

I DIDN'T BRING YOU HERE FOR THE VIEW

"Wow. This is...modern."

A freshly showered Max, his damp hair slightly tousled, beams when Colton closes the door behind me. His dark pants and blue button-down shirt are very businesslike. Is this what he wears to relax at home? Maybe I should have worn something dressier. My flirty black skirt and gold silk tank, Christmas gifts from my fashion-conscious mom, seemed plenty dressy at home. At least I'm wearing heels.

Colton takes my jacket and I walk into the open-plan living area. Holy cow. Why does he need all this space? The living room alone could hold fifteen or twenty people.

For the first few minutes, I can only stand and stare. The three separate seating areas are all decorated with casual, comfortable-looking sofas in muted shades of gray and beige, dark wood coffee tables, and industrial lamps. Wide brown leather chairs and soft Berber area rugs unite each separate space. A granite-topped bar with seating for six complete with wall-mounted television is surrounded by potted palms.

My heels click over giant, cream marble tiles, and I run my hand over the smooth, shiny surface of the giant mahogany dining table. The gray leather dining chairs have low backs and wide padded seats. As with the rest of the room the furniture is masculine but inviting. A modern man cave.

"The top level is essentially a complete home." Colton smiles when I spin slowly around. "Although there are three levels, the master suite, kitchen, breakfast room, living room, dining room, and library are all on this one floor."

"There's more?" Just the space I can see is about ten times bigger than my entire house.

"Oh, yes." Colton gestures down a wide hallway ending in double doors. "The master suite is about the same size as the main living space. Upstairs you'll find the en suite guest bedrooms, and downstairs we have the media room, gym, home theater, staff quarters, and wine cellar."

"Wow." I can't think of anything else to say.

Max settles me at the bar and excuses himself to make a call. Colton offers me a drink but I decline alcohol in favor of diet soda. I don't want to embarrass myself in Max's fancy home.

We chat about the house, Colton's living quarters downstairs, and the five bridge views from the wraparound patio. I chase down the diet soda with an entire bowl of nuts.

Max has still not returned by the time I finish plundering the snack tray, and I talk Colton into letting me join him in the kitchen while he puts the finishing touches on the meal.

"Dinner will be ready in a few minutes," Colton says, as we leave the bar. "Tonight we're having lobster cocktail, tomato salad, grilled free-range chicken with roast field mushrooms and asparagus, and chocolate mousse for dessert."

My mouth waters. And to think I had planned a dinner of cereal and skim milk before Max texted me this morning. "You cook too?"

"A butler takes on whatever duties are required. Mr. Huntington travels a great deal and did not wish to employ a full-time cook. I enjoy being in the kitchen. It works out very well."

I follow Colton through the house. Although the man cave is cozy and comfortable, I don't see any personal objects. No photos. No magazines. No coffee cups, slippers, or blankets. Everything is pristine and perfect. Definitely not the kind of place to relax after work with a good book and a pint of Chunky Monkey.

The kitchen is the size of the entire living area of my new apartment. The walnut island could easily fit six stools, and ceiling-high white lacquer cabinets line the walls. Antique industrial lights and stainless steel accents give the kitchen an artsy feel.

Dream kitchen. And I don't even like to cook.

I sit at the island while Colton stirs the contents of a large pot on the stove. Tantalizing aromas waft my way and my stomach gurgles.

"Can I help you with anything?"

"No, thank you, Miss Makayla. We don't make our guests work when they come to visit."

"It's not work." I join him at the stove. "I would feel more comfortable if I had something to do."

"I don't know if Mr. Huntington would approve."

"Please, Colton. I'm used to a house filled with people, a floor piled with pizza boxes, and crumbs on every surface. Silence and sitting make me nervous."

A reluctant grin spreads across his face. "The lettuce needs a wash. There's a spare apron in the cupboard beside the fridge."

My shoulders drop into a relaxed slump. "Lettuce washing sounds perfect." I grab a blue and white checkered apron from the cupboard and head to the sink.

"Have you worked for Max very long?" I cannot find any way to turn on the tap. It looks like a giant swan neck with a cage attached to its beak. Maybe I should honk.

"About six years. I was in service to a family in Yorkshire and he enticed me away." Colton waves his hand in front of the tap and water shoots out the swan's nose. Classy.

"I have not regretted the move for a second," he continues. "America is indeed a land of opportunity, and Mr. Huntington is a very generous employer."

We chat about Colton's work while I rinse the lettuce. Colton hands me a pink, plastic lettuce knife and a cutting board, and entertains me with stories of butler school while I chop. Butler school. How cool is that?

"Colton." The sharp crack of Max's voice slices through our camaraderie like a lettuce knife through lettuce.

Colton's head jerks up and he pales.

"What is Makayla doing in the kitchen?"

I position myself between a shaken Colton and a fuming Max, and plant my hands on my hips. "I asked if I could help out. Colton said no.

I insisted. I wanted to do something to keep busy while you were on the phone. I'm not good at being idle."

"Learn."

My breath catches in my throat. "What did you just say?"

His eyes narrow. "I said learn. You are a guest in my home. Guests relax. I don't want you working. That's Colton's job."

"I want to be here." I keep my voice low but my tone firm.

Max ignores me and glares at Colton. "I'll speak to you outside."

"I'm sorry, sir. It was my mistake."

"No. It wasn't your mistake." I walk up to Max and fold my arms. "It was my decision."

"Makayla! This is a staff matter. It doesn't concern you."

"It does if Colton is reprimanded for something I did. If you want to fire someone, fire me. I've never been a good lettuce chopper."

Max huffs out a breath. "I'm not going to fire anyone."

"Good." I shift my weight from one foot to the other as we stare at each other. Now what? I've never done drama queen before. Should I leave? No. He needs to listen and understand. That won't happen if I run away.

I clench my teeth and exhale loudly. "I like that you want to look after me but not if it means you're going to be all bossy and controlling. I can't handle it. Sometimes you need to back off and trust that I can make my own decisions."

Max frowns. "This is my house."

I slide my hands up his chest and around his neck, pulling him down until I can feel the heat of his breath on my lips. "This is your girl. And if you want your girl to stay in your house, you'd better apologize to Colton."

His eyes darken and he wraps his arms around me. A low rumble starts deep in his chest. "My girl."

I brush my lips lightly over his. "Yours," I whisper. "And you are mine."

"I apologize, Colton," Max says abruptly. "I was out of line."

"Much obliged, sir." Colton unties his apron and hangs it on the peg. "The meal is ready at your convenience. I'll go and set the table."

"He's very discrete," I murmur against Max's lips.

Max lifts me up and settles me on the island. He trails his fingers along the sensitive skin of my inner thighs, pressing them gently apart to accommodate his hips. "He likes you."

"How do you know?" His fingers trace lazy circles closer and closer to my center. I put a hand on his shoulder to steady myself as desire spirals through me.

"You're in his kitchen. He never lets anyone in his kitchen. But I'm not surprised. You have a way of making people feel comfortable. You listen to them. Really listen. I'll bet you know as much about Colton after your short time with him as I do. It's one of the things I like about you."

"He's had an interesting life."

Max chortles. "And you're an interesting girl."

"I'm a hungry girl." I point to the pots on the stove. "I would hate for his meal to get wasted. He put a lot of time and effort into it."

Max wraps his arms around me and kisses me long and deep. "Food is about the last thing on my mind, but you'll need your energy for later."

My breath catches in my throat. "What happens later?"

He gives me a wicked grin. "You'll have to wait to find out."

I run my finger along the top edge of his belt, stopping at the center of his belt buckle. "What if I don't want to wait?"

Half an hour later, the Agusta glides to a stop at the top of San Francisco's most famous peak. The city twinkles below us, and the stars are so close in the dark night sky, I could almost reach up and touch them.

Max gently pulls my helmet over my head and places it on the stone retaining wall.

I look around and snort a laugh. "I can't believe you brought me to Twin Peaks."

"Why?" He takes off his own helmet and places it beside mine.

"This is *the* makeout spot in Oakland. No one comes to Twin Peaks at night for the view."

"I didn't bring you here for the view," Max rumbles. He pats the seat in front of him, and my legs turn to jelly.

Wary of the hot exhaust pipes, I climb onto the seat facing him. The space is so narrow I can barely squeeze in front of him and Max has to ease himself back along the pillion seat. My heart pounds against my ribs when I meet his smoldering gaze. "Max Huntington. Did you take me up here to make out?"

He cups my face between his hands. "Dinner first. Then dessert." My stomach flutters at his words, and a shiver wracks my body. My need escapes with the softest moan.

"God, Makayla." He leans down and slants his mouth over mine. Everything inside me softens. His tongue parts my lips and sweeps inside my mouth, stroking, touching, tasting. Even better than last time.

"Don't tempt me," he murmurs against my lips, "or you'll never get your dinner."

"Don't want dinner."

"You'll need the energy." His voice drips with sensual promise and I only just manage to restrain myself from ripping my new leathers off my body and begging him to take me right on his motorcycle.

He unhooks the saddlebag and pulls out two tall tin containers divided into sections. Each section swings out to reveal a different part of the meal. Delightful. I need one of these for my lunch bag. Charlie would be so jealous.

We eat our meal facing each other and only occasionally glancing over at the view. Although the food is delicious, my body thrums with anticipation. I want the promised dessert. I want more kisses. I want more fondling. I want more Max.

"What did you think of the house?" He spears a piece of roast chicken with a small silver fork.

"It's…um…modern and masculine. Cozy. And…nice. Well-decorated."

Max raises an eyebrow. "Be honest with me."

"I love it, but it doesn't seem like you. Not that you've told me a lot about yourself, but I didn't see *you* anywhere. I saw Max you but not Torment you. I don't know if that makes any sense."

From the smile creasing his face, I assume that was the right answer.

"I use it mostly for entertaining. I meet a lot of potential clients, and I usually have them stay with me so I can get a better feel for the people I'm dealing with. I couldn't do it without Colton. He handles everything so I can talk business."

"Where do you go if you just want to kick back and relax?" I spear another vegetable. I don't know what kind of vegetable it is, but its deliciousness changes my mind about vegetables forever.

"I'm building a suite on the second floor at the club. It's still a work in progress, but I've got all the basics in place. I go there when I want to get away."

"I'd like to see it," I say quietly. "I'd like to see something that is you."

His jaw tightens. "I don't take anyone up there."

Although his tone is gentle, his rejection stings. "Sure. Sorry. Forget I asked."

No longer hungry, I close up my little container and tuck it in Max's saddlebag. He follows suit and for a moment we just stare at each other in awkward silence.

"Fuck." Max slides one arm around my waist and hauls me up against him. He bends down and teases my mouth open, then runs his tongue in a sensual slide over my lips. My body flames in response.

He pulls away and rubs his thumb over my cheek. "That bothered you."

"No. Really. I totally understand. We all need our privacy."

"Not you. Not from me." He dips his tongue in my mouth and then plunges deep. His hand threads through my hair, and he tugs my head back, exposing my neck to the sensual caress of his lips. "Are you hiding something from me?" he murmurs.

My lungs seize up, and I fall back on the tried and true deflection technique. "Your tongue was just halfway down my throat. Does that seem to you like I'm hiding anything?"

"Always with the smart mouth." He runs his thumb over my lip and when my mouth opens he covers it with his own. This time he takes everything I give and demands more. My body melts into his. My back arches over his arm. My breasts press against his chest, begging to be freed.

"Every time I see you, I want to kiss your smart little mouth," he rasps in my ear.

I wrap my arms around his neck and draw him down. "Consider this an open invitation." I kiss him back, drinking him in. Our tongues tease and touch; our mouths meld. My fingers curl into his jacket, and I moan into his mouth.

"Need to touch you." He doesn't wait for my response. Instead, his hand finds my zipper and in one swift movement he has the jacket off my shoulders.

I shiver at the rush of cool, night air. My nipples pebble against the thin fabric of my tank top, and I arch toward his hand.

"You are so damn hot." He cups my breasts, one in each palm and rubs his thumbs over my nipples, drawing them into tight peaks. His tongue plunges in and out of my mouth—a teasing promise of what better damn well be coming soon.

Max slips his fingers under the spaghetti straps of my tank top and peels it down. The built-in bra means I am instantly bared for his viewing pleasure. He stares but doesn't move.

"Max?"

"So beautiful." He bends down and draws my right nipple into his mouth sucking and nibbling until I am clinging to him for dear life and panting like I've just run a marathon.

Too much. Too many sensations. His mouth on my breasts. His thumb circling my nipples. The soft brush of his hair over my chest. The beauty of the night sky and the breathtaking view of San Francisco spread below us like a blanket of stars.

"Ahhhh." I lean backward, arching uncomfortably over the gas tank, and away from too much sensation. My hair falls down along the fairing, my breasts thrust upward and my peaked nipples reach up for the stars. Max's hands freeze mid-caress.

"Christ. You are beyond tempting. If you don't get up now, I won't be able to stop."

"I'm not getting up."

"Then I'm not stopping, baby." He leans over, plants tiny kisses down my stomach, and teases my naval with his tongue. Heat pours off my body. His teeth nip my belly, and then his mouth dips lower.

My body tightens as need ratchets through me. Max slides one finger inside the waistband of the leather trousers he insisted I wear along with the leather jacket to stay safe on the ride. I wiggle to give him more room. The world shifts and tilts upside down.

"Whoa there." Max grabs my arm and saves me from a humiliating, half-naked gravel nose dive.

My cheeks flame. "I'm afraid I haven't kept up my making-out-on-a-motorcycle skills."

Max studies me, his eyes thoughtful. "I have an idea."

Five minutes later I am back in position, but now the rear wheel is secured with some kind of collapsible swing arm stand and Max is standing beside the motorcycle with a coil of rope in his hand.

"Are you going to pull a rabbit out of that pack next?" I ask as he tugs my tank top over my head.

"You like rabbits?" he murmurs.

Do I ever. But not the fuzzy kind. Not that I would ever let him know.

I am too hot to be cold, but when he eases me back over the gas tank, I hiss in a breath at the sensation of cool metal kissing my skin. His hands slide to my hips, and he positions me with my bottom on the seat in a semi-reclined position, then he kisses me long and hard.

"Do you trust me to keep you safe?" he whispers.

"I trust you."

His eyes flash with sensual promise. "Will you do exactly as I say, baby? If you don't, you might slip off. I don't want you to get hurt."

"I'll try."

He lifts my arms over my head and slips the rope around one of my wrists, fastening it to the handlebars. Then he does the same with the other. I tug. The handlebars twist. My forehead creases. Hmm. Hands tied out to the sides. Seems kinda kinky. Never done kinky before. "I don't know about this," I say. "If I fall off, the motorcycle will fall on top of me."

"I won't let you get hurt." Max rakes his eyes over my body. "Think of a word that tells me you want to stop what we're doing. Something to tell me we've gone too far. A word that means something to you."

"Why not just 'stop'?"

He presses a kiss to my belly. "Sometimes in the heat of the moment 'stop' means 'go.'"

I suck in my lips and look around. What means something to me out here in the darkness? Not much. Maybe I should choose a word that means something to Max. Then he'll pay attention.

"Agusta."

Max smiles. "Your safe word is Agusta. Don't forget it."

A warm breeze caresses my cheek, blowing my hair. I try to brush it away, but when I jerk my arms they only move an inch before the rope tightens. Reality hits me hard. I am tied to his motorcycle. My heart pounds at double speed.

"Don't move. Stay still for me."

I swallow past the lump in my throat. "I…don't think I like this."

Max leans down and takes my breast in his mouth, teasing my nipple with his teeth. Lust rips through my body and I shiver in the cool night air.

"Do you like this?" He nuzzles my other breast, flicking his tongue over my nipple until it becomes painfully hard and sensual lightning bolts shoot straight to my core.

"Yessss."

He strokes his hand down my stomach to the waistband of my leather pants, and flicks open the snap. Inch by agonizing inch he tugs the pants and my skirt over my hips. Un-sexy leg contortions follow, and within a minute I am wearing only a brand new pair of shiny emerald panties that match my eyes. The familiar tingle of adrenaline courses though my veins. Something pokes into my back.

His eyes rake over my body and he groans. "You are even more breathtaking than I imagined."

He imagined me naked. My discomfort gives way to my delight at being the subject of Max's fantasies.

His lips slide down over my abdomen and then along the top edge of my panties.

I moan my approval and try to encourage him to keep going by tilting my hips up toward his hot, wet kisses.

"I told you not to move." His smooth voice takes on a sharp edge. "There is a price to pay for not following the rules."

Hmmm. I like the sound of that. I hope the price involves removing my panties.

Max walks to the front where I can't see him. "Five minutes," he calls over his shoulder. Gravel crunches, fading into the distance, until I can hear nothing but the wind in the trees.

"Max?" I tilt my head backward trying to see but the windshield is in the way. "Where are you?"

My pulse speeds up as my lust-sodden brain struggles to process what is happening. Is this what he means by paying a price? Leaving me tied to his motorcycle in the dark? Is he joking?

"Max?"

Silence.

"Am I supposed to be turned on by this? If so, I'm not really feeling the heat. I'm actually feeling the cold. You might remember I'm not wearing very much. Also, your motorcycle isn't very comfortable in this position. It's quite hard and something is sticking into my back. I think it's the gas tank."

He can't have gone far. He wouldn't leave his precious Agusta. But would he leave me? My lungs tighten at the thought.

"Did I mention my stepfather is the chief of police in Oakland? Not that I'm threatening you, but if someone were to find me like this and I dropped your name, he might not be too happy. Ever been in jail, Max? I hear it's less comfortable than being tied naked to a motorcycle on Twin Peaks."

A frisson of fear, cold and low, slithers up my spine. What if he has a car nearby? What if someone was waiting to take him away? What if this is all some elaborate sex game he plays with women? What if he teases them and kisses them and leaves them to be found in the morning?

Oh, his kisses. Such delicious kisses. Kisses on my lips. Kisses on my throat. Kisses on my breasts. Kisses on my panties. Everything below my waist tightens and suddenly my senses heighten. The hard metal gas tank presses into my back, a contrast to the soft leather of the saddle under my bottom. Traffic hums in the distance, and I catch the odd flutter of wings overhead. Stars twinkle in the night sky, bright pinpricks in a sheet of black velvet. The air is fragrant with pine and salt and the sharp scent of gasoline. Max's taste is on my tongue. My pulse beats steadily between my thighs.

Seriously? I'm tied to a motorcycle in the dark, and I am so aroused I want to scream? What the hell is wrong with me? Maybe I *should* scream. As I draw in a huge breath, Max's mouth covers my own in a brain-searing kiss. The scream dies in my throat. Why didn't I hear him coming?

"Time is up. You did well, baby."

"You left me on purpose?"

"You didn't follow the rules."

Red sheets my vision. My hands clench into fists above my head, and my arousal fades away like a dream in the morning light. All manner of swear words pop into my head—the usual ones children learn at school, a few others I picked up in books, and some really filthy language I can't believe I would contemplate letting fall from my lips. I toss them around in my brain and discard them all. I won't let him do that to me. I will not be reduced to swearing.

"Untie me. Now."

Max tugs on the ropes and they slither off my wrists. He reaches out to help me up, and I slap his hand away. "Don't you dare touch me."

After I ungracefully dismount the motorcycle, I stomp over to the wall toward my jacket with as much dignity as I can muster wearing only wet green panties. I. Am. So. Out. Of. Here.

Before I can tug the jacket on, Max is behind me. He slips one arm around my waist and pulls me into his body. Skin to skin. He must have removed his jacket and shirt when I was terrified and alone. How presumptuous.

"You were so sexy lying across my bike," he murmurs in my ear. "Do you know what I wanted to do to you? Do you know where I wanted my hands, my lips, my—"

"Stop. I don't want to hear it." I spin around to face him. "You scared me. That wasn't fun."

He studies my eyes so intensely I look away to the sweep of lights in the city below.

"Tell me the truth." His deep voice, though soft, is filled with demand.

"I am telling you the truth. You scared me. I'm so angry right now, I'm thinking about slapping you."

His expression becomes carnal, predatory. He presses me backward against the retaining wall. The cold, rough stone scrapes against my skin. He cages me with his body and locks his eyes with mine.

"Slap me."

"No."

"You just said you wanted to slap me."

My body trembles when he leans over me. "I said I was thinking about it."

His eyes soften. "What else are you thinking, little fighter?" He cups my head with his hand and strokes his thumb over my cheek.

"I'm thinking you have a terrible seduction technique," I grumble. "You started off well—motorcycle ride, Twin Peaks, picnic under the stars—but you lost me when you decided to play cowboy and rope yourself a filly."

Max chuckles. "Did I lose you, or did I arouse you? Are you angry because you were scared or because it turned you on and you don't like that it did?"

"That's ridiculous." I shift my weight from foot to foot. "Who would get turned on by being tied to a motorcycle and left alone in the dark?"

"You." His hand slides down my stomach and over my mound to cup my damp heat. I suck in a sharp breath, but moving away is not an option. My betraying hips tilt toward him, asking for more.

He strokes his finger along the edge of my panties and then shoves them aside. I press my hands against his chest, intending to push him away, but my hands also aren't following the program. Instead, they slide up his chest and circle his neck, pulling me closer to the heat of his body. Max's finger slides along my folds and then it dips inside. My eyes slit closed and a shudder ripples through me.

"You're so wet, baby," he groans. He trails my wetness down my inner thigh. "Your body knows what it wants. You just need to free your mind."

I bite my lip and turn my head away. He's wrong. He has to be wrong. I'm not into kinky stuff. Not that I've ever had a chance to find out. My three sedate, ultraconservative boyfriends never tried anything except the missionary position.

"My body and my mind agree that I want to leave."

A smile ghosts Max's lips. "One kiss and we'll go. You have my word."

Desire whispers through my veins with promises of pleasure. I clench my teeth and fight it back. Bad Desire. Go away. "Fine. One kiss."

Max's eyes darken. He slides one hand around my waist and pulls me tight against his chest. Sparks shoot straight down my spine, and a warm, liquid sensation ripples through my body.

His breath whispers over my cheek, and I press my lips together. He is going to get a chaste kiss. A disapproving kiss. A kiss that says I like to kiss, but I don't play those games.

"Open for me, baby." His words send a surge of moisture between my legs. He glides his thumb over my bottom lip and presses down. I succumb instantly, like a kid in a candy store. I part my lips and allow his thumb to dip inside, and then greedily suck it like a lollipop.

"Good girl."

His words send goose bumps dancing along my skin. Soft words. Approving words. Condescending words. I can't muster the energy to reprimand him while his thumb is sliding in and out of my mouth making me think of other things. Naughty things.

He curls his fingers around my neck and tilts my head back, his thumb now caressing my cheek. I can't look away. My entire being is focused on him. He leans down and covers my mouth with his, sending quivers of excitement rippling through me. His tongue glides along my lips and then dives inside, thrusting deep and filling my mouth. My brain fuzzes at the startling sensation, but he gives me no chance to recover. His fingers tighten on my neck and he draws me closer, kissing me until I can barely breathe.

Oh God, I want him. Bad. I tighten my grip on his neck and mold my body to his.

And then he pulls away.

"No." My voice rises almost to a whine.

Max's eyes glitter fever bright, and his chest rises and falls so quickly I worry for a second he might hyperventilate. "I gave you my word. One kiss and we would go."

"I don't want to go."

"Then tell me the truth," he rasps. "Admit it made you hot. It made you wet. You are coiled so tight I could slide my hand down your panties and make you come before you could tell me to stop."

Sexy words. Dirty words. Cocky words. They burst the dam holding back my desire. With a low groan I lean up and press my lips against his. "Yes," I whisper.

Max gives a self-satisfied grunt. He slips his hand down my panties, pressing the heel of his palm against my sensitive spot. His fingers slide through my folds, and then dip inside.

Oh. My. God. My breathing stops and fire shoots through me. I whimper and rock myself against him, needing more.

"I've got you, baby." His breath is warm and moist in my ear. "I know what you need."

Max pulls his finger out and thrusts two fingers in, ripping a cry from my lips. His fingers plunge in and out while his thumb rubs the sides of my sweet spot until my legs buckle. Max's arm tightens around me, holding me up.

So close. So damn close. I need release so badly, I groan.

"Let it go." Max brushes his thumb over my throbbing center. Once. Twice. Three times is all it takes. "Come for me, baby."

His deeply erotic words catapult me to orgasm. It hits with such force, I scream. My first-ever orgasm scream. Thunder roars through my ears, and my sex spasms around his fingers, each contraction sending lightning bolts of pleasure through my body. But he doesn't stop. His fingers continue to work their magic, drawing out my orgasm until I go limp, and only his arm keeps me from slumping to the ground.

When he finally withdraws his fingers, I am seized by uncontrollable shivers. Max wraps his arms around me and holds me tight. This is not how I ever imagined my first non-Makayla-induced orgasm would be. No soft bed. No gentle touching. No slight quiver and a tiny burst of pleasure. This was wild. Uncontrolled. There were ropes and metal and cold and fear.

My blood chills. Fear has no place in the bedroom or even on Twin Peaks. I stiffen in Max's arms and pull away. God, I'm a mess. "Can we go now?"

Max's brow creases. "What's wrong?"

Stomach churning, I scoop up my clothes and tug them on. "Nothing. I'm good. Just…cold." Damn. I forgot my skirt. I ball it in my fist and stuff it down the front of my pants.

"Come here, baby."

"Okay. All ready to go." I plaster a fake smile across my face.

Max stalks over to me and cups my face in his hands. "It's okay to be afraid."

"I'm not afraid of you."

His eyes soften. "Maybe not, but you are afraid of you."

Chapter 13
I'M NOT THAT KIND OF GIRL

I AM AWAKENED BY the jarring buzz of my phone. I fumble around until I locate the offending device and hold it to my ear.

"Good morning, Ms. Delaney."

At the sound of Sergio's voice, I come fully awake. My alarm clock reads ten a.m. Sun streams through the crack in my curtains. I am naked in bed. Alone.

"It's Sunday. Why are you calling me on a Sunday? There must be laws against harassing people on the weekend."

"I am permitted to call you between eight a.m. and nine p.m. seven days a week, as many times as I wish so long as you do not feel harassed. Do you feel harassed Ms. Delaney?"

"Yes. I have two days to sleep in every week and you have just ruined one of them. I most definitely feel harassed."

Sergio chuckles. "I didn't want you to sleep the day away. The sun is shining. The birds are singing. The debts are growing."

"How thoughtful."

"I am thoughtful," he croons. "My thoughtfulness has motivated me to call you this morning to remind you about the payment due tomorrow."

"I'm glad you called. Just give me a minute." I scramble around the room looking for my notes from the calls I made to various government agencies about student loan debt collection.

"Take all the time you need, Ms. Delaney. You are my only call of the day."

After retrieving the papers from the bottom of my backpack, I make myself comfortable on my bed.

"I understand if I am on the rehabilitation program, I have twenty days to make each payment from the day it is due. So, in fact, I have twenty-one days to make the payment due tomorrow."

Sergio huffs into the phone. "I do so hate debtors who think they know the law. That provision kicks in only AFTER you make the first payment. You aren't getting out of it so easily."

"No way. I researched it."

"Not well enough."

My heart sinks. "I can't pay it all. Only some of it."

"Beg, borrow, and steal, Ms. Delaney. I can assure you the last thing you want is for me to run down to court and get an order to seize your parents' home and your paycheck."

"What about the Education Commission? Did they contact you about my complaint? Are the payments frozen yet?"

I hear a familiar rattle on Sergio's end of the phone—like a hospital gurney. More rattles. It is a hospital gurney. Maybe he's visiting a friend. Do debt collectors have friends?

"They were very efficient with your file," Sergio says. "Apparently, after you accepted your new position, they reevaluated your file and canceled the deferment. They sent you a letter to that effect informing you that your payment obligations had been reinstated."

"I didn't get it."

"It seems from the file, they sent it to your previous address."

"What?" My voice rises in pitch and I throw the covers off. "I told them my new address when I moved."

Someone coughs in the background on Sergio's end and I can hear the tinny sound of a PA. Definitely a hospital. Why would he call me from a hospital? Is he that dedicated to his work?

Sergio sighs. "You have issues with them, you deal with them. All I care about is the money you owe."

"Please, Sergio. Can I pay part of it? I've got extra work and I'll be able to pay the rest next week."

"Unfortunately for you, I get a big fat bonus if you make all your rehabilitation payments on time, and an even fatter bonus if I get all the money at once, say from a foreclosure. And I need that bonus—" He cuts himself off, choking on his words.

Seriously? He's getting upset over the possibility he won't get his Porsche?

"Has the clock started ticking?" I scramble to find a way out.

"I beg your pardon?"

"Is your bonus calculated from the day I make the first payment or the day you first called me?"

Sergio gives a thin laugh. "Clever. I'll be honest with you. It's calculated from the day of your first payment."

"What if I tell you a really good joke? Can I have an extra week? It won't affect your bottom line. I've never sworn at you or called you names or hung up on you. It must be hard to have people be nasty all day. But if you're nice to me, I'll be nice to you."

Silence.

"Sergio?"

"I'm thinking. This is quite novel. I'm trying to decide if it would affect my bonus."

Jeez. This guy's materialistic streak makes me ill. But I can do obsequious like the best of them. "I've seen the lineup for next year's Porsche collection. To be honest, you would do better to wait."

"You know about cars?"

I fall back against the pillows. He hasn't said no, which means he might say yes. "My stepfather is into cars. I go with him to all the auto shows."

"You continue to surprise and delight me, Ms. Delaney. Tell me your joke. If it makes me laugh, I'll give you an extra week. It won't affect my bottom line, and I could use a joke right now."

I squeeze my eyes shut and try to slow my racing heart. Although our conversation has been cordial, I can't ignore the underlying threat. My brain blanks. This is all so new. So foreign.

And that reminds me of a joke.

"Three debt collectors are captured by cannibals..."

Pick up. Pick up. Pick up.

Amanda answers her phone on the fourth ring. "How was dinner? Did you sleep with him?"

"No. I need—"

"You didn't sleep with him?" Her voice rises with incredulity.

"No, but the debt collector called my house, and I need—"

"What happened?" she interjects yet again. "It was the perfect set up. Cozy dinner at his house. Talk about the relationship. Engage in hot and heavy makeup sex."

"Amanda. I have a problem."

"You sure do, honey. If you haven't been able to get Max into bed by now, you need some special help."

"He tied me naked to his motorcycle at Twin Peaks and walked away, and I liked it," I blurt out.

Silence.

"Amanda?"

"I just knew he was kinky," she breathes. "Like Drake, who is, by the way, in my kitchen getting a glass of water to rehydrate after our night of festivities."

"Doctor Drake is at your house?" My voice rises in pitch. "You slept with Doctor Drake?"

"Jake is avoiding me," she snaps. "It won't do. And since we're broken up, Drake was more than happy to help a girl in need. He knows the score."

"He's my boss!" I shriek. "You can't sleep with my boss."

"Ooops. Too late. The deed is already done. Multiple times."

"Nooooo!" I am reminded of Edvard Munch's painting *The Scream*. No doubt his muse was someone who discovered her best friend was sleeping with her boss.

"He certainly has creative ideas about how to use a thermometer," she giggles. "And a stethoscope and—"

I hold the phone away from my ear. "Don't tell me. Don't tell me."

"You should try it sometime." Her voice takes on a teasing lilt. "You might like it."

I wrap the sheet tight around my body as if she might suddenly appear with the aforementioned medical instruments. "I won't. I'm not into kinky stuff."

"How would you know? Yesterday was your first experience.

When you do finally get Max into bed, he's going to think he's the luckiest man alive. You're like a virgin minus the virginal bit. A blank slate. He can mold you to fit his kinkiest desires, and you'll think it is normal."

My body heats imagining Max's kinkiest desires. Suddenly, the sheet is too hot and I kick it off, letting the cool air soothe my burning skin. "I'm not totally unaware of what goes on in the bedroom."

"Trust me, you are."

I suck in a breath. "Do you think Max is into…kinky stuff?"

"Did any of your other boyfriends strip off your clothes and tie you to a motorcycle?"

"No."

"Did he just happen to have some rope or other restraining device handy?"

My stomach sinks. "Yes."

"Then I diagnose a severe case of kinkiness, and you're going in the deep end." She giggles and whispers something intelligible.

"Is Doctor Drake in the room? Are you letting him hear our conversation?" I bolt upright in the bed.

"He's just gone out again to look through the pie cupboard where I keep my sex toys. We didn't spend much time in the bed—mostly in the kitchen, on the couch, the dining table, the shower, and out on the balcony. You missed out big time. He is kink on a stick. And with his knowledge of female anatomy—"

"I don't want to hear it. What about Jake? If he was pissed off with your games before, I can't imagine he would be happy to know you are sexing it up with my BOSS."

Amanda snorts a laugh. "Since when did you become the expert on men? I thought you just told me you didn't even get Max into bed. What happened?"

I twist the sheet in my hand. "I…it was so intense it scared me, and I didn't like that he made me like it. I tried to talk to him about it afterward, but I couldn't explain myself and he didn't seem to understand. It kind of ruined the mood. Eventually we decided it would be best to call it a night."

"Poor Max," Amanda chortles. "He must have had a hard night after dropping you off."

"Amanda!"

"Text him. Let him know you're okay."

"I'm not okay. I'm confused."

"Tell him that too. And for the record, he didn't make you like it. You like it or you don't like it. It's all up to you."

I wriggle under the covers and pull them over my head. I am going to hide here all day. No debt collectors. No kinky fighters. No friends sleeping with my boss. "You aren't making me feel any better, and he wasn't even the reason I called. I have another problem—"

Amanda's voice drops to a low rasp. "He's sucking my toes."

"Ewww. TMI. And I'm sure he can hear you. Does he know it's me?"

"No," she whispers. "And he can't hear me. He's under the covers."

"Please. Take me away," I whimper.

"You're safe. He's just slithered out of the bed and is racing toward the kitchen. He's so exciting. I never know what he's going to do next."

My stomach churns. "Don't tell me any more. Every time I look at him at work I'm going to have inappropriate images in my head. What if I blurt out something without thinking? What if we're in a meeting and someone says something about toes? I won't be able to control myself."

"Oooooo. He's been through my toy stash and now he wants to play," she murmurs. "He's holding things up one by one to—Bad dog. Get off the bed. Stop. Don't bite the pillows. Oh, wait. Those aren't pillows." She bursts into laughter. Well, at least one of us is having fun.

"I'm hanging up," I say morosely.

"No wait. The debt collector." She mumbles something and I hear the unmistakable sound of a bed creaking. "You have to find a way to shut him down."

"But—" I have too many questions and I need her full attention. "Do you have time to meet up for coffee?"

Amanda giggles. "I think I'll be staying in bed today. Drake has brought in a bowl of ice, a bag of clothespins, a packet of twist ties, a cucumber, and a bottle of hot sauce. Ooooh. And a pair of handcuffs. Where do you think he found those?"

I sigh. "I don't think he would have had to look too hard."

"Oh wait, someone's at the door. Hold on. I'll be able to give you my full attention once I'm out of the bedroom."

She breathes into the phone and I imagine her walking through her country chic living room filled with pastel antiques and cozy chintz. A lock clunks. A door creaks.

"Jake!" She gives a squeak of horror.

My pulse races. "Get him out of there," I whisper. "Don't let him see—"

"Who's that?" Jake's voice is so loud I hold the phone away from my ear. "Damn it, Amanda, you didn't waste any time did you?"

"You wouldn't see me." Her voice is thin, high, and almost unrecognizable. My eyes prickle with tears.

"So you jump into bed with the first guy who comes along?" he shouts. "When the going gets tough, Amanda gets laid? Is that about it? Is that how you handle a relationship? Is that all I meant to you?"

"Jake," she whispers. Her voice is thick with horror and regret.

I slap my hand over my mouth. In all the years I've known her, I've never heard her sound so desolate.

"If I never see you again, it will be too soon." The door slams.

Amanda draws in a breath and a sob rips from her throat.

"I'm on my way, honey." I end the call and jump out of bed.

No Max for me today. Tension eases from my shoulders. I have a little breathing room.

—~~—

Hi Max

How is my girl today?

Ok

Just okay?

Just ok

Because of me?

U and other things

I'm coming over

U can't. I'm going 2 c Amanda

We should talk

She needs me

I need you

She needs me more

frowns I want to see you

I'll send you a picture

Now?

No. I'm not dressed

Waiting for picture

You want me to sext you?

Waiting for picture

I'm a sexting virgin

Waiting for picture

I might get hurt

How?

Your phone is so big **trembles**

True. Phones don't get any bigger than mine

So modest

Waiting for picture

I'm not that kind of girl

What kind of girl are you?

Naked kind

Max likes naked kind

Confused kind

Max likes confused kind

Sorry kind

Don't be sorry. I shouldn't have pushed you

I was scared

I know

But also **blushes**

Max likes **blushes**

I have 2 go or I'll miss the bus

I'll send Lewis to take you. He'll wait until you want to go home

No need. Bus is fine

You take care of Amanda. I'll take care of you

———

"Mac, I have a favor to ask." Dr. Drake flips my desk sign to *Closed* and rounds the partition to join Big Doris in my cubicle.

My stomach twists and I clasp my knees together and look down. After the unwanted glimpse into his sexsational life, I've been trying to keep my distance from him for the last two days. But fate has seen fit to reward me with Big Doris and Kink on a Stick in my cubby at the same time.

"Good morning, Doctor Drake." Big Doris blushes and looks down at the stack of green slips in her hand. "I was reprimanding Mac yet again. She had two pens point up in her pen box. It violates our health and safety protocols. We don't want employees to accidentally drop a hand on the pen box and get stabbed. She whips a green slip from her pad and drops it on my desk.

Dr. Drake frowns and grabs the slip. "I hardly think that is conduct worthy of a green slip."

Big Doris's nostrils flare but she recovers quickly. "Of course. What was I thinking?" She gives me the sweet smile of a fox about to rip the head off a chicken. I predict a hailstorm of green slips coming my way. "Perhaps I could help you." She lays her hand on Dr. Drake's arm and bats her tiny, pale eyelashes.

Ignoring the quivering Big Doris in front of him, Dr. Drake drops a gold envelope on my desk. A meaty hand snatches it up. "What's this?" Charlie asks, coming up behind me.

Seriously? My cubicle is barely big enough for one, much less three. I slide my chair to the corner and hold my knees to my chest.

Dr. Drake raises an eyebrow. "Mr. Brown, don't you have work to do?"

Charlie shakes his head. "No."

"Are there not patients who require admitting?"

"Not by me."

Dr. Drake sighs. "I suppose you could all help me out. The

hospital is having a black-tie charity fund-raiser at the Regency Center on Thursday night. We need people to circulate and solicit donations. We also need people to help with the heart auction."

"Heart auction?" Charlie's eyebrows fly up. "Someone's donating their heart?"

Dr. Drake rolls his eyes. "The hospital has solicited famous artists, jewelers, and sculptors as well as patients and the public to create and donate a heart in any material or on any medium to be auctioned for the benefit of the hospital. It is most entertaining. No one knows the provenance of the heart they have bid on until the end of the auction."

"I heard last year someone bid one hundred thousand dollars for a glass heart, thinking it was a Chihuly, only to discover it was bought at a dime store and painted by one of our four-year-old patients," Big Doris titters. "Count me in."

"Me too." Charlie gives Big Doris a wink and she shudders.

"What about you, Mac?" Dr. Drake snatches the invitation from Charlie's hand and slides it across the desk to me. "We could use all the help we can get."

I want to help, but I've spent every evening this week consoling Amanda. Max will not be pleased if I cancel our date so I can spend the evening with Mr. Humping and Pumping.

"Um. I'm sorry. I've got other plans."

Dr. Drake tilts his head to the side and studies me. "The money will be used to buy badly needed equipment for the children's ward. The more people we have, the better chance we have of making the fund-raiser a success. I could authorize overtime pay for all of you. Triple time. It is a work function, after all."

I make a quick calculation. Triple time plus two nights at the club would more than cover the next payment to Sergio and then some. I sigh a dejected sigh. "Count me in."

Dr. Drake beams. "Done. I can give you a ride. I saw you a few times at the bus stop after work. Charlie told me you sold your car."

Charlie whistles and looks away from the fierce scowl I shoot in his direction.

"I can take the bus," I protest.

"You can pick *me* up," Big Doris booms.

"I'll pick you up." Charlie pats her shoulder and she shrugs him off.

Dr. Drake's lips curl into a smile. "Excellent. Mr. Brown, you can take Doris, and I'll take Mac."

"No, I—"

Charlie cuts me off with an exasperated groan. "He won't bite, Mac."

Dr. Drake winks. "Not unless she asks nicely."

Chapter 14

ARE YOU MY GIRL?

Hi Max

Hi baby. I'm back. I'll pick you up after work

*Have 2 cancel. Work function tonight **sniffs***

Work on Thursday night?

Charity event for the hospital

I'll come

Invitation only

I'll get one

You'll distract me. No Max allowed

frowns

*U need 2 learn some new text expressions like **smiles with understanding***

frowns

See you 2morrow?

No. Tonight

After the charity event?

Now

Inspiration hits me. I run over to the doorman and ask him to take my picture with my new phone. He poses me by a potted palm and I fan out the floor-length silver dress Amanda loaned me. I should have worn higher heels but three and a half inches is my limit. I turn sideways so Max can see the dress has no back—daring, even for Amanda.

"You look good enough to eat," the doorman says when he returns my phone. I wish I could keep him when we move back to our house.

I check the picture and smile. I don't look too bad. The dress hugs my curves, and with the help of Amanda's magic curling tongs, I have created a hint of a wave in my hair. I am a movie star version of myself. Maybe once Max has seen me all dressed up, he'll forgive me and meet me afterward. Or maybe I'm just playing with fire.

I email the picture to Max and wait.

I wait and wait. Maybe he isn't checking his emails. Maybe it didn't go through. What if he doesn't like it? Maybe I'm deluding myself about how I look.

A black BMW pulls up in front of the building. Dr. Drake honks twice and then exits the vehicle. He is drop-dead gorgeous in his tux, and from the way he is walking, all swagger and rolling hips, he knows it. I step out the door and he stops in his tracks. He throws a theatrical hand over his heart and falls to his knees.

My lips quiver with a repressed smile. Okay. He's mildly amusing, good-looking, apparently hot in bed, and for some strange reason hot on me. And yet all I can think about is Max and why he didn't email me back.

Two hours of schmoozing at the Regency and I'm ready to call it a night. I have solicited donations from politicians, businessmen, philanthropists, and the cream of San Francisco society and all with Dr. Drake's hand plastered to my bare back in a gesture that is at once solicitous and overly familiar.

Dr. Drake is called up to the stage, and I gratefully drop into one of the circular, red benches scattered throughout the Lodge Room. The Heart 2 Heart fund-raiser is in full swing. I lean back and admire the open-beam ceilings, dark-paneled walls, and stained-glass windows. The room has the feel of a gothic church. I almost expect someone to sit at the huge pipe organ and play a hymn.

I ease my aching feet out of my shoes and rub them through the plush carpet while Dr. Drake arranges the charity hearts on tables at the side of the stage. The creativity of the heart donors is astounding: big hearts, little hearts, six-foot tin can hearts, and tiny sequined hearts; hearts made of concrete, glass, wood, metal, and paper; painted hearts, video hearts, even a photo of a real heart mounted in a silver frame. My favorite is a picture of a heart, painted with three red brush strokes, and the words "My Heart" penciled in the corner. Likely it was made by one of the children in chronic care, but it could also be one of the multimillion-dollar hearts donated by famous artists.

Dr. Drake waves me over. I slip on my shoes and join him at the tables along with Charlie, Big Doris, and the assorted other staff members he roped into helping tonight.

When everyone is assembled on the stage, Dr. Drake clears his throat. "One by one you will select a heart and walk it down the runway, doing everything you can do to heat up the bidding. It's easier if you choose a heart that speaks to you. Make sure everyone can see it. Show it at every angle. We will have a screen projection behind you. If you like being in the spotlight, this is your chance to shine. Pose, blow kisses, dance, sing—do whatever it takes, and remember, sex sells. This is for a great cause, so give it all you've got."

"What about you?" I ask. "Will you be parading around the stage with a heart in your hand?"

Dr. Drake's eyes gleam. "Full of fire tonight, aren't we?"

"Heh, heh, heh." I try to dampen my laugh in case anyone thinks we're together, although after playing sex toy for him this evening, I doubt my efforts will have any effect.

"Don't fear, beautiful," he chuckles. "I'll be on that stage and the female patrons will be beating each other back to get what I have to offer." Arms raised, Dr. Drake rolls his hips in a circle and then thrusts them forward and yells, "Boom! One hundred thousand dollars for Doctor Drake's heart."

I inelegantly snort a laugh. The crowd disperses and Dr. Drake holds out an arm to help me down the stairs.

"You liked that, did you?" he murmurs.

"It was mildly amusing. I dare you to do it on stage."

A grin splits his face. "Don't you know I can't resist a challenge?" His eyes soften. "*You* are a challenge. We would be good together, and you just can't see it. We share a passion for healing, a sense of humor, and a conservative world view—"

Conservative? Him? With clothespins and hot sauce and medical instruments being used as sex toys?

"And a distaste for violence," he continues. "What could be more perfect?"

"Max." The name drops off my lips before I can stop it.

He cocks his eyebrow. "Your surly friend from the bar? He's too aggressive, too controlling for you. I thought I'd have to take him outside and teach him how to treat a woman. You need someone who will respect you, treat you with kindness, and nurture you."

Does tying a woman to a motorcycle and leaving her alone in the dark count as nurturing?

"Like you?"

He leans forward and brushes his lips over my ear. "Like me."

Twenty minutes and three speeches later, the first heart is auctioned off for a paltry two thousand dollars. The next one fetches only nine thousand, and the one after that only ten.

"This doesn't bode well for the rest of the auction," Dr. Drake grumbles. "Last year the bidding started at twenty-five and went up from there."

"Doris is up next," I soothe. "Maybe she'll get the bidding going."

Big Doris selects a twisted metal heart covered in barbs. How appropriate. She shuffles to the front of the stage and holds it in the air. Her Jell-O green suit glows under the stage lights.

Silence.

Sucking in her lips, she spins around and then walks up and down the runway. Still no bids.

When her face tightens and her bottom lip trembles, a queasy sensation rolls through me. I raise my hand in the air and pray Sergio doesn't ask for even more money. "Five hundred dollars."

Dr. Drake looks down at me and smiles. "You have the biggest heart of anyone I know, but I can't let you spend money I know you don't have." He waves his hand in the air. "One thousand dollars."

Big Doris looks over and her eyes widen. She flashes Dr. Drake a relieved smile and parades up and down the runway flogging her iron heart. With Dr. Drake's nudge, the bidding picks up and voices fill the air.

Big Doris's heart sells for three thousand dollars. She leaves the stage with a smile on her face. Charlie is up next. Almost unrecognizable in an ill-fitting, polyester tux, he works the stage with the grace of a bear on a trampoline, and his giant balloon heart is auctioned off for a cool twenty-five thousand.

"Why won't they go over twenty-five?" Dr. Drake rakes his hand through his hair. "We need to spice things up." He stalks over to the tables and scoops up a giant, heart-shaped crystal vase. "Ladies," he calls into the audience. "Not only are you bidding for this priceless item by an artist unknown, you are bidding for dinner with me. I am a single, unattached surgeon with an empty heart." He holds the vase aloft and winks at the audience.

A collective gasp fills the room as he struts down the runway, his hair and teeth glowing like one hundred suns.

"Fifteen thousand."

"Twenty."

"Twenty-five."

Dr. Drake tucks one hand in his pocket. He prances. He spins. He smiles. His sharp black tux and Ken-doll good looks are a winning combination. The bids ratchet up at dizzying speed. When they plateau at thirty thousand dollars, Dr. Drake puts down his heart and eases his jacket off his shoulders. The band bursts into a jazzy rendition of Joe Cocker's "You Can Leave Your Hat On." Women scream. A fit of giggles overtakes me. Dr. Drake spins his jacket around his finger and tosses it into the audience. The jacket hits Janice from Radiology square in the face. She hugs it to her head and her muffled shrieks are swallowed by the frenzied crowd.

As the band plays, Dr. Drake loosens his bow tie and unbuttons his shirt to his naval. He eases it open. Dear God. He has an amazing body—all tight abs and toned muscles. No wonder Amanda let him into her inner sanctum. He flexes. His pecs ripple. Janice faints. The crowd goes wild. My stomach aches, but I can't stop laughing.

"Fifty thousand dollars," a woman's voice booms through the room. The music squeaks to a halt.

"Fifty going once," the auctioneer calls. The audience takes a collective breath. Heads turn, seeking out the bidder.

"Going twice."

The room stills.

"Sold to the woman in the lime green suit. Please come to the stage to collect your prize, or should I say, prizes?" the auctioneer chortles. Dr. Drake poses at the front of the stage holding the heart aloft.

The audience parts and Dr. Drake's smile fades when Big Doris climbs the stage and wraps her arms around him. Handing out green slips must pay better than I thought.

After Dr. Drake's performance, the bidding heats up. My painted heart on canvas goes for thirty thousand dollars, and a feather boa heart brings in a staggering forty-two thousand dollars. Dr. Drake joins me at the side of the stage, seemingly recovered from his recent shock, to tell me I'm up next.

"How did she afford you?" I cannot contain my curiosity.

Dr. Drake grimaces. "Her father is here. Some hotshot banker. Wanted to buy his baby girl a present."

"Lucky you."

"Think you can beat me?" He gives me a wink and hands me a vodka shot. "If you want to make the same dinner offer to spice things up, I'll foot the bill."

"I'll see how my heart does without any spice."

We clink glasses and I shoot my bolt of liquid courage before taking to the stage to survey the remaining hearts. I walk up and down beside the table twice but nothing calls to me. I am about to choose something at random, when a sparkle catches my eye. I push aside a velvet cushion heart and pull out the necklace peeking out from underneath. Wow! A huge heart-shaped ruby mounted on a diamond-encrusted heart and suspended on a gold and diamond chain. No way is it real. Something like that would be worth millions of dollars. I figure it has to be quartz, but still...I've never seen anything so beautiful. If it hadn't been hidden, I'm sure it would already have been auctioned.

I wipe my palms down my dress before I take to the runway, holding the necklace in my hand. I try to banish all thoughts of Big Doris from my head. The necklace is so pretty. Someone has to bid.

Dangling the pendant from my hand, I turn so the cameras can project the image on the screen behind me. Then I smile.

"Five thousand."

Darn. Even I know the necklace is worth more than that. Taking a deep breath, I swing the necklace from my finger and saunter down the runway.

"Ten thousand."

"Twenty."

"Twenty-two."

Twenty-two is a long way from fifty, and with Dr. Drake smirking in the corner, I need to do something to heat up the bidding. I saunter to the auctioneer and tell him to announce that I too will offer myself as a dinner companion.

My offer receives cheers and applause, a few whistles, and one catcall.

I put my hand on my hip, spin around and wiggle walk to the back of the stage giving everyone a good view of my backless dress.

"Thirty thousand."

Looking back over my shoulder, I give the audience a wink and then spin again and pose with the necklace laid against my chest. A smile tugs at my lips. This is kind of fun and in Amanda's dare-to-bare dress, I'm feeling the magic.

"Forty thousand."

"Forty five."

"Forty eight."

The bids continue to climb. The more I wiggle, the faster they rise. By the time they hit sixty, I'm sweating like I've spent an hour in the gym.

"Seventy-five thousand dollars," Dr. Drake shouts from the floor. He looks up at me and winks.

My face freezes mid-smile. Nonononononononono. Seeing him at work is one thing, but going on a date with him when he's made his intentions clear is another. And what about Max?

"Seventy-five thousand going once," the auctioneer calls.

Dear God, please let someone else bid. I'll be good. I won't gossip. I won't think mean thoughts about people. I'll call my parents every day.

"One hundred thousand," someone shouts.

Saved.

"One twenty-five," Dr. Drake counters.

No. Bad Dr. Drake. Sweat trickles down my back. My heart thuds against my chest. No. Please. Not an evening with Kink on a Stick. I like my toes unsucked.

"One fifty."

I roll my hips like a catwalk model, and I walk up and down the runway, imagining I don't have quite as many curves. By the time they reach two-fifty, my stomach has twisted itself into such a knot I may never eat again. Where does a surgeon get two hundred and fifty thousand dollars to throw away?

"One million dollars." A deep, rich voice cuts through the crowd.

Gasps from the audience. A sharp inhale of breath from Dr. Drake. A small sigh of relief from me.

"Well, I can't beat that." Dr. Drake throws up his hands and shrugs.

"One million once," the auctioneer calls. "Twice." He pauses and the crowd holds a collective breath. "Sold for one million dollars. Would our generous benefactor please step forward and collect your prize? Your contribution will help fund our new neonatal cardiac ward and we would all like to show our appreciation."

I would like to know who thinks this heart is worth one million dollars.

Or maybe, I already do.

A low murmur builds, rolling from the back of the room, gaining momentum as the crowd parts. I hold my breath, and a space clears at the front of the stage.

Max.

He looks up and catches my gaze. My eyes glisten with happy tears. My lips part and my grin stretches from ear to ear. He strides toward me, breathtaking in his sleek, black tux, thick hair still slightly damp and curling at his temples. When he reaches the stage, he closes the distance between us, taking the steps two at a time until he is standing in front of me.

He takes the necklace from my outstretched hand. "Mine," he whispers. "Yours. A million times over."

He reaches behind me and fastens the chain around my neck. His fingers brush lightly over my bare skin and a tiny shiver races down my spine. My hand flies to my throat to touch the most expensive piece of jewelry I have ever worn. "Max, you don't have to—"

"I want to."

The audience claps and cheers. Max spins me around to face them and slides an arm around my waist. "Are you ready for the big time, baby?"

―〰―

By the time the paparazzi are done taking pictures, I can no longer see. Max leads me off the stage and into a luxurious side room with a working fireplace, silk tapestries, and carved-wood ceilings. We sit on a red upholstered sofa built for two, and I stare at the fire and try to blink the spots from my eyes.

"I see you managed to get an invitation."

Max runs his hand up and down my bare back sending tiny shivers of need darting through my veins. "When I saw that picture I had to come. I would have stormed the castle if Colton had not managed to get me on the list."

I touch the necklace. "I'm glad you did. Seeing you walk through the crowd was magical. You took my breath away. It's a moment I'll never forget."

"I aim to please."

"And please you do," I whisper.

With the worst possible timing in the universe, Dr. Drake appears in the doorway. "Mac, we need you on stage. The bidding is cooling off. You've got to get out there and heat things up again."

Max bristles. "No."

"Huntington." Dr. Drake walks toward him and holds out his hand. "We meet again. I want to thank you for your contribution. It will help us purchase equipment that will save many lives, and I'm sure Mac will be an entertaining dinner companion."

He turns to me and gives me a wink. "Hopefully you can repeat the performance for the benefit of Geriatrics."

"No." Max's voice deepens and he rises to his feet. "She's not going back on that stage."

Dr. Drake's smile fades. "No?"

I tug on his sleeve. "It's for charity."

"I said no." Max folds his arms. The sleeves of his tux strain under the bulge of his flexed biceps.

Dr. Drake raises an eyebrow. "I believe it is Mac's decision. I might also point out this is a work function and she's being paid to do a job."

"I want to help." I stand up and put my hand on Max's arm. "It won't take long, and I promise not to offer any dinner dates."

"There you go." Dr. Drake smiles. "She wants to help." He puts his hand on my bare back and takes a step forward, leading me toward the door.

"Take your hands off her."

Dr. Drake freezes. "I beg your pardon?"

"You heard me." Max grasps my arm and pulls me toward him. I stumble sideways and trip on the hem of my dress. Dr. Drake's arm snakes around my waist and he catches me before I fall.

Max yanks me out of Dr. Drake's arms.

"Enough. This isn't a tug of war." I twist in his arms but he hugs me to his chest like a child protecting a toy.

"I believe Miss Delaney would like you to release her." Dr. Drake's voice is calm and even—a decided contrast to the low, threatening rumble emanating from Max's chest.

"And I believe if you have any sense of self-preservation, you will walk out that door and find someone else to help with the auction."

"You are overreacting." I rest my cheek against his twitching pecs. He smells divine. His cologne is fresh, spicy, and oh so masculine. His body vibrates with the rumble of his voice. He is in full protective mode and it fires my blood. But I can't let him interfere with my work.

"Are you threatening me, Huntington?" Dr. Drake gives Max an assessing look. "I'll have you know I was a two-time NCAA champion wrestler in college. I gave up on a professional career to become a doctor, but I still practice daily in the hospital gym." He air boxes his shadow, giving it a one-two punch. "You want to step outside?"

"No." I look from Dr. Drake to Max and back again. "I won't allow it."

"I wanted to step outside with you a long time ago, Drake," Max says ignoring me. "You can't seem to keep your hands off my girl."

"Is she your girl?" Dr. Drake asks in a cool voice.

"Are you my girl?" Max's voice drops to a low murmur, and he brushes his lips over my hair.

"Yours," I whisper.

Max gives a self-satisfied grunt and tightens his arm around me. "She's mine. She says so."

"That doesn't mean *obeys Max's every whim*," I add. "I'm going to do my job and help with the auction. You can glower by the stage and growl at anyone who dares breathe in my direction."

Dr. Drake chortles. "Looks like she might be too much for you to handle, Huntington. Maybe she needs a real man."

Max's body tightens and I slide my arms around his chest. "Don't—"

"Redemption," Max bites out. "MMA club in Ghost Town. Tonight after the auction."

Dr. Drake's eyes flash and he grins. "I'll be there. And lucky for you, after your defeat, when you're moaning in a pool of your own contrition, I will be morally obligated to tend to your injuries."

He extends his hand and he and Max shake.

"After the auction," Max snaps, "and you don't touch my girl again."

"After the auction. And I will if she wants."

Chapter 15

YOU KNOW THE RULES OF THE RING

THE AUCTION IS A roaring success. I walk the catwalk four more times, and my hearts raise another two hundred thousand dollars. Max escorts me on and off the stage. During the breaks, he keeps even Charlie away with his folded arms and menacing stare. I am forced to entertain myself by playing spot Big Doris as she swans around the room in her florescent green suit.

After the auction ends, the floor is cleared for dancing. I catch Charlie planting a smooch on Big Doris in the corner. Big Doris doesn't look pleased. She slaps him across the face. Good thing we're in a room full of medical professionals.

"Lighten up," I say after Max chases away an eighty-something-year-old man in a wheelchair.

"If you want me to lighten up then put on my jacket," he snaps. "I know what these men are thinking, and I don't want them thinking it about you."

"If I wear your jacket, will you dance with me?" Although I have doubts about the kind of music the band is going to play for the primarily post-sixties crowd, I never miss an opportunity to dance.

Max gives me a curt nod and slides his jacket off. He holds it for me and I slip my arms inside. The warm, silk lining glides over my skin, and I close my eyes and revel at the delicious sensation of being totally enveloped in Max.

We hit the dance floor and the band launches into an upbeat, old-time jazz tune. Max takes my hand and we shuffle a slow circle under a potted palm. He hums along to the song, his face soft and relaxed. A smile tugs at the corners of my lips. I've never seen him really enjoy himself.

"What is this song?"

"Nina Simone's, 'My Baby Just Cares for Me.'"

"Of course it is." I grin. "And you had nothing to do with the fact they decided to play it right here, right now."

The band segues into something soft and sultry. Max pulls me into his arms. He slides one hand under the jacket and caresses my back. His other hand intertwines with mine, and he holds them pressed against his chest. So damn sexy.

The beat slows, and I press my cheek to the smooth cotton of his shirt. "What's this one?"

"'Listen to Me' by Buddy Holly."

I snort a laugh. "How much did you pay them?"

Max chuckles and spins me around the dance floor. His hand massages its way up my bare back with firm, gentle strokes. My muscles relax into his warm caress until his questing fingers dive into the side of my dress to fondle the curve of my breast. I stiffen in his arms.

"Bad Max. I'm wearing the jacket to assuage your overly jealous nature, not so you can surreptitiously feel me up."

"You can't show me something all night, baby, and not expect I'll want to touch." His fingers slide farther into my dress and brush over my nipple. I gasp and try to pull away.

Max holds me tight and leans down, covering my mouth with his own, drowning my moan of displeasure. Or is it pleasure? I can't tell. His lips move, easing mine apart, and he kisses me, deep and tender. "Shhh, baby."

"I'll shhh when you stop being naughty."

"Can't. You're wearing a naughty dress. All I can think about is getting inside it." To emphasize his point, he slides his hand down my back and inside my dress to cup my bottom. He gives my ass cheek a squeeze and runs his finger along the inside of my thong before giving it a tug. "Don't need this."

"I do need it. I am not going commando at a swanky party."

"You won't be wearing it by the end of the night," he rasps in my ear. "I promise you that." He squashes my hips against him and his arousal presses into my belly, sending tiny shivers of need down my spine.

The band plays yet another old tune, and Max easily catches the beat. The music is not as bad as I thought, especially with Max caressing me into a frenzy of lust under his jacket.

He croons along with Sinatra, his deep voice rumbling in his chest. My body thrums with desire and the painful pleasure of unfulfilled need.

"You're in the mood for fighting," I correct him, when he pauses to take a break after the famous first line. "You've decided to throw away the opportunity to get Makayla out of her dress so you can indulge in a late-night pissing contest with Doctor Drake. I have to work tomorrow. There'll be no loving for you."

"Sassy girl. It works both ways. Do you really want to spend the night alone?" He feathers kisses along my jaw. I roll my eyes and pretend flames of need are not licking through my body.

"I have a Rabbit."

Max freezes and thrusts me away from him, eyes wide. "What did you just say?"

What did I just say? I take a little trip down memory lane. I do not like where I arrive. My hand whips over my mouth. NO. I did NOT just say that. Please, please, please let it not be true.

Max's eyelids lower to half-mast and he licks his lips. "We'll go to Redemption. I'll deal with Drake. Then we'll go to your place and play with your Rabbit."

I did say it. "Uhhhhgh." My voice catches in my throat. "I don't… you know—"

"You do now." His voice is warm, rich, and filled with promise.

"Can't you just forget about Doctor Drake?" I murmur. "We could go to my place—"

"He challenged me. I don't turn down a challenge. This is who I am, baby. I'm a fighter."

I stroke my hand along his jaw, trying to ease his tension. "It isn't who you are. You are so much more. I don't want you to fight with him. Please. Just walk away. Come home with me."

He shakes his head and draws my hand away. "Don't do this. Don't ask me to choose."

My heart sinks, weighted down by his unspoken words. If forced to choose, he won't choose me.

An hour later, I huddle in the backseat of the limo outside Redemption. Despite Max's best efforts, I refuse to go inside. If not for the fact it is impossible to get a cab at this time of night, I would not even be here.

Lewis turns around and holds up a flask. I shake my head. I might be patching up two morons tonight. I'll need a clear head to treat them, and my wits about me to scold them.

My phone buzzes and I take a call from Dr. Drake. He isn't coming. Big emergency at the hospital. He sends his regrets. Hooray! I might get some loving tonight after all.

I race into the club and find Max shadowboxing in the practice ring. His fight shorts cling to the curve of his ass, and his back glistens with sweat. I catch the fresh, lemon scent of cleanser and raw musk of hot, sweaty male.

"He's not coming."

Max shakes his head and jabs at the wall. His muscles ripple and swell as he lands each imaginary punch. Maybe he didn't hear me.

"Doctor Drake isn't coming," I yell. "He was called to the hospital to consult on an emergency heart surgery."

He lowers his arms and turns to face me. "Do you believe him?"

"Yes. If he wanted out, he would have thought up an excuse that wouldn't be so easy for me to check when I go to work tomorrow."

Max grabs a towel and wipes himself down. His hair is damp and curls just above his neck. As he moves, his tattoos undulate over his skin. Broad back, tight ass. All man. All hot. My mouth waters.

As if sensing the stirring of my desire, Max spins around, dark eyes hooded. "What are you thinking, baby?"

I put a hand on my hip. "I'm thinking it's time to go home."

His wicked grin shoots straight to my core. "I'm thinking it's time you came into the ring. If you aren't here in five seconds, I'm coming to get you."

I kick off my shoes and climb through the ropes. As soon as my feet touch the mat, he backs me into the corner and licks his lips.

"You look like you're about to devour me."

"I am." His mouth slants over mine and he kisses me. Hot. Wet. Hungry. I don't even try to resist. I curl my hands around his neck and pull him down for more.

"You know the rules of the ring," he murmurs. His tongue flicks against the seam of my lips, forcing them apart.

"No eye gouging. No biting. Nothing below the belt. No fish hooking," I say with pride.

Max chuckles. "Not the rules I was thinking about. Especially since there may be some biting and there will definitely be attention focused below the belt."

A soft "oh" escapes my lips. "I didn't know there were other rules."

"Our main rule is that no one leaves the ring unless someone goes limp or gives up. Which will it be, baby? I think we should go for limp—the replete with sexual satisfaction kind."

My lips part with a moan, and he dips inside, coaxing me open with his talented tongue. He tastes of whiskey and coffee. He tastes of me.

I slide my hands around his powerful torso and explore the hard ripple of muscle down his back. "You must have me confused with someone else," I tease. "I'm not that kind of girl."

"What kind of girl are you?" He sifts his hand through my hair and cups my head, holding me tight as he deepens his kiss.

"Hot kind," I whisper against his lips.

"What else?"

"Wet kind."

He slides his hand down my bare back, then lower until he kneads my bottom, sending a shock wave of pleasure over my skin.

"What else?" he demands.

I pull out of his grasp and step away. Before he can protest, I put my hands behind my neck and undo the clasp of my dress. The front falls to my waist, revealing its secret built-in bra cups and baring my breasts. Max's hungry gaze rakes over me, but before he can touch, I undo the clasp on my lower back and let the dress sweep down my body into a pool of silver sparkles. "Naked kind."

Max stares at me, his gaze traveling the length of my body and back again, so intense I feel the heat in my toes.

Boldly, I step forward. My breasts brush against his hot, hard chest, and my nipples tighten in response.

"I like naked kind. But you aren't entirely naked." His hands glide down my sides to my hips. His thumbs hook into the band of my lacy thong and he tugs. The thin fabric parts with a graceless ripping sound and then flutters to my feet.

Raw lust streaks straight to my core. "Animal! You tore off my panties."

Max cups my ass in his palms and squeezes lightly, rolling my cheeks. "I told you it would come off tonight."

"Is that how you seduce a woman? You rip off her clothes?"

"I thought you were seducing me," Max murmurs. He presses tiny kisses along my jaw and down my neck. "Best seduction technique is to get naked."

I rub my hip against the hard line of his erection. "Is it working?" I ask with feigned innocence. "I've never seduced a man before."

"And you won't again." His voice is deep and sexy, and I can't help but smile.

"That sounds serious."

"It is."

Max lowers his head and captures my lips in a hard, demanding kiss. Deep in my belly, need unfurls and licks softly through my body. I glide my hands over his chest, but when they move lower to trace the ridges of his six-pack, he stops me.

"No, baby. My turn." He pulls my arms behind my back, bracketing my wrists with one hand.

My body arches into him, my breasts brush against his chest. His free hand glides up my curves, and he cups my breast in his palm and squeezes gently. I moan and wriggle in his grasp. How can hands that are capable of such violence be so gentle and sensual on my skin?

"I'm not sure who is seducing who anymore," I pant.

"Maybe we're seducing each other." He turns his attention to my other breast, rolling my nipple between his thumb and forefinger until it peaks. A groan rips out of my throat.

"Then one of us isn't doing a good job, since he still has his clothes on." I trail a finger along the elastic of Max's boxer shorts and then freeze. Suddenly shy, I give him a questioning look from beneath my lashes.

His brown eyes smolder beneath heavy lids. "Tell me what you want, baby."

"I want to touch you," I whisper, dropping my gaze downward. I want to feel his desire in my hand, taste it in my mouth, and feel it inside me. Only then will I know it is real.

"Where?"

Heat sizzles through me. I bite my lip and press my hand over the erection straining beneath his shorts. "Here."

Max hisses in a breath and eases his shorts over his tight hips, sighing audibly as his erection springs free. He kicks them aside and I take a step back and stare at his incredible body—the lean contours of his muscles, the deep cuts of his narrow hips, the ripples across his abdomen, the tight, hard planes of his chest, and the trail of soft, dark hair leading down to his thick, heavy shaft.

"Touch me, baby."

Hand shaking, I circle my fingers around his girth and marvel at the contrast between his hard desire and the silky softness in my palm.

I slide my hand up his length, stroking lightly. Max groans. Sweat beads on his forehead and his hands clench and unclench by his sides. No man has ever been so aroused by my touch. Emboldened, I sink to my knees on the cool rubber mat. I press a kiss to his swollen head, and then a lick. Salty. Sweet. Sensual. Everything that is Max.

"You taste good." I open my mouth and slide my lips along his length, taking him as far as he can go.

"Makayla, baby. Stop." He threads his fingers through my hair and gently eases my head back. "I won't be able to hold out. I've wanted you for so long, and seeing you like this…here." His voice breaks. "A man can only take so much."

"But—" I want this. I want to taste him. I want to give him what he gave me.

He hooks his hands under my arms and yanks me up. I groan when his fingers slip between my legs.

"You're so wet." His voice deepens, thickens. "You liked having my cock in your mouth."

I should be shocked, maybe offended by his words. Instead, I am incredibly aroused. "I've been wet since you walked onto the stage at the gala. It seems to be my normal state around you, but yes, I especially liked having you in my mouth."

"My turn." Max nudges my legs apart and drops to his knees. He isn't going to…he can't—

He nuzzles my mound and my breath hitches. Oh God. He is. He can. I take an involuntary step back, but before I hit the ropes, Max grabs my hips and holds me still, his thumbs sliding to the juncture of my thighs. Fire races through my veins. He spreads me wide and his breath, hot and moist, whispers over my aching nub.

"Oh, Max." I thread my hands through his hair, and dig my fingers into his scalp. Max looks up at me and grins. He slips a finger inside me, and I rock into his palm. It can't get much better than this.

He leans forward, and his tongue sweeps along my folds in one long, wet, delicious lick. I gasp. It *can* get better. Much better.

"You like that, baby?"

My only response is a strangled cry.

Two fingers dip inside me, deeper this time, and then out, again and again, until my hips are rocking in time to his rhythm. I tighten my grip on his hair and try to get him where I want him to go.

"My girl is so damn hot when she's right on the edge," he murmurs. He slides his fingers out, but before I can protest, his tongue plunges into my sex, the sensation intimate and darkly erotic. I arch my back and moan.

"Hold on, baby." He captures my sensitive nub between his lips and sucks it gently into his mouth. I fall back against the ropes and scream as my orgasm hits me. But he doesn't stop. His teasing tongue continues to lick and he draws out wave after wave of mind-numbing pleasure.

A slight quiver in my thighs is all the warning I get before my knees buckle. Max catches me and pulls me down to the mat on top of him.

My breath comes in short, hard pants. "Weren't we just in this position a few weeks ago?"

"Yes. And I was thinking then exactly what I'm thinking now." He flips over, carrying me with him until I am on my back, caged by his tight, hard body.

"So was I."

"I'm going to make you feel so good, baby." He presses his palm over my sweet spot, and his fingers thrust and curl inside me. My body tightens around him. Tighter. Tighter. And then his fingers disappear and his erection prods gently against my swollen folds. I breathe a sigh. Finally.

"Open for me."

Sensation floods my body as he spreads me wide.

Finally.

I've waited for this for so long. Dreamed about it. Fantasized about it…

"Damn."

"Max?" Half-dazed, my face crumples when he draws away. "What's wrong?"

A pained look crosses his face. "I don't have a condom."

My tension instantly disappears and I melt into the mat. "I do."

"Where?"

"In my purse." I point to my evening bag long abandoned beside my dress.

Max pushes himself up and grabs my bag. "I am both pleased and displeased to know you left home tonight with a bag full of condoms." He hands the bag to me.

I pull out a condom and hold the open purse for him to see. "Not a bag full. Only three. I like to be safe."

He tears open the packet with his teeth and sheaths himself. "*Only* three? Drake and who else did you plan to seduce tonight?"

I grin and ruffle his hair. "I like jealous Max."

"I like Makayla with only one condom in her purse. For me." He settles himself between my legs, holding up his weight on his elbows. His erection presses deliciously against my entrance. I lean up and flick my tongue along his tattoos.

"I like these," I whisper. "Do they mean something?"

"Failure." The self-loathing in his voice startles me. I look up at him, but the pained expression on his face freezes my tongue. So many tattoos. So many failures. Why does he feel the need to ink them into his skin?

My mouth opens to ask him to explain, but Max cuts me off with a kiss. He nuzzles my neck and trails kisses down my throat and then around each of my breasts. He laves first one nipple then the other, and my arousal ratchets back up in an instant. I arch my back and whimper.

"There we go," he rasps. And with one thrust, he's inside me, pushing deep, deeper than fingers, deeper than his tongue.

"You feel like velvet. So hot. So wet." He shudders and pulls back slow and easy. My body protests by tightening around him, ripping a grunt from his throat. He thrusts deep again, filling me, stretching me. Possessing me.

"Don't stop." I wrap my arms around him and pull him down, crushing his mouth to my own. Max groans and fills me again. I tilt my hips to take more of him. When I whimper my need, his pace changes. Faster. Harder. I am climbing again, higher and higher, until searing pleasure rips through me, and I am soaring in Max's arms.

Max's body tenses and he thrusts hard and deep, climaxing with a husky groan.

When I regain a semblance of consciousness, Max is staring down at me. His eyes are soft, warm, and free of shadows. His lips find mine and he kisses me long and deep.

"Hot kind. Wild kind. Sweet kind," he whispers as he rolls to his side.

"Your kind." My fingers brush along his jaw, prickly with a five o'clock shadow.

A smile ghosts Max's lips. "Mine."

Chapter 16

SEX IS NOT REALLY THE PROBLEM

Max, are u awake?

No

U make a very comfortable bed

Time to sleep

No sleep

No choice. You only had 3 condoms

U don't have a single condom in ur house?

Sleep

Bad sleep. Want to go condom hunting

No

Text me a bedtime story

What story?

The story about the man who had no condoms in his house

MAKAYLA!

Did u just shout at me? **frowns**

Behave

You don't like my hand here?

I don't want to move. I like Makayla lying on top of me

I like Max getting up to find condoms

Max is happy like this

This part of Max is not happy

You shouldn't text in bed

Why?

This might happen

gasps I'll find condoms myself...naked

You win. I'll go

Yessss! **pumps fist in air**
But you will pay
Yessss! **pumps fist in air**
Like this
Oh **whimpers**

The soft, slow glide of a tongue circling my nipple awakens me. For a moment I am totally disoriented. Dark. So dark. I take a deep breath and smell spicy cologne, wood polish, and the lingering scent of sex.

Max's room. Max's bed. Still night.

His tongue laves my nipple, drawing it into a hard peak. Warm, relaxed, and still half-asleep, I sift a languid hand through his hair. Desire flickers through my body. How can I be wet already?

"Bad Max. I have to work tomorrow."

He turns his attention to my other nipple, pausing briefly to say, "It is tomorrow. Do you want to play, baby?" He rolls to his side and kneads my breast before he runs his hand down my body to the juncture of my thighs. I startle at his firm, demanding caress, so unlike the gentleness of the night's previous encounters, but the effect is the same. My nipples harden and moisture pools between my thighs.

"Yes, Max. I want to play."

"That's my girl." The deep rumble of his voice vibrates against my chest sending a wave of heat through my body.

He cups the curve of my sex and drives two fingers inside me with a hard, sharp thrust. No build up. No teasing. No warning.

"Ahhh." I arch my back and my hips come off the bed at the intimate invasion.

"Wet and ready for me. Good girl." His voice, warm and smooth as bourbon, slides over me like the blanket now missing from the bed.

When I moan, he leans down and slants his mouth across mine. His kiss is hard and urgent. Demanding. He thrusts his tongue between my lips and takes my mouth in long, firm, unyielding strokes.

The hair on the back of my neck prickles. Where is soft, gentle Max who whispers in my ear and nibbles at my lips? Where is playful, sensual Max who teases me to orgasm and holds me until I come back down?

He nips my bottom lip. "Do you trust me, baby?"

Um. No. Not when his manner has suddenly changed from sweet and loving to dominant and sexually demanding.

As if sensing my concern, he brushes my hair over my shoulder and nuzzles my neck. I giggle when his chin dips into a ticklish spot.

"I'm not sure which Max we're talking about."

His presses a soft, sweet kiss to my lips. "Same Max. Different style."

"I liked the old style." I wriggle my hips on the bed. "But right now I need—"

He spreads my moisture up and around my sensitive nub, while his fingers continue to stroke inside, teasing me until my thighs quiver.

"I know what you need, baby. Let me give it to you the best way I know how."

My body aches. My nipples throb. The air around us charges with electricity. I slit my eyes closed and whisper, "Yes, Max. Okay."

"Arms over your head." His tone changes in a heartbeat, from a soft cajole to a brusque command. "Now."

My breath leaves me with a sharp exhalation. He positions himself astride me, straddling my hips. His erection, hot and heavy, rests just below my breasts. As if someone else is in my body, someone carnal and wanton, I do as he commands. I raise my arms.

He gives a satisfied grunt and reaches behind the bed. Movements behind me I cannot see. He attaches a soft strap to my wrist and secures it to the bed frame. I tense and the steady rhythm of my heart quickens.

"Wait."

He doesn't wait. He attaches a second strap to my other wrist and secures it to the other side of the bed frame, spreading my arms wide.

My heart bangs a warning against my ribs. I yank on the straps. No give. Unlike the rope on the motorcycle I don't for a moment think I'll be able to wriggle myself free, and there is little chance of anyone coming to save me except Colton.

Bang. Bang. Bang. My ribs ache from the pounding of my heart.

My lungs tighten and I fight for every breath. Last night was nothing like this. Last night was fun and sweet and tender. Last night was normal.

"Makayla, look at me." Max's deep, compelling voice draws my eyes to his. "What's your safe word?"

Safe word? My brain clicks into gear, remembering our night at Twin Peaks. "Agusta."

He strokes my cheek and smiles. "Trust me not to hurt you, baby. Trust me to give you what you need."

Trust him? I don't know him. I know cool, bossy Max the businessman. I know sexy, playful Torment the fighter. But this man—his tattoos glistening on his powerful body—ignites my deepest, most carnal desires and my most hidden fears. I am drawn to his flame, unable to resist.

"I trust you, Max." The lie falls off my lips in the wake of overpowering need and insatiable curiosity.

Max slides down my body and kneels at the foot of the bed. "You're okay, baby. We've done this before. I'm just going to take you a little further this time."

His words speak to something dark inside me. My sex clenches, and I try to resist the pull. "It had a purpose before—to keep me on your motorcycle. I'm not about to fall off your bed."

"It had another purpose—to see whether you liked being restrained and touched." He slides a finger along my folds and shows me the wetness glistening on his fingers. "You do."

My cheeks burn and I turn my head away. What the hell is wrong with me?

Max slides his hands up my inner thighs and bends my legs one at a time. He plants each heel on the bed and sits back and studies me. "Open yourself for me."

My body flames, but I do as he asks and spread my knees wide. My thighs quiver. Cool air rushes down below but does nothing to dampen the burn of my desire. For the first time ever, I feel utterly vulnerable, exposed. The sensation is at once frightening and arousing.

"You have a pretty pussy, Makayla. I want to see it. Don't move your legs. If you do, there will be consequences." He smacks my thigh so smartly, I jump, and a disconcerting wave of heat rushes through me.

"If you want to stop, use your safe word." His eyes shine fever bright in the shadows. His body thrums with energy. He is alive in a way I have seen only in the fight ring. And, alarmingly, so am I.

When I shake my head, his lips curl into a smile. He runs his hand down my body from my neck to the juncture of my thighs, and then in and out my curves and over my breasts. His strokes are firm, uninhibited, and entirely possessive. The sweep of his hand etches his ownership into my burning skin.

Unable to stand the rush of sensation, I close my eyes. Max slides one hand under my neck and lifts me into a fiery, demanding kiss. As his tongue thrusts, ravaging my mouth with firm even strokes, he slides two fingers into me hard and fast.

"Ahhh," I moan into his mouth, arching my back, trying to get away, but his lips press against mine and his fingers dive deeper.

"Feel me," he whispers, sliding his mouth to my ear. "Feel me everywhere."

My body trembles. My hips buck against the steady rhythm of his fingers. Desire ratchets through me like a firestorm.

I need more. I tilt my mound into his palm seeking even the smallest bit of friction. Max jerks his hand away. "No," he barks. "Not until I say."

My thighs shake uncontrollably. His words, his bourbon smooth voice, his taut, lean body impaling me with pleasure, all combine to undo the threads of my control one by one. I slide my foot forward to leverage myself closer to his hand.

"Are you sure you want to do that?" Max warns. His voice is low and cool.

My heart pounds. A sharp stab of need sizzles all the way to my core and I slide my foot back.

"Better." Max slicks a third finger inside me, stretching me as his thumb strokes over my sensitive nub. He spreads my wetness around and around the throbbing bundle of nerves, until there is no part of my body free of quivering need.

Move. I need to move. But Max holds me tight, and I get only what he wants to give.

"Max. No more. I can't take anymore." My vision blurs and the painful, desperate need to orgasm obliterates every thought, releasing my mind to float in the endorphin rush.

Dark. Quiet. Shadows in the corners. Where is he?

I creep across the lino tiles to the body on the floor.

"Wake up," I whisper. "He's coming."

Soft hair, red and golden brown spills over a creamy shoulder. Her gold necklace, M for mother, M for Mary, dangles on the floor.

A creak behind me.

"Come back. Come back to me."

My vision clears. Brown eyes laced with gold study my face. "You okay, baby?" His soft, gentle tone chases the flashback away. Max. My Max. Not the voice in the shadows. His face is etched with concern, not anger. I am safe. I am wanting.

"I need you."

He hesitates. "What happened?"

"Nothing. Just…lost in the moment."

His brow furrows, and then he slides his hand under my back, arching me up toward him. He takes my mouth and plunders his way to the back of my throat. His fingers dip inside me, pounding in and out harder than I ever thought possible. His thumb circles closer and closer to where I want it to go.

"Give it up to me," he murmurs against my lips. "Give me everything. Surrender to me." He thrusts his fingers deep and slides his thumb over my sweet spot. Finally, I break with a shriek, falling to pieces, as a fireball of pleasure explodes inside me and wave after wave of scorching heat carries me away.

Before I have time to recover, Max has sheathed himself. He braces his forearms on either side of my head and enters me in one hard thrust. He angles himself to hit my sensitive spot, and I grow even slicker and hotter than just moments ago. Pleasure pain sears through me. Erotic. Unfamiliar. I want to get away, but his hips keep me open to him, and his weight pins me to the bed.

He pulls back and then moves inside me, in and out with gentle thrusts. My sex pulses and throbs, and I build again. Max presses deeper, filling me, taking my breath away. I close my eyes and give myself up to him with a moan.

"That's it, baby." He changes to a hammering pace and catches my nub gently between his fingers. One stroke and I am undone. My sex closes around him. My body tightens and pleasure sears through me. Max loses his own control. He roars his climax, the sound drowning out the echoes of my release.

Moments later, Max releases my hands and lies on the bed, pulling me across his chest. For the longest time I can't move, a combination of exhaustion, confusion, and shock. My mind churns, trying to make sense of the hottest and most disconcerting sex I've ever had.

Max strokes his hand up and down my back. "You did well."

His words squeeze my heart and relieve the ache, but now there is something new. A sense of disquiet. He has awakened something in me, deep and dark, and it wants to rock my world.

"You're so quiet." Max chuckles. "No jokes or smart remarks. Where is my Makayla?"

"I don't know," I answer honestly. "Lost, I think."

I try to pull away but Max tightens his arms around me. "I have you, baby. I won't let you go."

"Makayla. Come back here." The voice gets louder and louder. I tremble on the floor beside Mama. Why is she sleeping when Dad is so angry? She knows what he will do.

I shake her, gently at first and then harder. She doesn't wake. Something is wrong. I kneel beside her and catch sight of the gash on her head. Blood trickles out. She needs a doctor. I don't know how to fix her.

"Mama. Get up. He has a bat this time; the one Grandpa Joe gave me for my fifth birthday last year. And he smells of that smell. We have to run."

Mama doesn't move. Something is wrong. Mama said if something bad happened to her I should call 911. Is this what she meant?

"Makayla. Where are you, girl? I would never hurt you. I just want to talk."

I peek around the corner. His face wavers from round and bloated to square and defined. His hair darkens from auburn to brown. But his eyes remain black, hard, and cold.

———

Pulse racing, I jerk out of my nightmare and take a deep breath. My eyes slowly adjust to the dim light. The first fingers of the day creep through the blinds, gliding over the dark, cherrywood furniture in Max's massive bedroom. Beside me, Max breathes the slow, steady rhythm of sleep.

I ease myself away from his warmth and sit on the edge of the bed, my arms wrapped around my sweat-drenched body in a tight hug. I need to get out of here. Now. I tiptoe across the floor, grabbing my clothes and my purse along the way. By the time I reach the bedroom door, I am fully dressed, purse in hand, torn panties scrunched in my fist. I take one last look at Max asleep on the bed behind me and then I close the door with a gentle click.

My heart pounds as I cross the great room toward the door. *Please don't let him wake up. Please don't let him wake up.* Four weeks ago, I could never ever have imagined I would be sneaking out of a man's house after a wild night of sex. But four weeks ago, I had not met Max.

I lean against the front door and slip on my shoes. Will he be angry when he wakes up and finds me gone? Disappointed? Will he care? Would he understand my confusion, the maelstrom of emotions swirling through my brain, or the black hole sucking at my chest?

"I'll drive you home, Miss Makayla." Colton appears in the hallway, fully dressed, coat and keys in his hand.

I gasp and stagger back, my heart pounding. Where did he come from? Why is he dressed and ready to go?

"It's okay." I wave him away. "I saw a bus stop down the hill. It's almost time for the early morning bus. I didn't mean to disturb you."

He gives me a warm smile. "I was already up. It's no trouble at all. In fact, I insist. I am certain Mr. Huntington would terminate my employment without hesitation if he found out I had let you go home alone."

Colton or the bus ride of shame? Not much of a choice. I swallow hard and nod.

Colton leads me to the four-car parking garage and starts up a black SUV. As we pull away from the house, a light goes on. My heart races and I silently urge Colton to put his foot on the gas. If it is Max, I'm sure I'll find out soon enough.

We drive in comfortable silence through the empty streets. I lean my head against the window and bite my lip to fight back the tears. Why am I crying? We had wonderful, sweet, intimate sex and then we had rough, mind-blowing sex in which Max manipulated my body, my mind, and awakened something in my very soul.

A sob catches in my throat and Colton reaches over and gives my hand a quick, gentle squeeze. "Don't give up on him."

He says nothing else for the rest of the trip. Not even good-bye.

Friday morning passes in a blur. Charlie and I whisper through the public relations course we are forced to take every six months, sharing details of our plans for the afternoon off the hospital gives all staff on training days. I say nothing about what happened after the gala. I say nothing about Max. For the first time ever, Charlie doesn't push for details. Maybe he can sense I am so close to the edge, I might crack.

After lunch he drives me to La Sanctuaire, Amanda's favorite spa, located in the heart of the Marina District. Still distraught after Jake's unexpected visit, she insisted I join her for a little beauty therapy to take my mind off Max.

After Charlie roars away in his rusted Ford Escort, I step through the frosted-glass doors into a haven of peace and calm. The soothing trickle of a waterfall echoes in the quiet space. Birds twitter in the background. The exotic scent of incense perfumes the air, and my skin glows golden under the soft lights. Tension eases from my muscles. The perfect place to regain perspective—at least until I have to see Max at the club tonight.

Amanda waves me over to the front desk and gives me a big hug.

"This is so nice of you," I say. "I'm sure your client expected you to use your vouchers for yourself on your afternoon off. What did you book for us? Massage? Pedicure? I could really do with some relaxation."

Amanda shakes her head. "You sounded so distraught this morning, I thought a massage might not be the best thing for you—too much thinking time involved. You need a distraction, so I booked something that will fully occupy your mind. Something I knew you would never do yourself."

My body tenses. "What?"

"A wax."

"What are we waxing?"

"It's a surprise."

"Is it going to hurt?" I ask, my voice rising in pitch. "Is that why you told me to have vodka for lunch?"

A beautiful, perfectly coiffed woman seats herself behind the desk and gives me an assessing look before turning her attention to Amanda. "*Bonjour*, Amanda. Eees thees the friend you told me about?"

Amanda nods and shoves me forward. "Mac, meet Giselle. She's one of the most experienced aestheticians at La Sanctuaire. She'll be looking after you today. She's French."

"I wouldn't have guessed."

"*Bonjour.*" Giselle holds out an elegant hand. Her nails are beautifully polished, something I dare never do with my nail-biting habit.

"Hi," I grunt through clenched teeth.

Amanda gives me a condescending pat on the shoulder. "She's a little nervous," she explains to Giselle. "She's never had anything waxed before."

Giselle stands up and peers over the desk. Her eyes travel the length of my body and linger on my bare legs. "So I see."

I narrow my eyes. Better to look natural than like some kind of painted doll. Does she draw her eyebrows on every morning?

Giselle ushers us through another set of glass doors and into the spa. "Zee Hollywood might be a bit much for a waxing virgin. Maybe we should start her off with a bikini wax?"

I freeze midstep. "What is a Hollywood?"

"She's tough," Amanda says to Giselle. "She can handle it."

"Handle what?"

Amanda wraps an arm around my shoulders. "You're going all the way. Dare to go bare. No point going through the pain if you leave anything behind."

I gasp. "She's going to take everything off? Down there?"

"You'll be fine," Amanda assures me. "It's all part of the plan."

"She eess so nervous," Giselle interjects. "It reminds me of my first wax when I was ten years old."

"Seriously?" I turn to Giselle. "You had something to wax down there when you were ten?"

"I'm French." Giselle huffs through her nose and leads us down a cream, tiled corridor.

"What plan?" I ask Amanda when Giselle is out of earshot.

"The assure-you-there's-nothing-wrong-with-liking-kinky-sex plan," she whispers.

"And this is going to be achieved by luring me to a spa on false pretenses and having me shorn like a summer sheep?"

Amanda laughs. "Don't get sarcastic with me. I know what I'm doing."

"I'm sure you do, but you can't help me. He makes me do things I don't want to do and he makes me like them."

"Then they aren't things you don't want to do," she answers. "They are things you have never thought of doing and can't believe you quite like."

Giselle leads us into a cozy room with cream walls, potted plants, and dim lighting. Not quite the shearing pen I had imagined. A partition separates two padded, beige spa tables. Giselle leaves us to remove our bottoms while she finds Amanda's aesthetician.

I strip down and ease myself onto the freezing cold, vinyl surface. Goose bumps erupt over my skin. "How am I supposed to position myself?" I call over to Amanda.

"On your back. Knees apart."

"Like a frog?"

She giggles. "Ribbet."

"I feel very exposed."

"You are exposed."

"I don't like to be exposed." I cover myself with a thin, paper privacy sheet.

"I know. That's why I thought this would be good for you. You'll realize you can't die from exposure."

"Max is all about exposure," I complain. "The minute I let my guard down he starts to push. I'm afraid to tell him anything in case it's used against me in some twisted way in the bedroom. When we were in the limo on the way to his place, after hotting it up in the boxing ring, I mentioned I like strawberry jam. Guess what? He decided to have a midnight snack—Makayla and jam."

Amanda snorts a laugh. "I told you at the beginning he was the kind of man who needs boundaries. If you don't set limits, one day he'll push too far."

"He already did."

Giselle returns with Amanda's aesthetician, Lulu, and two pots of what I assume to be boiling wax. She takes a seat beside me and puts the boiling wax within spilling distance. "I'm not so sure about this," I warn her.

"It's a little uncomfortable at first," Amanda admits. "But we'll be talking, so after the initial shock you won't notice."

"I won't notice when she pours boiling wax on my most intimate area and then rips it off?"

Giselle chortles and then whips off my paper privacy sheet. She takes one look at my nether regions and slaps a hand over her mouth.

"Eeek."

Eeek? Is that a French word?

"Don't you trim?" she asks, her face a mask of horror.

"Of course I trim." I bend forward to check out the situation down below. Neatly trimmed. Why all the theatrics? My thicket didn't scare Max away.

Giselle jumps up and disappears behind the privacy screen. "Lulu, darling, I need your shears."

Shears? My body tightens and I imagine Giselle hacking away at my lady garden with a giant pair of clippers, a wicked smile on her face.

She returns a moment later with a small pair of scissors and proceeds to snip off a few curls.

"In America, we call those manicure scissors," I inform her, in a clipped voice.

"In France, we call this *une épaisse tignasse*." She taps her scissors on my freshly trimmed mound.

I scowl at what must be an insult, although it sounds sexy when she says it. I should learn how to speak French.

Giselle sprinkles baby powder between my legs and then stirs her pot of wax with the zeal of a witch over a cauldron. I hear a ripping sound from behind the screen, and Amanda exhales loudly.

"I'm not into pain," I say to no one in particular.

"From what you've told me, I don't think Max is either," Amanda answers. "Just light bondage and domination stuff. He definitely has control issues."

"Amanda!" I shriek. "The stuff I told you on the phone this morning is PRIVATE."

"We're in an estrogen enclave. If you can't get good advice here, where can you go?"

Giselle raises an eyebrow as she paints hot wax over my mound. "Sounds like your man likes la BDSM."

I hiss in a breath at the initial burn, but it quickly fades to a tingling warmth. I manage to unclench my teeth to answer, "I wouldn't know. We never discussed la BDSM. But I don't think he's into that lifestyle, or if he is, he didn't mention it. I didn't see any dungeons or whips or crosses on the wall. I think he's just…very dominant and…adventurous in the bedroom."

Giselle presses white strips over the wax and pats them down. "You like to be adventurous in the bedroom?"

I shift around the table and scowl at the partition hiding Amanda from my wrath. "I don't really know. I'm not as *experienced as Amanda*." I shout the last few words.

Amanda just laughs. "If you keep going out with him, you will be."

Giselle checks her watch and tests the wax. "You like to give the man control?"

"I don't like to be bossed around."

"But in the bedroom," she persists, "do you like the man to be in charge?"

My body tenses. "I'm not really comfortable discussing this with a stranger."

Giselle pats me down below and chortles. "Do you allow strangers to touch you here?"

She touches me there. I guess that means we're friends.

"I don't know if I like him to be in charge even in the bedroom. I have issues with controlling men. I've never actually dated one before. I usually go for easygoing, even-tempered, B-type personalities."

"Yawn." Amanda fakes a yawn to go along with her insult. "Her boyfriends were so boring. Even she got bored of them. She would text me an hour into her dates and beg me to have an emergency so she could escape."

"Nice. Thanks for sharing. Lucky me to have such a discrete and understanding friend."

Giselle tugs on the edge of a white strip and I wince. She raises a painted eyebrow. "If it didn't hold some appeal, you would have run away screaming."

"I did run away. I didn't scream because I didn't want to wake anyone up."

"You can scream now." Her voice is calm, reassuring.

Riiiiiip. Brain freeze. Pain. Someone screams. Me. I just screamed. "You…you…horrible woman," I shout at Giselle.

Everyone laughs. "Is that the best you can do?" Giselle taunts.

She rips again. I roar. "Rah."

"Rah?" Giselle lifts an eyebrow. "Like a baby tiger?"

"That's all you get. I have manners."

Amanda laughs. "He wanted her to talk dirty. But she was too shy."

"Amanda!"

"Say it in French," Giselle offers. "Everything sounds better in the language of love." She says a few sentences in a low, sultry voice. My mouth drops open.

"So beautiful. What did you say?"

Giselle translates, and I suck in a sharp breath. "That's absolutely filthy."

"I will teach you. You will whisper in your man's ear and *voilà*. La sex."

"Sex is not really the problem," I inform her. "Now that I've been forced to bare my most intimate moments, I think the problem may be that he likes to be controlling all the time and I only like it…some of the time."

"In the bedroom!" Giselle says, as if she knew it all along.

For the next fifteen minutes, Giselle waxes and rips, over and over and over again until my throat is hoarse and tears stream down my face. At least I have overcome my good manners and reticence to talk dirty. By the time she tells me there is only one strip to go, I have called Giselle every filthy name I know.

Her cold fingers pat down over something cold fingers shouldn't touch. Good thing we're friends. "I always save the landing strip for last," she says.

I peer down below. Oh God. No. Not there. Not there. "Let's just stop now. I like this look. Sort of like a shorn sheep with a five o'clock shadow on his back."

Riiiiiiip.

"Ahhhhhgh." My scream strangles me. "No la sex. Never again. I'll never even be able to look at a man after this."

Giselle soothes lotion over the torture site. "Your man won't complain."

"He's not my man. I ran away. He'll probably never want to talk to me again. He'll think I'm a love 'em and leave 'em kind of girl."

"If you mean something to him, he'll come looking for you," Giselle says. "And when he does, you can beguile him with the new you." She holds a mirror in front of my nether regions and angles it for me to see. "*Finis!* What do you think?"

I gasp. "I look like a plucked chicken."

Giselle nods, her face grim. "Yes, you do. You should stay away from him for at least a day. This is not so appealing to men and not so pleasant when it comes to la sex."

"So, how do you feel?" Amanda emerges from behind her partition fully clothed and without a hair out of place.

"Exposed. It's not a comfortable feeling."

Amanda smiles. "Don't worry. It's worth it in the end."

Chapter 17

WHERE IT ALL FALLS DOWN

By seven o'clock I am at Redemption, bare, sensitive, and ready to work. For the first hour, I hide in the first aid room in case I bump into Max. If I wasn't so desperate for money, I would never have shown up tonight.

Rampage stops by to tell me Max is caught up in a business deal and won't be at the club tonight. My shoulders sag and I slump back in my chair. Thank God. Even after my chat with Giselle, I am still not ready to face him.

I open the cupboard to inventory the supplies for the tenth time that evening. A cough alerts me to Rampage's continued presence in the room.

"Was there something else?"

Rampage clears his throat. He smoothes the sheet on the bed. He polishes the doorknobs on the cabinet with his T-shirt. He leans against the door frame and tells me Homicide's wife has been at the club three times this week, and Homicide is now a contented man. Nudge, nudge. Wink, wink.

"I'm happy for him," I say.

Rampage sighs. "Guess I'd better get going." He turns and shuffle hops to the door.

"Something wrong with your leg?"

He whips around and smiles. "Yeah, doc. I think I twisted my knee."

Curious. I would have thought he would be disappointed—devastated even—to have an injury. An injury means less training time and fewer fights.

Rampage leaps up on the bed with an enthusiasm I have never seen in an injured fighter. While I examine his knee, he inveigles advice from me about how to win the heart of the fair Pinkaluscious. I am more than delighted to help him divert her attention from Max, even if he never wants to see me again.

If I can't have him, neither can she.

I tell Rampage I can't find anything wrong with his knee. He pats me on the back and assures me he won't hold it against me. He shuffle hops out of the room, this time favoring the opposite leg.

Hmmm.

Half an hour later, I am inundated with fighters suffering from injuries ranging from a sore finger to a splinter. For every fighter with a semiserious injury, I treat at least three more who present with fake injuries for the sole purpose of extracting relationship advice from me. Men, it seems, have as many issues and worries as women—maybe more.

After the club officially shuts down, the core members haul out the beer kegs, and I am invited to join the party. Rampage cuts loose and leads the Electric Slide in the ring. The Blade Saw—he insists I call him Blade Saw, even if it means putting up with my laughter—runs up and down the bleachers, screaming and punching his fists in the air every time he reaches the top.

We consume copious amounts of alcohol. Pinkaluscious and I become best friends. She gives me the scoop on Max's past relationships but says nothing about what happened between them. I become depressed and drink some more. I teach Eugene "Hammer Fist" Smits how to mambo. A few of the other fighters try to teach me some moves on the practice mats. Due to my inebriated state, I spend most of the lesson giggling on the floor. Rampage dares me to stop Blade Saw's incessant running by flipping my skirt and flashing my cheeks. I comply. Blade Saw stops and screams at my ass. It is the best party ever.

Max doesn't show at the club on Saturday either. My impromptu counseling service, however, is a huge success. I have to fight my way through the crowds of fighters outside my door to tend to actual physical injuries, including two broken bones and a dislocated shoulder. I give hugs and peck cheeks. I squeeze hands, and several times, I even wipe tears. I love my new job.

By the end of the evening I hate women. Why do we nag men when they come home from work and just want to sit in front of the television with a beer and a home-cooked meal? Why do we ask them to participate in household chores when there is a game on TV? Why don't we dress up in a French maid's outfit to vacuum the carpets? And what the hell is wrong with a quickie? I resolve to be different. But first, I will have to learn how to cook, clean, and give up orgasms.

I am invited to another party after the club shuts down. It is even better than the last one. Tequila replaces the beer kegs. I lead ten rounds of "Row, Row, Row Your Boat." Rampage and I do the Twist with the grapple dummies. Blade Saw teaches me to drink upside down. Hammer Fist breaks a board over my head. We all play strip poker. I lose hand after hand.

When I am down to my bra and panties, Max arrives. He looks yummy in his T-shirt and low-slung jeans, but maybe a little annoyed. I toast him by shooting tequila from my cleavage. Annoyed becomes angry.

Max stalks over to us. I tell him I just lost the last hand of poker. I ask him to help me undo my bra. His face turns an interesting shade of red. Or is it purple? Grown men shout and scatter, knocking over their chairs in the process.

Max picks up the card table and throws it across the mats. My sense of self-preservation kicks in. I jump up, fold my arms, and scowl. Max doesn't notice. He is too busy rampaging after his friends like an enraged bull. I wish I had a red cape.

"Leave them alone." I raise my voice. "We were just having fun."

"Get your clothes on. Go to my office. And stay there." He drives his fist into a punching bag.

My jaw clenches. "Not until you stop this. You are totally overreacting."

His voice turns to ice. "Get your clothes on. Go to my office. And stay there." He spins around and slams an elbow into one of the practice dummies hanging on the wall. Homicide laughs. Max takes a step toward him. Homicide screams and runs away.

"If you seriously injure any of them, I will never speak to you again." I stride across the mat and put myself between Max and a gasping Homicide. "So I took off a few clothes. These are your friends. If you can't trust your friends, who can you trust?"

"They are men," he barks. "I know what they are thinking, and if you even had an inkling of what that might be, you would have been in a cab and home hours ago. You are tempting enough sober and clothed. Now. Last time. Get your clothes on. Go to my office. And stay there."

"Make me." My hands clench into fists on my hips. My heart thuds in my chest. I stand my ground and glare at Max. Yay, for alcohol loosening my inhibitions! I am brave tonight.

The room stills. The fighters who haven't run away suck in a collective breath. Maybe challenging him wasn't such a good idea.

Max's eyes narrow. His body tenses. He stalks toward me, scoops me up, and throws me over his shoulder like a sack of rice.

"Put me down." My efforts at escape are futile. He has my legs pinned tight, and the thud of my fists on his back does not even warm his skin.

When we reach his office, he dumps me unceremoniously on the couch and stands in front of me, his massive arms folded. "Stay."

"No." I push myself to my feet. Max steps in front of me to block my way.

"Are you going to run out on me again?"

Guilt makes me immediately contrite. My cheeks flame. "I'm sorry I left. It was all too much. I was…overwhelmed."

He cocks an eyebrow. "*You* were overwhelmed?"

I shrug. "Everything you do overwhelms me. You're big. You're strong. You're covered in incredible tattoos. You ride a monster motorcycle. You have a tendency to glare and shout and stomp around when things don't go your way. You're bossy and controlling. You take overprotectiveness to the extreme. But even with all that, I think I can handle you."

He walks across the office and swings the door closed so hard the pictures on the wall rattle. "You can handle me?"

I grab a blanket from the couch and wrap it around myself. "I think I can handle you because inside you are caring and compassionate and funny and sweet. And I like that you are protective and possessive. And I like that it's not just about me. You're a great teacher. You look after your guys. You are the first one on the floor when someone is hurt. You know who needs you to pull your punches and who needs you to let go." I cross my fingers behind my back and meet his gaze. "Like now. You weren't going to hurt anybody, were you?"

His face softens the tiniest bit. "Maybe not."

"But most of all, when I've asked you to back down, you backed down. Except today."

"You were standing half naked in a room filled with drunk guys. There is nothing you could have said that would have stopped me from taking you out of there. You were in danger."

My cheeks flame. "Maybe not the most sensible thing I've done."

"Definitely not."

"Where it all falls down…" I continue at double speed to hide my embarrassment, "and what I can't handle, is in the bedroom."

Max freezes. "The bedroom?"

I twist the blanket in my hands and study the tiles on the floor. "I like it when you…um…take charge. It makes me…well…hot. But the fact that I like it scares me. What if that means I like you to be controlling outside of the bedroom? What if I stop asking you to back down when you cross the line? I can't let that happen. I can't ever put myself in that situation." I cut myself off before I give myself away by saying "again."

Silence.

I look up. Max is studying me, thoughtful, intense. "What happened to you, baby?"

My heart thuds in my chest. *Nonononono.* I didn't want to have *this* conversation. I don't talk about what happened. Ever. It's a family secret. Part of it even from me.

"Nothing. I was just trying to tell you how I feel."

He reaches over and tugs on the blanket, drawing me to him like a fisherman reeling in a fish. With a sharp yank, he unravels me and folds me in his arms. "Something happened to you that made you afraid to embrace who you are."

"I know who I am." I squirm, trying to get away, but Max tightens his hold and rests his chin on my head.

"I'm not so sure you do," he says. "But I'll tell you what I know. You are different from any other women I've been with. You don't listen to me. You won't do what I say. You won't do anything you don't want to do, and once you've made up your mind about something, you won't change it. It is irritating as hell, but I admire your strength and conviction. You are caring, compassionate, sweet, and damn sexy. You live life. You experience it. But you do it on your own terms. I don't think a woman like that ever has to worry she might find herself in a situation she doesn't want to be in."

"Are you talking about me?"

Max chuckles. "Yes, baby. I'm talking about you."

"I don't think you know me at all. The guys I went out with were all nice guys, but boring and dull. I gave up a chance to go to medical school, and now I'm stuck in a dead-end job. Does that sound like someone who is living life?"

"It sounds like someone who doesn't know what they want. But when you do know what you want, you take no prisoners, and along the way, you enjoy the ride."

The fact he has spent any time thinking about me, analyzing me, makes my toes curl.

"Why aren't you angry I left yesterday morning?"

He pulls away and cups my jaw with his palm. "I told you I could never be angry with you. I was frustrated and disappointed with myself that I had pushed you so far that you felt you had to leave. I've never had a woman walk out on me, and you walking out felt like being stabbed in the gut. If Colton had not come home when he did, I might have destroyed a good portion of the house. He convinced me you just needed some time, and by the end of the day I thought he might be right. I pushed you too hard. I didn't consider your level of…inexperience."

I bristle. "I'm not that inexperienced."

Max chuckles. "Trust me, you are. But I'm not complaining."

Apparently not, since his hands have somehow found their way to my breasts and he is kneading them so gently I want to scream.

"You have beautiful breasts," he murmurs. "But they are only for me to see. If anyone had touched you, I can assure you I wouldn't have been pulling any punches."

"Men are hardwired to like any and all breasts."

Max leans over and draws my nipple into his mouth. "Not true. I have no interest in doing this to any breasts but yours." He nips gently and I gasp.

"I'll bet you say that to all the girls."

Max chuckles. "What girls?"

"All the girls you've dated. Sandy told me you had been with over almost thirty women in the last three years. She says you like a taste, but you don't want the main course."

"If I had been with thirty women in three years, I doubt I would have had time to run two businesses, much less leave my bed." He teases my other nipple into a tight, hard peak with his finger and thumb. My knees shake.

"I don't just want to be an amuse-bouche," I whisper.

Max hugs my face in his warm hands. "You are my amuse-bouche, my appetizer, my main course, and my dessert." He backs me up to the couch and presses me down to sit. With easy grace he kneels between my legs and slides his hands up the insides of my thighs, easing my legs apart. "Open for me, baby."

My panties dampen and I widen my legs. God, the things he says make me almost crazy with lust.

"You are my cheese sandwiches, pizza, and mashed potatoes with lots of butter," he whispers, brushing his lips softly over my ear. "You are my salmon mousseline, oysters in sea foam, frilled cod, and flying beets."

"Don't mention the beets," I giggle. "I still have nightmares."

Max nibbles my earlobe and traces lazy circles up the insides of my thighs. "You are the richest chocolate, the most decadent dessert, the smoothest coffee, and the most intoxicating wine." He kisses his way down my throat and circles each of my nipples with his tongue. My body melts and I arch my back, offering more.

"You, Makayla Delaney, are a buffet of sensual delights. A feast for my eyes, my ears, my hands, my nose, and my tongue." He slides his finger over my panties and brushes it gently over my sweet spot. I suck in a breath and my thighs clamp onto his hips.

"So responsive," he murmurs.

"You forgot ice cream," I point out. "If anything, I want to be your ice cream."

A wicked smile curls his lips. He points to a small bar fridge in the corner. "I have ice cream in the freezer. I bought it for you."

I lick my lips. "What are we waiting for?"

"We're waiting for you to get your ass off the couch and bring it to me." He pushes himself to his feet and pulls me up with him. Spinning me around, he smacks my bottom. Hard. "Go."

"Max!"

"Now I know you like it, baby, there will be no holding back." He tugs off his T-shirt and tosses it to the floor. I pause midstep to ogle the rippling muscles and the brush of dark hair running across his chest and down below his belt. He is a perfect canvas for the beautiful tattoos scoring his skin—not failures but works of art.

His eyes narrow. "Now."

"Woof," I grunt, feigning annoyance with a frown and a hand on my hip.

Max undoes his belt and shoves his jeans over his lean thighs to reveal the massive erection straining against his boxer shorts. Everything inside me turns liquid with arousal.

"If you're fast enough, I'll give you a bone."

"MAX!" My cheeks burn and I race for the fridge. Behind me, Max roars with laughter.

A minute later, I return with the tub of Chunky Monkey. "Do you have a spoon?"

"We won't need a spoon. I want my Makayla *à la mode.*"

My breath catches in my throat. "Which part of Makayla do you want *à la mode?*"

Max scoops me into his arms. "All of her."

He carries me and the ice cream to his big oak desk. With one sweep, he knocks everything to the floor—papers, files, pens, even a coffee cup. He seats me at the edge of the desk and grabs a pair of scissors from one of the drawers.

I scramble back on the cold, wood surface. I've had enough of sharp objects near my intimate areas. "What are you going to do with those?"

He slides the scissors along my skin, first one hip and then the other, cutting my panties in half.

"Nice," I huff. "You owe me so many pairs of panties it's not even funny."

Silence.

I look up. Max is looking…down there. He isn't breathing. I follow his gaze and remember my Friday afternoon activity.

"Surprise," I whisper.

"Makayla, baby, what did you do?" Max drops into his desk chair and continues to stare. I shiver and ease my legs together.

"Don't close your legs when you're with me," he murmurs absently. My legs jerk open. Moisture floods my sex. Does he have a script of things to say that arouse Makayla beyond belief?

"You don't like it? Amanda thought it would be a good experience."

"Fuck." He rakes his hand through his hair. "I liked you the way you were before, but this"—he exhales—"has certain advantages."

Not really the enthusiastic reaction I had hoped for. I haven't really checked out the situation below in any detail since yesterday. Maybe I didn't wait long enough. Maybe I've still got the plucked chicken look going on. I slide my fingers down and have a little feel.

Max inhales sharply. His hands grip the arms of the chair so tight his knuckles are white. "What are you doing?" His voice is a low, husky whisper.

"Touching myself."

The sound that erupts from his throat is a cross between a moan and a growl.

Hmmm. He likes that.

Keeping my eyes fixed on Max, I slick my fingers through my folds. My skin is so soft and smooth. I could touch myself for hours. Max had better get with the program or that's what I'll have to do. His body tenses and stills. He is either frozen into inactivity or he is about to pounce.

He swallows hard. "Stop, baby."

"A little late for that now," I groan. My finger slides over the little bundle of nerves already begging for attention. Watching Max watching me is arousing beyond belief, and I am building so fast I have no desire to stop.

"Aaaagh." Max jumps up from his chair, grabs my wrists, and pushes me back on the desk. The cool wood soothes my burning skin, but the press of Max's hardened length against my sensitive nub is almost unbearable. I rock my hips against him and moan.

"I need you inside you me. Now."

"You are irresistible and uncontrollable." Max scrapes his hand through his hair. "What are we going to do with you?"

I grit my teeth and writhe on his desk. "I'll give you three guesses."

He draws in a ragged breath and yanks open one of the desk drawers while still holding my wrists over my head. "I have a better idea." He pulls out a coil of soft rope and leans over my body to tie my wrists together.

"You always seem to have a rope handy. I, myself, keep only pens and paper in my desk, but maybe I should throw in some rope in case of emergency."

He snorts a laugh and runs his hand under the ropes to ensure they aren't too tight. His erection is now pressed so firmly against my nub I'll be able to get off with just a few strokes. I plant my heels on his desk and grind against him.

"Christ, Makayla. Stop. I'm going to lose control."

"Join the club."

"No." He pulls away and takes a few deep breaths. "I want ice cream." He rips open the container and swirls his finger inside.

"You don't want ice cream," I groan. "It's full of sugars and unnecessary fats. You want sex. With me. Here. Now."

Max gives me a wicked grin and paints cold, sticky circles around my breasts and over my nipples.

"Ahhh." I arch my back and my nipples tighten into rock-hard peaks. Max leans over and draws one into his mouth, licking and sucking until I am writhing on the desk.

"Stop. Stop. Stop. Please. I don't want to wait anymore."

He stops his incessant licking and glances up at me. "Do you need to use your safe word?"

I narrow my eyes at the hint of challenge in his voice. If he can hold out, so can I. "No. I'm fine. Just practicing for later."

He sucks. I wiggle. He bites. I writhe.

"Hmmm." Max finishes his ice cream with a final lick. "I can't enjoy my ice cream when my dish is squirming underneath me."

"I'll be still. I promise."

He gives me a cheeky grin. "Yes, you will." He uncoils more rope and dangles it above me, and then his smile fades. "Are you okay with this, baby? I went too fast with you before. I don't want to—"

"If you don't tie me up right now, I'm going to take care of things myself," I snap. Seriously? What does a girl have to do around here to get a little loving?

Ten minutes later, I lie trussed on the desk like a Thanksgiving turkey. Soft ropes around my thighs, ankles, and waist are tied to hidden D-rings on the desk, which hold my legs up and open. Where does a person get a desk with D-rings embedded all over it? How many women has he trussed in his office while pretending to do the club accounts? Most importantly, when do I get my stuffing? I could ask, but I don't want to know if the answer isn't NOW. I squeeze my eyes shut. I can't bear to even imagine how I look. The position is definitely not forgiving of my love of desserts.

"You don't actually have to do this," I whine. "I want sex. Right now. You don't have to work for it."

Max chuckles and sits down in his big leather chair. "I can control you better this way. I can give you more pleasure than you ever thought possible."

"Modest, aren't we?"

He pulls his chair right up to the desk. "Do you know how hot you look? You have such a pretty pussy." He slicks a finger through my folds and spreads my wetness along my inner thigh. "Your body is on board. Time to free your mind."

My eyes slit open just as he dips his finger in the ice cream. He paints a cold, sticky line down my throat, around each breast, and over my abdomen. A shiver races down my spine as the ice cream melts and trickles over my skin like the soft brush of feathers.

Max tips the ice cream container and pours creamy liquid into my belly button and down over my mound. Cool, little rivers trickle through my folds with soft, gentle, sensual tickles.

"This position is particularly good for eating ice cream." Max peppers little kisses along the insides of my thighs. "Especially when there is nothing in the way."

"You're not—"

Max bends down and licks the ice cream from my throat. His tongue laves its way around my breasts, pausing only to suckle my nipples, before continuing its featherlight descent down my body. His soft lips brush over my abdomen and then press against my mound. Anticipation ratchets through me.

"My favorite part is coming next," he whispers. "Be very still."

As if a trussed turkey can move.

He blows a warm breath over my mound and then his five o'clock shadow scrapes over my now ultrasensitive spot. I gasp and rock my hips against him.

Max chuckles. "If you're going to react like that before I even get where I want to go, I'll have to restrain you further."

More restraint? My heart won't be able to handle it. "This is good," I pant. "I'll be still."

He studies me and his eyes twinkle. "No you won't." He bends down and strokes his tongue through my folds and up over my throbbing bundle of nerves in one long, wet, sensuous sticky lick.

I shriek. My hips jerk but are held fast by the restraints. Bolts of white lightning shoot through my veins.

"Did you like that, baby?" He settles himself between my legs and brushes tiny kisses over my sex. I moan and pull myself closer to his tormenting tongue with my heels.

"Behave," he whispers. His breath is hot and moist, and I whimper my need.

Max groans. "You know I can't resist when you make those sounds."

I giggle and whimper again.

"You do like to live dangerously," Max rasps. His tongue slides over my folds and circles my sensitive nub. Before I can jerk up, he grabs my hips and holds me down, his palms pressing against my hip bones and his fingers brushing lightly over my abdomen. "You are mine to pleasure now."

"Yours," I breathe. My body melts under the gentle ministrations of his tongue.

He slides a finger deep inside my entrance. All coherent thought flees from my brain. He teases and torments, his tongue circling my sweet spot with lazy little licks, but never on the one place I want him to go.

I want to touch him. I tug on the restraints holding my wrists, but I can't get free. Blood roars through my ears. My heart thunders in my chest. I squeeze my eyes shut and suck in a breath through frozen lungs as darkness claws at my brain.

"You had your chance, Makayla. I'm coming for you now."

He is close. Just in the other room. My lungs burn from trying to keep quiet. He steps on Susie's doll and it starts to cry. Where is Susie? Is she still hiding upstairs? Or did she get out of the house like Mama said we should?

"Mama. Pleasepleaseplease wake up."

"There you are," he barks. "Get away from her."

His big hand grabs me from behind, jerking me into the air. I scream and kick. My foot hits something soft. He grunts and drops me. I fall on Mama's arm and she groans.

Run. I should run. But I can't leave Mama. She needs me.

I crouch beside her facing him and hold up my little hands. "Don't hurt us. Please."

The sound he makes, something between a choke and a sob gives me the courage to look up, but I don't know that face. Dark hair, dark eyes. Familiar.

He grabs my shoulders and shakes me. "I would never have hurt you but…"

"Let me go."

"You made the wrong choice." He grabs me and throws me through the air. I am falling, falling…

Someone far away is talking. His voice is smooth and soft. Comforting. He asks me something about a safe word. What is safe? Warm arms wrap around me. Hold me. Catch me. The scent of soap and spicy citrus cologne brings me back. Max.

"You're, okay, baby. I've got you."

When I open my eyes, Max is studying me. His eyes are tight; his brow creased with concern. The ropes are gone. I am free.

"What happened?" he asks

"I need you," I whisper. "I need you now."

He shakes his head. "Not this time. I want to know what's going on with you."

I shrug. "Sometimes I get flashbacks of my childhood. It's no big deal. I'm fine, really. Well, actually, not fine. I need to be close to you. No games. Just you."

Max's brow furrows in consternation. He takes a deep breath and shakes his head. "I don't want to do anything to hurt you, baby."

"You're hurting me by not doing anything." A groan tears through me. "Please, Max. I'm not going to run away this time."

He draws in a ragged breath and kisses me softly before sheathing himself. He grips my hips and enters me in one hard thrust. I arch up my body to take more of him. I am so deliciously, completely filled.

"Ah, baby. So hot. So wet."

I wrap my legs around him, holding him deep. My body trembles with need. With a groan, he withdraws and then pushes forward, driving into me. Faster. Harder. He gives me what I need. I build quickly, and when my body stiffens, he slicks a finger over my throbbing nub and I fall over the edge. Pleasure crashes over me, sweeping me up in a rush of sensation so intense, a shriek rips from my throat. Max stiffens, and his fingers dig into my hips. He comes with a roar, hard and fast and deep inside me.

For the longest time neither of us moves. I am sated and warm with Max lying on top of me. Finally, he pushes himself away to dispose of the condom. When he returns, he carries me to the couch, wraps me in the blanket, and holds me in his arms.

"That's twice, baby. Tell me what happened."

"I don't know," I lie.

He stares into my eyes and shakes his head. "You do know. I can see it in your eyes. Tell me. I'm here for you."

I bury my forehead in Max's chest and breathe in his scent of sex and musk and soap. I don't want to scare him away with my half-formed memories or my troubled past. I don't want to relive the nightmare. I want to move on. Forward, not back. With Max.

"It's nothing. It's all new to me so I got a little scared."

Max tucks his finger under my chin and tilts my head back. He stares into my eyes and his smile fades. "I trust you, baby. I trust you to tell me if there is something I need to know. The last thing I ever want to do is hurt you."

Funny. That's what my father said before he threw me into the wall.

Chapter 18
FROWNS

It's Monday morning and Sergio is in a terrible mood. After we exchange greetings, he snarls and growls about payments and due dates until I cut him off.

"I thought you'd be happy I sent in the payment. You're that much closer to getting the Porsche." I turn all the pens in my pen holder to point up and mentally calculate the number of green slips it might cost me.

"Unfortunately, your payment was insufficient," he says. "I went through the financial documents you sent me—rental agreement, bills, expenses—and by my calculation, your monthly payment should be higher." He tells me how high. My hand flies to my mouth, knocking over the pen box. A sea of pens washes over my desk. Points sideways.

"You've got to be kidding. I made a rough calculation myself. I should be paying less not more. Your new payment leaves me without money for rent, food, or expenses."

Sergio sighs. "I'll email you my calculations. You'll see I was doing you a favor by asking for the minimum payment. Now I'm forced to ask for more. This is what happens when you try to be too clever, Ms. Delaney."

"You can't do that." But already my brain is scrambling to find a way out. Maybe Max will let me work at the club every night. Maybe not. He's already paying me way more than I'm worth.

"I can do anything I want."

"I'm going to appeal," I say. "I want to speak to your manager."

"Go ahead. The appeal process is all set out on our website." Shouts echo on Sergio's end of the line. Someone yells "Code Blue."

"Are you at a hospital?"

Sergio growls and I hear a door slam. "Where I am doesn't concern you. The only thing that should concern you is paying me."

"Sorry." I immediately regret my curiosity. But why is he calling from the hospital? Again? Something about this whole thing is definitely off.

"I have to have that payment tomorrow, Ms. Delaney. Even if you appeal today, it will take several days to process your request."

"I'm going to call my friend. She's a lawyer. She'll tell me if what you're doing is legal."

Sergio gives a bitter laugh. "Go ahead. Even if I've crossed the line, what are you going to do? You don't have the money to start a lawsuit. And even if you find someone to take your case for free, it will be at least a year, maybe two, before you get into court, by which time the interest and penalties will have increased and your credit will be ruined because the default will continue to show up on your credit report. It's a no-win situation for you, Ms. Delaney. No. Win. Just pay the money."

His last few words come out in a shout. So emotional. So unlike the Sergio I've come to know. Where is the boredom? The professional detachment? The compassion and humor?

"I thought we were friends, Sergio," I whine. "Give me a week. I'll have the money."

Sergio sighs. "I have spent more time talking to you than all my debtors combined. I have bent over backward for you. I can't do any more than I have already."

"Bend just a little further."

"From what I know of you, Ms. Delaney, you wouldn't pay the price. You're just a little too straight up. You play by the rules. You don't take risks."

Straight up? After being with Max? I think not, but I'm not sharing those thoughts with Sergio of all people.

"What does a joke buy me? I have a feeling you might be in need of a joke today."

The sound Sergio makes, almost like he is choking back a sob, makes my heart lurch. He's not himself. He's in the hospital. Clearly distressed. Already I know I'm going to regret what I'm about to do.

"You know what, Sergio. I'm going to tell you a joke anyway. If you want to give me that extra week after I'm done, I'll be very grateful. But if not, I hope it brightens your day because it sounds to me like you need some cheering up."

He draws in a ragged breath. "You're hard on my mind, Ms. Delaney, and hard on my heart. You're like the mythical debtor everyone has heard about, but no one has seen. The debtor who sends presents at Christmas and flowers at Easter. Pleasant, cheerful, accommodating—"

"Desperate and broke."

Sergio sobs a laugh. "You have your week and you have bought yourself some goodwill and a smile you can't see. Tell your joke, Ms. Delaney. You're right. I could use some cheering up."

I mentally sift through my joke collection to find something that will make him laugh. Aha. I have it. I take a deep breath. "A debt collector parks his brand new Porsche outside his office to show off to his colleagues—"

⸺ⁿⁿⁿⁿ⸺

By the end of my day, I have filed an online complaint with his company, yelled at a lady at the Education Commission who insisted they had no record of my change of address, and called two consumer help agencies who advise me Sergio has not done anything wrong. Amanda is in trial but she promises she'll look into the case as soon as the trial ends. The Better Business Bureau and the Federal Trade Commission recommend several avenues of appeal, but by the time I finish talking to them, I have almost lost the will to live.

Thank God for Charlie. If he hadn't covered for me while I obsessed all day, I would have had a desk full of green slips and probably a pink dismissal slip too.

The easiest solution would be to make the payments, and for that I need a second job. Not so easy to get in this economic climate. I count sixty-seven job applications in my outbox and sixty-seven corresponding rejections in my inbox. My only hope is Redemption.

But can I ask Max for more work?

What if he asks why? I can't tell him how bad the situation is. And I don't want him to think I'm interested in him only for his money or that I'm using him to get a job. Still, the lure of working at Redemption with Max and his fighters is hard to resist.

I swallow my pride and text Max.

Are u busy tonight? Need to talk to u

At work. Negotiating a deal. Might go late. Tomorrow?

Can't wait

Should I be worried? **frowns**

☺

☺?

Turn that frown upside down

Will send Lewis to pick you up. You can wait at my office

*Looking forward to seeing ur office **jumps up and down***

Looking forward to seeing you **does not jump up and down because in meeting**

What should I wear 2 ur office?

Nothing

*Naughty Max **shakes finger***

Hard Max **shakes something else**

gasps

That's what I like to read

So...nothing? Seriously?

Nothing. Seriously

What about ur clients?

Will deal with clients

U r kidding right?

Max?

Max?

An hour later I step out of the elevator and into the offices of IMM Ventures, situated on top of a historic building in the South of Market neighborhood of San Francisco. I am greeted by the scent of lemon polish and a sea of white, broken up only by the occasional exposed brick wall and the wood-beam ceilings. The furniture has none of the features I usually associate with furniture. Chairs and couches lack backs, arms, or cushions. Tables jut out from walls like planks from a pirate ship. The reception desk appears to hover in midair. The last vestiges of daylight filter through huge iron-latticed windows. It is minimalism to the extreme.

A tall, willowy receptionist wearing a skintight red dress rises from the floating desk to greet me. Her ultra chic blond bob swings gently as she walks across the wooden floor on four-inch stilettos. Her face is so perfect she doesn't need makeup. Or maybe she's wearing her makeup perfectly. Regardless, she shouldn't be here in Max's office. She should be on a runway somewhere far away. Like Milan. Or maybe the Moon.

"Mr. Huntington asked me to stay until you arrived, Miss Delaney." Her smile is as cold as my heart. Why couldn't he have hired a frumpy receptionist with unkempt hair and a couple of extra rolls? Maybe a mole on her cheek.

"Thank you for waiting." We shake hands, my soft, warm fingers closing around her long, bony ones. Her hand is so thin, I could probably break it with just one squeeze.

I imagine we say so much to each other with that handshake.

"So you're the new girlfriend?"

"Hands off, bitch. He's mine."

"I've been after him for months. I don't know what he sees in you."

"I'm naked under this trench coat."

"I'm not even worried. Look at you."

"Completely naked. Except for these heels."

"One month and he'll come running to me."

"Not after I take off this coat."

"Or maybe, he won't even wait."

"I'm going to make him suffer first."

"You're hardly a threat. Sniff."

"When I'm done with him, he won't even know you exist."

She breaks the shake first. "May I get you something to drink, Miss Delaney?"

"No, thank you very much, I had a drink in the *limo* on the way here."

"May I take your coat?" She gives me a tight smile.

"It's a bit chilly in here. I think I'll keep it on."

Pleasantries over, we share a glare and then she sighs.

"Well, I'll be going then. Do make yourself comfortable. The meeting is in the boardroom. You can see all the action from the reception area."

We exchange farewells. I hope I never see her again.

I take a seat on the most uncomfortable bench I have ever had the displeasure to sit on. The slab of cold, hard marble juts out from the wall like a gigantic tongue. But it does give me a good view of the glass-fronted boardroom. Max is sitting at a long, white table facing me. He looks mouthwateringly hot in his blue shirt and red striped tie. An assortment of suited businessmen are sitting on the other side of the table facing him. How did he get six men to all sit on one side of the table? Did he entice them with the view through the massive arched window in the brick wall behind him?

Max glances up and his lips curve into a faint smile. Other than that, he gives no indication he sees me.

My phone buzzes.

Hi baby. I like your coat

Not my coat. Colton chose it. You paid for it. Lewis brought it to me

You're wearing it

I didn't think you were serious

When it comes to you, I'm always serious

When it comes to u, I'm always shocked

Are you undressed to play after the meeting?

Maybe. Maybe not

frowns

You're cute when you **frown**

I stand up and stretch, letting my coat fall open just a tiny bit so he can see what isn't underneath.

You're cute when you do as I say and sit on the bench until I'm done
Not tonight
FROWNS

He should frown. It is his game, but this time we'll play by my rules. Bondage ice-cream sex on the desk has loosened my inhibitions, and tonight I'm going to fly.

Someone speaks directly to him, and he puts down his phone. I wander around the reception area looking at…nothing. There is nothing to divert the eye except the view. No pictures, no magazines, no television, no area rugs. Like the restaurant, the focus is on the food—or in this case, the work.

I glance over at the boardroom. Max is talking, but his eyes are on me.

Showtime.

My, it's getting hot. I fluff my hair and lean against the cool brick wall across from the board room. I unbutton the first button on my trench coat and fan myself. Still hot. I unbutton the second button and flap the coat to let cool air brush over my skin. No response from Max. I slide my hand into the coat and cup my breast.

My phone buzzes. I struggle to repress a smile.

What are you doing?
I'm hot
Turn down the heat. There's a thermostat at Cindy's desk
I like heat
AFTER the meeting

Someone hands him a file folder, and he tears his eyes away. I saunter over to Cindy's desk facing the boardroom and perch on the front. Hmmm. It's a bit too high for comfort. I drag her chair around and sit on the desk with one foot on the chair and one foot on the floor. I rest my elbow on my thigh in Rodin's "Thinker" pose. But I'm not thinking intellectual thoughts. I let my trench coat fall open, just enough to reveal the shadow of my modesty.

My phone buzzes angrily. This is just way too much fun. Why did I never do anything like this before?

What the FUCK are you doing?
Pondering where the thermostat might be
It's on the other side of the desk
Ooops. Silly me

I slide off the desk and spin around. The thermostat is indeed on the wall behind the desk. Why waste time walking around? I bend over and lean across the desk. I spread my legs for balance. I flip up the convenient back flap of the trench coat. Then I give a little wiggle. I am a bad, bad girl.

BUZZ

I am laughing too hard to answer the phone.

BUZZ

Also, I can't reach it in my current position.

BUZZ

I relent and push myself up. He is in a meeting after all. I should really turn it down. Maybe he's hot too. I check my messages.

STOP
STOP
STOP

I bite my lip to stifle my laughter and return his messages.

Bad Max. Shouty caps hurt my ears
What the hell has gotten into you?
Sorry, couldn't reach the thermostat
You're going to be a very sorry girl when I'm done here
Promises, promises
On the bench and don't move

Yeah. I'll do "on the bench." I undo yet another button on my coat as

I walk over to the marble slab. I am hot now, for real. He must know what his words do to me. I lie on my side, one leg out, one leg bent at the knee, shoe on the bench, hand propped up on my elbow in the traditional sex kitten pose. My coat slides over my skin, revealing things that are for Max's eyes only. The phone buzzes in my hand. Why did I never notice it had such a powerful vibration?

Behave. We're almost done

I stare at the phone. Suddenly, I have an idea. A delicious idea. A naughty idea. I send Max a text.

Call me. If I don't answer, call again

I turn the ringer to vibration and swing my legs down so I am sitting on the bench facing him. I part my legs. Max frowns. I slip the phone into my coat and secure it at the juncture of my thighs. Max's eyes widen. He chokes. One of his clients pushes a glass of water across the table. Max glares at me and shakes his head. I slide one hand into the coat and fondle my breast. He closes his eyes and sucks in his lips.

Then he calls.

The vibration isn't great. Not like my Rabbit. But it isn't bad. And coupled with the fact I am naked under the coat with six men in front of me who could turn around at any moment, I don't need much more to get off. I hope the phone is waterproof.

I roll my nipple between my thumb and forefinger. Zings of pleasure shoot to my core. I close my eyes and shift position. The slippery slide of the coat's silk lining brushes over my skin in a gentle caress. My body tightens. I've never brought myself this close this fast. I suck in a breath and press my lips together as I teeter on the edge. The sultry, strawberry taste of Vivacious Vixen lip gloss bursts over my tongue.

The vibrations stop. Damn. I pull out the phone and read the message.

ENOUGH

Ha. Ha. I don't think so. I put the phone on the bench and slide my hand into the trench coat. I stroke my sweet spot and my body tightens again. I should stop. What if someone turns around? But I can't stop. I am heady with the knowledge he wants me and can't have me. Aroused beyond belief. My head falls back and I slip one finger inside my sex. Jeez. I'm so wet.

The office door crashes open. The glass walls shake.

I whip my hands out of the jacket and sit up straight, eyes wide, innocence personified. Max stalks toward me, his face so taut, I can see the blood pounding through the veins on his temples. He grabs my arm and yanks me out of the seat.

Without so much as a hello, he drags me across the reception area and slams his hand on the elevator button. The elevator opens instantly as if it knows Max is no mood to be trifled with. He pounds on the ground-level button and the doors slide closed.

"Are you angry?" My blood still runs hot with desire. I place a tentative hand on his chest. He hisses in a breath and steps away.

"Don't touch me. Don't talk to me."

My cheeks flame. Uh-oh. Really angry. My stomach clenches. It was just meant to be a game.

The elevator reaches the ground floor. Max grabs my hand and pulls me through a maze of corridors until we reach a battered metal door. He throws the door open and I follow him out into a dark alley.

The streetlights from the main road lick the darkness but don't quite reach our toes. Although I can see cars and people, they can't see us. But I can see Max and he can see me. His eyes gleam under the soft faint exit light above the door, and he studies me, a predator assessing its prey.

My heart pounds so hard I fear it might break my ribs. Angry Max. Dark alley. Maybe I pushed him too far.

Suddenly I am up against the wall, the rough brick digging into my back. Max pins me, one hand on my chest, the other making fast work of the buttons and belt on the coat. He yanks it open, exposing me to his heated gaze. His eyes rake over my naked body as cool air brushes over my burning skin.

Fear and arousal blend into a potent cocktail of need. A whimper escapes my lips. In an instant, I am in Max's arms, my body pressed against his.

"I've never seen anything as fucking hot in my life. You were killing me in there, baby." He threads his fingers through my hair and yanks my head back. His kiss is hard, almost punishing, but quickly it gentles, softens. A tremor runs through me.

"So goddamned fucking sexy," he whispers against my lips. "I thought I was going to explode."

My body sags as relief courses through my veins. Not angry. Aroused. As am I.

Boldly I stroke my hand over his erection, hot and hard, straining against his fine wool trousers. "What a hard cock you have Mr. Huntington."

He sucks in a sharp breath and his body goes rigid. "What did you just say to me?"

I lean against him and press my lips against his ear. "I said you had a hard cock, and I want it."

"Fuck." He has a condom in his hand and his pants down before I can catch my breath.

"I thought you didn't like to talk dirty." His voice is rough, gravelly, and hoarse with need.

"I thought the circumstances warranted a little dirty talk. We are in a filthy, garbage-strewn back alley after all. You sure know how to show a girl a good time."

"Christ." He rips open the condom and sheaths himself. "Every time I think I've figured you out, you do something that makes me think I don't know you at all."

"I didn't know this about me either," I whisper. "You've made me into a wild, wicked, wanton woman."

He slides his hands under my bottom and lifts me. I wrap my legs around his body and the coat swings around us, hiding us from view.

"You were always a wild, wicked, wanton woman," he chuckles. "You just needed someone to set her free." He slides inside me with one long, hard thrust.

Oh God. So good. So big. So hard. I groan and tighten my arms around Max's shoulders.

A sharp nip on my lip makes me gasp, and then he thrusts his tongue inside me, easing it in and out with the promise of what is to come. The ache of need burns through my body. He pulls his lips away and drags his mouth over my nipple, teasing it between his teeth until it peaks. Then he nips gently, and my body turns liquid.

A thin whine escapes me. I manage one slide up and down before he pushes me against the wall and grabs my hips, holding me still.

"I won't last, baby. And you're not ready."

"I am ready. I've been ready since I put on that trench coat and walked into your office."

He slides his fingers between us and strokes around my swollen nub. "I want you to come as hard as I'm going to come. After what you pulled in there, I want to hear you scream."

His hot, wet mouth closes around my other nipple. He sucks it into a peak then bites carefully. Pleasure pain shoots to my core, and my sex clenches around him.

"God, baby, I like to feel your response." He bites again. I clench and moan.

"Please, don't torture me."

His eyes crinkle. "Almost there."

Another kiss, harder this time, demanding, possessing. Trembles start in my core and spread outward to my fingers and toes. My eyes slit closed and I rock my hips against him.

"Now, baby. Let's go for a ride." He moves. Finally. In and out, the rhythm of his thrusts sending shockwaves through my body, winding me tighter and tighter until my fingers are pressed deep into his flesh.

"Don't stop. Don't stop."

With a low laugh, he puts his hand between us and slides his thumb firmly up and around the aching bundle of nerves at my center. Up and around, over and over, slicking so near where I want him to go, I want to scream with frustration.

My voice becomes one long, uncontrollable whimper as he continues to pound into me. I am overwhelmed by sensation. The rough wall in my back, the cool silk brushing over my skin, the sharp tang of his cologne mixed with the sultry fetid scent of the alley, the sensual taste of him on my tongue, the intense, all-consuming need for release. My mind blanks.

"That's it, baby. Just feel." His fingers slide over my clit and he pinches. Hard.

Suddenly the alley sheets white and I explode. Spasms of intense pleasure rip through my body, and I arch my back and scream.

Max's mouth covers mine, swallowing the sound of my orgasm. His hands slide under my bottom and he drives farther, deeper, changing to a hammering pace. With one last forceful jerk of his hips, he groans and swells, pulsing against my sensitive, swollen tissue. Another wave of tingles rolls through my body.

He holds me tight against him and presses his forehead against mine.

"Christ, Makayla," he mumbles. "What you do to me."

What I do to him? What about what he does to me? Never in my wildest dreams would I have ever imagined having sex in a back alley with a man I know so little and care so much about.

After one last, soft, sweet kiss, he lets me down and we straighten our clothes. He leans against the wall and holds me, his chin resting on my head, as if he doesn't have a boardroom full of clients waiting for him. The traffic hums past, people laugh, a bird tweets overhead. We hold each other in comfortable silence until finally, he pulls away.

"You'll never get rid of me now," he says as we head back into the building.

"I wasn't planning to get rid of you. Who else will appreciate my new penchant for dirty talk?"

We reach the elevator and he spins me around to face him. "You said you wanted to talk about something."

My cheeks flame. Will he think I tried to seduce him to get my way? "I...um...it's not that important."

"It's important to me."

I bite my lip. "I...was wondering...if maybe you needed someone to do first aid at the club during the week, or even during the day on the weekend. If you did...I'm free. You wouldn't have to pay me what you paid me before. I'm not really worth that much. But—"

His eyes soften and he cups my jaw and strokes his thumb over my cheek. "You want to work more often at my club?"

I nod, not sure where he's going with this.

"Despite your issues with violence?"

I nod again. "Working on gym and training days isn't really a problem. The problem is watching the fights."

"So I would see more of you?"

My lips quiver. I hadn't really thought of that. "I suppose so."

"And this is a request you thought I might refuse?"

I shrug. "You might not need another employee or not want to take one on. It's just…I enjoy being at the club. I like being able to help people. I like the guys and I like spending time with you. But I understand—"

His hand fists in my hair and he tilts my head back, cutting me off with a gentle kiss.

"If you need money, just ask. But I know you're proud and if you want to work for it, you work as many hours as you need to. You are an incredible asset to the club. Everyone loves you. The pay stays the same."

My eyes fill and I try to pull away, but he cups my face with his hands and holds my gaze. "Anything you want from me, Makayla, baby, you can have."

Ah. So sweet. The moment is ruined only by the hum of a floor polisher, the ding of the elevator, and the slither of guilt up my spine. If I didn't need the money, would I have offered to work at the club? But more troubling, do I feel the same way about him?

Chapter 19
THIS ONE IS QUITE WET

FOUR DAYS LATER, I spill the entire debt collector story to Charlie over a box of donuts at a local donut shop. He offers to help. I refuse. My mother never once accepted money from friends or family when we were on our own, and I can't bring myself to do it either. Self-reliance is one lesson I learned well. I already feel like I'm betraying her by working for Max and being overpaid.

"So what are you going to do?" He licks each of his fingers before sticking them back in the box.

"I've got a second job at Max's club."

Charlie waggles his eyebrows and picks up a chocolate dip. "Why work for the billionaire boyfriend? Why don't you just hit him up for some cash? You could promise to work it off in the bedroom."

"He's not a billionaire." I bite into my sugary sweet honey glazed. "No private jet. No yacht. No helicopter. No glider. No security team shadowing his every move. He has a successful company, and he seems to be financially comfortable, but our outings so far have been pretty sedate. He's as close to a regular guy as they come." Except for the ropes and D-rings on the desk.

Charlie frowns. "I thought you said he had a butler and a chauffeur and a limo and a kick-ass pad."

I shrug. "He said he entertains a lot of clients. I think those are all business expenses. And his club is just a big warehouse. It isn't like those top-class MMA facilities with mirrored fitness studios and high-tech equipment. He's not really the type of guy to splash money around."

Charlie snorts a laugh. "That's why he blew one million bucks to keep you out of Doctor Drake's clutches at the auction."

"He bought a necklace."

"He bought you. A man spends money like that, a man thinks he owns you. Don't forget it." He licks chocolate off his fingers and pulls out a cruller.

The door opens and a cool breeze dissipates the thick yeasty smell of baking donuts. I shiver and shrug on my sweater. A man in a brown jacket with sandy brown hair takes a seat at the table beside us and orders a coffee.

"You still haven't told me where he's taking you tonight."

"The Symphony Gala." My lips quiver with a repressed smile, and I blow on my fingernails and rub them on my shirt.

Charlie's eyes widen. "No way! That's *super* swanky. I wouldn't call that sedate."

I grin and lean over the table. "I KNOW. I'm so excited. I've never been to a society event before. He's even buying me something to wear from a little boutique he knows."

"DO NOT drink anything." Charlie's smile fades and he waggles a finger at me. "You know what happens when you drink too much. You need to act classy. Don't embarrass him."

I lean back in my chair and sigh. "Don't be overly dramatic. I've matured since the beer pong incident."

Charlie snorts a laugh. "I thought you said he caught you playing strip poker on the weekend."

"That's different. I knew what I was doing. I can even remember some of it."

The man in the brown jacket chokes on his coffee and dabs at his lips with a napkin.

"Moving off the topic of my drunken exploits," I say, "you've been chomping at the bit to tell me something, so spill." I bite into a Bavarian cream and watch my thighs expand. Charlie licks his fingers and spears another chocolate dip.

"I slept with Doris."

"You're kidding!" I lean right over the table. "You and Big Doris?"

Charlie blushes. "We had a lot to drink at the Heart 2 Heart benefit. One thing led to another and suddenly we were in her bedroom."

I snort and spew donut across the table. "Naturally. After a woman slaps you in a public place for stealing a kiss, of course you would want to sleep with her."

"Anyhoo." Charlie leans in and breathes donut in my face. "This is where it gets really interesting."

"I was interested from the second you said you 'slept with Big Doris.'"

Charlie looks around and then takes a bite of his donut. "The minute the door closed, she was all over me. She tore off my clothes in a frenzy of lust and then she—"

"Big Doris?" I interject, more to save my innocent ears than for clarification.

Charlie nods.

"Big Doris tore off your clothes in a frenzy of lust?"

"Check it out." Charlie lifts his shirt and treats me to a view of his jiggly white belly covered in a smattering of hair, and eight long red streaks cutting across the middle.

"Holy cow."

He drops his shirt and lowers his voice. "She ATTACKED me like a wild animal."

"Did you call pest control?"

"I couldn't."

"Why not?"

Charlie's cheeks redden. "She had me in a…compromising position."

Oh God. All my stress and anxiety disappear in a snort of laughter. My head bangs on the table, and the man in the brown jacket drops his donut in apparent alarm.

"It's not funny," Charlie says, miffed. "I was afraid. She was totally out of control. She isn't sane."

I lift my head to wipe away the tears. "If you really thought that, you wouldn't have put yourself in a compromising position. I mean, who does that? Who puts their most precious and delicate…item in the jaws of a crazed wild animal?"

"A desperate man," Charlie moans.

"So after you extricated yourself from the compromising position, why didn't you throw her back into the wild?"

"She wanted to have sex."

"Seriously?" I widen my eyes in mock horror. "She is crazy."

Charlie frowns. "You don't know what it's like. I had a long dry spell. A parched man does not turn down a glass of water even if the glass is broken."

"So how was it?" I shouldn't, but I have to ask.

"Wild," he rasps. "But afterward, I snuck out."

"Smooth. Love 'em and leave 'em. You've become a real player."

"It wasn't like that." He leans forward and lowers his voice. "In the heat of passion, she called me by the wrong name."

"Oh. My. God. How crass. Whose name did she call?"

The door opens. Heads turn. Max appears in the doorway. He spots us and his eyes narrow. Charlie drops his donut. "Hot damn he looks so good in that suit."

"Paws off, tiger. He's mine. I can hardly wait to see him in his tux again."

Charlie dabs at his cheek with a napkin. "He's not looking too happy. Maybe he thinks I'm putting the moves on you, or maybe he doesn't like his girlfriends eating carbs."

My cell buzzes, but before I can check the message, a glowering Max is hovering over our table. The man in the brown coat looks up from his newspaper. His eyes widen when he catches sight of Max and he turns away.

"What the hell is this?" Max holds up his phone and I catch sight of a run of tweets.

"Hey!" I give him an encouraging smile. "You're finally on Twitter. Good for you."

"THIS." He holds the phone closer to us and Charlie whistles.

"Hey, Makayla, that looks like your ass."

Max shoots daggers at Charlie. "How would you know what her ass looks like?"

Charlie doesn't miss a beat. "I see it every weekend when we play strip poker."

Before Max can react, I snatch the phone and check out the picture. Yup. That's my ass. The picture is titled "Makayla's Ass" and is posted courtesy of @Toots69, who must have been at the Redemption party on the weekend when I flipped a cheek at Blade Saw.

"Looks like someone was drinking again." Charlie pokes me in the shoulder. "And you told me you had matured."

I pull out my own phone and check my messages. Oh God. So many. Everyone has seen my ass on Twitter—Amanda, Rob, all my house-mates, work colleagues, friends, my fifth-grade pen pal from Norway, Susie in London, and my cousin in Nebraska. I hate social media.

"It's trending," Charlie shouts, holding up his cell phone.

The man in the brown coat has given up any pretense of pretend-ing not to overhear. He stares at us, following our conversation with avid interest.

Max frowns. "What does that mean?"

"It means Makayla's ass is very popular and is going around the world at lightning speed." Charlie grins.

Max's jaw clenches so hard I fear he might break his teeth. "What the hell were you thinking? That's my ass out there."

Charlie chortles. "I like your purple panties, Huntington. They looked good with your green skirt."

Max leans across the table and grabs Charlie's collar. I jump up and push him away with two hands. "Max. Listen to me. I didn't post that picture on Twitter, and if you even understood how it worked, you would know that."

"Who posted it?"

"I don't know. Someone with the handle @Toots69."

"Aaaargh." Max slams his fist on the table so hard our mugs fly off and crash to the ground. Charlie's eyes widen and he squeezes my hand.

"I should have known she would do something like this," Max bellows. "And calling herself @Toots69!"

@Toots69 is a she? There was only one other *she* at the Redemption party besides me.

Everyone in the donut store pulls out a phone. No doubt @Toots69 is suddenly going to get a lot of followers, and my ass is going to get some extra viewings.

Max pounds his finger on his phone. Seconds later he holds his cell to his ear and shouts loud enough for everyone to hear, "What the hell were you thinking? You take it down right now. I don't care what you want. We're finished. I made that clear. And if you ever do anything to hurt her again, I will never—" He storms out the door and we miss the rest of the conversation.

"He's pissed." Charlie snatches the last donut. "He's going to yell at you next. Doesn't bode well for the evening."

I grab my sweater and slide out of the booth. "I can handle him."

Charlie raises an eyebrow. "You can always call me if you need a ride home."

"I can handle him."

"Don't drink anything until after he's blown off some steam. You know what you're like."

"I can handle him."

"Yeah? So why are you shaking so badly?"

"Take a deep breath, baby. The feeding frenzy is about to begin."

Max helps me out of the limo and onto the red carpet outside Davies Symphony Hall. Cameras flash and people stare, as San Francisco's high society parade down the sidewalk at one of the city's most anticipated society events. And me. Makayla Delaney. Imposter. What I wouldn't give to be home on my couch in my sweats eating ice cream. I concentrate on not catching my three-and-a-half-inch emerald stilettos on the carpet.

"Huntington, over here."

Max stops and turns us to the right, his hand firm around my waist. "Pose and smile," he whispers. Millions of cameras flash, and suddenly I can't see.

"Aaaagh. Turn off the sun." I throw my hand over my face to shield myself and Max grabs my arm and pulls it down. "They want to see your face, not your hand."

"I didn't realize a look of sheer terror would sell papers," I mutter under my breath.

Max gives my name to no less than a dozen reporters and introduces me as his girl. Usually, I like to be Max's girl. Today, however, the endearment grates on my nerves. In this strapless A-line taffeta and organza cocktail dress, my face caked in three inches of makeup, and my hair ironed and teased, all courtesy of the resourceful Eva and her swanky boutique, I feel much older than a girl—at least twenty-five.

"Maybe you should introduce me as your woman," I tell him when we step inside the lobby. Although only five o'clock, the black-tie gala is already in full swing, with a sparkling wine reception and a string quartet.

Max chuckles and hands our ten thousand dollar tickets to the usher at the door. "You want me to say, 'this is my woman'? Should I grab your hair and grunt too? Beat my chest?"

"Mmm. I'd like to see that."

Brushing a kiss over my hair, Max whispers, "No one will doubt you are my woman. You are exquisite. You're going to knock their socks off."

"None of the women are wearing socks."

"Then you'll knock off their panties."

"Max!" I give him a gentle shove. "What's got into you this evening?" He is over-the-top playful tonight. So playful his good humor almost seems forced. Maybe he's still angry about Assgate. He still hasn't chewed me out. Best get him drunk and stay cheerful, and maybe he'll forget about it.

"Just looking forward to an evening with my woman."

Once inside, we are thronged by curious patrons. I grip Max's hand and plaster myself to his side. He introduces me to politicians, movie stars, directors, authors, CEOs, an assortment of chairwomen, and a dirty dozen young blondes with bad nose jobs. I perfect air-kissing by imagining I am a chicken. Heeding Charlie's warning, I turn down the copious amounts of champagne in favor of water. By the time we are called for dinner in the Tent Pavilion, I am ready to float away.

The tent has been decorated with yards of azure, draped fabric and thousands of blue peonies, which are also scattered over linen-covered tabletops.

"This is unreal," I breathe, spinning around.

"This is unreal." Max slides his hand under my skirt to caress my bottom. "It's so short. Barely enough to cover you, and yet it does."

"Stop it." I slap his hand away. "What if someone sees you?"

"They'll wish their hand was up your easy-access skirt too." He leans over and whispers in my ear, "Go to the restroom and take off your panties."

"What?"

"Take them off."

"Are you on drugs?" I stand in front of him and check his eyes to see if his pupils are dilated. Nope. Normal, except for the wicked glint. "I don't do things like that."

He runs his hand up and down my bare back, his fingers tickling my spine until I arch toward him. "You did this morning and last night, and the night before that, and the night before that." My body goes from calm to shaking with sexual hunger in a heartbeat.

Max threads his fingers through my hair and tugs my head back, exposing my neck to his featherlight kisses. "Bring them to me," he rasps.

My heat rises quickly as if he had kindled my fire. I take a deep breath and pull away from him, my body trembling inside and out. My token resistance is crushed beneath his creativity, and my body's unquenchable need to be devoured by him again. I am a bad, bad girl.

Ten minutes later, I am back at the table, bare. My panties are tucked inside my tiny apple-shaped evening bag. "I hope we don't have a car accident on the way home," I grumble. "My mother would be horrified to find out not only was I not wearing clean panties, I wasn't wearing panties at all."

Max pulls out my chair and leans over to whisper in my ear. "Don't sit on your skirt."

"Why?"

His voice drops, nearly to a whisper. "It'll get wet."

All the blood in my body races downward. Moisture pools between my thighs. I surreptitiously flip up the back of my skirt and take my seat. The soft, silk chair cover is cool on my heated skin. Naughty sensations ripple through my core. I am going to ruin this chair, and I can hardly wait.

Wine is poured and the parade of tiny, artfully presented dishes arrives, starting with a caviar and egg thing. Yech. Fish eggs. Disgusting. I brush the tiny, black, gel-like mass off the egg with my fork.

"That's the best part," my dinner companion points out. Seated to my left, he is tall and slim, with thinning, silver hair and a long nose. He has a shiny gold tooth and thick glasses. He looks familiar, but I can't place him.

Max slides his hand under my skirt and traces lazy circles up my inner thighs. I glance down to ensure his naughty meanderings are hidden by the tablecloth. My relief is short-lived. His fingers reach their target. I jump in my seat and squeal.

"You really have an aversion to caviar," Gold Tooth chuckles.

Max strokes his finger along my folds. "This one is quite wet."

"True. I do prefer mine dry."

Breathe. In. Out. Slow. Easy. My teeth are clenched so tight the Jaws of Life couldn't pry them apart. Yet another phrase to add to the "How to Intensely Arouse Makayla" list.

My white wine is replaced with red. Food comes and goes. I talk to Gold Tooth's wife about the hospital and the lack of funding. The table conversation turns to whether children should be allowed two or three horses each and where the best place is to buy a fourth home. Max's fingers continue their incessant stroking, slicking through my folds and around my swollen nub. Sweat trickles down my back. My body is coiled so tight I am sure I will detonate.

When Max's finger slides inside me, I can't stifle my gasp. My hips jerk at the unexpected intrusion, and every nerve in my body jolts into awareness.

"I thought I saw the president," I explain when everyone looks at me. Heads turn in the direction of my gaze, and I slap Max's hand away. He pushes out his chair.

"I think we'll step outside for a breath of air before the next course." Max excuses us and escorts me out of the tent.

Five minutes later, we are locked away inside a small storage room at the end of a long, marble hallway. The room is packed with music stands, boxes, musical instruments, and an assortment of costumes hung from a rail attached to chains in the ceiling. A mirror, a big table, and a few chairs fill the rest of the dusty space.

Max locks the door and turns to give me a wicked grin. "Alone at last."

"How did you find this place?"

"Advance scouting."

"You planned this in advance?"

Max wraps an arm around my waist and pulls me into his chest. "I like to be prepared for all eventualities."

"What if I didn't want to play your game?"

"You always want to play, baby. That's what I like about you." He slides his hand under my dress and along my wet folds.

"Bad Max. I can't believe you did that at the table."

"Bad Makayla," Max whispers, his breath hot and moist in my ear. "Running around a big society event without any panties. You need to be punished." He spins me around and pushes me down on the table. My breasts and belly press tight again the hard surface. He flips up my skirt and runs his warm hand over my cheeks. "You have such a beautiful ass, baby. It just begs to be spanked."

I glare at him over my shoulder. "Don't you dare."

"You showed it to the world. Why shouldn't I get a little bit more?"

Oh God. Charlie was right. He is pissed at me. I naively thought he was going to let it slide.

He holds me down with a firm hand on my back. My heart beats frantically against the table, and I shudder so violently my teeth chatter. "No. You're angry. Please. Not when you're angry."

"What's your safe word?"

My entire body goes rigid. My lungs tighten so hard I can barely speak. "Ag—"

Something soft and fluffy tickles my legs, running over the backs of my thighs and then down again. Soft, sensual, and very arousing. My breath whooshes out of me and I slump on the table.

"What is that?" I look back over my shoulder. Max grins and holds up a giant feather duster. He tickles it along the juncture of my thighs, and I squirm on the table as abject terror becomes abject need.

"More?" he whispers, brushing the soft feathers along my folds.

I moan at the delicious sensation. "More."

Max puts down the duster and removes all the costumes from the rail. He tugs on a rope at the side of the wall and the rail lifts into the air, swinging back and forth on the chains.

"Go hold on to the rail, baby. I won't restrain you this time. Something is going on with you and until you tell me what it is, the farthest I'll go is honor bondage."

"Honor bondage? Sounds like a bad Japanese film."

Max snorts a laugh. "Go. Stop cracking jokes. You're spoiling the mood."

"What mood?" I ask as I round the table. "The Makayla pretends to be a monkey on a flying trapeze mood? I had other ideas about what might happen in here."

The sound of Max wheezing in a breath startles me. I spin around just as he doubles over with laughter and clutches his stomach. *Yes.* I pump my fist in the air. I cracked the uncrackable Max.

"Stop looking at me," he barks. "Go and hold on to the rail."

I grasp the bar overhead with two hands. "Like this?"

"Take a few steps back so your weight is forward."

After I'm in proper trapeze position, Max tugs the rope and the rail lifts, pulling me up along with it until I am standing on the balls of my feet. I am stretched so high my stomach now forms a highly desirable concave, but my strapless dress is sliding down too far for comfort.

"Um." I manage to say before my breasts burst free. Classy. I am so cut out for high society.

"Don't let go."

"Is that 'don't let go in case you hurt yourself' or 'don't let go or you'll be sorry'?"

Max comes up behind me and brushes his lips over my ear. "What do you think?" he purrs.

"Not really thinking right now, which is my usual state around you."

Max chortles. "If you move, this"—he strokes the feather duster along my folds—"will become this." He smacks my bottom with his bare hand and shoots me into shocking arousal.

"Not moving. Not moving."

With a gentle tap, the feather duster hits my bottom. Max brings it down again and again. Tap. Tap. Tap. How irritating. The impact is barely a whisper, a tease, an amuse-bouche for my behind. I wiggle, seeking more sensation.

"Do you want to be spanked, baby?" He brings the duster down harder and the tickle turns into an itch. Arrrgh. It makes me almost want to say yes. But I don't. Never really having been spanked before, I have no frame of reference to answer his question.

His hand slides over my bottom, and he brushes a finger through the crevice of my cheeks. I shudder at the intimate touch, but by the time I've recovered his finger has moved on, gliding into the wet center of my body. I moan, so ready for him, I can barely stand it.

"Yes, you do," he rasps.

"Max! Please!" I rock my hips against his fingers as he teases me toward my peak.

"No 'Max please,'" he murmurs in my ear. "I want to hear 'yes, Max,' and nothing else." He nibbles my earlobe and feather kisses along my neck.

"Yes, Max."

"Good girl. You get a reward." He kicks my legs apart and slides his erection, hot and heavy, along my folds.

Jeez. When did he undress?

The violent gesture combined with the erotic sensation of his hot, heavy shaft between my thighs sends a firestorm through my blood. My body trembles with need and the exertion of holding the rail and balancing on my toes. Too much. Too many things to think about. I whimper softly and moisture trickles down my thigh.

"Hold on, baby." He pulls away and I hear the crinkle of a condom wrapper. Then he is back, easing me open to accommodate his girth.

"Yes, Max," I groan.

He laughs, low, deep, and sexy, and then he fills me. Slowly this time. He eases himself into my body and sinks deep. I sigh, relieved to finally have him where I want him. Now, if he would only move.

"I could stay here forever," he rumbles. Not the words I want to hear.

I angle my hips and push against his pelvis. I need him so badly I ache and throb inside.

"Aaaaagh," I groan my frustration.

"So impatient," he whispers. "I know what you want, but it's better if you wait."

Better for whom?

His hand slides over my hip, brushing over my mound, before settling on teasing circles around my sensitive nub. My core spasms. He drives and he strokes, building a rhythm, building my need.

My body arches into the sensation, but it isn't enough. I tighten my grip on the rail and push against his movement. "Harder," the word comes out before I can stop it. "More."

He freezes and his voice sharpens with warning. "What did you say?"

My pulse races. "Yes, Max."

He groans and pinches my sweet spot with firm, gentle pressure, the one touch I was waiting for. My release comes hard and fast, my sex convulsing around him as waves of sensation explode through me.

Max slides his hands to my hips and grips them hard. He increases his pace, driving into me with such force, I can barely keep hold of the rail. My body tightens and I near the peak again. So good. "Yes, Max. Yes. Yes—"

Just as I think my body can't get any tighter, the sensations any stronger, Max angles himself to thrust against a spot so sensitive my eyes slit closed. My orgasm explodes from me, sending ripples of liquid heat through my body.

With a shout, Max shudders and swells inside me, pumping hard and deep. When he finally stills, he pries my fingers from the rail and pulls me back into his chest. After a few minutes, he gently eases away and disposes of the condom. Then he returns to hold me some more.

I melt into the warmth of his arms. "You're very creative when it comes to sex."

Max chuckles. "I used to bartend at a sex club when I was younger. I was curious and wanted to check the scene out from a safe distance. They gave me a few ideas."

"Are you…into BDSM?"

"I enjoy it as a game, especially the dominance aspect, but not as a lifestyle. I like to be in control in the bedroom and take it right to the edge. Just like in the ring."

My breath whooshes out of me and I swallow hard. What does that mean? Whips and chains and spankings? *Oh my.*

We dress in silence and straighten the room. As I reach for the door, Max cups my face in his hands and kisses me, a long, soft, tender kiss. A kiss that says more than words.

———

We make it back to the table just before dessert, a delightful combination of cherries jubilee and chocolate cake. After dinner, music fills the tent and we follow a troupe of dancers into the hall for a Champagne Promenade, followed by a two-hour concert during which at least half the men fall asleep.

By ten o'clock we are back in the tent for the after party. My head is spinning from the overload of sensation and way too much alcohol, but I manage to drag Max to the edge of the dance floor through the hoards of overbearing mothers and their undernourished daughters all trying to get a piece of what's mine.

"I like jealous Makayla," Max whispers, when I scowl at another couture-clad matriarch desperately trying to get Max's attention.

"I'm not jealous."

"I think you've left fingerprints across my hip."

"Don't flatter yourself. It's hard to balance in these shoes."

"Those shoes put you at a perfect height." His fingers brush under my skirt, and he pinches my cheek.

"Ow."

"Max, darling, are you bothering this girl?"

One of the grand dames of the gala kisses Max firmly on both cheeks and then turns her gaze to me. She holds up a thick pair of glasses on a stick and peers at me through at least three thick inches of lens. I shudder under the scrutiny of monster-size eyes and return her stare. She drops the glasses and huffs her derision with an inelegant snort.

"Really, Max. This? Instead of my Tootles?"

"Tootles?" I have to ask.

"My granddaughter. She was with Max for—" She cocks her head to the side and her eyes narrow. "How long was it?"

"I can't recall, Moira," Max's voice is cold and stiff.

"Longer than anyone else. I do remember that." She peers at me again through her enormous lenses. "They were engaged. Did he tell you that?"

"Engaged? You were engaged? To Tootles?"

"No."

"Don't be shy, Max." The grand dame's voice becomes decidedly cold. "There's nothing to be ashamed of. There aren't many men the family would even allow near Tootles. She has one of the finest pedigrees on the West Coast."

A giggle escapes me. I imagine Tootles as a pedigreed poodle prancing around at a dog show. I should be upset at the revelation, but instead I am amused at the thought of Max with a woman named Tootles. Maybe I've had too much to drink.

"Enough, Moria." Max grabs my arm and pulls me away, but curiosity holds my feet to the ground.

"What happened to Tootles?"

"The same thing that will happen to you." She sniffs. "He'll have his fun with you in the storage room, just like he had with every other girl he's brought to the gala, but in the end, he'll leave you and marry his own kind."

My mouth drops open and my heart drops to the floor. My good humor dies a thousand deaths.

"Makayla." Max touches my arm and I yank it away.

"Look around this room, girl," she continues. "This is Society with a capital *S*. These are his people. He can have his pick of any of these women. I can tell by looking at you that you don't belong. Why would he want you except to have a bit of fun?"

Blood thunders through my ears, the rush so loud I can barely hear. For the first time in my life, I have nothing to say—no jokes or quips, sarcastic comments or smart remarks. All that I am has been sucked into the black hole in my chest.

"MOIRA!" Max's fists clench and his shout attracts all sorts of unwanted attention. He turns on the grand dame and gives her a piece of his mind. But I'm not interested in what he has to say. I slip through the crowd and out the door, just as the clock chimes twelve.

—᷍᷍—

Makayla, where are you?

—᷍᷍—

Just let me know you're safe

—᷍᷍—

I've checked with Amanda, your parents, your doorman, and your housemates

—᷍᷍—

Where are you?

—᷍᷍—

You don't have to tell me where you are. Just tell me you're okay

—᷍᷍—

I'm worried about you, baby

—᷍᷍—

I should have told you

—᷍᷍—

I'm sorry

Chapter 20

COME WITH ME

FRIDAY NIGHT. FIGHT NIGHT at Redemption. If Amanda had not offered to come with me, I would never have been able to step foot through the door. She stands guard outside the first aid office with the sole purpose of warning me when Max arrives.

My first patient walks in before I even put down my purse. He introduces himself as Obsidian. His voice is so low he should be narrating the introduction of every Hollywood film. I run my hands over his delicious, dark skin to check for broken ribs. He is broad and heavily muscled and I regret he has not pulled a muscle in his groin. Guilt does not nag me while I indulge in lustful thoughts about Obsidian. He is no rich, society playboy. He would know how to treat a woman.

Unfortunately, he also knows how to treat a man.

He confides in me about his problems with his boyfriend, Raoul, and his bit on the side, Bulldog. He shares very intimate confidences. Too intimate. I recommend toys without sharp edges. After he leaves, I want to grab the bleach and give my ears a good scrub.

Amanda flits in and out, oblivious to the trail of panting men behind her. In a white sheath dress and sparkly gold stilettos, her golden curls tumbling down her back, she looks like a goddess. In my functional stretchy pants and pink Lycra tank, I look like I'm going to yoga class.

The constant stream of patients keeps me busy until an hour before closing time. I have just finished treating Jeff "Jackhammer" Jones for a twisted ankle when Max appears in the doorway. My heart sinks. What happened to my bodyguard? I had an escape route all planned.

Max leans against the door frame until Jackhammer limps away. He steps inside and closes the door behind him.

I jam my hands into my armpits and back up against the wall.

"I'm glad you're safe," he murmurs.

I tighten my lips and stare at the ceiling.

"We need to talk."

"I have patients waiting outside. This isn't the time."

Max frowns. "You work for me, Makayla. If I say it's time, then it's time."

"I have an ethical duty to help people in need. It overrides anything a dishonest, playboy boss wants."

"She was lying," he says, his voice strained. "That is how high society works. Everyone watches everyone else. Someone saw us come out of the storage room and gave the information to the person they thought was in a position to do them the biggest favor. In this case, Moira. These are people who will befriend you one minute and then turn around and stab you in the back the next. It's why I want nothing to do with them and part of the reason why I left all that in my past."

"I might have believed you if I hadn't heard something similar from Sandy. Go away."

Max takes a step toward me. "I understand you're angry, baby. What she said was hurtful, cruel, and directed at me. She hasn't forgiven me for splitting with her granddaughter."

I frown. "Sandy is Tootles."

"Yes."

"You were engaged to her."

"Not exactly."

I tap my foot on the tiled floor. "What does that mean? You either asked her to marry you or you didn't."

Max sighs and leans against my examination table. "She only knew me as Torment. We pretended to be engaged so she could get a break from her family's incessant match-making. I went along because she was my girl. Neither of us realized her family would check into my back-ground and uncover a family history I had gone to great lengths to hide."

His words are like a slap across my face. Sandy, the society darling, was his girl. Makayla, the poor admin clerk, is not even in his league. A bruise of sadness forms in my chest.

"Get out."

"Baby—"

"Don't call me that. I don't belong in your world. Money was tight when I was a kid and it was tighter when I went to college. I never even rode a horse much less had four horses, and we never even had a house until Mom met Steve. I'm not telling you that so you feel sorry for me. I want you to understand we are different—too different. I had deluded myself into thinking you were a regular guy. You're not. You need someone like Sandy. Not someone like me."

The skin around Max's eyes bunches and his face softens. "What's really bothering you? It isn't finding out about my society ties."

"You lied to me."

He shakes his head. "I never lied to you. I didn't think it was important."

"It's important to me. Ex-society fiancées who hug and kiss you and party with your friends and tweet my bottom around the world are important to me. Your background, understanding who you are and where you're from, is important to me." I take a deep breath and continue. I am on a roll. "We have great sex and fun together, but you never talk about yourself. It hurts to find out from a stranger you were engaged to Sandy. It hurts to know you were keeping secrets from me. I thought we were close. I thought we shared something special. I was wrong." I am righteous in my fury and drowning in hypocrisy.

A solemn expression crosses his face. "You mean more to me than you could possibly imagine. You want to know who I am, I'll show you." He holds out his hand. "Come with me."

"No. It's too late. It won't change anything."

He gives me an impatient look. "Come."

"No." My bottom lip trembles. "Just leave me alone."

"I won't take no for an answer." His voice breaks. "I'm not losing you over this." He picks me up and throws me over his shoulder.

"Put me down," I screech.

"Not until you see what I want you to see."

"You can't leave the first aid office unattended. What if the regulators show up? They will shut you down for good."

"I'll ask Rampage to find someone to fill in."

Tears spill from my eyes. "Stop, Max. I don't want this. It's not funny."

He ignores me and strides toward the door.

"Please, Max." I choke back a sob. This is worse than hearing about Tootles and the storage room, worse than knowing I don't fit in. He is taking away my choice, my control.

He reaches for the doorknob.

"Agusta," I whisper.

Max freezes. He takes a deep breath and then he drops me gently to the ground. I take a deep breath and lean against the bed. My panic subsides.

"Getting to know me, giving us a chance, is more than you can bear?" His voice is raw with emotion and my heart gives an empathetic thud. He listened to me. He said I mean something to him. He wants to share a piece of himself with me. How can I refuse?

"I want to walk."

His breath catches in his throat. "You'll come with me?"

"I'll come because I choose to come, not because you made me."

He sucks in his lips and studies me for the longest time. "What made you so strong, Makayla Delaney?"

I shrug. "If I was strong, I would have said no and meant it."

He tucks my hair behind my ear. "A strong person faces their fears. A weak person runs away."

"Like I said, weak." I tilt my head into the warmth of his palm. He hisses in a breath and pulls me close.

"Like I said, strong." He clasps my hand and leads me through the warehouse to a small, circular flight of stairs in the back corner. We climb at least fifteen feet, and Max unlocks a heavy metal door and flicks on the lights.

Wow! A loft space has been created at the top of the warehouse. Floor to ceiling windows meet exposed beams and wood paneling overhead. Highly polished tigerwood angles across the floor space. Exposed brick walls are interspersed with textured drywall, and a black, wrought iron staircase runs up to a half-finished second floor. Stone and brick dividers separate multiple living spaces. A bed is tucked behind a wall made of glass bricks, and a huge, modern kitchen stands half-built in the middle of the open space.

"Max. This is you," I breathe. Rustic and modern, hidden and exposed, rough and classy. He has a foot in two worlds, and this place combines the best of both.

Max's face softens. "I've never brought anyone up here. I've done all the work myself."

No one else has been up here. No Pinkaluscious. No girls. No friends. Just me. Butterflies flutter in my stomach and I squeeze his hand. "You've done an incredible job. It's beautiful."

I wander to his makeshift living area: couch, television, bookshelves, a soft shag area rug, and…pictures. My mouth waters at the thought of getting a glimpse of the real Max. "Are these of you? Can I look?"

"Anything you want." His voice is a soft rumble. "I brought you here because you said you didn't know me. Here I am."

I drop to my knees in front of the table and sort through the pictures. I pull out a grainy, faded photograph of Max as a toddler, chubby and cute. He poses for the camera in kid-size boxing gloves beside a beautiful woman with long, dark hair.

"She's beautiful. Is she your mom?"

"Was."

I have so many questions, but this isn't the time. I pick up his preschool picture and smile. His chubby cheeks are gone, but his face is still soft and recognizable as my Max. He grins from a makeshift boxing ring surrounded in bushes. I find a few pictures of young Max at the beach and playing at the zoo, but mostly the pictures are of Max boxing or holding up trophies or medals.

I shuffle through the pictures. "Do you have any brothers or sisters?"

"No. It was just me."

"Where did you grow up?"

"The South."

I raise an eyebrow. "The South. Well, that narrows it down."

Max sits on the couch behind me and tucks me between his legs. His arms slide around my waist and he squeezes me tight as if we're on a roller coaster and he's hanging on for dear life.

"You didn't lie when you said you started boxing young." I hold up another picture of toddler Max.

"My father wanted me to follow his dream."

"Looks like you were very good." I point to all the pictures of Max and his medals.

"I was."

"You are." I look over my shoulder and brush a kiss over his cheek. He has bought his forgiveness by letting me into his inner sanctum, and I want him to know I appreciate the gift.

He shudders and murmurs into my hair. "I wasn't good enough."

"Is this your dad?" I hold up a picture of five-year-old Max at his birthday. His mom is pressing a kiss to his cheek while beside them, an intense-looking man glowers at the camera. He could be Max but smaller, thinner, and not as handsome. But I know that scowl.

Max rests his cheek against my head and tightens his arms. "Yes. He was a professional boxer but was kicked out of the circuit after a series of injuries. He had worked his way through his savings when he met my mother. She was high society and very well-off. They fell in love and eloped. The family turned against her. They thought he was after her money so they disinherited her. She didn't care. They were happy together until I was born." His voice catches in his throat, but as I turn to face him he redirects me to the table and folds his arms around me.

"What happened? It looks from these pictures like you had a happy childhood."

"I did. My dad worked as a boxing coach at a local gym. He didn't make much but he wanted me to have the shot at stardom he never got. All his money went to pay for coaches, trainers, gym time, and equipment. My life revolved around school and boxing. I didn't mind because I wanted to make my dad proud. But no matter how hard I tried, I was never good enough."

The pain in his voice cuts me like a hundred little knives. My arms ache to hold him. I try to turn, but he tightens his arms and rests his chin on my head.

"As I got older, I never thought to ask how a coach got the money to pay for all my training. Turns out he borrowed it from the local mafia at an exorbitant interest rate, and one day, when I was fourteen, they came to collect. Only Mom and I were home. "

I gasp and my hand flies to my mouth.

"You remind me of her," he murmurs. "You have the same hair. You are beautiful and headstrong and self-reliant. She never asked for help. She never listened to anyone—not even me—when it mattered most."

My heart pounds. "What happened?"

"Four mafia enforcers broke into our home to collect the money my father owed them. I think he had hoped my winnings would cover the payments, but it wasn't enough. They found my mother and me hiding in the bedroom. They saw her engagement ring. It was a huge diamond. I don't know how my father ever afforded it."

"Oh no," I whisper.

"They wanted it. She refused. She said it was all she had left to remember my father the way he used to be—when they were young and in love and nothing else mattered."

"She was a romantic."

"They all had knives but she wouldn't let me protect her." He takes a deep breath and exhales slowly. "I pushed her behind me. I knew how to fight. I had a wall full of trophies and championship belts to prove it. But she wouldn't stay out of the way. And she wouldn't give up the ring. I tried so damn hard…" He buries his face in my hair.

Tears spring to my eyes. "Oh, Max. I know you did."

"I managed to knock out two of them, but by then the other two had her. They tried to pull the ring off her finger, but she fought them off. One of them threw her against a glass cabinet. It shattered and a piece of glass cut her throat. There was so much blood."

My stomach clenches. The glass must have cut her carotid artery. She didn't have a chance.

"I couldn't protect her. I couldn't save her." His voice is so low, I can barely hear him. "I should have fought harder. I should have made her listen. If she had done what I said, she would be alive today."

Tears stream down my cheeks. "Max, honey, you were only fourteen. You were her baby. I'm sure she was just trying to protect you."

He draws in a ragged breath. "My father didn't see it that way. He blamed me. He said I had failed her. I wasn't good enough. After all the training, when it really mattered, I failed. He shot himself that evening."

"Oh God." I twist, breaking his grip, and turn to throw my arms around him. I hug him tight. "I'm so sorry. To go through that at fourteen."

Max stiffens. "It was a long time ago."

"What did you do?" I press my cheek against his, and tighten my arms.

"I lived with my aunt and uncle until I was old enough to leave. Then I took my inheritance and never looked back."

"You didn't stay in touch?"

"My father's family were scattered all over. They weren't close. My mother's family blamed me for her death. I could see it in their eyes. I could hear it in their voices. They didn't want me around."

My heart aches for him. I wish I could do something to ease the pain I see in his eyes. I sit back and run my fingers over his chest. "Is that what your tattoos are about? Is that why you say they represent failure?"

"Not just that night," he rasps. "I ink every failure into my skin so I remember."

I press my lips against his chest. "What you think are failures are beautiful to me," I whisper. "They make you who you are. They make you my Max."

Max's body tenses. He slides his hand to my shoulders and holds me at arm's length. "I won't go through it again," he says, his voice thick. "I've worked hard to get to the point I know I will be able to defend the people I love." His voice drops to a husky whisper. "I love you, Makayla. I couldn't bear to lose you. I want to protect you and keep you safe, but you need to let me in." He cups my face in his hands and gently tilts my head back. Tears spill over my cheeks. His eyes are filled with pain and tenderness. He slants his mouth over mine and our lips brush in a gentle, soft kiss.

He loves me.

He loves me, and I can't say it back.

He kisses away my tears and then our lips meet once more. His tongue slides inside my mouth, stroking, searching for something I don't have to give.

"So beautiful," he whispers. "Heal me, Makayla." He picks me up and carries me to his bed, rumpled and cool and smelling of Max. We undress each other, slowly, gently, and then we make sweet love surrounded by memories and sawdust in the very heart of Redemption.

―⁓―

Three hours later, we descend the stairs into chaos. The Friday night Redemption party is in full swing. Max keeps one arm around my shoulders, and we mingle with the fighters. He introduces me to his venture capitalist business partner, Jason. Taller than Max and leaner, with blue-gray eyes, dark hair and a chiseled jaw, he would send Amanda into a flirting frenzy. How does Cindy get any work done?

"So have you talked Max into fixing up this dive and making it into a proper mixed martial arts facility?" His voice is deep and low. Definitely Amanda-worthy.

"I didn't know he was considering it."

"I'm not," Max interjects. "I like it the way it is."

Jason shakes his head. "I've told him again and again, he could make some serious money if he fixes the place up and gets all the proper licenses. He lost a lot of guys to sanctioned clubs, and yet he still has a waiting list. He's a great instructor and he's hired some great people. With very little effort, this could be one of the top MMA training facilities in the state."

Max shakes his head. "I've told you before, too many rules, too many regulations, and too much money."

"Don't you want to test yourself against the best?" I ask. "Don't you want to train your fighters to fight against the best? And you wouldn't have to worry about anyone shutting you down."

"It's not going to happen, baby." Max gives my shoulder a squeeze. "I would have to stop the unsanctioned fights. It was my dad's dream to run a club like this. I don't need anything more."

"What about your own dreams?"

Before Max can answer, Blade Saw starts a game of Shake Shake Bang Bang, and our attention is drawn to the crazy man banging a shaken beer repeatedly on his head. However, instead of the usual hole forming in the side of the can, the top pops off and beer sprays all over me. Rampage, Obsidian, Homicide, and Jackhammer try to hold Max back. They fail. Blade Saw apologizes profusely when I bandage him up in the first aid room. I promise him he will be back to fighting in a few weeks.

Jake shows up with Pinkaluscious attached to his lips. Amanda flips out. I have no idea where she has been since she let me down at the door, but from her slightly disheveled appearance, I can guess. She deals with her first experience being dumped as anyone would. She becomes totally inebriated. After leading two rounds of the Chicken Dance in the ring, she races Hammer Fist up and down the bleachers, challenges Rampage to a wrestling match, and makes it through a few rounds of beer pong and quarters before collapsing on the bed in the first aid room. Max insists we take her home together in his limo. After I've tucked her into bed with a jug of water and a bottle of aspirin, we go back to his house. This time we don't make love. We have sex. Wild, wicked, passionate, soul-cleansing sex. Afterward, we cuddle. We are back to normal. There is no more talk of love. I like it better that way. I think.

Chapter 21
I WANT MINX

IT'S SATURDAY MORNING AND I have a post-party hangover. My mouth tastes like glue. My eyes feel like sandpaper. I have a pounding headache and my face is greasy with makeup. At least Max took off my dress, although if I remember correctly his reasons were totally selfish.

Max pushes a button and his electric blinds go up, letting in the evil sun.

"Bad sun. Bad Max," I groan into the pillow. "Turn it off."

Max chuckles and skims his hand down my bare back. "I have to be in Fontana at noon for work. One of our target companies is testing a new remote control device at a racetrack."

"So is this the 'wham bam thank you, ma'am, get out of my bed I have to work on a Saturday good-bye' speech?" I groan.

"This is the 'you wanted to know about me so now you get to see my work and you'd better get your ass out of bed and come with me or you'll be sorry' speech."

"Too many words. Hangover brain overload."

Max chortles and slaps my bottom. "Get up. We have to get you dressed, fed, and in the limo in an hour."

"Fontana is at least a seven-hour drive," I moan. "I'm not so good at sitting still for long periods of time while hung over and with a slapped bottom."

Max rips the covers off the bed, exposing me to the cold air. "We're going by plane. The flight is just over an hour. There's more bottom slapping in your future if you don't get up."

I don't budge.

"Makayla." His warning tone makes me giggle.

"I'm thinking."

"Don't tempt me, baby. I've been waiting a long time for sufficiently bad behavior to warrant a spanking." He caresses my bottom and
my body heats up, yet again. Will it never end? Will we get to the point
where I'll come just from him looking at me? I flip over to remove the
temptation of my overly round cheeks.

"Your personal plane, oh rich society dude?"

Max chuckles. "No. We chartered a plane for the trip, but Jason
told me last night he can't make it."

"I was planning to wash my hair today, but I *suppose* I could come
with you on a private *plane* to a *racetrack*, but I…uh…need underwear
and clothes that aren't covered in beer."

"We'll stop at Angel's Bike Shop, just outside the airport. We'll buy
you some panties, and once we're in the plane I'll rip them off you."

"How romantic."

"I'm all about romance." Max leans down to suckle my breast, and
pleasure licks up the inside of my thighs.

"You're all about sex."

He raises his head and locks his dark, dangerous eyes with mine.
"With you, baby, I can't be anything else."

Riding on a private plane with naughty "Biker Chick" emblazoned underwear hidden under my clothes is enough to send me into a frenzy of
excitement. "Look!" I shriek and bounce in my cushy leather seat. "I can
see the Golden Gate Bridge…and the ocean." I sip my champagne and
smile at the flight attendant who must be wondering how she landed
a job with a drop-dead gorgeous passenger and his overexcited puppy.

"Santa Cruz…Monterey…Ventana…" I rattle off the names of the
major cities and parks along the coast proudly demonstrating just why
I got an A in geography.

No, I chastise myself. Do not embarrass Max. Try to appear cul-
tured and sophisticated. Classy.

I take a chocolate-covered strawberry from the plate and nibble at
the tip. So delicious. The chocolate breaks off and falls on my new yoga

pants. No problem. Biker-style polyester cleans easily. At least that's what Angel told me this morning in her deep, gravelly voice as she detached her heavily muscled arms from around Max's waist. For some reason, I didn't feel jealous this time.

I dab at the chocolate and check my stretchy, pink tank top for similar disasters. Safe. As is my Harley-Davidson hoodie. I am so glad Eva was out of town. The mean-looking Tweety Bird wearing a Harley-Davidson skull cap and leather vest printed on my bra and panties, would probably have given her a heart attack.

"We'll have some more champagne please, Linda," Max says, his voice all smooth and mellow.

Luscious Linda, the well-endowed flight attendant giggles. She manages to tear her eyes off my man and disappears into the tiny galley.

"She has a last name. It's on her nametag. You should really call her Miss Slutzsky. Linda is too familiar, unless you know her very well. Maybe you do. Maybe that's why you used your sexy come hither voice when you were talking to her and gave her the 'I'm going to devour you with my eyes' look."

Max laughs and then hums a few bars of the Black Crows' "Jealous Again."

"Don't flatter yourself." I ram the rest of the strawberry in my mouth.

"Do you know why I sent her for more champagne?" Max tongues my earlobe and then nibbles around the shell until my body shivers with pure unadulterated lust.

"You're thirsty?" I push him away. "Or you like leading women on?"

"Only one woman." Max removes his napkin and tosses it over my lap.

"Linda Slutzsky?"

"You." He slides his hand under the napkin and down the front of my yoga pants, not stopping until his fingers are secured behind Tweety Bird's head.

"Max," I shriek. My legs jerk up, hitting the tray table. With the kind of coordination only seen in a circus, Max saves the tray with his free hand, while simultaneously stroking behind Tweety Bird's fluffy bottom with the other. His fingers push aside the panties and slide between my folds.

The curtain slides open with a loud rattle. Max continues to stroke. I draw in the deepest, most ragged breath and try to imagine I do not have a man's hand down my pants in a ritzy private airplane.

Ms. Slutzsky looks at Max. Then she looks at me. My cheeks flame. My lungs burn for air. How twisted is this?

"I think we'll pass on the champagne for now, Linda. Makayla is feeling a little lightheaded." Max graces her with his award-winning smile. "We'll call you if we need you."

Linda's smile does not reach her eyes. "I'll be in the galley." She yanks the curtain closed.

My breath leaves me with a whoosh. "She knew what you were doing. She'll think I'm a—" I can't say it. I can only call myself a slut in my head. "Minx," I blurt out.

Max chuckles. "You are a minx. *My* little minx. And the only thing she should be thinking about is whether we need more champagne." He presses a finger inside me and groans. "You're so wet, baby. I think my little minx likes a bit of danger served with her sex."

"Don't talk like that. It does things to me."

"What things?" Max slides a second finger through my folds and my insides melt.

"Naughty things."

"Tell me naughty things," Max whispers in my ear.

My hips rock in time to the gentle thrust of his fingers, rubbing my sensitive nub against the heel of his palm. The sensation is so delicious my head falls back on the seat, and I grip the armrests so hard my knuckles turn white.

"I can't…talk…when you are doing that."

"Then I'll stop."

"Nooooooo. Don't stop. Please, don't stop."

Max withdraws his fingers and pushes back our table trays. "I have to stop. Hot, wet Makayla moaning and writhing with naughty things on the tip of her tongue is more than any man could bear." He motions me out of my seat and I follow him down the aisle to a small, partially enclosed seating area containing two leather loungers. Max settles himself on the lounger nearest the window and undoes his fly. His erection springs free—hard, heavy, and swiftly sheathed before I can even catch my breath.

"Max." I look at him aghast and check over my shoulder for Luscious Linda. "What are you doing?"

"Guess."

"You don't waste any time, do you?"

"Up here, minx." Max pats his lap. "Come and whisper naughty things in my ear."

"But…Linda…and the pilot and copilot—"

"Are busy flying the airplane." Max reaches over and slides my yoga pants and Biker Chick panties over my hips, then eases them down to my ankles. "I'm going to fly you."

"Let me take them off." I bend down to slide them over my shoes, but Max grabs my hand.

"Leave them where they are."

"But I won't be able to move very much."

Max tugs me onto his lap, positioning my knees on either side of his hips. "Good. I want to be able to last out the flight." He slides the straps of my tank top over my shoulders and undoes the clasp of my bra, sliding them both down to my waist. Cool air brushes over my skin and my nipples harden.

"I don't feel very sophisticated right now," I complain, while he palms my breasts. "Look how easy it was for you to get into my pants."

He trails kisses down my throat. "I don't want sophisticated," he murmurs. "I want minx."

"I want to be like the women I saw you with on the Internet—the models and society girls who know all the right things to say."

"I don't want to hear the right things." He lifts my hips and positions me just over the tip of his erection. "I want to hear minx things." He pulls me down and thrusts deep inside me. The dual sensations overload my brain.

"Oh. My. God." He fills me so completely, so deliciously, I don't want to move.

"That's a start."

Drawing me up, he laves my nipple and yanks me back down again. My tongue hits the back of my throat and I choke out an elegant, "Gah."

"Tell me what you want and I'll give you a present."

"I thought you just gave me the present." I wiggle on top of him, delighted when he groans.

Max tucks his hand into his pocket and pulls out a shiny, silver box. "This is almost as good."

I stop wiggling. "Open it."

His lips curve into a sinister smile and he taps his ear. "Naughty things."

I lick my lips and then rattle off a few of the French phrases Giselle taught me on my way out of the spa. The look of shock on Max's face is almost worth the hefty tip I gave her.

"Well, if that's what you want, baby."

My eyes widen. "What? What do I want?"

"These." He flicks the lid off the box and pulls out two tweezer-like silver objects with silver chains and beads attached.

I frown. "What are they?"

"Nipple clamps."

"I don't like the sound of that. Some things are not meant to be squeezed too hard."

Max bends down to draw my nipple in his mouth, licking and sucking it into a hard peak. He slides the tweezers over my nipple and tightens them with a little ring.

Mind numbing, burning, searing pain shoots through me. I cry out and Max covers my mouth in a soft kiss.

"Take it off. Take it off." I pull away and reach for the dangly chain. Max grasps my wrists and restrains them behind me with one hand.

"Give it a chance, baby. It won't hurt for long." He sucks and teases my other nipple and releases my wrists to slide the other clip over the hardened peak. Another zing. Another burn.

"No, Max." I shake my breasts, trying to dislodge his torture devices, and the little chains tug gently. The pain blurs into searing, fiery pleasure. My sex clenches around Max's erection, and he groans.

A bell rings. The seatbelt sign flashes on. Ms. Slutzsky addresses us by name over the PA system and requests that we return to our seats and fasten our seat belts because of minor turbulence.

Max pulls out his seat belt and fastens it around both of us. He lifts my hips and slides deeper inside me. Although slightly constrained by my Tweety Bird thong foot restraints, and the seat belt around my back, I manage to gain some leverage and move up and down. Max hisses in a breath. The plane shakes and veers slightly to the left. So do my breasts. The nipple clamps tug as I sway, sending jolts of erotic pleasure straight to my core. My heart pounds. My hands fist Max's thick, soft hair. So dangerous. So exciting. So arousing.

"You are one goddamned hot little minx," Max rasps. He tugs the little chains and fire zings through my veins—a confusing mix of pleasure and almost pain. He slides my moisture up and around my sweet spot over and over until I am hovering over the edge of a cliff so high I can't see the ground. My nipples throb, my sex aches, and my body is coiled tight.

"What are you doing to me?" I moan.

"Go, baby. Fly for me," he whispers. He swipes his finger over my swollen nub. I fly apart. My orgasm crashes over me like a tidal wave. Max stiffens and groans, and I take him with me in a blaze of slutty glory.

Chapter 22
I WASN'T AFRAID

A LIMO DROPS US off at the Speedaway Exotic Car Racetrack, located at an abandoned airfield about an hour outside Fontana. We are greeted by the owners, Crash and Dirty Dan, both allegedly bikers. However, with their short, cropped brown hair, matching blue-and-white coveralls, mirrored aviator sunglasses, and perfect smiles, they look more like male models. Maybe I should tell Amanda to join a motorcycle club.

They walk us over to a tall, chain-link fence and show us the track. The runways have been resurfaced and joined to form a giant oval. At various points, straight stretches of pavement run for miles into the horizon, marked only by hay bales and orange netting. Skid marks indicate where drivers have gone off the track and spun out into the grass. At least there are no trees or buildings for anyone to hit.

We tour through massive warehouses filled with a mouthwatering array of exotic cars, from Lamborghinis to Porsches, and Ferraris to Audis. I walk around the Aston Martin, James Bond's vehicle of choice, and imagine myself behind the wheel.

"What are you driving today?" Dirty Dan asks, coming up behind me.

"If I had a choice, it would be this." I stroke the hood of the Aston Martin. "But I don't think Max will agree.

Dirty Dan gives me a wink. "I've always wanted to see a pretty girl behind the wheel. How about I get you prepped and ready to go? Max's clients aren't due for another half hour, which gives us plenty of time to run through the short course we inflict on all our drivers for insurance purposes. With that face and your training and safety certificates in your hand, he won't be able to say no."

He holds out a hand, and his cheeky grin is all the encouragement I need to follow him to the main clubhouse.

By the time we're done, an hour later, Max's clients have arrived and are in the process of setting up their equipment. Max explains they have developed a system to remotely control the vehicles so racetracks and driving schools can operate without an instructor in the vehicle. I join everyone on a shady viewing platform overlooking the track while Crash suits up and climbs into an Audi R8.

At a signal from one of the clients, Crash hits the gas and the Audi roars around the track. The clients stop and start his vehicle, and then make it perform a dizzying array of tricks. When Crash pulls up in front of us, everyone cheers.

"Might be worth the investment they are seeking after all," Max muses.

We spend the rest of the afternoon watching Crash and Dirty Dan test the system on different vehicles. Max's eyes light up when it passes the final test in my Aston Martin. He excuses himself to talk to his clients, and Dirty Dan climbs up to the viewing platform and tosses me the keys, a helmet, and a pair of coveralls.

"Try it out," he says with a wink.

My mouth waters. Me…in an Aston Martin going as fast as I want. The temptation is almost too much, but I've learned my lesson about Max's overprotectiveness. "I'd better ask Max. He has strong views on things he thinks might be dangerous." I say the right words. I will do the right thing. But in the end, if he says no, I'm going anyway.

I catch Max between conversations. "Is it okay if I take the Aston Martin for a spin? Dirty Dan gave me the safety lecture. I have my certificate." I hold up the white and gold embossed paper with my name printed neatly in the center. To my dismay, Max doesn't even glance at it.

"No."

"I'm a good driver. Steve had me take the same driving course as the police cadets. I promise I'll be careful."

He shakes his head. "It's a new technology. I came here because Crash and Dirty Dan are experts. They can handle any emergency."

"But it worked perfectly on every test," I complain.

"No."

"I'll go with her," Dirty Dan interjects. "If the system fails, I'll be there to take over. It will be no different from any member of the public going out on the track."

I throw my arms around Max, tilt back my head, and bat my eyelashes. I am not above all-out begging to get behind the wheel. "Pleeeeeeeeeease."

A smile tugs at his lips. He looks from Dirty Dan to me and back to Dirty Dan. His jaw tightens. "One hundred miles an hour. Tops."

"Come on, Max! It has a top speed of two twenty. You can't expect me to get in a car like that and not—"

"One hundred or nothing."

"Fine," I sulk. He won't be able to do anything once I get behind the wheel.

Max grunts and looks at Dirty Dan. "No risky maneuvers. Just a few laps around the oval, and keep an eye on her. She's hard to control."

"She's standing right here." I wave my hands in his face. "You don't have to talk about her as if she doesn't understand what's going on."

Dirty Dan snorts a laugh and leads me down to the vehicle. A thrill runs through me when I slide into the form-fitting bucket seat and breathe in the new car smell of polish and leather. The gray interior is all curved lines and soft angles. The high-tech dash looks like something out of a spaceship. Dirty Dan helps me adjust the seat and runs through the instrument panel, but all I really care about is the speedometer.

We pull on our helmets and Dirty Dan points out a few more features. "It will do zero to sixty in 4.7 seconds, and we've put in paddle shifters because most people don't know how to operate a manual transmission."

"I do."

Dirty Dan grins. "Why am I not surprised?"

My hands shake as I turn the key and start the engine; I glance at the window and wave to Max. Even from here I can see the tension in his body. Poor Max. He thinks he is tense now. In zero to sixty seconds, I'll show him tense.

"Ready to go?"

I nod and hit the accelerator. The vehicle roars to life and I am thrown back in my seat when we shoot down the speedway. It takes me half a lap to get a feel for the vehicle, but once I am comfortable, I press the pedal to the floor and the speedometer needle creeps upward. One hundred. One twenty. One fifty. One seventy-five. I glance over at Dirty Dan and he gives me a wink.

"Doing well. Just keep it steady. No sudden moves."

When we hit one-eighty, my grin stretches from ear to ear, and excitement takes my breath away. Everything outside us is a blur— Max, his clients, the clubhouse. My only reality is here—Dirty Dan, the Aston Martin, and me.

"You are one hot little package," Dirty Dan murmurs. "Look at you go. No fear in you at all. You handle the vehicle better than most of the clients I've taken out. Why did Max never bring you here before?"

"We haven't known each other long."

The steering wheel jerks suddenly to the side and I glance over at Dirty Dan. "What was that?"

He shakes his head. "Don't know. Maybe you hit a rough patch. Make sure you keep your hands at ten and two."

I slide my hands into correct position and the steering wrenches again, this time turning so sharply I almost lose my grip. The car veers to the edge of the pavement.

"Crap," Dan mutters. He pushes a red button, frowns, and pushes it again. "Looks like something is wrong with their remote system and the manual override. Slow down and pull over."

Before I can hit the brakes, the steering wheel spins out of my grasp.

"Look out!" Dirty Dan grabs for the steering wheel just as we fly off the track. We spin, round and round and round across the grass. It takes both Dirty Dan and I to hold the wheel straight until the vehicle is under control. We finally come to rest at the side of the track, and I take a huge breath, adrenaline pumping through my veins.

"Wow!" Dirty Dan unbuckles our seat belts. "They have some serious bugs in their system. Good thing you decided to go for a spin."

I swallow hard and nod. My heart is pounding. My body is trembling. What a ride!

"You okay?"

I flash him a smile. "I'm good to go again. Maybe this time we should take a car without the new system."

His eyes widen and he grins. "Damn girl, if things don't work out with Max—"

Uh-oh. Max.

The door flies open and Max reaches inside and drags me out into the big, bright, sunny world. He rips off my helmet and runs his hands up and down my body.

"I'm fine, Max. There was a problem with the system but we got it under control. I want to go back out but in a normal car."

"Absolutely not."

"I loved it. It was so exciting."

"I said NO." His voice carries across the racetrack and draws the attention of everyone in the vicinity.

He spins around and slams Dirty Dan against the vehicle. "You were supposed to keep her speed down. What happened?"

"She's a great driver," Dirty Dan protests. "She handled that car like an expert. I didn't think it would be a problem, especially with the new system in place."

"Max." I place my hand on his arm. "I wanted to go fast. Just…chill."

"Chill?" His icy tone freezes my blood. He grasps my elbow and leads me away from the group. "I brought you here. You are my responsibility. You could have been seriously injured. Something happens to my judgment around you. I knew better than to let you drive."

His jaw is tight. His eyes are hard. He bristles with protective anger. Adrenaline still pounds through my veins, and the entire experience has left me inexplicably and incontrovertibly aroused. I curl into his body and press myself against his heat. "I wasn't afraid. Not for one second. There's nothing to hit out here, and Dirty Dan knew what to do."

His body stirs against mine, and he closes his eyes and takes a deep breath. "It will never happen again," he says.

We hold each other for the longest time. Max's heart slows to a steady rhythm and his muscles relax. He rests his cheek on my head. "There was nothing I could do."

"I know, Max. I know that was particularly hard for you. But life is like that. You can't control everything."

He tightens his arms around me. "I can control you."

"I'm afraid I'm uncontrollable." I laugh lightly. "I like dangerous and exciting. That's why I like you."

Max chuckles. "Am I dangerous and exciting?"

"Very dangerous." I slide my arms around his neck. "And very exciting when you go all-protective alpha-male crazy. It makes me"—I search for the right words—"want you. So much. Now."

My words have the desired effect. Max grabs my hand and half walks, half drags me to the car warehouse. Once inside the cool, dark space, he locks the door. Light filters through cracks in the joints and shines through the small windows dotted around the massive space. Beautiful, exotic cars in a rainbow of colors gleam in two neat rows.

We stare at each other for a long moment. With a groan, Max pulls me into his chest and covers my lips with a hard kiss. I thread my fingers through his hair and pull him down for more.

"Fuck." His first word in five minutes isn't exactly what I wanted to hear, but I'll take what I can get.

"Yes," I breathe against his lips. "Now." My heart pounds. My pulse races, and with Max in my arms, my arousal soars.

"You push me right to the edge." His husky murmur inflames my desire, and I rub myself against the evidence of his need as it strains against his fly.

"I thought you liked it right on the edge."

He makes a choking sound, and in ten seconds flat he has me stripped and pressed up against the door.

"Which car should we ride, biker chick?"

My words catch in my throat. "Lamborghini?"

"Too low for what I have in mind."

He takes my hand and leads me to a brilliant red Audi. "Over you go, baby." He leans me over the hood of the vehicle, and my nipples tighten at the erotic sensation of hard metal against my soft flesh. I twist to look over my shoulder and Max presses me back down. "Stay still. Hands on the hood in front of you."

My pulse races and need licks through my veins. I position my hands on the Audi's smooth surface.

"What is your safe word?"

I tense. Why do I need to remember my safe word now? "Agusta."

Max strips off my yoga pants and biker chick undies. Then he caresses my bottom cheeks. I tremble. I want him so much, I am ready to beg.

"You disobeyed me," he murmurs. "You put yourself in danger. You need to be punished so you learn not to do it again."

"What?" A thrill of fear ratchets through me.

"You didn't trust my judgment," he continues. "I set the speed limit to keep you safe."

"Please," I whimper. "No games. I need you."

"I have needs too. I need to know you won't do anything like that again. Ten smacks for disobeying me." He brings his hand down across my behind, smacking me hard. Pain explodes across my cheek and I shriek.

"Max, no. You're angry."

"Do you need to use your safe word?"

My entire body trembles even as a burning flush spreads outward from my bottom. Moisture trickles down my thigh. The nightmare dances at the fringes of my consciousness. Anger and violence. We were always heading in this direction. This is the last step before the end.

No. This is not the same. He cares for me. He loves me. He promised he would never hurt me. "No."

"Good. Because I'm just getting started." He strikes again, this time low on my other cheek.

I gasp and try to wiggle free. Max's hand tightens on my back. "Don't move or I'll punish you for that too." He smoothes a hand over my flaming cheeks and my tension eases. Two smacks. Not so bad.

Smack. Smack. Smack. He alternates cheeks and strike zones. Nowhere is safe. My bottom flames and I press my hips against the metal, trying to find stimulation for the throbbing bundle of nerves between my legs.

"No you don't." Max kicks my legs apart and pulls my hips back. "First punishment. Then pleasure."

He slides his hand between my legs and through my wet folds. "Damn, baby. You're so wet. I knew this would excite you." He flicks his finger over my sweet spot and the shock of pleasure makes my knees buckle.

"Not yet. I'm not done with you." He repositions me on the vehicle and lands two more swats on my flaming skin. "Why are you being punished?"

"Because I scared you?"

"No." He strikes again, harder this time. "Because you didn't trust me to protect you. Never again are you going to put yourself in danger. Understood?"

Pain and pleasure flow over my body. My sex quivers. My knees shake. Need coils in my belly so tight I can barely think, much less respond.

SMACK. "Answer me."

Part of me wants to tell him to go to hell. Another part wants to turn around and make him give me what I want. But the part of me consumed by lust answers, "Yes."

"Last one," he rasps. The air whistles and the final smack sends a firestorm racing beneath my skin. I scream out my frustration, my need, and my pain. Max releases me and flips me over. He lifts me and seats my burning bottom on the cool, metal hood.

"You did so well, baby." He plants a soft kiss on my forehead and I jerk away. I don't want tenderness. I want release and I want to leave. In that order.

Max shoves his clothing down to his knees. His erection springs free, hot, heavy, and pulsing with need. He rips open a condom packet with his teeth and sheaths himself.

"Open for me." He spreads my thighs with his firm fingers and grips my hips. "Look at me, Makayla. I want to watch you come."

My eyes widen at the fierce possessiveness of his gaze.

"Mine," he rumbles. "Say it."

Dazed with need, I whimper, "Yours."

He eases inside me and flicks his thumb over my throbbing bundle of nerves. One slick flick. One long, hard, delicious thrust. I am filled and stretched. I am possessed.

"You feel so good," he groans as he pounds into me. "So slick and tight."

Already on the brink, it takes no more than that to set me off. I throw back my head and let loose a guttural scream as my orgasm rips through me, sending white hot bolts of lightning through my veins. My sex clenches and pulses. Max angles in deep and drives into me with quick, hard thrusts. Seconds later, he tenses and shouts his release. The throb and pulse of his climax send me into a new wave of rapture, and I bite down on his shoulder to stifle my moan.

So hard. So fast. So unlike anything we've done before. So disconcerting. I have to force myself not to pull away.

We hold each other while the fire dies down. A chill creeps through me, winding its way through my body to my heart until I can no longer bear to be touched. I ease Max away and dress without saying a word.

While he hunts around for his shirt, I wander through the cars until I find an Aston Martin identical to the one I just drove. I slide down until I am sitting on the floor beside the vehicle, my cheek pressed against the cool, metal door, my hands around my knees.

Stones crunch over cement, and Max bends down in front of me. "Makayla? Baby?" The pain and hesitation in his voice tear at my heart, but still I hold up my hand, palm forward to keep him away.

Max sits on the floor across from me, his back against a red Ferrari. I tighten my lips and study his face. His distress is etched into the lines around his eyes, concern in his wrinkled brow. He scrapes his hand through his hair. "Let me hold you."

I shake my head and close my eyes again. I breathe in the scent of rubber and paint, new leather, and old memories.

"Baby—" His voice cracks and his pain spills between us. My heart aches in response. I am hurting him with my silence. Hurting is not what I do. He told me he trusted me to tell him if there was something he needed to know. There is something he needs to know, and he needs to know it now.

"I used to have nightmares about what happened the night my dad died." I keep my eyes closed and my cheek pressed against the Aston Martin. If not for the rasp of Max's breathing, I could be alone.

"I was six years old. My dad was an abusive alcoholic. He shouted and swore, and hit my mom when he was really drunk. One day he came home from the bar worse than usual. When we saw he had a baseball bat, Mom told us to run. Susie and I hid in the upstairs closet."

Max sucks in a breath but doesn't interrupt.

"We heard shouting and screaming and then a thud," I continue. "When we crept to the kitchen, Mom was lying on the floor, bleeding from her head. She was moaning, so I knew she was alive, but I didn't know how to help her. That's the first time I knew what I wanted to do with my life."

"Go on, baby."

"I tried to wake her up, and he came in and saw us. Susie ran away, but I couldn't leave my mom. He said I could trust him and we would run away together. He said he would never hurt me." I draw in a ragged breath and squeeze my legs tight. "I said no and held up my hands to ward him away. He was so angry. He lifted me by my wrists and pulled me into the air. I kicked out and hit him, and he dropped me. He was really angry then. He picked me up around the waist and threw me into the wall."

Max makes a choking sound. Stones crunch and suddenly his arms are around me and my cheek is against his chest. I shudder into his warmth.

"Keep going," he whispers. "I'm here for you."

I swallow hard and dig my fingers into his arm. "I lay on the floor and watched him hunt for the bat. I thought we were all going to die. I closed my eyes, and I don't know what happened next. I guess I gave up. Next thing I remember is Susie slapping my cheek. My father was lying on the floor, out cold but still breathing. We got Mom up and we all ran away with nothing but the clothes on our backs. Despite everything, it was exciting to run away in the dark, knowing we would never be afraid again." My body tightens. "That's how I know I'm not a fighter. They needed me and I gave up. It has always stayed with me."

Max's fists clench and unclench against my back. His voice lowers and thickens. "How did he die?"

"We found out later he got in the car—presumably to chase after us—but he was so drunk he hit a post. He died instantly."

"What about Susie? Couldn't she tell you what happened?"

I shake my head. "She never talked about it. I don't think she remembers. She left home as soon as she could."

"Why didn't you tell me?" His voice wavers. "No wonder you have issues with violence and being restrained. I would never have asked you to work at the club. I would never have—" He chokes on his words. "Christ."

I close my eyes and breathe in his warm, sexy Max smell. "I like being with you, Max. You make me feel alive. I like the things we do together. I won't lie and say they don't scare me. They do. But I trust you, and that trust turns the fear into something thrilling. The flashbacks only come when I've lost control—like when you tie me up."

Do I tell him my real fears? That he needs a level of control I can't give, or that he will turn his violence on me? Was today a game or a warning?

Max pulls me up and holds my face between his hands. "What we do together is totally different from what happened that night. You are in total control. One word and it stops. The only problem would be if you didn't trust me enough to know I would stop when you said the word."

"That's what happened today," I whisper. "You were angry at me. I couldn't tell if we were playing or if it was real, and if it was real then I was afraid you had lost control and you wouldn't stop. Like him. Violence and anger together scare me more than anything else."

Max dips his head and presses his forehead to mine. "I told you before, I could never be angry with you, baby. You are who you are. I was angry at myself for not managing the situation better, but the minute we stepped through the door I put it aside. You were so wound up, I thought you could handle something more intense. I am a violent man, but I don't want you ever to worry that I'll be violent with you. I would rather cut off my hand than hurt you."

I close my eyes and take a deep breath. "Okay."

"You don't sound convinced."

"I think I just need a bit of time."

His brow creases with worry. "Are you…do you want to—"

I kiss him softly. "No, Max. I'm not running away this time."

Chapter 23
YOU DIDN'T TRUST ME

WE MAKE IT BACK to the club just before opening. I have just prepped the first aid room when my phone vibrates. I check the Caller ID. Max. He tried to be respectful of my need to be alone on our trip home, but now that we're back, my brief respite appears to be over.

Where are u?

First aid room. U know this **raises eyebrows**

Just checking

Okay

Do you need anything?

No, thanks

Medical supplies?

No

Are you thirsty?

No

Hungry?

No

Cold?

No

Lonely?

No

I miss you

U just saw me ten minutes ago

Ten minutes is a long time

This is true

Do you need more time alone?

If I did, I wouldn't be here

Good. I'm coming to see you

Bad Max. Injured fighters only

I am injured

U r not **folds arms**

I need minx medicine

Have to go. Amanda calling

Within ten seconds of speaking to Amanda on the phone, I deduce she is drunk. She only ever calls me Makayla when she is over her limit.

"What have you been up to this afternoon?" I ask after she mumbles something unintelligible into the phone. "It's only seven o'clock on a Saturday night. You're wasting your weekend."

"We settled a big case and the clients took us out for a few drinks."

"On a Saturday?"

"Time has no meaning in a law firm," she admonishes me. "You know that."

"Where are you now?"

She giggles. "In a cab on my way to the Geek Club. I need to speak to Jake. I want to know if we would have had a chance if I hadn't called a break."

Oh God. "You don't want to do that, honey. He's done with you. He's moved on. You're just going to embarrass yourself and get hurt in the process."

"I need closure," she snaps. "I need to understand what went wrong. How could he choose that skinny society bitch over me?"

"You hurt him."

"I didn't mean to," she says quietly.

I fiddle with my first aid kit, repacking things that don't need packing. "Couldn't you go another night? Maybe when you haven't been drinking all afternoon? Max and I could come with you."

"I'm going now. I need to get it over with."

I ball my skirt in my fist. "You can't go there alone. It's dangerous. What if Jake isn't there?"

She groans into the phone. "Seriously? You worry too much. I'll go in, see if he's there. If he is, I'll talk to him and leave. I'm not sticking around for the fights. And it's not like I'm going alone to Ghost Town. It's an upscale residential neighborhood. What could possibly happen?"

"Something bad enough to cause Max to make me promise never to go there again."

Amanda snorts a laugh. "If Max had his way, he would probably wrap you in cotton and lock you up so nothing could ever happen to you. He takes overprotectiveness to the extreme."

"He's not that bad."

"Just sayin'."

"If I wanted to do something dangerous, he wouldn't stop me," I lie. "We have an open relationship. We would discuss it and he would understand my point of view."

"I thought I was the inebriated person in this conversation," she laughs. Amanda knows me too well to be fooled. "Have a nice evening surrounded by hot, sweaty men."

"Wait," I bark into the phone. "I'll come with you. Promise you won't go in until I get there."

"Don't you have to work?"

"I'm not leaving my best friend to wander drunk into a dangerous fight club looking for an altercation with her ex."

"You're so sweet," she sighs. "I remember seeing a bus stop about half a block away. I'll wait for you there. DO NOT tell Max where you are going. I don't want him to tip off Jake."

"But—"

"If you tell him, don't bother coming. If I find out Jake skipped out because you couldn't keep a secret, I'll be so mad at you…"

My heart sinks. "Just promise you won't go in without me."

"Pinky promise."

"I'll be there as soon as I can."

―⁓―

"Max?" I knock on the door to his office and peek inside. Max points to the phone in his hand and waves me in.

I take a seat on the big, comfy leather chair in front of his desk and wait for him to finish his call. His office reminds me of his suite upstairs—polished-wood floors, exposed-brick walls, modern fittings, and the big oak desk covered in D-rings. Only the paintings on the wall behind him don't fit with the wood and stone decor. Both are framed tribal prints, one red and one green. They remind me of his tattoos.

"Minx. What's up?" Max asks after he finishes his call.

I bite my lip and stare at the floor. The lie I had prepared sours on my tongue. I don't want to lie to Max, but I can't let Amanda go into the Geek Club alone. Maybe I can fudge it.

"What's wrong?" Max voice drops, and I look up just as his brow furrows.

"Amanda needs me," I say in a rush. "She's about to do something crazy. I know this is unprofessional, and I would never normally ever ask—"

"Go, baby. I'll find someone to cover for you."

My tension lifts and I exhale the breath I didn't realize I was holding. "Aren't you going to ask where or why?"

Max grins. "I trust you. I can be reasonable, except when it comes to your safety."

My lungs tighten. I could have dealt with angry, shouting Max, but his kind understanding is almost too much too bear. I am an awful, horrible person. I am betraying his trust. He deserves better than me.

I push myself up and 'round his desk. "Thank you." I press a kiss to his forehead, but before I can turn away, he sweeps me into his lap.

"That's all I get?" he teases, and his dark eyes warm. "I suffer through an afternoon of silence and manage to restrain myself when my girl wants to disappear on a mysterious errand, and all I get is a kiss on the forehead?"

"Maybe you get a kiss on the cheek too." I brush my lips over his cheek, scratchy with his five o'clock shadow and smelling deliciously of cologne.

Max frowns and twists his lips. "Hmmm."

"Maybe you get a kiss here too." I trace the outline of his lips with the tip of my tongue and nibble and suck his bottom lip. When he threads his fingers through my hair to pull me closer, I press my lips against his and dip my tongue into his warmth. Max moans into my mouth. A hot surge of need rushes through me.

My phone rings and I look over at my purse on the chair. What if Amanda decided not to wait?

"I'd better go." I push myself away but Max holds me firm.

"I might need more convincing." He kisses me so hard and deep, my toes curl.

My phone rings again, and I wiggle off his lap. "That's probably Amanda." I race over to the chair, grab my phone on the last ring, and accept the call. "Amanda. Don't you dare go without me," I bark into the receiver.

"Ms. Delaney. Name is Ty. I'm a collector at Collections R Us. I've taken over your file from Sergio. Says here you missed a payment on Monday. I'm after our money."

My blood runs cold. "Where's Sergio? Why are you calling me now?" I can't disguise the horror in my voice.

"You know why I'm calling." His voice is low, rough, and nothing short of menacing. "Sergio is away to deal with a family emergency. I'm handling his files for him, and I want the fucking money."

"But...it's Saturday night...you're harassing me."

Ty makes a tsk tsk sound. "I'll fucking call you whenever I fucking want, you little deadbeat. Don't think you'll be putting me off the way you did to Serge. You had him twisted around your little finger but that crap doesn't work with me. The money better be in our account first thing Monday morning or I'll be taking a part of your paycheck for the rest of your fucking life and selling your parents' house so fast they won't know what hit them."

My hands shake so hard I have to grip the chair. "You aren't allowed to threaten me. I'll report you."

He snorts a laugh. "Christ. Like I haven't heard that one before. How are you going to prove it? You got a record of this call? No fucking way. You got money to go to court? I don't think so. I want my money, honey, or you and I will have a date at your workplace Monday morning, eight a.m."

"Please," I choke back a sob. "You'll have your money. Just please leave my parents alone and don't come to my work…"

Work. Oh. My. God. I'm in Max's office.

I spin around. Max is standing behind me, only a few feet away. When I catch his gaze, his expression hardens into stone.

"Give me the phone." His face and his voice command compliance, and right now, I'm not up for a fight.

"I have someone who wants to speak to you," I say to Ty. I hand over the phone.

"Who is this?" Max thunders.

Ty talks for at least a minute. Max's lips press into a thin line. His body stills. His face turns purple. Anger rolls off him in waves. His fury at my strip poker shenanigans was nothing compared to this. My thighs quiver and I curl up in the chair with my arms wrapped tight around my knees.

"Tell me how much? The full amount." After thirty seconds, he barks, "You'll have your money on Friday and you will NEVER contact her again. Give me the account details." He stalks over to his desk and writes the numbers on a piece of paper, and then he ends the call.

I shake my head. "I can't take your money, Max."

"You will."

"It's my problem. I'll deal with it."

His jaw clenches. "You don't deal with people like that. He'll run you into the ground and your parents too."

I nod and tears trickle down my cheeks. "That's why I needed the second job."

His face stills and my heart skips a beat.

"So take the money," he shouts. "My company makes more than that in an afternoon."

"I can't. I don't want you to ever think it was about the money."

He closes his eyes and takes several deep breaths. "I know that, baby. I never thought for one minute you were like the others."

"I forbid you to make that payment, Max. If you do, I'll never speak to you again. I'll find a way out of it myself. I don't want to be indebted to you. I don't want to feel I owe you anything." And I have to know I can walk away. If there was one thing I learned as a child, it was that.

"Aaaargh." Max throws the phone against the wall. I jump at the sharp crack as it hits the exposed brick and slides to the floor with a soft thud. "Of all the stubborn, irrational..." He rounds on me, striding toward my chair in a blaze of fury. "Why didn't you tell me? After what they did to my family, how could you not let me know they were after you?"

I exhale a long, slow breath. "It wasn't him before. It was a guy named Sergio. He was different. More accommodating. We had a bit of give-and-take going. And with the second job I was pretty sure I could make the payments. There was no reason to involve you. And after you told me about your family, I didn't want to put you through anything like that again."

"Christ." Max rakes his hand through his hair. "Do you even understand? He will stop at NOTHING to get his money. I went through this when I was fourteen. He will harass you and torment you. He will show up at your work, your home, even if you go for a walk in the park. He will make your life a living hell."

"I'll find a way. If it means I have to get another two jobs, then that's what I'll do. I owe the money. I intend to pay it back. If he had just let me make reasonable payments, it would have been fine. Plus I've filed all sorts of appeals and Amanda's going to help me out. She's just finished a big trial."

"Take the money and pay me back."

"I don't want to owe you anything. My mother never borrowed a cent off anyone. Even when things were at their worst, she always found a way to get by. I admired her for that. I would be happy to have half her character."

Max slams his hand against the wall. "You didn't trust me. Again. You didn't think I could help you. No matter what I do, you won't let me in."

"That's not true."

He pulls open his door and looks back over his shoulder. "I am paying that debt, Makayla, whether you want it or not. I will not let you suffer the way my family suffered. I won't have him chasing after you or threaten your life. I'll save you even if it means losing you."

The door swings closed. I am alone.

An hour later my cab pulls up at the bus stop outside the Geek Club. I have tested my phone and although it seems to have a few glitches, I have been able to text Amanda, check the weather, and find the nearest pizza joint.

I step out of the cab, and Amanda tosses the driver a roll of bills and then throws her arms around me. "I'm so sorry you had a fight with Max. I can't believe you still came."

My bottom lip quivers and I fight back the tears. I can cry later. Right now, Amanda needs me.

We walk up the sidewalk to the Geek Club. Light shines from the edges of the blacked-out windows, and loud punk music almost drowns out the sounds of the fight going on inside. The night is cool and still. Wind brushes through the treetops. The street is eerily deserted.

The side door is locked with no attendant in sight. Amanda suggests we walk around the garage and look for another entrance. We slip through a side gate and follow the wall around to the backyard. I am about to turn the corner when Amanda grips my shoulder and pulls me back behind a bush. The hushed murmur of voices carries toward us, and I peek through the leaves to see what's going on.

Three men, all wearing jeans and dark T-shirts, are huddled in the corner. One man opens a shopping bag and pulls out four brick-size packages containing what looks like white powder.

Oh. My. God. I gasp in a breath and stagger backward, pulling Amanda with me. "Drug deal," I whisper. "We have to get out of here." We turn to run, only to find the gate blocked by a bald giant in a leather jacket.

I grab Amanda's hand and we run back into the garden. I glance over my shoulder. The bruiser has been joined by the three drug dealers, and they are gaining on us. I wheeze in breath after breath and stumble over a toy truck and onto my knees. Amanda hauls me up and we keep running. The fence in front of us is about eight feet high and scalable if we find a foothold.

Wham. Someone slams into me from behind and throws me up against the fence. A thick hand clamps around my neck and I suck frantically, trying to get air.

"Gotcha." My captor leans in to stare at me, his bald pate glistening in the moonlight. A smile creases his round, heavy face and his jowls jiggle as he laughs. His breath smells of garlic and onions. He brushes his humongous red nose against my cheek and sniffs as if he's looking for truffles. I name him Pig.

"They saw you," Pig grunts to the three drug dealers who have just joined us at the wall. "Grab Blondie and we'll take them down to the cellar."

Pig spins me around and covers my mouth with one hand. "You're gonna walk to the cellar doors over there, nice and slow. You mess with me and I'll cut off your air. You understand?"

I nod. Then I ram my foot into his instep and bite his hand.

"Fuck." Pig jerks his hand away and staggers back.

I scream as loud as I can and run at the guy holding Amanda. Just as my fingers touch his jacket, something hits my head and the world goes black.

Chapter 24

Everyone not tied to a chair jumps up

I OPEN MY EYES and for a second I think I am dreaming. I am in a huge, dimly lit room filled with boxes, barrels, and crates. Three guys—one redhead, one blonde, and the other with curly black hair are huddled over a table in the far corner, all dressed in cheap printed T-shirts, flip-flops, and torn jeans. A naked bulb swings from the ceiling. The air is fragrant with the rich scent of earth and the fusty aroma of dried herbs. It is almost surreal.

However, Amanda, tied to a chair in front of me, the burn of ropes around my wrists, and the pounding in my head are very real. So real, I groan.

"Mac," she whispers. "Mac. Are you okay?"

"Aside from the fact I am tied to a chair and probably concussed, I'm fine," I moan. "What happened?"

"The big guy hit you over the head with something. We're in the cellar under the Geek Club. He's gone to get the boss."

I struggle against the ropes on my hands and feet, but they are secure. As is the room. Aside from the tiny windows along the edges, the only way out is up the steps.

The door creaks open and Pig comes down the stairs followed by a giant. A familiar giant.

Misery.

My heart pounds in my chest. He seems even bigger in the enclosed space than he did at Redemption, his head just clearing the ceiling. He storms over to the men at the table. "What the fuck were you doing taking the stuff out of the club? You are all fucking idiots."

He looks Amanda up and down, and then his gaze falls on me. His eyes narrow. "I know you." He leans down and grabs the guy with the curly black hair by the collar. "Who is she? Why do I know her?"

Curly wilts. "She's Torment's girl."

"Fuck." Pig spits on the ground, as pigs do. "I thought I recognized her."

"Who's Torment?" the blond asks.

Curly swallows. "He works the underground circuit. One of the top fighters. Used to be a professional boxer. Mean. Nasty. Hard as nails. He's crazy. I've seen him take down three men here at the club without breaking a sweat."

The blond whistles. "What were they packing?"

"Hard-drive casings, keyboards, laptops, external drives, a couple of flat-screen monitors, and a whole roll of HDMI cable."

Red whistles. "Serious fight. HDMI cable isn't cheap."

"Geeks." Pig rolls his eyes, making no effort to hide his derision.

"I heard Torment once shoved a hard drive down a guy's throat," Red interjects.

Curly's eyebrows wiggle like two dancing caterpillars. "What capacity?"

"Four terabytes."

"No way. That must have just been in the last few months. They haven't rolled the fours out to the public yet."

"Shut the fuck up." Misery shakes Curly like a rag doll and tosses him to the floor. Curly's phone skitters across the concrete. The sleek, silver design is familiar.

"Amanda," I whisper. "I have an idea."

"I'm so sorry I got you into this," she sobs. "I don't know what I was thinking. I went a bit crazy."

I give her a half smile. "That's why I came. I couldn't let you be crazy alone. Now give me a distraction before we both start sobbing. Something to get them near us."

Amanda nods.

"If we let them go, Torment will come here on a tear." Pig's voice wavers. And well it should. Max could eat him for supper.

Misery responds with a sharp bark of laughter. "I'm not fucking afraid of Torment. He ran out on our last fight." He looks me over again. "Maybe we should send him a message to keep his bitch in line. Draw him out to finish the fight."

I look Misery straight in the eye. "I'm not his bit…girl anymore. We broke up."

Misery gives me a cold smile. "Even better. I can enjoy you without having him show up on my doorstep."

"Nice one, Mac," Amanda spits out. "You just threw away your only bargaining chip. You had value as his girl. Now we're going to die because of your self-pity." She gives me a wink. Operation Distraction has begun.

"What?" My voice rises. "We wouldn't even be here if it wasn't for you mooning after your guy like a lost puppy. You screwed up with him. Get over it."

We banter back and forth, drawing the attention of everyone in the room. No man can resist a catfight. Too bad we didn't have a couple of bikinis and a mud pit. They edge closer to us, and I spot my purse under the table.

When they are all as far away from the phone as they will ever be, I suck in a breath and scream, "CALL 911."

Everyone freezes. No sound emanates from my purse. Is the leather too thick? Is it broken after being smashed against the wall? I take another breath, just as Curly's phone starts dialing.

"Fuck," Misery shouts. "She's trying to set off your damn phone. Shut it off."

Curly scrambles over the floor, grabs his phone, and shuts it off with a loud sigh.

I glare at my purse. I have to give it one last try. Maybe it didn't recognize the numbers. "CALL MAX CELL," I scream. My phone starts dialing.

"She's got one too. Find it, you idiots." Misery storms across the cellar and hits me across the face. "Shut it off."

My head snaps to the side and blood trickles down my lip. Fire screams across my cheek. "No."

He hits me again. This time, his palm connects with bone. The pain brings on the darkness, whispers of memories, someone yelling my name. A whimper.

No. Not now. I fight away the nightmare and snap back to reality and a whole lot of pain.

"SHUT IT OFF!" Misery yells.

"No."

His third hit almost knocks me out of the chair. Amanda screams for him to stop. Something trickles down my cheek. I can't tell if it is blood or tears.

"Makayla, baby?"

Tears spring to my eyes when Max's voice, deep and low, echoes in the room. Red crawls under the table and grabs my purse.

I take a deep breath and scream, "MAX. HELP. MISERY HAS ME AND AMANDA IN THE CELLAR OF—"

Thwack. Misery hits me again. The sharp, bitter taste of blood fills my mouth. My vision blurs. Red triumphantly holds up my phone and then smashes it on the floor. This time, it does not survive.

Misery gives a satisfied grunt. "Even better. He knows I have you but not where. Looks like I'll get to send him a message after all."

I slump against the chair. Amanda sobs. Misery pulls out his phone and makes a call. He orders a couple of pizzas—no anchovies—and a side of wings. I guess message time will be delayed.

———

An hour has passed. The pizzas have been eaten. Misery and Pig debate what to do with us. Pig wants to kill us. Misery thinks this is a bad plan. Body disposal is not easy, and he just had his Jeep cleaned. He also has a slipped disc. My wrists and ankles are raw from trying to get out of the ropes. My head aches. My jaw throbs. I wish I could have seen my parents one last time. I wish I could have given Max one last kiss. I wish Misery would have given us some pizza. I'm starving.

The cellar door creaks and everyone looks up. Misery sends Curly to check it out. Curly doesn't return. Red goes next. We wait. No Red. As if we were in a bad horror film, Misery decides to send the blond. The blond doesn't want to go. He knows the score. Dark night plus disappearing friends usually equals axe in the head. I suggest he put on some sexy lingerie and run out screaming like a co-ed. Misery tells me to shut my mouth or he'll shut it for me with something so big I'll never be able to talk again. I hope it's a big slice of pizza.

Brave Pig goes up the stairs. He returns head first. No axe. All body parts intact. He is followed down the stairs by Max, Jake, Rampage, and Homicide. Yay!

Everyone not tied to a chair jumps up. For a moment, the room is still and quiet. Relief wells up in my chest and explodes in a sob. Max's head jerks around and his eyes rake over my swollen, bleeding face and then travel over the ropes on my hands and feet. His nostrils flare and his lips pull back, baring his teeth. The air around him ripples and changes. His body tenses and swells; his muscles and veins strain against his skin. I almost expect him to change form—maybe a werewolf or werebeast. I have seen his anger and it scared me. This is not anger. This is rage.

Max explodes into motion. He barrels toward Misery, tossing chairs and crates and the blond out of his way. One of them hits the wall with a sickening crunch—a chair, not the blond.

Jake throws a punch at a recovered Pig. He squeals, as pigs do. Rampage and Homicide untie Amanda and me and usher us into the corner. They tell us there are more men fighting outside and we are safer in a small, confined space with four raging, out-of-control giants attacking each other. I disagree. I am outvoted.

Max attacks Misery with the kind of vigor only reserved for really dirty ovens. Fists fly. Bones crunch. He does not hold back. My stomach clenches tighter and tighter. This is nothing like the club. This is real. Forget the werebeast; Max is violence with a capital *V*.

Misery pulls out a knife. Not just a knife. A dagger.

"Oh God. Max is going to be killed."

Rampage laughs. He cups his hands around his mouth and yells, "Yo. Torment. Misery's the one who beat on your girl."

Max stills, and for a heartbeat, I imagine fear flickers across Misery's face, or maybe it was just a muscle twitch. In a blur of motion, Max closes the distance between them and lets loose. My body convulses and I grab the wastepaper basket, retching over and over again. Amanda holds my hair and rubs my back. Rampage hands me a bottle of water.

By the time I can sit up again, the fight is over. Misery is down and groaning on the floor.

Max surveys the room. His eyes skim over me, pausing briefly on the basket. Then he stalks across the room, grabs my hand, and yanks me up the stairs.

Sirens sound in the distance, drawing near. Someone must have called the police.

"How did you find me?"

"Tracking device in your phone."

Max drags me across the lawn to a garden shed surrounded by trees. With one kick, he breaks down the door and pulls me inside. He slams the door closed and my eyes adjust to the dark. Thin, wavering filaments of light from houses and streetlights find their way through cracks in the wood. Enough to see the fury in Max's face. His eyes are wide, the pupils almost black. His neck is corded with tension. His face is all hard planes and angles, dark with shadows. I barely recognize him.

"You promised you would never come here." His body shakes so violently, I am afraid to touch him. He is barely in control, and a shiver of fear winds its way up my spine.

"I couldn't let Amanda come here alone."

"You promised you would never put yourself in danger."

"I had no choice. She's my best friend."

His nostrils flare, and he folds his arms across his chest. "Take off your clothes."

My heart pounds frantically against my ribs. I've never been claustrophobic, but in this tiny, dark shed smelling of gasoline and grass clippings, and with Max looming large in front of me, I can barely breathe.

"I don't want to be here."

"Take off your clothes." He forces every word through clenched teeth as if speaking is an effort.

"Why?" My voice is thin and high, almost a whine.

"Goddamn it, Makayla. For once, just do what I say. Take. Off. Your. Clothes."

I step backward until I hit the safety of the wall. My eyes flick to the door behind him. He catches the direction of my gaze.

"You aren't leaving until you take off your clothes."

I wrap my arms around myself in an effort to stop trembling. "No."

"Fuck." He closes the distance between us in two long strides, and grabs my shoulders. He slants his mouth over mine and kisses me hard, crushing my lips, banging my teeth. Fierce kiss. Frightening kiss. The smell of his rage fills my nostrils, thick and suffocating like wood smoke. The world tilts. He grabs my top and yanks it over my head. Cold air blasts against my skin. Fear and confusion freeze my brain.

"Max," I whisper. "Please. No." Instinct screams for me to run. He is out of control. But part of me still believes he won't hurt me.

His hands drop to my waist, and he jerks my yoga pants over my hips and shoves them down to my ankles. He steps back, and his eyes rake over my body, cold and detached. Not the look of a lover, but of a stranger.

Although I am still wearing my bra and panties, I instinctively try to cover up. I wrap one arm around my breasts and the other over my hip. My hand fans over the juncture of my thighs.

"Don't cover yourself from me." He enunciates each word, shooting them at me like arrows.

A sob wells up in my throat. I drop my arms and look away. I cannot bear to look at him or to see this stranger looking at me through Max's eyes.

Max grasps my shoulders and pulls me away from the wall. His hands slide over my body, his touch rough, perfunctory, and impersonal. His hands linger over my belly. I bite my lip and tears trickle down my cheeks. He spins me around, and his cold assessment continues over my back, my buttocks, and my legs. By the time he is finished, I am sobbing out loud. A black hole has formed inside me. I have never felt so alone or, disconcertingly, so ashamed.

He steps away and his hands fall to his belt. He undoes the buckle and yanks the belt off his jeans with a loud crack. He motions me toward him with an abrupt wave of his fingers. "Come here."

I back away.

"Come here now." The undercurrent of barely controlled anger in his voice sends me scrambling back into a shelf. I stumble over my yoga pants and fall to the floor. Flower pots and water cans tumble to the ground around me. Max strides across the shed. I hold my hands up and turn away. "Please, Max. I'm sorry. Please don't hurt me."

He stops short and looks at me aghast. "Is that what you think?"

I look from him to the belt and back to him. Tears stream down my cheeks. "I don't know what to think anymore."

With a roar, he throws his belt across the room, and then sweeps the workbench clean with his hand. Tools clatter over the concrete floor. "What can I do, Makayla?" he shouts. "What can I do to get you to trust me?"

"Not this."

He pushes open the door. Pausing, he looks back over his shoulder, and breathes slowly, in and out, as if trying to calm himself. "When I got your call, I thought…then I saw you in the cellar…tied up…your face—" His voice breaks and he scrubs his hand over his face. "It was too much. I couldn't think…talk." He takes another deep breath and grips the frame of the door so hard, his knuckles whiten. "I needed to see if you were hurt anywhere else. I needed to hold you. But when I saw the bruises on your stomach and your back, I took off the belt so the buckle wouldn't hurt you."

He steps out into the night, and the door slams behind him. I collapse, sobbing, in a heap on the cold, stone floor.

~~~

For the next few hours, the Geek Club bustles with activity. Geeks scatter far and wide. Amanda and I sit on the front porch of the house, and give our statements to the police. Pig and the drug dealers are hauled away. Misery, who turns out to be the CEO of a major tech company, is handcuffed and thrown in the back of a police car. Max and Jake are questioned about the fight.

"Hey, it's my favorite EMT." Ray drops to his knees beside me and pulls out his paramedic kit. "You're looking all banged up."

"I'll be fine."

"She was hit on the head and lost consciousness," Amanda interjects. "The big guy also kicked her stomach and back when she was down." I glare at her. I already told her I didn't want anyone to know. I can take care of myself.

Ray raises his eyebrows and feels along my scalp until I wince.

"How are you feeling? Any symptoms of a concussion? Maybe we should take you to the hospital and get you checked out."

"I just want to go home."

Ray takes me to the ambulance and does a thorough check of all my bruises. He cleans up my face and gives me some ice. "I'll let you go home if you have someone to stay with you for the next twenty-four hours. You know the drill."

"Sure. I'll work something out."

He packs up his kit and hesitates. "Listen, my offer still stands. If you need any help or advice about qualifying as a paramedic, give me a call."

By the time he leaves, the street is empty. The bad guys are in jail. I haven't spoken to Max since the incident in the shed, although he has never been far away. I wander back to the porch and huddle in a deck chair.

Jake squats beside me and clasps my hand. "I'm going to take you home, and Max will take Amanda on his motorcycle."

"Sure." Numb and emotionally drained, I don't need to ask why.

"He's not thinking clearly right now," Jake offers. "And it's probably best for you too. I think you need some time to come to terms with the fact he is capable of a level of violence you can't tolerate."

I shrug.

Jake sighs. "I'll tell him to bring the bike to the front to pick up Amanda."

"Wait." I grab his arm. "Aren't you going to talk to her? You are the reason we came here tonight."

Jake presses his lips together and shakes his head. "Not going to happen."

"Why?"

"She's not the only one hurting."

Two hours later, I toss and turn in my bed. I can't sleep. My head aches. My jaw throbs. My brain is sore. I briefly consider joining Jake in front of the television, but I don't feel like talking. I wish Amanda hadn't told him I wasn't supposed to be left alone.

Where is Max? Did he stay at Amanda's house? Images of them together appear unbidden in my mind, and I push them away. Amanda would never hurt me. I trust her implicitly. But what about Max? Do I trust him? Would he ever turn his violence on me?

I groan and turn to my side. A deep longing claws at my gut. A longing stronger than fear.

The soft click of the bedroom door startles me. I look over my shoulder and my heart leaps. "Max!"

He puts his finger to his lips. His leathers creak as he eases himself into the armchair in the corner of the room. He sits back and the shadows flicker around him, shades of black and gray.

I toy with the sheet, winding it around my hand. I wait for him to take off his clothes and come to bed, but he doesn't move.

"Max?"

He draws in a ragged breath and shakes his head. His eyes are bleak and desolate, all traces of their usual warmth gone. My breath leaves me in a rush, and dread creeps its way up my spine. I sit upright in bed and pull the sheet around me. He is wearing his leather pants and a white T-shirt, stained with blood.

"You're hurt."

He looks away and my blood chills. His face is taut; his jaw clenched so hard it quivers. His lips are pressed together in a thin line. His hands are balled into fists on his lap. Anger or anguish? I can't tell.

"Talk to me. Please. I'm sorry I misunderstood your intentions."

He scrubs his hands over his face. "Sleep, baby." His voice is raw and strained with emotion. His body is tense. He won't meet my gaze. And suddenly I understand why he is here. Despair hits me like a punch to the gut.

"You came to say good-bye." A statement, not a question.

His chin dips, just barely, but I don't need the nod. The answer is in his eyes.

"Can I hold you one last time?" I ask softly.

He shakes his head. Tears trickle down my cheeks and my throat tightens. "You're going to watch over me tonight and then you'll go?"

He grips the arms of the chair, his knuckles white, and he presses his lips together, tilting his head back to stare at the ceiling.

Tears run down my neck, staining my top. "I'm sorry, Max." My shoulders quake and I sob into my hands. "I'm sorry I can't be who you need me to be. I'm sorry I can't give you the trust you need. I'm sorry your violence scares me so much."

"I'm sorry too, baby." His voice is so low, so broken, I can barely hear it.

I curl up on the bed facing him and wrap my arms around myself. I study his beautiful, haunted face. I try to memorize every plane and angle of his jaw, his strong chin, the curve of his lips, and the crinkle at the corners of his eyes. I imagine I can feel the scratchy stubble on his cheek and smell the spicy scent of his cologne. I close my eyes and imagine the warmth of his body and the light caress of his hand over my skin. I remember the deep rumble of his laugh and the low growl of his voice. I imagine I am in his arms. Safe. Cherished. Loved.

When I open my eyes, it is morning.

Max is gone.

Chapter 25

A DECENT KINDA GUY

MONDAY MORNING. SEVEN FIFTY-SEVEN a.m. My eyes are bleary from a lack of sleep. My head aches. I see Max everywhere—on the bus, on the street, in the coffee shop. My heart leaps and crashes at every false sighting. I can't bear the pain anymore, and it's only been two days.

"Late. As usual." Big Doris tears a green slip off her pad and drops it on my desk.

"I'm not late."

She tears another green slip off her pad, and another and another until my desk is littered with paper.

"What are these for?" My voice rises as the green slips continue to fall.

She presses her lips into a thin line. "You ruined EVERYTHING— the dinner on the weekend, the date…He's supposed to be mine and all he talks about is YOU."

Huh? What did I ever do to her? Who's she talking about? Charlie?

As if on cue, Charlie pokes his head around the partition. "What's going on? Are you okay, Doris?"

"Don't speak to me." She spins on her heel and marches down the corridor.

Charlie stares after her and then turns his gaze to me. "Hey, Mac. You look like shit."

"Back at you."

My phone rings. My heart thuds and I stare at the receiver. The phone rings and rings.

Charlie pokes his head over the partition. "Hey. You gonna pick that up?"

"No. New debt collector. Mean, nasty one."

"He'll call your cell next," Charlie nods at my purse.

"Don't have a cell. It got smashed on the weekend when I was tied up and beaten by a couple of drug dealers in the basement of a fight club."

Charlie stares at my cut and bruised face. "No shit. I thought maybe you'd walked into a door."

"I wish I had."

The phone rings again and I throw my jacket over it.

"Won't work," Charlie offers. "My brother had a debt collector after him for years. He kept changing his phone numbers, but the collector came to his house. Sometimes he sat outside in his car for hours. My brother lost it one day and smashed all the windows of his car with a bat. Collector just added it to the bill."

"Maybe I'll move back to my old place. It's still being renovated. He won't think to look for me there."

~~~

Twelve hours later, I am back in my old room. I unpack the boxes in my as-yet unrenovated lilac sanctuary and dig out my old phone. After talking to Dr. Drake over lunch in the canteen, and agonizing about it all day, I've decided to apply to medical school, and I want Amanda to be the first to know.

"Hi, Mac," she says. "Guess what? I'm on a date with Kink on a Stick. I needed to rebound from Jake, and Drake was totally on board. We're sexually but not romantically compatible so we've decided to become friends with benefits."

A roar fills the speaker and I hold the phone away from my ear. "What's that?"

"We're at a mixed martial arts club. After his pissing contest with Max, Drake is all gung ho to get into the circuit, and he really knows how to work a crowd. They love him. He held his own in the last fight for almost two minutes. He really did wrestle in college. Apparently he even won a few titles. You should see him. He's fast and so light on his feet."

"Is Max there?"

"No. We're at some fancy club in Palo Alto. Not as big as Redemption, but it's been done up with wood floors and high-end equipment. All licensed and sanctioned." Her voice drops to a whisper. "Have you heard from Max?"

A lump forms in my throat. "No. His good-bye was pretty clear. And I'm not sure I even want to. I just can't get over my violence issues. I think we aren't meant to be together."

"Maybe you should call him. Talk to him. Find a way to build a level of trust where you aren't terrified he'll turn into your father, and he isn't terrified to give you some space."

"It doesn't matter now." I sigh. "I'm going to send a fax to the collection agency on Friday that says I don't consent to Max making the payment. He'll be furious. I'm sure the new collector will be too."

"Don't you worry about that collector. I'm in the game now."

"Why are you whispering?" I play with the heart-shaped pendant around my neck. I should probably take it off. Maybe even sell it, but I've never had a piece of jewelry that meant so much to me. It reminds me of the night Max first said, "Mine."

"We've snuck into the first aid room. Drake said he needs personal medical attention. He's gone to his car to get his supplies. I'm not sure what he expects me to do. I'm an attorney, not a doctor." She bursts into laughter and I can't help but smile.

"I'm thinking of taking him up on his offer to help me get into medical school," I tell her. "He can help me get a full scholarship and get my application through on the fast-track. If it goes well, I could be in med school in just four months. If I can hold off the debt collector until then, my payments will be waived while I'm in school."

"And if you can't?"

"I'll be in a position to buy my parents a new house when I graduate."

Amanda sighs. "I thought it wasn't what you really wanted to do."

I bunch my sweater in my fist. "It's not, but I don't have any other options."

"This is my fault," she says, her voice flat. "You didn't work on Saturday because of me. You and Max broke up because of me. I was too busy with my trial to help you when you needed me."

I curl up on my bed and wrap one arm around myself. "Don't ever think that. You're my best friend. I was there because I wanted to be there, and I would do it again. This was going to happen anyway. I just can't think of another way to get out of it. I can't take Max's money, especially now."

"Too bad you don't know an attorney who owes you a big favor."

My chest tightens. "I don't need you to fight my battles either. This is my mess. I have to sort it out."

Amanda groans. "I'm not offering to fight your battles. You are going to fight your battles, but I am going to help you. That's what attorneys and best friends do. And lucky for you, I have a space on my pro bono list for a best friend who has been there for me and had my back since I was four years old, even when it cost her everything, like now."

Tears well up in my eyes. "Stop. You're making me cry."

"Good. You made me cry, and now when Drake comes back with his fake medical supplies, my face will be all puffy and red. Not a good look for playtime. I'm going to have to run to the washroom to freshen up. In the meantime, you need to think about getting some leverage."

"I owe the money. I don't have any leverage."

"The law is your leverage." Her tone switches to full-on lecture mode. "There are laws about how he can collect the money. He can't harass you; he can't threaten. The list goes on."

"I thought it took a long time to run these things through court."

"It does. Unless you have friends in high places. And you know I do."

A door closes in the background. Amanda giggles. "Drake is back. He's pulling a nurse's uniform out of his bag. Hmmm. I've never seen a nurse's uniform with only two inches of skirt and breast cutouts. What else does he have? A pair of rubber gloves, a giant syringe with no needle, twine, a roll of plastic wrap, a crescent wrench, battery cables, a plastic whale, and…I don't even know what the last object is, but it moves."

Laughter wells up in my chest and spills out in a snort. "You're making that up to cheer me up."

"I couldn't make that up if I tried." Her voice drops so low I can barely hear her. "I don't think he's really injured."

"Maybe in the head."

"Are you sure you don't want him? He still holds a torch for you, and I think you could learn a few things."

"No. Definitely not. I have issues with plastic animals being used as sex toys. He's all yours."

"Ooooo. He's showing me where it hurts. That's a very big owie. Maybe nursie should kiss it better."

"LEAVING NOW," I shout into the phone. "TMI."

"Bye, honey," she whispers. "Don't worry about the debt collector—" She cuts herself off. "Bad patient. Stop running around or nursie will have to spank you. Oh, I see. You brought your own paddle. Gotta go, Mac. Things are heating up."

Dr. Drake beams when I walk into his office after work the next day. "Look who's here. It's my favorite med school applicant."

"Hi, Dr. Drake." *Don't think about whales. Don't think about whales.* Images of plastic whales float through my mind. *Bad whales. Go away.*

He gestures me over to a round table in the corner and takes a seat beside me. "I am so glad you decided to take me up on my offer," he says. "After you called this morning, I had my secretary put together two files—one for scholarship applications and one for medical school applications. I thought we could fill them out together, and I could give you tips about what they'll be looking for."

"Great." I plaster a fake smile on my face and try to convince myself this is really what I want to do. "I can't thank you enough for all your help."

Dr. Drake throws his arm across the back of my chair. "Don't thank me yet. Thank me when you get that big fat scholarship and the acceptance letter to medical school. Just think. In seven to ten years, you'll be a fully qualified doctor working in the emergency room. We can lunch together every day."

A scraping sound in the hallway startles me, and the hair on the back of my neck stands on end. I spin around and look at the open door. No one there. My disapproving subconscious is giving me the jitters.

"Ten years." I swallow. "Looking forward to it."

"Would you mind grabbing the medical school listing?" he says, as he sorts through the files. "Top shelf. Red book with blue letters."

"Sure." I push my chair away from the table and catch the sound of tapping in the hallway. "Is someone there?" I walk to the door and look left and right. Nothing. I am definitely getting paranoid. I head back to the bookshelf and stretch up on tiptoes to ease the book down.

"Sorry, Mac. I forgot it was so high. Let me help you." Dr. Drake comes up behind me and reaches for the book. He is so close I can feel the heat from his body against my back.

A snarl from the hallway sends a shiver down my spine.

"Someone is out there." I slide out from under his arm. "Did you hear that?" I race out the door but the hallway is empty.

"Who is it?" Dr. Drake joins me.

"I don't know. I kept hearing noises outside, and then I thought I heard a snarl."

"Maybe it's just nerves."

"Yeah. That must be it."

Dr. Drake turns me to face him. "It isn't nerves, is it? Your heart isn't in this. I could see it the minute you walked into my office, and I can see it in your eyes now. You sparkle when you are enthusiastic about something. You sparkle when you talk to Charlie. You sparkled at the auction when you were with Huntington, but you didn't sparkle with me. That's when I knew it was time to back off."

My mouth falls open. "No. Really. I want to do this."

Dr. Drake shakes his head. "Why don't you give this decision some more thought? I'm always here. I'm very happy to help bring a new doctor into the fold. But if you do decide to go ahead, I want to see sparkle. I want you to be living your dream."

My heart clenches. "I've given up on dreams."

Dr. Drake tilts my head back with a gentle finger under my chin, forcing me to look up at him. "Never give up on your dreams. You see something you want, you fight for it." He pauses and frowns. "That reminds me, I owe Huntington another round in the ring. Tell him to give me a call."

I swallow and look away. "We broke up."

His face softens and he runs a finger lightly over the worst of the bruising on my face. "I'm sorry to hear that. I hope these bruises weren't part of the reason."

"No." I shake my head so hard my ears ring. "Max would never hurt me."

And suddenly, for the very first time, I believe it.

~~~

The hospital is in an uproar when I arrive at work on Friday morning. Everyone is talking. No one is working. Security has been doubled. The police are everywhere. I weave my way through the crowds and head straight to Charlie. If anyone knows what is going on, it will be him.

"You've come to the right place," he says, when I ask about the whispers in the corridors. He leans back in his chair and steeples his fingers. "I am the heart of the hospital. You need information, you come to me."

"I'm here," I snap. "Now spill."

Charlie's smile fades. "Someone attacked Doctor Drake last night in his office. The hospital has been trying to keep it all hush-hush. They don't want people to panic."

"Is he okay?"

Charlie shrugs. "He's in critical care. Apparently he was hit over the head with a fire extinguisher. He never saw his attacker."

I grab Charlie's arm. "I was with him Thursday night. I was sure I heard someone in the hallway."

"Who would want to hurt Doctor Drake?" Charlie muses. "I heard his office was untouched. His wallet was still on his desk. He was still wearing his expensive watch. He's a nice guy. Too good-looking for my taste, but decent. Although he is the competition." He leans forward and whispers, "It was his name Doris called out that night."

Nausea roils in my belly. "Do they have any leads?"

"Not so far. They have fingerprints from the fire extinguisher, but not much else."

I head back to my desk and scrub my hands over my face. I can't imagine who would want to hurt Dr. Drake, but I know in my heart it wasn't Max.

The day drags. All I can think about is meeting Amanda at Doctor Doctor to talk about Max and to plan our attack on the debt collector over a few drinks on her client expense card. But when my shift ends, she calls to say she's stuck in a meeting and won't be able to make it.

Bubble bath and ice cream time.

I send my fax to Collections R Us and throw my pack over my back. My phone rings again. I check the Caller ID. Unidentified caller. Could it be Ty on a different number? I grit my teeth and answer on the last ring. I make a pathetic attempt to hide my surprise when Jake says hello.

"I need your help," he says, ignoring my high-pitched squeak, "Torment challenged the Pulverizer to fight tonight. The Pulverizer is ranked number one on the U.S. underground fight circuit. Torment flew him in just for the fight."

"If he wants to fight, he'll fight. I won't be able to stop him."

Jake hisses in a breath. "You don't understand. He went crazy this week. It's like he had a death wish. He challenged the three guys in the state ranked above him. He opened the club every night during the week for the fights. He won every match, and now he's number one."

"I thought that was his dream." I stop just outside a convenience store and lean against the wall. "He said he wanted to be number one in California. He said he would be happy when he got to the top."

"It wasn't enough."

Of course not. His father's words must still haunt him.

"Why do you need me? We aren't together anymore."

"You have to come to the club, Makayla." Jake's voice takes on a pleading tone. "The Pulverizer has sent every one of his opponents to the hospital with life-threatening injuries. He trains for months before a fight. He's won his last fourteen matches all by knockout. He's been undefeated for six years. But he's a dirty fighter. If he wasn't on the underground circuit, he would have been kicked out of the professional leagues. Torment is the first real threat he's faced in years. He'll come prepared."

"Max...Torment can handle him. He's a good fighter. The best now."

Jake groans. "Max isn't ready for this fight. He's tired, he's injured, and he's unfocused. He's fought more this week than the Pulverizer fights in a year, and he won because he was willing to take risks he normally would never take. He can't fight like that with the Pulverizer. The guy is good. He's ready. He's rested. And he'll fight dirty. One wrong move and Max will be toast."

My stomach clenches. "What do you want me to do?"

"Come to the club and talk him out of it. I tried. Rampage tried. Hell, we all tried. Even Sandy. He says he'll be number one if it kills him. And it might kill him. He's not thinking clearly, and if he can't focus, he can't fight."

"We broke up. He doesn't want to see me."

"Please."

A sob wells up in my throat. "I'm sorry, Jake. It would just prove to him we were never meant to be together, and it wouldn't change his mind."

"You're making a big mistake," Jake snaps. "If that's what you think, then you never really understood him at all."

Too distressed to go home, I head to the critical care wing of the hospital to visit Dr. Drake. I have a book of green slips in one hand and a paper clip heart in the other. I hope he gets the joke.

The hallway is cool and quiet. Critical care is a place of emotional extremes. Lives teeter in the balance. One way and families rejoice. The other and they despair. There is a lot of despair here today and only five rooms are occupied.

Dr. Drake is not in his room. They have taken him for CT scans. I sit in a chair in the hallway to wait, and a man in a brown jacket walks into the room across from me. I recognize him from the donut shop, but he isn't eating donuts today.

The woman he is visiting must be related. They share the same olive skin, dark hair, and patrician nose. She is on life support. Asleep. The machines in her room whir and beep. The man sits by her bed and holds her hand. A nurse goes in to check the monitors and they share a few words. As she leaves, he calls out, "Thank you, Ms. Maloney."

His voice is familiar. Very familiar. I walk up to the door and check the name on the chart. Gloria Martinez.

"Excuse me?"

The man looks up. Not a man. A boy. No more than twenty. His eyes are dark circles in a sunken face. A face without hope.

"Are you Sergio?"

I catch a flicker of interest in his eyes and he nods.

"I'm Makayla Delaney. You were chasing me for a debt."

Myriad emotions cross his face. None of them particularly pleasant. "What are you doing here?"

"Visiting a friend." I take a wild guess given his age and the similarity of his appearance to the woman in the bed. "Is this your mom? Is she the reason you were always calling from the hospital?"

His face crumples. "Yeah. She's dying. She needs a new heart. But she doesn't have any medical insurance."

My heart aches. "I'm so sorry."

"I've sold everything I have to pay for her treatment," he says, "but I don't have enough money to get her on the transplant list. If I'd been able to collect enough to get the bonus, I could have bought her a heart."

He turns his face away and wipes a tear from his cheek. Sympathetic tears well in my own eyes, and my throat tightens.

"Would my payment have made a difference?"

He shakes his head. "Even if I had pushed all my debtors into making their monthly payments, I wouldn't have had enough. I needed a big windfall—like someone paying the whole loan off at once."

"I'm sorry."

His cheeks redden. "I saw you in the donut shop a while back. Your friend was saying your boyfriend was a billionaire. I thought maybe if I pushed you harder, he might pay off your loan. But you were so nice. I couldn't go through with it."

I slump against the door frame. "He's not a billionaire. And he's not my boyfriend anymore."

Sergio gives me a half smile. "Trouble in paradise?"

"We didn't gel. He needed trust and I couldn't give it. He's a violent guy. I was afraid he would hurt me or try to control me."

"Sounds like Ty. I heard he got your file. That guy is crazy. Always in trouble with the law. Always pounding on people for no reason. Flies off the handle for the smallest things. Threatens people to get his way."

I take a seat in the chair near the door and frown. "Max isn't like that. I've never seen him hurt someone who didn't deserve it or ask for it. He never threatened me. He's controlling in a protective kind of way. He wanted to pay off my loan and I wouldn't let him."

Sergio's eyes widen. "Sounds like a decent kinda guy. Too bad it didn't work out."

Understatement of the year.

"I almost quit this job after the first day," he says. "I'm not Ty. I couldn't do what he does. I couldn't handle the screaming and swearing. But we needed the money. My mom told me sometimes you have to see to the heart of a person. Look below the surface. So when they were swearing at me I would listen, and I would try to find out what they were really afraid of. I couldn't do anything about it. I still had to collect the debt. But it helped me deal with the anger on the surface. And when I could make it easier, I did."

My breath catches in my throat. I have seen to the heart of Max. I have seen his kindness and compassion. His fierce need to protect. He would never hurt me. I was just afraid to believe it.

"My mom is all I have," he says quietly. "My dad died when I was little. No brothers or sisters. The rest of the family is in Italy."

Tears stream down his cheeks, but this time he doesn't turn away. I fish around in my purse for a tissue and see the fax receipt.

Suddenly I have an idea. A windfall for Sergio. Forgiveness for me.

I hand Sergio the tissue. "I think I may be able to help you, but we'll need to go to your office and intercept a fax. And I need a ride to a fight club in Ghost Town."

"You a fighter?"

My lips curl into a smile. "I am a fighter and I'm going to fight to win back my decent kinda guy."

Chapter 26
DON'T YOU DARE
LEAVE ME AGAIN

SERGIO PULLS UP OUTSIDE the front doors of Redemption. His face is tight with emotion. Max's payment went through, and now that we retrieved the fax, it won't be sent back. His mother will have a new heart and a chance at a longer life.

"Are you sure you want me to leave you here? It seems kinda rough for a girl like you."

"It's perfect for a girl like me."

Sergio leans over and grabs my hand. "I don't know how to thank you. I was such a bastard on the phone, and it killed me. I wasn't lying when I said you were the nicest debtor on my list."

"You'll have to thank Max. He's the one who made the payment. I told him once I thought people were essentially good. It never occurred to me I wasn't giving him the same benefit of the doubt."

"Good luck."

"Bye, Sergio. Stay in touch and let me know how your mom is doing. You know where to find me."

I close the door and race over to Amanda, waiting at the entrance.

"I finished up at work just before I got your text," she says. "I got here just a few minutes ago."

"Where the hell have you been?" Obsidian booms when we push open the door. "I stalled the lockdown as long as I could. The main event is about to begin. Grab your kit and let's go."

"That's one hell of a voice you've got there." Amanda follows us to the first aid room and waits while I grab my kit.

"He's gay," I say over my shoulder.

"Doesn't bother me."

Obsidian laughs. "I've already got twice as much trouble as I need, but when I'm free again, kitten, I'll look you up. I've always had a soft spot for angels."

We race through the training area and head toward the ring. Redemption is packed. Standing room only. The air is thick with anticipation. The club smells of stale sweat, cheap perfume, plastic mats, and disinfectant.

We skirt around the crowds and make it as far as the pen before Jake blocks our way. A black bandana holds back his mass of curls and the light glints off his oiled six-pack, visible above his low-slung jeans.

His eyes flick from me to Amanda and back to me. "Where the fuck were you? You're too late."

In the distance, flesh slams on flesh. The crowd cheers.

"Get out of the way. I need to see him."

Jake folds his arms across his chest. "He doesn't need to see you. Not now. He delayed the fight as long as he could. After I told him I called you, he was sure you would come. He didn't want to fight unless you were here. Now, you'll just be a distraction. You'll never change his mind."

"I'm not here to change his mind. I'm here to support him. And if he gets hurt, I'll take care of him."

I try to get around him but he stops me with a heavy hand on my shoulder.

"Jake. Let her through. There's no need to be cruel." Amanda finds her voice and Jake turns in her direction. There is so much heat in the look they share, I take an involuntary step back.

"You would know about cruel. You broke up with me over nothing and jumped into bed with someone else so fast it made my head spin. I was just a game to you."

Amanda sucks in a breath. "It wasn't like that. You don't understand."

Jake steps toward her and takes her chin between his thumb and his index finger. He tilts her head back, forcing her to meet his gaze. "I understand. Perfectly. You don't respect men. You reel them in, you play with them, and you throw them away. But I'm not like the others, sugar. It doesn't work that way with me. When I want a woman,

I don't play around." His chest heaves and his body trembles. For a second I think—no, hope—he will kiss her, but then he lets her go and steps away.

Amanda sucks in a breath and swallows. "You're making a mistake."

Jake folds his arms. "You made the mistake, Amanda. We had something special and you threw it away."

Her face crumples. "Why didn't you tell me how you felt?"

"I thought you knew." He runs his hand through his hair. "I thought you felt the same way."

Someone groans. A body hits the mat. I push past Jake and run toward the ring, using my first aid kit as a battering ram. When I reach the raised platform, I stagger back in relief. The warm-up fighters are just leaving the ring. I'm not too late after all.

Max and the Pulverizer climb into their corners. The crowd cheers. Max's tattoos gleam in the overhead light. A sweaty Pulverizer glows like a honey-glazed ham.

Amanda comes up beside me, and her eyes widen. "Ohmigod," she breathes. "He's a mammoth. They must have just pulled him out of the ice. He's three times the size of Max. Look at his hands. They're like bricks." She lifts an eyebrow. "You know what they say about the size of a man's hands."

"Amanda! Do you ever think about anything except sex?"

She rolls her eyes. "Yes. I think about debt collectors chasing my best friend, the occasional legal brief, but that's it."

"Max is a good fighter. He'll use brains instead of brawn."

"Brains aren't going to save him," she hisses. "One hit from the Pulverizer and his head will split open like a melon."

"Amanda!"

"Sorry. It just doesn't seem like a fair fight."

The crowd hoots and hollers. I turn back to the ring; Pinkaluscious climbs through the ropes, clad in her trademark pink Lycra. Her horse-hair ponytail flaps in the nonexistent breeze. She trots over to Max and throws her arms around him. This time, however, she doesn't stop at a hug. She presses her mouth to his lips and gives him a deep, long, wet kiss. The crowd heckles. My stomach heaves.

"Maybe I made a mistake."

"No." Amanda grabs my arm and holds me fast. "They aren't together. He still wants you."

"How could you possibly know that?" My voice rises high enough to attract the attention of the people around us.

"Because he's looking at you," she murmurs. "And his heart is in his eyes."

I glance up. Max is watching me. Like magic, his hard eyes heat and soften. A smile ghosts his lips. In that split second, I know I am forgiven. And I know something else.

I love him.

Obsidian clears out the front row with a low growl, and we take our seats behind the Pulverizer. I drum my fingers on the first aid kit until Amanda smacks my hand to make me stop.

The bell rings. Max and the Pulverizer dance around, feeling each other out. The Pulverizer moves forward with a jab and front kick, and Max comes back with a one-two punch. The Pulverizer staggers back and Max hits him again, this time in the jaw. My stomach clenches but I refuse to take my eyes off the ring.

The Pulverizer shakes his head and charges in with a few more right hooks. Max avoids them easily, but the Pulverizer is unstoppable. He tries to take Max down, but Max evades him and gives him another double punch. He moves in and out so fast it looks like he's dancing.

"Max…Torment seems to have the edge so far," I whisper to Obsidian.

"That's because he's dominant in boxing. As long as he stays on his feet, he'll be able to hold his own. But he'll be in trouble on the mat. The Pulverizer is known for his grapple technique. He used to be a pro wrestler."

The Pulverizer attacks Max with kicks from his long legs. Max sidesteps them and jabs him in the nose. Blood trickles over the Pulverizer's lip. The round ends and Max retreats to his corner. Jake, Homicide, and Blade Saw give him water, pat him down, and talk him up.

The bell rings and Max goes on the attack, thudding his knee into the Pulverizer's solar plexus and then taking him down to the mat.

"That's a double-leg takedown," I say to Amanda. She snorts a laugh and shakes her head. "You've been hanging out here way too much. I never thought I'd hear you of all people describing fight moves to me."

"The Pulverizer is going for a guillotine," Obsidian says.

Sounds scary. I clutch the handle of the first aid kit so hard, my knuckles turn white.

The fighters break apart and grapple on the mat. Obsidian lets out a long, low whistle. "Didn't slow Torment down. He's looking for a kimura now."

"Watch," I say to Amanda. "He'll twist himself around the Pulverizer like a pretzel."

The pretzel never happens. Instead Max gets on top of the Pulverizer and hammers him with punches.

The second round ends and I take a deep breath. So far so good. I'm still here. My dinner is still in my stomach. Max isn't seriously injured.

The Pulverizer starts the third round with a slew of desperate punches. His long arms windmill around and Max gets caught. He reels back, and the Pulverizer moves in with one brutal punch after another. He drops to the mat, and the Pulverizer keeps on him. Punch after punch. Max's face is covered in blood. He rolls toward the ropes, but he doesn't tap out.

My entire body seizes up. I scream at Obsidian to stop the fight. I yell for Jake. Homicide. Anybody. I run up to the ring. Amanda is right behind me.

Shilla the Killa in her striped referee shirt calls a halt. She waves the Pulverizer to the corner nearest us and crouches down beside Max. Sweat drips off the Pulverizer's back and splashes on the floor. Our noses wrinkle. The Pulverizer reaches behind him and digs into his shorts. Amanda and I share a glance and mouth to each other, "Gross."

What is not gross, however, is the set of brass knuckles he pulls out of God knows where. Only Amanda and I, standing directly behind him, see him slip them on seconds before Shilla says the fight can go on.

Max struggles to a crouch. The Pulverizer strides across the mat toward him.

"Max," I scream. "He's got a weapon." But I'm too late. The

Pulverizer smashes his fist into Max's skull. One hit is all it takes. Brass knuckles are illegal for a reason. Max sags to his knees, and I am up the stairs and in the ring, running, running across the mat. I throw myself between them. I hold up my hands and scream.

"Enough. He's down. Leave him alone."

No one steps into the ring. No one comes to help us. Jake leans over the ropes and shakes his head. Max is down, but he isn't limp and he hasn't tapped out. I'm breaking the rules.

I don't fucking care.

Light streams into my eyes casting the Pulverizer in shadow. Darkness flickers at the corners of my mind. He grabs my wrists and lifts me up in the air and away from Max. I kick. I scream. My foot hits his sternum. He drops me and I crawl back to Max. The Pulverizer grabs me around the waist and tosses me through the air.

My back smacks hard against the pole. Dazed, I slide to the mat. My vision wavers. I fumble behind me, trying to orient myself and then I feel the handle of the first aid kit slide into my hand. I look over my shoulder. Amanda.

"He needs you," she says quietly.

I push myself to my feet. My missing memories come flooding back. Susie pushing the bat into my hand. My father lunging at my mother. My first pathetic attempt to slow him down. My second swing, from up by my ear like Grandpa Joe showed me. The crack as the bat hit his head. Susie and I watching him crumple to the ground, moaning. I wasn't a victim. I had fight. I didn't give up then. I won't give up now.

I stalk across the mat. The Pulverizer is kicking Max in the ribs. Max is moaning, too far gone to tap out. I don't hesitate. I break into a run and aim the end of the first aid kit at his diaphragm, exactly where Max hit Homicide. One hit had Homicide down on the mat. I don't need to be strong. I need to be accurate. I never thought my EMT training would be so useful.

The Pulverizer does not see me coming. My strike is dead on. He falls to the ground, gasping for air. He taps out and his handlers run in to help him.

I drop to my knees beside Max. He isn't moving. His face is gray and his skin is clammy. I check his pupils and sit back on my heels. Dread winds its way up my spine and through my body to squeeze my heart. He's going to die. I never got to tell him I love him.

Amanda climbs into the ring and sits beside me. "Do something. Help him."

"I'm not a paramedic. I can't help him. Call 911."

"Jake called them already, but right now, you're all he's got." She opens my first aid kit. "Tell me what to do."

"Pray."

"No," she shouts. "You can do this. You can save him."

Max's eyes flicker open. He looks around and his eyes meet mine. He lifts his hand and strokes my cheek. "Baby," he whispers, "I'm glad you're here." His eyes close and his body goes limp.

I can't see through the tears streaming down my cheeks. "Max!" I grab his shoulders. "Max. Don't you dare leave me again. Once was enough."

Amanda fumbles in my first aid kit. "I guess I'll have to treat him myself. Looks like he needs a bandage on his head."

She unrolls a tensor bandage, and I grab her wrist. "You can't wrap that around his head. We need gauze."

"Gauze it is." She hands me the sterile package, and I tear it open and press it to the bleeding wound on Max's head.

"I guess we should poke him with something next." She pulls out an epinephrine injector. "This looks painful. Where should I stick it?"

"No." I grab the injector and throw it back. "That's not what he needs right now."

"What does he need?"

"Ice. Stabilization. I need to check his pulse and breathing. I need a blanket." I glance over at her smiling face. "I know what you're doing."

"Good," she says. "Now he has a chance."

Four hours later, Max is wheeled into his room in the ICU. Colton and I jump up from our chairs. The attending physician informs us the tests are clear. No fractures or brain damage. He diagnoses brain swelling and a severe concussion. He can't predict when Max will regain consciousness.

"Mr. Huntington has a hard head," Colton murmurs after the doctor leaves.

"The hardest."

Colton snorts a laugh, and I manage a half smile.

"Am I missing the party?" Pinkaluscious pulls back the curtain. Although she is almost unrecognizable in dress pants, pearls, and a silk blouse, I would recognize that fake, platinum blond hair anywhere.

"Sandy." Colton holds out his arms.

"Oh, Colton." Pinkaluscious evades his arms and air-kisses him. The urge to toss her out on her bony ass surges through me like a tidal wave—or maybe I should take a picture and post it on Twitter.

"What's she doing here?" Pinkaluscious asks, her eyes flicking to me.

"You know why she's here. She's Max's girl."

"I'm Max's girl," she snaps. "He told me he broke it off with her. He was coming home with me tonight."

I hold my breath hoping her mascara will run as she fake sobs beside Max's bed. Or maybe one of her false eyelashes will come off. Better yet, she might trip over her four-inch stilettos and chip a tooth.

"You were," Colton says quietly. "You aren't now."

"She's the reason he's lying in that bed." Pinkaluscious glares at me. "She drove him to it. He couldn't deal with the stress. Normal fights weren't enough." She looks over Colton's shoulder and gives me a self-satisfied evil bitch grin. "She sent him back to me."

My hands clench into fists and my jaw twitches. I will not lower myself to her standards. I will not catfight. I will hold up my head and walk away.

"I hope she suffers," she continues as if I wasn't standing in the room. "Look at Max. Look what she did to him. She should crawl back under her rock and leave Max with his own kind."

"What kind is that?" My seething and inquiring mind wants to know.

"The better kind. Society."

Colton excuses himself and leaves the room, mumbling something about catfights. I should have told him Makayla Delaney does not do fights—catfights, fistfights, or otherwise.

Or maybe I do.

"He told me he wanted no part of it," I say.

"That's why we should have been together." A tear trickles down her rosy cheek. "We were perfect for each other."

"So what happened?" *Please tell me. Please tell me. Please tell me.*

"He said I wasn't the one. I wanted more than he could give."

"What could you possibly want that he wouldn't give?"

She turns to face me, her eyes devoid of expression. "Pain."

"Pain?"

She sighs. "Never mind. You couldn't possibly understand. He just…couldn't hurt me."

Gah. TMI. Where's the bleach?

"To be perfectly honest," she continues, "I don't know what he sees in you. You have nothing to offer him. You don't have a pedigree or money or even connections. And I can tell by looking at you that you sure as heck can't give him what he needs in the bedroom."

"I can give him love."

She rolls her eyes. "And how's that working out for you?"

"I'll let you know."

She searches through her insanely expensive Birkin handbag and pulls out her phone. A piece of paper falls out. She bends down to pick it up. Her bony ass waves in front of me. I whip my old phone out of my jacket pocket. The antiquated camera takes grainy pictures at best, but I don't need twenty megapixels to get my point across.

Don't do it. Don't do it. SNAP. I do it.

She kisses Max lightly on the forehead. "Tell him I said good-bye. I found a way to break with the family. He knows how to find me."

"He wasn't going home with you tonight, was he?" I say on a hunch.

Pinkaluscious shoves aside the curtain and then looks back over her shoulder and sighs. "He said there was no chance we would ever get back together. He said he loved you."

I wait until Pinkaluscious is gone before I tweet her ass. I'll bet it doesn't trend,

I sit beside Max and stroke his hand, careful not to touch the IV tube taped to his wrist. A warm orange glow from the hallway streams under the privacy curtain, and the fresh, sharp smell of disinfectant assails my nostrils. Machines beep. Nurses murmur. Crocs squeak on the tiled floor.

Max stirs and I jerk my head in his direction. I have never watched him sleep before. His face is relaxed, peaceful, and more sensual in its softness. I brush my hand over his cheek and his head moves. My heart pounds wildly. I glance up, hoping to see him looking at me, but his eyes remain closed, and his heart monitor continues to beep in a steady rhythm.

"I know you can hear me," I tell him. "I've read about the unconscious mind. You might not process the information in the same way, but you understand." I wait for a response, but when it doesn't come, I continue talking. Words spill out of my mouth, tumbling over each other so quickly they are almost unintelligible. I tell Max about my childhood and how the happiness of each day was dependent on how much my father drank. I tell him about hiding with Susie in the closet on the bad nights and listening to the sickening thud of fists hitting flesh, knowing the next day Mom wouldn't be able to go out because of the bruises.

My stories run together: Christmases good and bad; the happy days when my dad took us to the beach and played with us in the waves; and the few times Mom smiled. I tell him about the thrill of sneaking away into the night and the years of hardship that followed until Steve came into our lives. I tell him how Mom was so focused on supporting us financially that she forgot all the little things that hold a family together. I tell him how I tried to hold our family together with humor and how Susie drifted away. I tell him how I always longed for a big family full of warmth and laughter. Sort of like Redemption.

Finally, I tell him I remember what happened the day we ran away. I tell him I didn't give up. I am a fighter, just like him.

"I love you," I whisper into the stillness.

The monitor beeps and the green numbers rise slowly, indicating an increase in heart rate.

I giggle. "I knew you were there."

I pretend he is really listening. I sing him a few songs. I tell a few jokes. I share my brief and few sexual experiences. I ask him to tell me his secret.

Who is Max Huntington?

I trace my finger over the tattoos on his shoulders, and then slide the sheet away to follow the lines and swirls over his chest and down his abdomen. Failures to him. Beauty to me. His heart rate rises again; the machine beeps a faster rhythm.

"Don't get any ideas," I murmur.

My fingers run over his tattoos again and again. The longer I stare, the more I see. Here and there, little embellishments have been added to the lines. I lean forward and trail my fingers across the tattoo running over his shoulder. Are these feet? And a tail? I tilt my head and look into the face of a dragon, hiding in a wavy sea.

I know this dragon. The last time we met, he was green and hanging in Max's office.

Hands shaking, I tug up the sheet. Only then do I notice the skin on the unmarked side of his body is red and inflamed—a small square just over his heart. I walk to the other side of the bed for a better look. He has a fresh tattoo—a new failure. Two stylized lines forming the rough shape of a heart, and inside is written "Makayla."

Chapter 27
SHHH. IT'S ME

UTTERLY DRAINED AFTER SPENDING twenty-four hours straight sitting by Max's bed, I take Amanda's advice and go home to eat, shower, and change, confident that the nursing staff will heed both my instructions and my threats and call me immediately when he wakes. By the time I'm finished, it is dark and I decide to splurge on a cab. The driver's arms are covered in tribal tattoos, very similar to the tattoos on Max's body…and the paintings in his office.

On a whim, I redirect him to Redemption for a quick look at the paintings before I go to the hospital. We make good time through the city, but when we arrive, the parking lot is empty and yellow police tape crisscrosses the front door.

"You sure you want me to let you off here?" the taxi driver asks. "Looks like it's closed."

I open my mouth to tell him to drive away when Rampage and Blade Saw walk across the parking lot.

"Could you wait just a minute?" I slide out of the taxi and race toward them.

"Hold up. What's going on?"

They look up and their grim faces tell me everything I need to know. "Permanently shut down?"

Rampage nods. "Ambulance crew and hospital reported the use of an illegal weapon and an unsanctioned fight. The police arrested the Pulverizer before he got on the plane. CSAC shut us down last night."

"So what are you doing here?"

Rampage grins. "Sneaking in."

"Can I sneak in too? There's something I wanted to see in Torment's office."

"Good thing you're here," Rampage says, nodding. "After I'm done with Blade Saw, he might be in need of medical attention."

I pay the taxi driver, and we wait until he has disappeared before we head around the building to one of the back doors. Rampage pops a key out of a compartment in the door frame, and we hurry inside. When I reach to close the door, Blade Saw grabs my hand.

"Leave it open. Obsidian, Hammer Fist, Homicide, and Jake are joining us. Jackhammer is bringing a keg. We're gonna toast Torment, get pissed, and beat the shit out of each other."

"Sounds like fun."

Rampage raises an eyebrow. "You're welcome to join us. Torment's girl should know how to fight."

I give him a half smile. "Maybe later. I have stuff to do first."

I walk through the silent warehouse to Max's office. The door is unlocked, and I flip on the light switch. Empty. A week ago Max sat in that chair. He told me he trusted me, and I let him down. My chin quivers and I close my eyes, breathing in the faint scent of his cologne and the fainter scent of him. I miss him so much. I never knew hearts could really hurt.

But I have investigating to do. I walk behind the desk and lift one of the paintings from the wall. Now that I've had time to study Max's tattoos, the similarities are remarkable. The same swirls, curlicues, and patterns from his tattoos appear in the painting, even the dragon's face. I flip it over. A small printed card on the back identifies the artist as Suzanne Morgan Huntington. His mom. He inked her into his skin as the biggest failure of his life. My poor Max.

I replace the painting and take down the other one. The designs on this one match the tattoos on Max's back. When I flip it over, I find the same card, but this one has the word "Dallas" penciled in beside the name. My Max is a Southern boy after all.

By the time I leave the office, the illicit party is well under way. Homicide and Obsidian are wrestling on the mats. I take a seat on the bleachers, and Rampage hands me a cup filled with warm beer.

"I used to think I didn't have any fight in me." I sip the beer, and the warm, bitter liquid slides down my throat. "I thought I had no fire. I drifted through life never knowing where I was going or what I wanted. Then I met Torment. He made my life exciting. He opened my eyes. He made me see I had fight."

"You're a fighter to the bone," Rampage says. "The way you climbed into the ring on the first day you were here…not a hint of fear…hell, that's when I knew you belonged here. Torment saw it. We saw it. I'm glad you finally see it too."

I rest my palm on his massive shoulder. "I want to learn how to fight. Really fight. I don't want to be afraid. I want to know I can hold my own against anyone. I want to be able to watch Torment fight and know when he pulls a punch and when he lets go."

Rampage grins. "You want a lot of things."

"I'm just getting started."

"You've come to the right place," he chuckles. "Follow me."

My heart thuds as I hurry after him down to the practice mats. He is alarmingly determined, moving faster than his size would suggest possible.

"Yo," he booms. "Makayla wants to learn how to fight. We're gonna teach her. Everyone has a specialty. You teach her that. Anyone hurts her, you answer to me."

"If she wants to fight, she needs a ring name," Obsidian interjects.

They all stare at me in silence. I shift from foot to foot, sensing the importance of this moment and yet wanting to get it over with so I can get down to training.

"Doc." Homicide says with a grin.

"I'm not really a doctor."

Blade Saw gives me a warm smile. "You are to us."

"Everyone agreed?" Rampage asks to a sea of nodding heads. "Right. You are hereby christened Doc." He dumps his beer over my head. Everyone cheers. I laugh until my stomach hurts. The only thing missing from this perfect moment is Max.

—∿∿—

On Wednesday, just after lunch, the ICU nurse calls to tell me Max is awake. I grind it out at work until my shift is done. The second the clock strikes five, I race through the hospital and burst into his room. Max is sitting up in bed. He looks tired, thinner, but still impossibly handsome.

"Max! You're awake!" I throw my arms around his neck and sob into his shoulder.

"It's so good to see you, baby." He strokes my hair. I cry harder.

Max chuckles. "It would be good to see you if I could actually see your face."

Turning away, I fish through my purse for a tissue. "Not now it won't."

"Turn around," he says softly. "Your tears are beautiful to me. They tell me you care."

I turn around and look at my Max. My lips quiver again. More tears. More tissues.

"Shhh. It's okay. I'm okay." He cups my cheeks in his palms and wipes my tears away. "I guess you care after all."

"I love you, Max."

Max's eyes soften. "You don't know how long I've waited to hear you say that."

I sniff and wipe away the last of my tears. "Can I kiss you?"

"You don't know how long I've waited to hear that too."

Our lips brush together. Soft. Tender. He curls his hand behind my neck and pulls me closer. "Say it again."

"I love you."

He captures my lips and kisses me long and sweet, and then he buries his face in my neck and whispers, "Makayla."

"Ahem."

Cheeks burning, I pull away when Nancy, the shift nurse, breezes into the room to check the monitors.

"Heart rate up." She peers over her glasses and gives me a wink. "You're not going to be a very good paramedic if you make the patient's heart rate go up instead of down."

"You decided to enter the paramedic program?" Max's eyes warm.

"I could have done so much more for you, but I didn't have the training. It almost killed me. And since you paid off my loan, I thought you might be accommodating of a long-term payment plan. I'll be making a lot more money as a paramedic."

"I'm proud of you, baby, for following your dream." He cups my cheek and I lean into his warmth.

"Took me a while to figure out what that dream was."

Nancy finishes her checks and discreetly disappears. Max trails his fingers along the line of my jaw.

"Rampage stopped by this afternoon. He told me what happened. He said if you hadn't stabilized me, it could have been much worse. As with Frank, you made a difference." He pulls me down to sit on the bed beside him, nuzzles my neck, and nibbles at my earlobe. "You smell so good. Like flowers in the sunshine."

"Max. Stop. What if someone comes in?"

"They'll wish they could nibble your earlobe too," he chortles.

I huff through my nose. "I was telling you something important."

"I was listening, baby."

Mollified, I allow him to nuzzle my neck while I talk. "You made me realize the reason med school didn't interest me was because I need excitement. And I need it now. Not in ten years. You made me feel alive. I want that from my career, but I still want to heal people. I called Ray and we worked out a deal. I volunteer with his crew and his company will pay for my paramedic training."

"Do you think you might be able to squeeze in a few shifts at the club? After Rampage told me we had been shut down for good, I decided it was time to go legit. I've already called my attorneys. We've applied for a license. We'll be a sanctioned MMA club, and I'll need a doctor and medical staff—you."

The door swings open and a well-groomed, middle-aged couple join us in the room. Max glances up and his face darkens. "What the hell are you doing here?"

I hold out my hand and introduce myself to Max's aunt and uncle, Richard and Elizabeth Morgan.

I swallow hard, appalled at his outburst and embarrassed for his family. "I called them, Max. I was looking at your tattoos when I remembered the paintings in your office. I got your mother's details and did some Internet searching. I thought you would be happy to see them."

"Damn it, Makayla. I left for a reason. If I wanted to see them again, I would have contacted them myself."

My bottom lip trembles. I had nurtured a faint hope this wouldn't go badly. I imagined tears and laughter and forgiveness and joy. Not anger or the self-hatred I can see in Max's eyes.

"You were unconscious. The doctors didn't know if you would make it. I thought you should have your family with you."

"You were wrong."

His words sting, but I press on. "No, you're wrong. I talked to your aunt and uncle. Not one single person in your family blamed you. No one thought a fourteen-year-old boy should have been able to take on four seasoned mafia enforcers—no matter how good a boxer he was. And your mother wasn't disinherited. Her money was put in a trust for you at her request. She chose to break with the family. They didn't choose to break with her."

Elizabeth gives my shoulder a squeeze, and I find the strength to carry on. "I called your father's family too. They never blamed you either. Your aunts and uncles are on their way here from Georgia. You have family, Max. They love you. Even though you don't believe it, you deserve to be loved."

Heart aching, I grab my purse and push open the door. "Love is a gift. Don't throw it away."

—∿∿∿—

The next few evenings pass in a blur. I go to work. I sneak into Redemption for fight training. I spend the night kissing the mats. I drink too much beer with the guys. I go home and pass out. I arrive exhausted for work the next day. Max doesn't contact me, and I don't contact him.

Friday night, Homicide brings in a bottle of tequila. I am an amazing fighter under the influence of tequila. I resolve always to drink tequila before a fight. By ten p.m. I also resolve never to drink tequila again.

Rampage decides I should have a little rest in Max's suite while everyone else plays strip poker. He pulls out a hidden key from behind a brick and ushers me inside. After he leaves, I strip off my clothes and climb into Max's bed. I breathe in his scent and imagine he is with me.

I must have drifted off because I am awakened by a warm hand sweeping over my back. When it curves around my bottom, I stiffen and push myself up.

"Shhh. It's me." Max's deep voice echoes in the stillness.

"Me is supposed to be in the hospital," I mumble into the pillow. His warm hand on my skin is delicious. Almost as delicious as tequila, which I am never drinking again.

"I got out early for good behavior." His delicious hand sweeps along the side of my body and strokes the curve of my breast. Even more delicious. I flip over and offer my full self for his caressing pleasure.

"How are you feeling?"

Max chuckles. "Well rested. How about you? You seem a little tipsy."

"Smashed, actually." I push off the sheet so his hand does not face any impediments and is free to travel where I want it to go.

"You're very responsive when you're smashed." His fingers slick between my folds, and he holds them up so I can see them glisten.

"Mmm. Pretty." I draw his hand down to my mouth and wrap my lips around his finger. I suck gently and slide my lips back and forth. I taste sweet and salty.

Max groans. "Don't do that, baby."

I drag my lips away. "Why?"

He swallows. "I just…it's hard."

I roll over and nuzzle his crotch. He is very obviously erect. "Yes, it is. Let's do something about that."

Max snorts a laugh. "I don't want to take advantage of you in your drunken state."

I flip over again and lie spread-eagle on the bed. "Please do. I wish you to take advantage of me in every way possible."

His voice deepens to a low, guttural groan that just adds to my itch. "Don't tempt me, baby."

"I'm trying my best here. You gotta give me something back." I stretch and wiggle on the bed. Max cups my breast in his warm hand and tweaks my nipple.

"I'm still very annoyed," he murmurs. "Arranging for my family to visit was a shocking surprise."

I arch into his hand. "Annoyed is good. You want to spank me or tie me up? I'm pretty much game for anything right now."

"How about we sleep?" Max stretches out on the bed beside me, fully clothed.

"How about we don't sleep?" I unbutton his shirt and ease it open. "How about Makayla lies on top of you and licks all your delicious tattoos?" I follow the dragon marking down his chest with my tongue, but stop when I am parallel to his heart. "Why did you get this?" I trace a gentle circle around my name.

Max sifts his hand through my hair. "I thought we were done. I failed you like I failed my family. I couldn't get you to trust me."

I ease myself on top of him and wiggle until his erection is nestled tight between my thighs. "You didn't fail me. My issues were my own. I was worried you were like my father, but I thought about it a lot when I was sitting with you in the hospital, and I spent a lot of time with the guys downstairs. My father's violence and your violence are totally different. You have purpose and control, whether you fight for sport, protection, or defense. His violence came from anger and fear. You never hurt anyone without reason; he always did."

Max strokes his hand up and down my back then palms my bottom and squeezes my cheeks. "What about when we're together? Our play always sets you off."

My tongue glides over his bottom lip. He tastes minty and fresh. He tastes like Max. "I was afraid of losing control. I didn't really understand that 'Agusta' put me in the driving seat until you explained it. And now it doesn't matter because I know I have fight. I won't be afraid to tell you to stop." I take a deep breath and bite my lip. "Maybe we could…try again."

Max cups my head and pulls me down for a long, hard kiss. "Don't worry, baby. We'll try again. You need to be punished for springing all my relatives on me like that. But not while you're like this."

"Threats and promises." I push myself down his body and unbuckle his belt.

Max groans. "We should get some rest."

My restless hands slide his clothes over his hips and toss them on the floor. "No rest. You've had a week to rest. Now it's time to play." I crawl up his body and flick my tongue over the swollen head of his shaft. "How about this? Any problems with inebriated Makayla engaging in this sort of behavior?" Max's hands fist on my back, and his body tenses under me.

"I'll take that as a no," I whisper.

"You can take it as your two-minute warning. Two minutes and I'm taking over."

I look up and smile. "I can do a lot in two minutes." I lick a circle around the head of his shaft and then slide my tongue down its length. "You taste good," I murmur.

He becomes impossibly hard and I struggle to take him all in. "Makayla, baby—" His body strains upward, and I wrap my hand around his throbbing erection and stroke him in counterpoint to the slide of my lips. His hand sifts through my hair, pulling tight. I suck him hard, taking him deep.

"Fuck. I won't be able to hold out." He tugs my head back, and in one smooth wrestling move, he flips me onto my back.

"I thought I had two minutes, not two seconds."

His eyes rake over my body and the look he gives me is nothing short of carnal. "My bed. My rules."

"Wipe that self-satisfied smile off your mouth," I grumble. "You have only the illusion of control."

Max throws back his head and laughs. "You tell yourself that, baby."

Ten minutes later we lie groaning side by side on the bed.

"What do you mean, you don't have any condoms?" I moan.

"I didn't come here expecting to find you naked in my bed. Where's your purse full of condoms?"

I edge away from him in case the heat of his skin sets me back down the road of no release. "It must be downstairs. Rampage had to carry me up here."

"Rampage carried you and put you to bed?" Max pushes himself up and glowers at me.

"Why, yes, he did," I sigh. "I see getting hit on the head has not diminished your overprotective nature in the least."

"Some things are not going to change. Better get used to it."

My eyebrows fly up to my hairline. "So, if I want to be with you, I'll never be allowed to put myself in danger; I'll have to ensure no man looks at me if I'm naked or in a state of semi-undress; and I'll have to trust your judgment and do what you want at all times?"

Max gives a satisfied grunt and nods. "And always let me know where you are."

"I was joking."

"I wasn't."

"Maybe this won't be a happily ever after." I fold my arms across my chest.

Max unfolds my arms and leans down to lave my nipple. "It will be if we find some condoms."

My lips quiver with a repressed smile. "Rampage and I shouldn't have used them all up. It was quite thoughtless of us."

Max flips over and lands on top of me, his weight crushing me into the bed. He pins my wrists to the pillow and presses his forehead against mine. "Not funny."

"I'll tell you what's not funny," I rasp, "aching to have you inside me and not having a condom. Now, get off me. You're turning me on."

"Everything turns you on. I almost can't keep up, and that's saying something." Max lets me go and slides off the bed. He grabs his jeans and shirt from the floor and dresses before I can get up.

"Everything *Max* turns me on," I correct him.

"I'll meet you downstairs."

"You're going to pound out your frustrations on poor Rampage, aren't you?" I tug on my clothes as fast as I can.

"He touched my girl."

"He took care of your girl." I walk over to him and slide my arms around his neck. "I have a better idea. Let's go to my place. My house is closer than yours, empty, filled with condoms, and we have never had sex there before. "

"You mean *my* house."

I suck in a sharp breath. "You bought the house? You're the mysterious new landlord?"

Max laughs. "I couldn't let you live in a hallway. I also bought your apartment at Sunset View. Why don't we go there?"

"How about both? The night is still young."

Frowning, Max grumbles, "The bed in your house is barely big enough for you."

I give him a wicked grin. "I wasn't thinking about using the bed."

—◇◇◇—

Are you awake?

No

What are you doing?

I'm watching you sleep

I'm not sleeping

Then I'm watching you awake

How do I look?

Beautiful

Flattery will get you in my pants

You're not wearing pants

That's right. You tore them off

Max likes torn off pants

Makayla has no pants left for you to tear off

Good. Easy access

Behave

You're mine. I don't have to behave

BAD MAX. Keep your hands to yourself

I'm not using my hands

Chapter 28
I HEART MAX

FRIDAY NIGHT. FIGHT NIGHT. My favorite night of the week.

I arrive early at the club and head straight to the first aid office. Our shiny new MMA club license is posted just outside my door. My days are busier than ever. When I'm not in paramedic training or volunteering on the ambulance crew, I run the first aid office at the club.

Except for the days Max doesn't let me out of bed. Or the days we go down the coast on his motorcycle, or drive at the racetrack, or have picnics on the beach, or visit Max's relatives in the South, or barbecue with Amanda and her latest squeeze on the terrace at Max's house.

By the time I have prepped my office, the line has formed. With twice as many classes and twice as many fighters, I rarely have a moment to myself. The evening passes quickly. When my last patient walks out the door, it is almost closing time and I have only a few minutes to walk the floor and say hello to my friends.

Rampage waves me over to his post by the red line. "Hey, Doc."

"You got a new smiley face shirt."

Rampage pats his belly. "The other one disintegrated. Musta been poorly made. I got this one for five bucks at a dime store."

"Try washing it once a week."

Rampage frowns. "What'll that do?"

"Make it clean."

His eyes narrow. "Are you planning to step over the red line, Doc?"

I grin. "With both feet."

"You know the rules."

"One round in the ring with Torment. Looking forward to it. Blade Saw taught me some new moves." I mock up my new fighting stances.

Rampage chortles and looks me up and down, making a show of checking out my tiny red spandex shorts and fringed bra top. "If you're planning to fight wearing that, you won't need new moves."

"That's the idea." My hand slides to my bottom where I am still feeling the aftereffects of my last attempt to wear something tight and sexy in the fight ring.

Rampage shakes his head. "You got balls to take him on like that."

"He's got to learn not to be so overprotective."

"You're fighting a losing battle. He's wired that way. I'm surprised he hasn't just locked you up in the house to keep you safe."

I snort a laugh. "He tried that. Didn't go down so well for him."

A short, stocky man with overly tight shorts pushes past me and almost knocks me over. Rampage growls and grabs him by the collar. He lifts him high in the air and holds him right in his face.

"You almost knocked Doc over. You don't disrespect Doc. You might need her someday. And she's Torment's girl. You don't want to mess with Torment. You got that?"

The guy nods and Rampage drops him, clamping his hand around the guy's arm.

"You new?"

He nods again.

"You fight?"

The newbie shakes his head. "I was just taking a look around. I'm on my way out. Name is—"

"Don't care what your name is," Rampage snaps. "Don't know how you slipped in earlier. Maybe cause you're so tiny. We have rules here. You come in. You fight. It's simple." He drags the guy down the aisle and yells, "Last minute newbie. Open the pen."

"Don't let him put you in the ring with Torment," I shout after Rampage's newest victim. "He's got no mercy. He'll tear you to ribbons."

Dr. Drake looks over and peels himself away from the punching bag. He meets me in the aisle and gives me a peck on the cheek.

"How are you?" I ask. "I was glad to hear you weren't in the hospital too long."

He touches his head. "Almost fully healed. The police arrested

Doris for the attack. Imagine. Doris attacking me. Apparently, she thought we were meant to be together, and she went crazy when she heard you and me in my office."

"I heard you signed up to be our new ring doctor."

Dr. Drake grins. "That's right. We'll be working together again. Plus it gives me a chance to do some real training. I finally got in the ring with Torment, and he kicked my ass. He said it was a warning. Apparently, I'm not to look at you or speak to you or breathe the same air as you. If I touch you, he'll hunt me down and kill me and bring you my head as a trophy. Only reason he took me on as a ring doctor is because someone told him I was good at what I do. Who could that have been?"

I give him a wink. "Can't imagine."

"You'd better get going before I get in trouble," he says with a grin. "Seeing you in that outfit makes my fingers itch and I like my head where it is."

I take a step away and then turn back. "Thanks for looking in on Gloria Martinez. My friend Sergio really appreciated the extra follow-up after her surgery."

Dr. Drake waves a dismissive hand. "I was happy to do it. It made me rethink my decision to move into administration. I'm meeting the board next week to talk about getting my admitting privileges back. I'm a healer, like you, Mac, not a paper pusher."

By the time I reach the ring, Max and the newbie are already in position. Rampage and Homicide are snickering in the corner. The newbie is quaking in his too-tight shorts. Max's face is devoid of expression, but I can see the humor in his eyes.

I take a seat in the front row beside Jake.

"Looking good, Doc."

"Back at you."

Jake gives me a lopsided grin, and for a second I forget I hate him for hurting my best friend.

"You here alone?" He shuffles his feet and twists the ring around his finger.

"You mean other than with Torment?"

Jake shrugs. "Yeah. Like, did you bring any friends? You brought that big guy last week—the one who wanted to get in shape."

"Charlie." I laugh. "He loved it. LOVED it. He goes to the hospital gym every day now to practice his Muay Thai moves on Drake. He's coming back this week to learn some Brazilian jujitsu." All paid for by his promotion to green slip manager.

Jake nods. "Drake is climbing the ranks pretty quick. Everyone thinks he's just a pretty face, but when he gets in the ring, he sure packs a punch."

So does Max. I look up just as he stalks over to the newbie. He growls and the newbie dives under the ropes and scrambles off the platform. Rampage catches him and roars with laughter. The newbie manages to crack a smile.

My phone buzzes and I check my caller ID. Amanda. She's going to freak when she finds out I'm sitting beside Jake.

"What's up?" she asks.

"I'm at the club. Max is intimidating a newbie. He still insists I come to every fight, even if he's just sparring. I can make it through anything less than five minutes so long as there is no blood. I'm pretty proud of that."

"You're too good to him," she chastises. "If you cave in all the time, he won't respect you."

"He respects me," I whisper. I slide off the bench and step out of Jake's earshot. "Once a week I get to be on top, and I insisted all sex toys have to be soft, pink, or have ribbons or feathers. It's kinky sex, Makayla style."

Amanda giggles. "Sounds like you're keeping him in line."

"Well, he did go out and buy a pink paddle. When he gets too bossy, I turn off my phone and do something crazy—like cliff jumping or skydiving. After the inevitable explosion, he grabs his paddle and we have wild punishment sex."

"I haven't tried that one." Amanda breathes. "I'll have to toss a few paddles Drake's way when he comes over tonight. He's doing an edible theme—edible panties, chocolate sauce, popsicles, dill pickles, pepperoni sticks, whipped cream…it will be a veritable feast."

"There's a veritable feast sitting on the bleachers," I whisper.

"Jake?" Her voice drops. "Did he ask about me?"

"In a roundabout way."

"Do you think he'll call?" Her voice wavers. "Should I tell Drake not to come over?"

I glance sideways at Jake, engrossed in the fight. "Not yet. Give him time. I don't think he's written you off."

A whistle blows. Rampage nods and I end the call and climb into the ring. Max is facing the other way, talking to Obsidian. Rampage clears his throat.

"We have a line crosser for you Torment. This one's trouble. I've seen her around before."

"Wait," the newbie yells. "You can't put her in the ring with Torment. She's a girl. She'll get hurt."

"I'm not afraid of him," I assure the newbie. Not anymore.

Max spins around. His eyes rake over my barely there skirt just covering my tiny exercise shorts and my even tinier fringed top. I shake my girls and my fringe dances. Obsidian catcalls. Rampage whistles. Max's jaw tightens.

"Club is closed. Everyone clear out," Max hollers.

Rampage gives me a wink and herds the last of the fighters out of the warehouse. By the time everyone has gone, I have almost lost interest in my own game. Almost. Not quite.

Max's biceps twitch like he wants to catch someone. "Ready?"

My heart pounds and I nod.

He stalks toward me, and I push myself back against the ropes as hard as I can. When he is close enough, I let go.

Whump. We're down on the mat. I am lying full out on top of Max. From the state of affairs under his shorts, he likes this position. A lot.

"One point for me," I whisper and wiggle.

The smoldering look in his eyes sends white-hot need ratcheting through me. We get to our feet, and I look down to adjust my top.

Whump. I'm down on the mat. Max is kneeling astride me. His eyes darken and my body heats in an instant.

"I like it when you mount me, Max." I lick my lips. "But that wasn't fair. I wasn't ready."

"You show up in my ring dressed like that, you know what's coming," he growls.

"Are you trying to turn me on?"

Max leans down and rasps in my ear. "You were turned on before you stepped into the ring. I know that flush on your cheeks, baby. You want something from me?"

"Just here to fight."

Max jumps to his feet and helps me up. I reach behind to pull my shorts down over my surprise.

Whump. Back down on the mat. This time Max gives me a full body press. He slides his knee between my thighs and eases my legs apart. My pulse skyrockets. I bite my lip and breathe in short pants.

"Um…this is a good submission. What's it called?"

Max studies my face and his lips quirk into a wicked smile. "It's called Playtime."

"Bad Max. Get off me." I wiggle underneath him. My actions only serve to inflame my desire. And his.

"Not bad Max," he hisses. "Bad Makayla. You're lucky I love you so much. The punishment for being inappropriately attired in the ring is very serious."

I stop wiggling and look up at him with interest. "How serious?"

Max's eyes blaze with sensual promise. "Tap out and I'll take you upstairs and show you."

My lips curve into a smile. "You tap out and I'll give you a present."

"What present?"

"The present tattooed on my ass."

Max sucks in a sharp breath and his eyes narrow. "You DID NOT get a tattoo. I strictly forbid it."

My smile broadens. "Oops."

We stare at each other, our bodies melded together, our hearts thudding in union. Max's face softens almost imperceptibly. "You never listen. What am I going to do with you?"

"I have a few ideas."

"Do those ideas include me ripping off your shorts so I can see the tattoo you were forbidden to get?"

"Yes," I whisper.

"What else?"

"Hugging me."

"What else?"

"Holding me?"

"What else?"

"Loving me."

Max kisses me soft and sweet. "Tap out and I'll show you how much I love you. I have a new spanking paddle upstairs."

"You tap out and I'll show you the tattoo on my ass."

Curious warm brown eyes lock on mine. "What does it say?"

"It says 'I heart Max,'" I whisper.

Max smiles and taps out. "I heart you too, baby."

ACKNOWLEDGMENTS

Many thanks to my editor, Leah Hultenschmidt, for loving this story and helping me make it shine, and to my agent, Laura Bradford, for her insight, patience, and guidance. To Louie "the Filipino Tornado" Grover for introducing me to the world of MMA, and to Cindy Davis for her em dash expertise. To CaRWA, for their incredible support, and especially to Dara-Lee Snow who gave me the courage to press "Send." Last but not least, to my family great and small, far and wide, for inspiring me, encouraging me, and tolerating my writerly ways.

ABOUT THE AUTHOR

Recovering lawyer, karate practitioner, and caffeine addict, award-winning author Sarah Castille worked and traveled abroad before trading her briefcase and stilettos for a handful of magic beans and a home in the foothills of Canada's Rocky Mountains. When she is not glued to her keyboard or e-reader, she can be found playing piano, shuttling munchkins, and burning dinners. Her steamy, contemporary romantic tales feature blazingly hot alpha heroes tormented and tattooed for your reading pleasure. Visit www.sarahcastille.com.

In Your Corner

by Sarah Castille

coming Spring 2014

A high-powered lawyer, Amanda never had any problem getting what she wanted. Until Jake. She was a no-strings-attached kind of girl. He wanted more. Two years after their breakup, she still hasn't found anyone nearly as thrilling in bed. And then he shows up in her boardroom…

Jake is used to fighting his battles in a mixed martial arts ring, not in court. He needs Amanda's expertise. And whether she knows it or not, she needs him to help her find true happiness.

"Smart, sharp, sizzling and deliciously sexy.
Against the Ropes is a knockout."
—Allison Kent, bestselling author of *Unbreakable*

For more Sarah Castille, visit:

www.sourcebooks.com

Awakening

by Elene Sallinger

He will open her eyes to the ultimate pleasure…

The minute Claire walked into his shop, she aroused every protective instinct Evan ever had. She looked so fragile, so lost. He ached to be the one to show her a world she'd never dreamed of, to awaken within her the passion she was so ripe to share. It only takes one touch for him to see how open and responsive she is to his dominant side. But the true test will be whether he can let go at last and finally open his heart…

Festival of Romance Award Winner

What readers are saying:

"If *Fifty Shades of Grey* intrigued you, *Awakening* will take you to a whole new level of desire, submission, and unforgettable romance." —Judge, Festival of Romance contest

"One of the absolute best BDSM novels I have read. (And I've read quite a few.) This one is absolutely amazing!" —Autumn Jean

"Finally! A well-told story that shows the characters' vulnerabilities and how they learned to trust and love again." —A. Hirsch

"Exquisitely beautiful, touchingly heart-wrenching, and hedonistic enough to keep your body on fire." —*Coffee Time Romance*, starred review

For more Xcite Books, visit:

www.sourcebooks.com

Restless Spirit

by Sommer Marsden

Three men want her. Only one can truly claim her.

When Tuesday Cane inherits a cozy lake house, she's not expecting to find love as part of her legacy. But how can she choose between Aiden, the loyal and über-sexy handyman she's known for years; the charming and wealthy Reed Green, a former TV star; and the mysterious Shepherd Moore, an ex cage fighter.

The only way to know for sure is to try them all… Surrounded by so many interesting men and erotic temptations, Tuesday has no intention of committing. But deep down she longs for that special, soul-deep connection. Only, which man can entice this restless spirit into finally settling down?

What readers are saying:

"An intense emotional and sexual journey
that is quite compelling." —Kathy

"One of the best adult/erotica books I have ever read.
The characters are real and believable, and the sex
scenes are absolutely scorching hot." —Rebecca

"Themes of domination and submission are fantastically well
varied throughout the story… Realistic and relatable characters
with steamy encounters at every turn." —Michelle

For more Xcite Books, visit:

www.sourcebooks.com

Control

by Charlotte Stein

When Madison Morris decides to hire an assistant to help run her naughty bookshop, she gets a lot more than she bargained for. Two very different men are vying for the position...and a whole lot more.

Andy excites her into grasping control, while Gabriel shows her how freeing it can be to just let go. Soon the lines are blurring and Madison is no longer sure who's leading and who's following. In the midst of kinky threesomes and power plays, she'll have to finally decide what—and who—she really wants.

For more Xcite Books, visit:

www.sourcebooks.com

Telling Tales

by Charlotte Stein

The only limit is their imagination.

Allie has held a torch for Wade since college. They were part of a writing group together, and everything about those days with him and their friends Kitty and Cameron fills her with longing. When their former professor leaves them his mansion in his will, it's a chance for them to reunite. But there's more than friendship bubbling beneath the surface.

As relationships are rekindled and secrets revealed, they indulge their most primal desires. With the stakes getting higher, Allie isn't quite sure who she wants…fun-loving Wade or quiet, restrained Cameron.

For more Xcite Books, visit:

www.sourcebooks.com

Sinners on Tour

Rock Hard

by Olivia Cunning

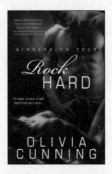

On stage, on tour, in bed, they'll rock your world...

Trapped together on the Sinners tour bus for the summer, Sed and Jessica will rediscover the millions of steamy reasons they never should have called it quits in the first place...

"A full, well rounded romance... another dazzling story of Sinners, love, sex, and rock and roll!" —Night Owl Reviews, *Reviewer Top Pick*

"Wicked, naughty, arousing, and you'll be craving the next page of this book as if you were living it for yourself!" —Dark Divas Reviews

"Hot men, rocking music, and explosive sex? What could be better?" —Seriously Reviewed

"An erotic romance that is rockin' with action and a plotline that keeps you on your toes." —Romance Fiction on Suite101.com

For more Olivia Cunning, visit:

www.sourcebooks.com

Sinners on Tour

Double Time

by Olivia Cunning

On stage, on tour, in bed, they'll rock your world...

On the rebound from the tumult of his bisexual lifestyle, notoriously sexy rock guitarist Trey Mills falls for sizzling new female guitar sensation Reagan Elliot and is swept into the hot, heady romance he never dreamed possible.

"Snappy dialogue, dizzying romance, scorching hot sex, and realistic observations about life on tour make this a winner." —Publishers Weekly

"Whether you like rockers or not, this story will get you thinking about becoming a groupie!" —Night Owl Reviews

"Hot rock stars, hotter sex, and some of the best characters I've read this year." —Guilty Pleasures Book Review

"Double Time gives us Trey's much anticipated happy ending, and all the sexual adventures along the way." —Fresh Fiction

"A sexy, steamy read about two rock stars and the man who loves them both. A great installment to this series, it left me anxiously waiting for the next one." —Romance Junkies

For more Olivia Cunning, visit:

www.sourcebooks.com

Sinners on Tour

Hot Ticket

by Olivia Cunning

On stage, on tour, in bed, they'll rock your world...

A man as talented as Sinners bass guitarist Jace Seymour needs a woman who can beat out his self-doubt. A woman as strong as Mistress V needs a man she can't always overpower. And in each other's tight embrace, an escape from harsh reality is always a welcome diversion...

"The heat and hunger between the two leads creates a palpable tension that will keep readers turning pages with reckless abandon and begging for more from this sizzling series." —RT Book Reviews

"Cunning develops her characters into real people who engage in a compelling and satisfying erotic romance. Their relationship builds amid a dramatic series of unexpected events." —Publishers Weekly

"Sizzling hot, tragically emotional, and totally rockin'. Only one more band member to go and I can hardly wait." —Fresh Fiction

"I said it for the first book and I'll say it again, these yummy guys are so hot that you'll want to rip your clothes off and join them. I hope this tour never ends." —Night Owl Reviews, *Top Pick*

"As Jace's story is told in Hot Ticket, *the reader is provided with the heart-wrenching and powerful backstory that formed the Jace we saw in the first two books of this series."* —The Romance Reviews, *Top Pick*

For more Olivia Cunning, visit:

www.sourcebooks.com

Where There's Smoke

by Karen Kelley

The Devil went down to Texas…

Sexy wannabe demon Destiny Carter has pissed off the people downstairs and has been kicked out of Hell. Now she's in Ft. Worth, Texas, with one week to corrupt a soul. Or else.

Lookin' for just One Soul to steal…

When smokin' hot Destiny strolls into The Stompin' Ground bar in a slinky red dress, she has a feeling her assignment might not be so bad. The cowboy at the bar looks pretty darn delicious and oh-so-corruptible.

But Chance Bellew is no ordinary cowboy, and Destiny gets way more than she bargained for when she rubs up against that sexy dark angel perched on a barstool like sin just waiting to happen…

*"Kelley burns up the pages… This book is witty, sexy, and a lot of fun.
Readers won't be able to wait to read the next installment!"*
—RT Book Reviews, *4 stars*

*"Bestseller Kelley (the Princes of Symtaria series) launches a sultry paranormal
series with this smoky, sweet, and surprisingly touching tale."*
—Publishers Weekly

For more Karen Kelley, visit:

www.sourcebooks.com